Kandoria

Carol L. Davis

Order this book online at www.trafford.com
or email orders@trafford.com

Most Trafford titles are also available at major online book retailers.

Note for Librarians: A cataloguing record for this book is available from Library
and Archives Canada at www.collectionscanada.ca/amicus/index-e.html

Printed in Victoria, BC, Canada.

ISBN: 978-1-4269-2001-1 (sc)
ISBN: 978-1-4269-2002-8 (hc)

Library of Congress Control Number: 2009937967

*Our mission is to efficiently provide the world's finest, most comprehensive book publishing
service, enabling every author to experience success. To find out how to publish your book, your
way, and have it available worldwide, visit us online at www.trafford.com*

Trafford rev. 10/16/2009

 www.trafford.com

North America & international
toll-free: 1 888 232 4444 (USA & Canada)
phone: 250 383 6864 ♦ fax: 812 355 4082

Dedication

To my dad, Richard Jasper Thorn—
A great teacher—1932-2004

To my second dad, Gene Anstee—
In other words—1930-2009

To my friend, Susan Moulton—
Do what you know—1961-2008

Acknowledgments

The author would like to acknowledge and thank my husband Todd Davis for his unwavering belief in me. One-step at a time.

Thanks to my sister Lauri Haskell for her kindness and skill with Microsoft. I am glad we travel this life together.

For my mom Gladys Anstee thank you for all your support and encouragement. Love sometimes sounds like a cat purring and reads like a good book.

A special thanks to my friend and copy editor, Sandra J. Marcano for her sharp mind and eyes. I have learned much.

For my friend Jessi Winburn thanks for teaching me how to appreciate the dictionary. You always know how to make it fun.

Many thanks to all my family and friends that have helped me along with this challenging and wonderful writing experience. Keep smiling.

My appreciation goes out to the staff at Trafford Publishing. Thanks.

Their eyes blazed with the raging fire, a crazed dance filled their moments, sealing their fate Farstar stepped back into the shadows of the night, a wisp of a smile on his face for this new journey begun.

I

"Where did you say Autumn found this?" Zyleon asked, looking at the photo.

"Sector C."

"I have to see this," said the Professor, unable to hide the edge of anticipation in his voice. "Care to walk with me," he more stated than asked, already exiting the tent.

"Nacoo tells us of a legend, that the region's native ancestors were visited and taught by beings from a distant star system, which could explain some of the mystery." Daj said.

"That's a hell of a history. This could date back thousands of years, most of which time it was embedded in solid rock — hmm, remarkable condition."

"The encasement is formed of astro-alloy, a form we haven't analyzed yet, and the crystal is of unknown origins."

"A piece of the enigma," Zyleon said as he massaged his chin. "Does Nacoo recognize the writing"?

"Not yet." Daj could sense the Professor's growing enthusiasm; a discovery like this would gain them recognition with the International Alliance of Archaeoastronomy Sciences.

Zyleon wiped his perspiring baldhead and took a deep breath as they entered the mountain cavern. Chipping and brushing of stone echoed softly in the relief of the shadowy coolness. Phosphorus stalactites and stalagmites glowed in hues of pink, green, and yellow. "What a pleasant place for an ancient community," he said, experiencing a touch of déjà vu. His mind filled with thoughts of finally finding proof of an alien race having once lived on Earth.

Autumn pointed with dust-covered gloves to an exposed artifact that rested in a wall notch. "Professor, I believe we have found another piece to this puzzle."

Zyleon ran a gloved finger over the wand's smooth, unfamiliar astro-alloy crown that cradled an equally unusual crystal. He took a step back and assumed his thinking pose, left hand holding his right elbow, while stubby fingers massaged his chin.

Autumn eyed Daj and gave a knowing grin.

"When I was a young man working on Space Station Eight, a group of astronomy scientists had just returned from a fifteen year exploration of the outer planets, and with them, they had brought back some very unusual artifacts. One of the items was a wand similar to this one, wrapped in alien material resembling silk. Daj, I need you to find that analysis for a comparison."

"What classification"?

"2098SP8-RDR2"

Daj opened his hyper-band. "Transmit code 2098SP8-RDR2 to Momma," he said. He nodded, flicked his oilskin Barmah, and headed for the entrance.

The jungle dripped with moisture, hot, hazy, and humid, a good day to keep the air on. Daj wiped a trickle of sweat from his nose with his bandana and entered the equipment tent.

"Ahh, the ranger of discovery has finally made it in to see me this fine morning," said Dawn, pointing to the screen. "I think we are on the verge of something extraordinary. The study remains Momma has brought up so far have the same structure as those classified 2098SP8-DNADR5. This is an amazing find!"

Daj leaned, palms down, on the table, where data sheets filled every inch of it. "Extraordinary might be too small of a word for this discovery," he said, pulling up a chair. He sat down next to her. "Since you are in the area, have Momma open rock-drawer two for me. Let's see if we can find the family this piece of astro-alloy belongs to."

"I can do that." She wiggled her shoulders, clapped her hands, and then rubbed them together.

Dawn's girlish excitability always made him feel like a first-year college student.

"I overheard one of the workers say the ancient teachings would one day be revealed to the world." She bit her bottom lip, as her fingers expertly tapped the keys and sweat trickled down the side of her freckled face. Nevertheless, she was oblivious to it.

Nacoo's baritone voice floated into the tent. "Where is the Professor"? He asked.

Daj looked into Nacoo's leathery face. "He's in the cavern with Autumn."

Nacoo left as fast as he had appeared.

"Ahh, here we are Year 2098, Space Station Eight, Rock-Drawer Two."

"I need a printout of the alloy and crystal formation analysis, Dawn — thanks," he said, moving toward the printer.

Excited voices and movement stirred outside. Radin the security work supervisor pushed open the tent flap. "There has been an accident in the cavern," he shouted. The two men and Dawn glanced at one another then Radin was gone.

Daj was first out the door, with Dawn, first aid kit in hand a step behind him. Nacoo met them at the cavern entrance, his voice rolling thunder. "You're never going to believe this, but Autumn has become stuck behind the wall."

Daj stopped in his tracks when he noticed Professor Zyleon's astonished expression. "She was brushing a pot over there in the wall, when I decided to remove the wand from its holding place. I moved it a quarter inch, and dust started to fly. Autumn asked me what the hell was going on, and then called for help. But by the time the dust settled and the crew and I could see; she had disappeared behind the wall."

They looked at the empty place Professor Zyleon had indicated and a long moment passed between them. The rhythmic dripping of water echoed through the eerie silence of the cavern, like a disturbing call to the soul.

"We'll start a search for another entrance," Radin announced, breaking the spell.

"The sun has reached its zenith," said Nacoo, whose gaze was upon the crystal, cupped in its astro-alloy crown. A tiny beam of sunlight shone through the ceiling, upon which was a sculpted map of the heavens. This small but precise ray, arrowed down, directly positioned on one of the furrowed symbols in the wall notch. With a finger, Nacoo air-traced a projection on the wand, comparing it with its matching sign on the hold in which it rested. "It's a key," he said with excitement. Using a feather-light touch, he aligned the two symbols. A cloud of dust exploded around them.

Daj covered his face with his bandana, waving an arm around, attempting to clear an area. A faint glow shone from behind where the wall used to be. He stepped closer, tipping at its edge. A vertical slant disappeared into a ghostly radiance and a peculiar feeling of having been here before crept over him.

"There are writings on the walls." Nacoo stood beside Daj. "It may be some kind of temple."

"I guess we don't need this," Dawn said, dropping the first aid kit. It hit the cavern floor with a solid clunk. She moved over to the opening and in a hesitant voice, called out for her colleague. "Autumn," she coughed, "Autumn, are you down there?" There was no echo and no response.

"Team — gear up. We are going in after her!" Professor Zyleon hit a pitch no one had heard before. "We've got to find that girl. She'll be the greatest damn discovery I've ever made."

Radin shouted orders to his men. Everyone scrambled, buzzing fervently about the cavern.

"The engravings are a mixture of cultural symbols," Nacoo said. He studied the hieroglyphics speaking softly into his hyper-band. "Eth, Keeper of the Key to Kandoria. Take each step of the journey in comfort." He air-traced an indented diagram of stairs descending to a pool. It matched one of the projections on wand. "I must have the key — pull it straight out." He motioned to the Professor.

The Professor gave Nacoo a serious glance. Bracing himself he pulled the wand straight out, away from its ancient embrace. "Well, that's a relief," he said, handing it to Nacoo whose onyx eyes reflected red in the dim light.

With resolute skill, he aligned the stair symbol on the key with its twin wall design. A soft glow filled the crystal, and again dust started to rise. Nacoo grasped the wand and placed it in an inside pocket of his vest. It was a perfect fit. "Just like it was meant to be there." Nacoo patted his pocket.

Dawn coughed again. "There goes my hair."

"Mastery at its best," Daj said, removing his well travelled, Barmah hat shaking the dust from it, catching the shine that was as bright as the phosphorous torches in the Professor's eyes.

"Let's not waste any more time… hard copy this," Zyleon waved a hand in front of his face, sputtering, "Where the hell is Radin. We need that equipment!"

"Right, as we speak a disc is burning. My hyper-band's been on relay, recording documentation under security mode since we walked into the cavern. I thought Momma could help analyze this situation."

"Good man, Daj, good man," said the Professor, patting dust from his shirt, ignoring Daj's haughty smirk.

Radin arrived with a few men shouldering packs. "You have essentials and back-up for hyper-bands," he said. He wiped his brow and motioned to a black pack. "Inside are small weapons — just in case." His eyes fixed on the staircase. "Good luck."

They gathered up their packs with a sense of nervous anticipation.

Daj took the first step, his boot disturbing a thick layer of dust. "There must be a ventilation system in here to keep it so dry," he said, glancing around for telltale signs.

"Momma is cautioning us to use silent mode, so everyone equip their hyper-band. I don't want a wall collapsing on us." Nacoo spoke in a hushed tone.

Dawn removed the tiny bung remote from her hyper-band and groaned as she plugged it into her sensory site, hidden just under her hairline, where the back of her skull met the right side of her neck. This always made her feel so violated, knowing everything she saw, felt, heard, tasted or spoke would be collected and sent to Momma, to be deciphered.

Daj caught Dawn's "I don't want to do this expression" and studied the dove-gray screen on his hyper-band. He enjoyed the way Momma could collect and interpret his thought waves. *"Professor Zyleon,"* he thought and pushed the send button. He watched as the words appear on the screen, *"do you think Autumn will plug in?"* The small screen lit up with the Professor's answer.

"She's a clever girl," Zyleon responded his heart aching at the thought of losing his only niece. *"We played many scenario games and placed them in her personal hard drive. She'll have access to that information if she can't get through to us."*

Suddenly, Daj longed to look into her golden-flecked, brown eyes.

Nacoo noted the walls as they descended. *"The cavern rock is not the same in here as it is up above."* Send to Daj.

"This appears to be made of a type of clay, unlike any I have analyzed before, maybe a mixture of three or four components." Return.

Nacoo nodded to Daj.

"Professor Zyleon, are you feeling okay?" Send.

"I'm fine, my girl, just fine." Return to Dawn. He lied; in fact, his head swam, his heart pounded and sweat rolled down from the top of his head. He felt close to passing out.

The dim glow of phosphorus torches gave his face a peculiar shine. Dawn struggled to concentrate. Her throat was dry, and she tried to wet her lips, she was so thirsty. She stretched forth her arms, touching the wall, it seemed as though the passageway was becoming narrower. Unexpectedly, she felt solid wall give way. "Nacoo!" she cried, gasping for air.

Nacoo stopped walking, did Dawn just call out to him? The walls moved in time with his breathing, they were alive and vibrant with color, swirling and enveloping him.

"Activation of emergency breathing apparatus initiated," Momma's emergency override kicked in forcing fresh air under their noses.

What was that noise? It sounded so mechanical so unreal — so — so — Momma! In the back of Daj's mind that sugary whirring voice broke through the mist, he had been walking in. The breather lay across his shoulder close for face contact. Cool air rushed beneath his nose, Momma flashed red on his screen. Daj sucked in sweet air and watched the mist fade and shadows grow into the shapes of his colleagues. He scuttled over to where Professor Zyleon lay and placed his breather under his nose, snapping it into place. "Breathe, Professor," he whispered.

Daj looked around in the dimness, seeing Dawn lying on her side he hurried over to her. "Dawn," he said, under his breath. Daj grabbed her breather lying next to her ear and placed it under her nose, Nacoo was kneeling by his side.

"Is she okay?" Nacoo clenched his hands into softball-sized fists.

"I don't know." Daj's hyper-band screen lit up with the words, *"Is everyone alright?"* "The Professor is," he whispered. Dawn moaned. "And I think she will be."

Nacoo readjusted his air piece and looked d at Dawn. "That was a close call," his voice deep and trembling.

"Woo what a ride! Thanks for that save Momma." Send. Daj walked over to the Professor.

Momma responded. *"You are welcome, Daj."* He shook his head and helped Professor Zyleon to his feet. "I think we should set control to environ scan."

Zyleon steadied himself, grateful for Daj's support. "I'm doing that now."

Nacoo slid an arm around Dawn's fleshy waist, gently helping her to her feet. His strength comforted her, and she nodded her thanks. Curly black hair, wet with perspiration, glistened against his face, and those onyx eyes penetrated her soul; she looked away, feeling her face flush.

"Everyone keep alert and resume silence," Zyleon's stubby finger hit the send button.

Daj looked around, realizing they had reached the bottom of the stairs. Scan mode showed normal environment levels. *"What do you make of that, eh?"* Send to all.

Dawn responded. *"Tomb dust is an oxygen robber."*

"Ha, ha, but by the looks of things, there is plenty of moisture down here," Professor Zyleon sent his return message with a smirk on his face.

A small pool of emerald water reflected in everyone's eyes.

Nacoo walked to the opposite side of the pool, where an engraved diagram on the wall reminded him of an old wagon wheel he'd seen at the Cartner and Plob Museum of Ancient History. At each spoke end were squares, a possible representation of rooms. He studied the wand, trying to match symbols. *"We seem to be in a hub, Autumn must have landed here, and yet I see no evidence of such or a way to use this key."* Send to all.

Carol L. Davis

Dawn moved to Nacoo's side pointing at the ancient inscriptions framing each doorway. What he deciphered caused Nacoo to feel at ease, as though he had seen and spoken the words many times: *"WELCOME TO KANDORIA."* "We are free to speak aloud, but everyone should stay plugged just in case," he said.

"There is a heat signature in this corridor," Professor Zyleon stood at the left of the stairs. "I think this will be a good place to start."

Daj knelt to pick up a stone chip, placing it in a container, sealing it for later examination. He followed through the same archway as the others, but they had vanished from view. "Hey mates," silence answered him, "Right, game's up." Silence once again. "Bloody 'ell," he switched to talk mode on his hyper-band. "Twas once was a voluptuous wench that lived by the forest dark," he said in his best drunkard singsong voice; still no answer. "Switching over to silent mode, you'll find me in lost and found." He grumbled and sent his message.

II

Dawn brushed away the hair that tickled her face. A soft breeze flowed through this passage, sending her thoughts to the last site she worked at. The tiny girl mummy, dubbed Toot, along with the rest of her small village, marked another in the path of migration that good old humankind had taken from the sunken land of the Pacific Ocean. Nacoo's voice brought her back to the present.

"Where is Daj?"

Everyone looked around.

"Daj," Zyleon yelled out. "Daj, where in the tellurium are you?" He waited for a response. "Isn't it just like the boy to be playing games at a time like this," he said, agitated.

"Professor, my indicator has two heat signatures up ahead of us." Nacoo sighed, "I wonder if Daj has found Autumn?"

Dawn shivered. "This place gives me the creeps. Daj was behind us collecting samples, how did he move ahead of us so fast?" Her eyes met Professor Zyleon's clear blues.

"Let's keep walking." Zyleon set the pace, scanning with his hyperband and his own senses. He also felt, as Dawn did, the same distorted strangeness of the place, but his physicist mind demanded answers. He couldn't let the place get to him. "I remember a similar feeling on Space Station-Three where I reworked the motion stabilizer system. Maybe the stabilizer is out of whack here."

"Yeah, maybe," Dawn mumbled.

Zyleon's thoughts drifted for a moment. "That was where I met and married Kuranna," he said. Thinking, whoa, even now she could knock his socks off. That brought a gentle smile to his lips.

"Maybe there's a bit more to that story then you're telling us." Nacoo chuckled.

The hallway ended and opened up to a twelve-by-twelve space. Straight ahead, the wall was solid and to either side hung a facsimile of the aurora borealis curtains. *"Momma, scan."* Nacoo whistled softly, "They are beautiful."

"The fields are magnetic filters." Momma whirred.

"Is it safe to move through?" Nacoo queried.

"The fields are safe to move through" Momma responded.

All eyes were on their hyper-bands. Moments passed without a signature appearing.

"This is all so weird." Dawn threw her hands up in exasperation. "Which way do we go?"

"Girl, your guess is as good as mine. Let's try this way. If it is a hub we will just circle the pool." Zyleon felt a dull ache in his legs. "Damned to get old," he groaned to himself.

The three passed through the curtains, first Professor, then Dawn. Nacoo stepping through last, colors danced around him and the air caressed his skin. Sweet voices' called to him. It was a good place. A safe place, a place he had always wanted to be.

"Professor Zyleon," Dawn reached for his arm and caught the belt of his backpack, "Can you see anything?"

"Yes, are you okay?"

Dawn was looking directly at the Professor and felt the solid fatherly hold he had on her shoulders. "Strange," she shuddered, "I lost sight of everything until I touched you. It felt like we were moving deeper into the cavern — and — and —" she turned to speak to Nacoo but he was no longer there. "OH, MY GOD," she gasped, bringing her hands to her face. "Nacoo isn't behind us anymore Professor." Unnerved, she retightened her grip on the Professor.

Zyleon rubbed his baldhead and tried to sound convincing, "Nacoo is an intelligent man, if something has happened, he will find his way. This place is a grand discovery, so let's stay calm and use our wits. Maybe he is reading some inscription?" He wished he could sit for a few moments. Then as if by magic, a white marble bench appeared in his peripheral vision. "Astonishing," he muttered.

Daj circled the pool whose water changed from a sea green to deep turquoise to soft sky blue. It fascinated him. It was warm to the touch and smelled of pine, reminding him of long hikes through the

Molay Mountains in search of the planet's unusual sharpay stone. The stone behaved as an energy collector, not unlike Earth's crystals. This particular stone, which he held in his hand, rubbing its smoothness, could reverse stored energy, enabling it to be used for healing or in stabilization systems.

"It's going to be a long wait," he sighed, letting his fingertips skim the top of the pool's surface. A sudden, overwhelming desire to dive into the mesmerizing water engulfed him; he fumbled, finding he couldn't move fast enough to remove his gear and clothing. In the back of his mind, a voice taunted him… *"come have fun Daj, come in, and swim with me."*

The water wrapped around his body massaging him, pulling him deeper — deeper — deeper — into its comfort; thoughts of Autumn swirled within his mind. He wanted to hold her, kiss those full red lips, stroke the soft curves of her body, drink her essence — yes — drink her essence, take in all of what she had to offer. *"Catch me if you can,"* the teasing voice lured him onward. He felt the feathery touches of the aquatic plants as he swam in this sea of changing color, unconcerned about the world or even his own breath. *"Daj,"* the voice reached deep into his soul opening the door of lucidity.

Nacoo had a grin he could not wipe off and laughter rolled from the very heart of his soul. "To my family and friends," he held up a shimmering champagne glass and drank deeply; it tasted so good, so real. People milled about in the muffled buzz of the room. Nacoo placed a hand on the mahogany table, which was smooth and cool to the touch — was it real. How could this be happening? Did he and his colleagues achieve High Honor?

A plaque sparkled on the table in front of him. He glanced around the room searching for his friends — a face to confirm their success.

Dawn's small fingers curled around his arm. "Congratulations," she said.

Nacoo smiled warmly at her, and then raised his head to look at the monster of a chandler. "Have we actually attained this?" Is this real, again, he wondered.

"Are you happy?" Dawn asked.

Her eyes twinkled like moonlight on ice. He let go of his inhibitions lowered his head and kissed her with a long awaited passion; her lips were cool and tasted of peppermint.

"Come with me," she said, grasping his hand like a child, leading him out into a marble lined hallway.

"Sweetness, this place is beautiful," he said.

"Come on, hurry!" She giggled.

Oh, she was cute, he let his eyes follow her small, plump backside; he just could not get rid of the smile on his face. They entered a room with the largest bed he had ever seen. Velvet maroon; curtains draped the walls, matching the bedcover and canopy screen. "By the gods," he gasped, "this is spectacular."

The lighting was dim, and soft music filled his ears. He hummed softly to its rhythm, as he lifted her up on the bed. Grasping the sides of her face, his desire surged, he didn't care if this was real. It felt good.

He watched her lips part and listened to her soft whimpers. Her skin was supple, the color of shadowy snow, fingers followed the curve of her breast finding and unbuttoning her blouse. What was she wearing the last time he saw her? His hands slipped the blouse from her shoulders and followed it down her back. One hand worked her skirt zipper; the other lifted her off the bed, allowing the skirt to fall to the floor. A shiver ran through him and he realized his own clothing lay on the floor. How can this be? He wanted to savor every touch, every sensation, and every moment of what was happening. He looked down at her silvery legs wrapped tightly around him. Was that a natural glow? A Groan of pleasure escaped him — he did not care — her essence consumed him.

The bench was a huge relief to Zyleon's legs; he sat with Dawn and studied his hyper-band instrument panel. "No signatures," he sighed. "This room is another twelve-by-twelve room according to the dimensions screen. We will go back the way we came," he said and patted Dawn's leg. "Maybe we should hold hands this time, but let me rest a bit first."

Dawn wrapped her arm firmly around the Professor's, saying in a barely audible voice. "To hell with hands, I'm staying closer to you than a wrapped mummy." Faint thoughts like hypnotic drumming played at the edges of her mind. Had she been here before? The walls stood white and bare like bones stripped of their meat. She shivered, tightening her hold on the Professor, "I feel so exposed in here."

"Have you noticed the silence?"

Dawn looked at the Professor's round face, white eyebrows as thick as the mustache under his bulbous nose. He made her feel a little more composed. "Creepy," she said.

"Kuranna told me before I left for this dig, that it would be my last one," Zyleon said. "Let's go girl," he grunted, standing up.

"Creepier," she breathed, keeping a firm hold on the Professor.

Shrouds of color played around them as they walked back through the doorway. It was cool and sounds of the ocean filled Dawn's ears, "Professor Zyleon, are you still with me?" She looked down at her hands.

"**D**aj, in what part of the constellations have you been?" Zyleon shouted, as he looked into shining, moss green eyes. "Boy, you need to stop those practical jokes." He took notice of his surroundings, but did not remember how he came to be in this hotel bed. "Where am I? What's happened and where is everyone else?"

"You need to stay calm Professor. After that fall, you took; it would be the wisest thing to do. I have placed sharpay stones on your legs to assist the healing, so just relax, Professor, and enjoy the comfort."

"What has happened?" He asked again, feeling the warm sensation of the stones. He thanked Daj, feeling sleepy, yet something wasn't quite right, although it was nice to be off his feet and let go of the worry.

"**I** was wondering when you would show up."

Dawn looked up into the eyes of her friend, "Autumn!" She squeaked. "We were so scared for you. Are you all right?"

The women embraced. "I'm fine, and why would you be scared for me?"

That was a crazy question. Dawn stared incredulously at Autumn. "What…" Dawn swooned and grabbed for a deck chair.

"Whoa, you must have had one too many drinks; I think sitting is a good idea." Autumn guided Dawn into a chair.

After the dizziness passed, Dawn became aware of the warm ocean breeze lightly tossing her hair; the table in front of her was set with chocolate-mint martinis and small gourmet sandwiches. She chose one of the cucumber quarters and began munching. "Oh, my favorites," she said, sipping the martini as if nothing in the world was wrong.

Dawn watched as Autumn picked a pepper sandwich noticing the way the space between her nose and lip crinkled when she chewed. She laughed, taking in the rest of the scenery. "This is nice; body watching is my favorite sport, those young men on the beach are beautiful! We should buy them a drink or two," she joked, continuing to munch and observe.

There was a faint echo in Dawn's mind a familiar whirring sound. What was that? Autumn's hair glistened with moisture. Dawn wondered if she had gone swimming.

"Come on Dawn. Let's go back in for a swim." Autumn offered her a hand.

Dawn looked at her bathing suit, realizing it was wet. "But how?" she whispered. She noticed the camber of Autumn's body as they moved away from the tables and out onto the warm sand. How did she keep her self so slender? She giggled almost uncontrollably as they ran like small girls across the beach, getting the attention of the men sun bathing there. Autumn looked devilish in her rose-colored suit. Her eyes glinted and a small crafty smile played upon her lips. She cocked her head toward the men and seemed to glide over to them. Was she leaving footprints in the sand?

Dawn shyly nodded no, but Autumn had already turned away. A thrill rushed through her when the men started walking back with Autumn. Dawn pushed her hair off to one side. Noticing the closer they came the more striking they looked, she swallowed hard. "Oh dear God, what am I getting into," she thought.

"These nice gentlemen agreed to have a drink or two with us," Autumn said, with a twinkle in her eye.

Dawn blushed. "Okay by me." She thought she saw the blonde rest his hand on Autumn's posterior. How odd she thought, Daj would spit over that. They reached the tables, and the dark-haired man pulled out a chair. He had a nice smile. "Thanks," she murmured, accepting his free hand. "My name is Dawn." His hand was very cool.

"Hank," he offered, settling in the chair beside her.

The couples sat and talked for a few hours. Dawn speculated how many drinks she'd managed. Autumn was full of life and flirtatious with everyone there. That was so unlike her, must be the drink, she thought, tipping her glass, catching the gaze Hank was sending her. She missed Nacoo — Hank's eye's appeared to glow — where was he anyway? She pouted.

"Come on," Autumn touched her arm. "Let's go inside."

Dawn plopped down on the couch, eyeing the blonde-haired man as he started a fire in the fireplace. "He has a nice butt," she thought, and rolled her head back. Hank handed her another martini. "Hoo," she let out a gusty breath. "Do you really think I need this?"

"Yes," Hank answered, sitting down beside her. "And me too," he whispered in her ear.

Dawn threw her head back laughing, drunk and loving it. She never let loose like this around strangers, and it felt good.

Autumn ran her fingers under Dawn's chin and kissed her forehead lightly. Dawn looked into her colleague's blazing eyes, not sure, why that just happened. She heard Autumn say, "It's alright, just relax, and enjoy the pleasures we offer."

Dawn closed her eyes; she felt Hank's cool hand untie her suit. Did Autumn say pleasures "we" offer or... Hank was kissing her — and she lost herself in that kiss, she tasted him — she tasted his essence.

III

Autumn pulled the bung remote from her hyper-band and plugged it in her sensory site. The room was dark and smelled of clover, her favorite smell. It was a special memory she had of ol' pa, he would set out at morns' break during the warm summer months and cut sweet clover for the rest of the day. Of course, he allowed Autumn to ride in his big tractor.

There wasn't much to do, just sit and watch the scenery, talk, listen, and sometimes play a game. The tractor was satellite controlled and needed just a touch or two of the control panel. He told her stories of antique tractors that ran on fossil fuel. "How awful," she would say, and he would chuckle.

"Momma, confirm connection." She delicately touched the swollen spot on her head, "ouch," wincing.

"Connection confirmed processing starts now."

Autumn shuffled through her work pack. She found the first aid kit with an ice pack inside, which made an audible crack when she snapped it on her knee, releasing the cold instantly. She sighed and placed it with gentle pressure on the wound. As she started to take inventory of where she was; a small blue light flickered through the gloom. Autumn struggled to stand, her head swimming in a whirlpool of agony. The light grew stronger, chasing the shadows back from whence they came; she held her breath, hearing only a faint whooshing sound. No footfalls, a shiver of panic threatened to come out in the form of a scream.

"Are you hurt?" It was a man's voice in the darkness.

The light shone in her eyes, blinding her to his unfamiliar presence. She lifted a hand shielding her eyes, squinting to make out any shape she could.

"Do you need healing?"

The stranger's words were almost lost to the sparks of pain shooting through her head. She moaned, "I hit my head."

"Can you walk?"

Her legs felt like rubber, but she dared not refuse and leave herself vulnerable to this man. "Yes," she answered, adjusting her pack.

"I can aid you, follow me." The shadowy figure shone the light on the floor, showing her where to walk.

Autumn hesitated, shakily placed her hyper-band in her vest pocket, and for reassurance, patted it, feeling for her sharp-bladed little jambiya Radin had given her two weeks prior. He was distrustful of one of his men. "This may come in handy," is all he'd said. She had thanked him and promised to keep it near her. "Okay," she answered, but as she began to walk; a wave of nausea swept over her, stopping her from moving. "No!" she gasped.

The light moved closer and a strong cool hand steadied her. "Come," the shadow, whispered, "I shall bring you home with me, and heal your wound."

"Who are you?" Autumn asked, allowing him to lead her. She had an odd sense that this had happened before.

"I am a friend," he said in a clear, reassuring voice.

When they entered into a brighter area, Autumn thought the blow to her head was more severe then she knew. She gazed upon a finely featured humanoid of pale, blue-gray skin, silver hair of silken texture and very slender body, with pupil less eyes that sparkled like diamonds; she was mesmerized. He guided her to a bed covered with a cottony-silk material, smiled at her, and silently asked if that was comfortable.

Autumn was stunned.

"Would you prefer I speak with my physical mouth?" The alien spoke in a musical tone.

All Autumn could do was nod, yes.

"Very good, I shall, and I shall return momentarily with preparation for your wound. Please take comfort." He placed a slim, six-fingered hand on her shoulder and stared deep into her eyes," suddenly she felt incredibly shy.

Autumn's head ached, and she wasn't even sure if she was conscious. The room had an arched ceiling, plain white walls, and the bed was concave. There was a dim glow but she couldn't find its source. Her head throbbed and she was dizzy.

He found Autumn leaning forward, holding the ice pack on her head. He sat down next to her, wrapping an arm around her waist and with little effort, pulled her close. She lay her head on his shoulder, as if she had known and trusted him, all her life; he then placed an otah-laden compress against her wound and permitted himself to sense her emotions and follow the flow of healing.

Autumn turned her face into this alien's shoulder. He smelled of mossy forest soil. Warmth flowed through her from the pack he placed on her head. Almost instantly, the pain lessened and the swaying stopped, which made her stomach feel much more stable. This must be a dream, she thought. Tired now, she willingly rested against this strange being's cool body, wishing she knew his name and wanting to know what he used to remedy her.

"My name is Farstar and the juice of the otah plant from my home planet is what I have comforted you with."

"How do you do that?" She asked, awed and strangely not afraid.

He considered Autumn's response, "I feel this in you."

Farstar placed the palm of his hand against Autumn's forehead, whispering strange words. Blackness swarmed at the corners of her eyes," she tried to look up, but darkness took her sight.

Just before Farstar put Autumn to sleep, her thoughts had met with the human male named Daj. He frowned, then with a gentle movement, laid her head down on the bed, and lifted her legs. "Rest now *zifla* ~ angel, and take comfort." He allowed a slender finger to slide down Autumn's bronze cheek.

Daj swayed at a sickening pace; he reached up, grabbing his head in hopes of slowing down. Gradually he came to realize the cold, stone floor beneath him and that he was fully dressed. He felt his vest, checking for his hyper-band and dagger, then his neck for the plug, and he sighed with relief. "That kangaroo kicked just a little too hard." He sat up taking inventory of his body, "not broken — what is this place?" He spoke to Momma.

There was no response. He shuddered against the chill, speaking once more to Momma, "give location of colleagues," he tried to remember what had just happened. "Momma respond," panic tempted him. Finding a light stick in his pack he snapped it creating a soft green glow, standing and slowly turning with the light held above his head, he took in his surroundings. The light reflected off the two glittering archways on either side of the room, he moved closer and touched the shining stone. "Crystal," he gasped.

Holding his hyper-band in front of him, "I hope this works," he said, tapping the directional guide, searching for signatures. Daj stood silently for a long time, as the screen remained inactive. Finally, putting it away, he took a deep breath, put the light in his shoulder strap, placed his fingers in his pants pockets, thumbs through the loops, and he started to walk.

His pocketed fingers pressed against his legs, half a smile graced his lips, thinking about Jack. Jack was his best mate during boyhood. The most fun they had together was when the two of them would sneak up behind Lucinda Green, pull her dress up to get a peek at her panties, and of course to see the expression on her face. She would scream obscenities at them and start to cry. They would run to the nearest alley rolling with laughter and mocking her girly cries.

Jack's father was the tailor who sewed Lucinda and her family's clothes, often reminding them that it was a good income and to leave poor Lucinda alone. Daj curled his fingers, crunching up the inside of his pant's cotton pocket. Jack's father frequently stitched in leather pockets for his customers and family. Said it would keep them from wearing out so fast. Nevertheless, Jack could wear out the thickest patch in a very short time, and Daj would tease him about it, which always ended up in a good wrestling match. He chuckled.

The passageway started to lighten, and the clicking from his boot heels became muffled. He noticed the stone had turned to moss and the walls now shrouded him in dense forest. Quick as a rabbit, he backed up against one of the tallest trees he'd ever seen, the golden-leafed branches drooped nearly to the ground. Somewhere in his mind, a story was coming to life. He reached for his dagger and found a short sword in hand, leather clothing outfitted him, and a foolish grin crept over his lips. The place was bringing his fantasies to life. "Welcome to Targ," someone said. "I hope you are ready for what awaits." His eyes met with eyes of diamonds.

Nacoo sat in the center of a white room; he shielded his eyes from its brightness. What had just occurred? He tried to think but his head pounded. "Ugh," he checked his hyper-band, "can anyone hear me?" He boomed, holding his head. "Ugh, I think I cracked my head. It hurts like it anyway." An empty gray screen met his eyes, sliding his hand down he felt for his plug. "Good, still there," he sighed. There were no doors he could see, just white everywhere. He stood slowly to his full height of six foot seven and moved unsteadily toward a wall. Placing his left hand upon it, he leaned slightly forward, holding his head with the other hand.

He felt his way around the room, hoping to find an oddity that could serve as a door. After nearly walking all the way back to where he had placed his hyper-band, he found a small indentation; he grabbed up his hyper-band and pushed a finger into the hole. The wall slid open. On the other side of the wall sat his ultimate dream. The Sunstream Flying Craft: the Sunstream was Earth's finest air ship as far as Nacoo was concerned.

The machine glistened in the brilliance of the room; he let his fingertips glide over the surface and whistled. "She's a beauty." He remembered seeing an antique Sunstream at an aircraft show his father had taken him to as a young man. The manufactured date was around the year 2025, making the model before him about one hundred and twenty-five years old. "Well kept," and with an enthusiastic grin, he forgot the ache in his head and pushed the door button. It slid along well-conditioned tracks a digital voice greeted him. "Welcome to Kandoria." Nacoo paused, caressing the wand inside his vest. "Kandoria, odd place," he thought.

Nacoo ducked to get inside, and once seated, found it comfortable and spacious. "Oh, Father, if you could see this. His large leathered hand gently wiped the control panel stopping to rest next to a small, bony, brown hand; he turned and looked into the eyes of his father. "Father," he said, barely audible. His mind reeled back to the last time he had seen him. "You're dead!" Fear caught in his throat.

"Son," his father's gentle voice met his ears. "Let us have this short time together," his small hand patted the big man's hand. "Get this baby flying," The old wrinkled face cracked into a familiar smile. Not knowing exactly why, Nacoo shook off the fright he felt and returned a smile to the old man. He pressed the lift button.

A small rumble shuddered through the aircraft as it lifted off the floor. The electro-magnetism was still in working order, the men grinned with shear excitement. Nacoo pushed the control stick forward rapidly raising the Sunstream. "And away we go," he cheered. Pushing the stick to the left, and swiftly they were above the jungle. Nacoo could see the camp tents set in a circle and the entrance to the cavern, which Radin's men guarded. He wondered if someone had found Autumn yet. "I should go back and continue my search, Father." He spoke to the old man, and without warning, a robust outpouring of laughter escaped him. "This is superb, Father." The old man's eyes sparkled like diamonds and he chuckled under his breath.

Zyleon sat looking out the large windows down at the pool, the ache in his legs had vanished, and swimming sounded like fun. He stretched, put on comfortable shorts he found on a chair, threw a towel over his shoulder, and slipped on a pair of sandals. He laughed. "He thought of everything; a drink is in order for that boy," he said, still puzzled about Daj telling him he had taken a fall. He certainly didn't feel like he whacked his head. The last thing he remembered was drifting away from Dawn and then Daj doctoring him. "Something's just not right about that," he mumbled massaging his chin.

The sun warmed his face as he lay back on the chair; a warm gentle breeze dried the water from his skin. This must be what Heaven is like, he thought. "May I get you a drink, sir?" A mousy voiced attendant asked him, and brought him out of his reverie.

He opened his eyes, blinking away the brightness. "Sure." He sat up taking the menu offered him.

"There is a gentleman wishing to speak with you." The server nodded her head in the direction of the shaded tables.

"I'll have a coffee, over there with the gentleman."

"Very good, sir," she said, walking away.

Zyleon moved with the ease of a twenty year old. He reached out to shake the stranger's hand. "You asked to speak with me?" His breath came short when the pale, blue-gray, slender, six-fingered hand took hold of his.

"My name is Thorb; I hope you are comforted with provisions given. We find that your experience can go no further until complete healing occurs, and you are more able to enjoy our offerings."

Thorb's eyes shone like the diamond on Kuranna's finger.

"We apologize for such harsh entry —" he paused. "We have not had this facility running for many of your human years. Tainted air of old artu; an *aresh* ~ essence, that brings on pleasant encounters of the mind, caused the quandary." The room he had sat in with Dawn materialized around him, stupefying the Professor even more. "Zyleon, your questions shall be answered but now you must rest for safety on your trip.

Zyleon thought he was in a dream; did he actually stand in front of an alien being?

"Please, come with me."

He cautiously accepted the offer, following the alien down a corridor of white and into a docking bay. The sweet smell of peach blossoms scented the air, causing an even dreamier feel to what was happening. They boarded a vessel; one that he did not recognize. They walked over to a tiny cabin, entering in; now clothed in a white robe —how — he wondered is this occurring. "Please take comfort here," the melodious voice said. He lay down without resistance; lids heavy and mind clouded, he allowed sleep to come.

Dawn awoke standing next to an ancient crypt looking into the hollow eyes of an alien figure. She blinked and took a step back. "Where am I?" she gasped, feeling for her hyper-band. Hanging lamps emitted a soft green glow; she shivered in this cool belly of the cavern. As an anthropologist she had learned to keep the heebie-jeebies at bay but this setting was especially eerie, gooseflesh crawled over her body. She raised her hyper-band to her lips, "Momma," she nearly croaked, "Report."

Dawn spun her head and through the fog of her apprehension, a familiar voice spoke. "Your equipment is temporarily disabled."

"Woo!" she jumped. Hank's eyes sparkled. "Where is this place, and what's going on?" She released a frustrated squeak. "And just what are you doing to me?"

Hank grasped her hand and Dawn sensed a shift in the air; a woodsy smell filled her nose. She looked up at the canopy of a great forest and in her awe became aware that she herself was clothed in a full-length leather cloak with a quiver flung over her shoulder. In her right hand, she tightly held a short bow; Hank squeezed her hand with an urgent grip. "Hurry, we must run."

Farstar sat on a bench that previously was not there. Autumn's honey-brown hair fell about her face and shoulders. She was ready for transportation and he needed to make sure she enjoyed her trip. He slipped into her dreams and found himself there.

"What is the purpose of the wand?" she asked him.

"It is the key to Kandoria." He smiled enjoying the rush of excitement that came from her.

"Key to Kandoria," she repeated softly.

Farstar devolved deeper into her mind. He desired to experience her thrill. This woman had a hundred questions, yet even in her dream, she carefully thought on each one that arose. "Kandoria is an *ootau* ~ comfort facility. It is a place to rest, heal, study and to take pleasure in what you imagine or allow interaction with others imaginations. The wand is but a key."

Autumn looked up through dreaming eyes, into Farstar's diamond eyes, and for a moment wanted to cry. He was so beautiful. "Oh," embarrassed she turned away from him. "What do you study?" she asked, and out of thin air, a book appeared in her left hand. Farstar guided her to a large comfortable chair, a small table sat next to it with a reading lamp already lit.

A fireplace was aglow with flames licking and caressing the logs. His essence filled her. "You are very beautiful, too," his voice mesmerizing, alluring her to places she never dared to go. Cool gray lips pressed against her forehead, "*ne ootau* ~ take comfort, in your study, soon we shall be past the Kuiper belt and into interstellar space; after a short time we shall arrive at my home planet, Targ, and there I shall show you its wonders."

Autumn grabbed for Farstar's hand in this misty land of dreams. "Where are my friends?" She stared into those shining eyes, "Are they coming? Do they know I'm safe?"

"*Va* ~ yes," he answered, "become still now and study for the answers you seek," placing his hand over hers he moved her hands across the book. The title Kandoria etched in gold letters met her eyes.

Once again, Farstar felt Autumn's sheer pleasure of discovery.

"My Uncle Zyleon would be most fascinated with this; after old pa died, the Professor would read me stories about the space stations and how someday we would meet a new race." Autumn murmured, dreamily gazing into Farstar's eyes. "What a discovery! This will change men's history and our view of the galaxies, most definitely." She giggled as though intoxicated. "What have you done to me Farstar? My mind fades in and out of clouds; does that otah give you a kick?" She leaned forward.

He held her shoulders, gently pushing her back into the chair, "you are dreaming *bu zifla* ~ my angel."

"You seem so real." She said, reaching up to touch his face.

"Our race has an area in our brains similar to your pineal gland, which enables us to feel other's thoughts and emotions; it is called blending." Farstar felt Autumn's mind quiver with curiosity.

"That is so fascinating." Pausing, she asked. "Will I remember this?"

"*Va* ~ yes," Farstar answered.

"Can you hear all the private thoughts floating around in my head?" She asked shyly.

"Va."

"Can you make them as real as you seem to me?" She felt so sleepy.

"Imaginations can be acted out or watched as a play; it depends on how deeply rooted the emotions are to such — private thoughts." Farstar was finding this conversation quite amusing.

"Ah, the difference between love and lust, "as Daj would say;" Love is the action, lust the play."

Farstar pulled back from her mind.

"What was that?" Autumn grabbed the arms of the envisaged chair. A wave similar to what occurred during a space-boat, locking in at a docking port, passed through her. "We are home, rest now." Farstar looked down upon the face of the sleeping female human, *"vuel ~ sleep,"* he whispered in her mind.

"**Foster's** the name," the tall slender man said from the shadows; he held a gloved hand out to Daj. "I think finding a camp for the night would be a grand idea," he stated, handing Daj a set of reins belonging to a black dale. "He's a fine ride and can carry his weight in gold." Foster chuckled.

"He's a beaut," Daj grinned, swinging expertly up into the saddle; he patted the dale on the neck. "This is some kind of fantasy, eh?" Daj asked his guide.

"You are quick to figure things out." Foster made a clicking sound with his mouth and lightly kicked the flanks of his mount. "This is an integration of real and unreal."

"What kind of an answer is that?" Daj flicked the reins. "Is this really happening or not?"

Foster chuckled again, *"tutal* ~ friend, what is happening to you right now is real, created between the two of us," he continued. "For you it is, as if, far away or long forgotten thoughts have come to life and for me it is as if I conduct a dream."

"So — this is akin to an interactive movie." Scents of moist soil and horse sweat filled his nostrils. Daj pushed his Barmah off his head letting the string hold it around his neck, and glanced around at the leaves growing on the knobby shaped branches of the trees, they appeared to change color in the shadowy coolness of the woods, adding ambience to this mystery.

"Va ~ yes," Foster answered.

"You're not human," Daj shifted in the saddle and stared at Foster's gray-blue skin and sparkling eyes. Just a story he thought.

"It is not a story, I am Targian." Foster bowed his head to Daj.

Startled at hearing this being's voice in his head, Daj remained silent while a slow acceptance of his situation settled in his mind.

The two rode through one forest trail after another, crossing creeks and ambling through rocky pathways, stopping only long enough to stretch. They rode on until dusk, when the path opened up to a small glade. "This shall be a good place to rest," Foster said. He dismounted, feeling every bit saddle sore.

Daj laughed, "A might long being in the saddle, when one hasn't ridden for awhile." He let out a grunt as his feet hit the ground.

Daj unsaddled and set the horses to feed on the dark, lush grass, he had blankets and cooking utensil unpacked when Foster returned with wood for a fire. The men ate dried fruits and drank an herb tea Foster brewed. Daj's mouth tingled with sweetness. "What do you call this?" He held up his cup to Foster, who was lying on a blanket on his side, one hand holding up his head, the other playing with a twig. The fire shadowed his face, adding new dimensions to his fine-featured looks.

"It is cu," Foster tossed the stick into the fire. "It shall give you strength to meet your battles."

Daj gazed into eyes that danced with the flames, "do you know of my colleagues?" he asked.

"Va, they are well."

Abruptly, blue smoke billowed from the fire, forming a cloud around them. Daj waved his hands back and forth in front of his face and tried not to breath. His eyes watered and he tried to stand up, instead he doubled over with laughter. He fell back onto his sleeping roll. "I'll be gob smacked, that's bottler smoke. There will be a need to get me some of that." He lay back down, hands behind his head, looking up at the stars through blurry eyes, wondering if he should trust what was happening, it felt way to good.

Turning his head, he could see Foster lying on his back, hands behind his head also, grinning from ear to ear, this caused another rumble of laughter to escape him, and he returned his gaze to the sky, "Foster why do the stars look so different tonight?" He chuckled not daring to look at him.

Foster let a moment slip by before he answered. "Because we are in my galaxy."

Daj yawned. "Your galaxy?"

"Va, we arrived here shortly after we met," Foster let out a small laugh, he chewed on a piece of grass, grinning foolishly.

"Arrived?" Daj sat up and removed his vest, laid back down tucking it under his head.

"You are on my home planet, Targ. Remember the corridor as it began to change?"

"Yes," Daj mumbled.

"That was when you stepped into my ship and when we reached the mouth of the glade — that is when we stepped out."

Daj looked over at his companion through half lidded eyes. "Well if that doesn't take the roo by the balls."

The two of them exchanged grins and gazed at the stars until sleep beckoned them.

It was not quite dawn yet when Daj awoke to Foster's voice in his head. *"Do not move; there is a wodevil standing over you."* He opened his eyes to see a monstrous hulk of a man shape, eyes flaming yellow, charcoal skin with great bulging veins that popped out everywhere and oozed with a putrid smelling fluid, a deep guttural sound came from the beasts' throat and every hair on Daj's body stood at attention.

Daj swallowed hard and again he heard Foster in his mind, *"DO NOT MOVE, NOT EVEN A BLINK OF THE EYE!"* The beast came closer, snorting and viciously snapping its slobbering jaws. Daj held his breath, the heat that emanated from it caused beads of perspiration to erupt across his forehead, and with the need for air he painfully, slowly inhaled the smell of a rotted corpse. His eyes burned and the bitter contents of his stomach rose in his throat, he swallowed hard. *"NOOO,"* Foster's voice screamed in his mind, the wodevil bared its razor sharp teeth, mucus dripped in globs from pinky-sized fangs onto his shirt. It lunged with the force of a laser whip, sinking its blackened teeth into Daj's right thigh. "AAAAHHH," he shrieked, the beast lifted him off the ground tearing a chunk of his leg as it did so.

Daj fell violently onto the ground. "AAAAHHH," he let loose another agonized scream, grabbing his leg, hot red blood, gushed between his fingers.

"I have your blade," Foster shouted.

The creature let out an earth-shaking roar, swinging its hideous head from side to side like a charging bull. It tore at the ground with talons of steel. Clods of dirt and grass flew as Daj scrambled toward Foster and his sword. The beast again let out an ear-splitting cry causing both Daj and Foster to cower and cover their ears. Daj looked for a route of escape within his field of vision, seeing in his tormented shock, a woman aim her bow; she released an arrow straight and true, in this violet morning light, and then another shattering wail came from the wodevil. It stood looking bewildered; the great foul beast collapsed to its knees then crashed face first across the sleeping roll Daj had been laying on moments before.

"What the bloody 'ell was that!" Trembling violently, he looked up at a shaken Foster.

"A plague on our planet," Foster answered, beleaguered, "they feast on any living thing." Splattered blood glistened on his pale skin. "If it were not for those two," he pointed to the woman and a man now walking toward them. "We may not have lived." Foster held his sword close, breathing hard, staring at the great bulk of beast. "It did not like the taste of your blood; that is why it did not strike twice." Foster knelt down beside Daj who was trying desperately to stop the bleeding from his leg and tied Daj's bandana tightly above the wound, making him wince. "Kolum trey," he whispered.

Daj watched dumbfounded as Foster placed his six-fingered hands around his leg; they grew intensely warm. Little strikes of blue lightning emitted from Foster's hands. A strong feeling of compassion swept through Daj, making him want to weep. Then the pain dissipated and the bleeding stopped. Amazingly, the missing part of his leg began to regenerate at a high rate of speed, nay leaving a scar. Daj was open-mouthed as he watched the miracle Foster had just performed; he gazed up into the face of his healer, a face that looked drawn but relieved.

"You have lost a lot of blood tutal," Foster panted, his chin lowered to his chest.

"I feel great," Daj stood testing out his leg and looked down at the stained, ragged tear in his jeans. "I don't know what to say or even how thank you," he said, and picked up his hat, running his fingers over the snap, Jack's father had sewn in for him, allowing him to snap up the right brim.

"I shall teach you, that is how to thank me," Foster answered, lifting his head and donning a pair of five fingered gloves.

"Why five fingered gloves," Daj asked, finding that rather curious. Foster entered Daj's mind, *"say nothing of the healing, or gloves to the woman."*

Daj felt dazed. "She will see the rip in my pants." It was strange to hear someone inside his head, but everything was strange lately.

"She does not know that I am Targian." The two men stood downwind of the wodevil and waited to greet their saviors.

Daj thought the woman's gait was familiar, a wisp of strawberry colored hair flitted out from under the hooded cloak. "Nice shot," he yelled, as they drew close.

Dawn lifted her face to look at the man whose voice was the same as her friend Daj. Tears filled her eyes as she pulled her hood from her head and ran toward him.

Daj stared in disbelief. Was it really Dawn, did she just save his life? The woman leapt into his arms, almost knocking him to the ground.

"Oh, Daj," she wept, "I thought this was a dream I couldn't wake up from. I didn't think I would ever see you or anyone else again."

"Hey spitfire," he laughed, grabbing her by both sides of her head. He kissed her cheeks, tasting the salt of her tears, and hugged her tight once more. "It's not a dream, we've been nabbed and are part of an interactive game, reasonably," he murmured, with a genuine inflection.

"Oh, Daj," she cried, her words muffled against his chest. "I've been so scared, very strange things have occurred. I was holding the Professor's arm when he disappeared." Dawn was sobbing.

"I know," Daj cooed, reassuringly, and held her until his shirt was wet and her eyes were dry.

Hank stood captivated, watching with a curious expression on his face.

Foster was very still.

"Do you know what you just did for us? I would never have thought you were an expert archer." Daj held her small hands, admiring them.

"That thing chased us all night," Dawn said weary, looking Daj up and down, "Hank said we could shake the beast from our trail when we came upon your camp. I didn't know it was you." Dawn wiped new wetness from her freckled cheeks. "We hid in the bushes until the thing made its move. I aimed at its silhouette and heard it scream; when it flailed its arms in the air, it gave me a better target," she said with a faint smile.

Daj gently squeezed her hands. "Yes it did, my saving angel, yes it did."

Bewildered, Nacoo found himself seated in the Sunstream, looking at the deck of an alien landing-dock. He shook his head thinking it only a dream when a slender of medium height, pale blue-gray skinned, diamond-eyed alien motioned for him to lock down the landing gear. He thought of his father and the twinkle in his eyes. "Ugh," he slapped the palm of his hand on his forehead. "This is a real alien abduction."

"What a strange way of putting it," said the now materialized alien beside him. "My name is Jax, I am your, umm — shall we say, tour guide."

"Tour guide?" Nacoo questioned and pushed the landing gear button following the hand signals of the alien flagman. "Where am I?" The Sunstream settled as graceful as a swan.

"You are a skilled pilot," Jax expressed with admiration. "This is my home planet, Targ. Come, we are expected at the reception hall." Jax smiled and opened his door, glancing back at Nacoo's astounded expression, and he laughed to himself. "You may find our accommodations to your liking," he said as he exited the Sunstream.

"Is the air breathable?" Nacoo asked, skeptical, as he watched the Targian's fine, silver hair, flutter airborne like dandelion seeds on the current of a summer breeze.

"You may feel like you are in a higher altitude, so breathe slowly."

"Breathe slowly," Nacoo, repeated, a betraying edge of uncertainty filtered into his voice.

The two walked into a lounge area where Jax motioned Nacoo to sit. Nacoo sat; feeling uneasy; *"where are you?"* He tapped the send button on his hyper-band but the screen remained inactive.

Jax returned a few moments later and gestured for Nacoo to follow him. "Come, I wish you to meet a *tutal* ~ friend, of mine."

As Nacoo approached Jax and his female friend, a strange but familiar sensation crept over him. She reached out her hand saying, "so we meet again, Nacoo."

When her cool slender hand slid into his, flashes of Dawn came to him. "You," he uttered, in a low tone.

"Mmm — I assume you've enjoyed our hospitality. I am Clamora, creator of your first fantasy." Her voice was musical. *"Come with us, we wish to show you much."*

Strangely, Nacoo heard her in his mind, humming a melody to which he could almost hear the stars twinkling, enticing him to follow her beauty.

A gentle hand stroked Professor Zyleon's face; *"you may awaken now,"* a voice came into his mind. *"Our journey has brought us safely to Targ, my home planet."* A lovely alien female looked deep into his eyes. *"Your physical infirmities have been healed and you shall be able to continue with y…"*

Zyleon raised his hand to hers. "No more dreams," he uttered, amazed that he could hear her so clearly in his thoughts.

"As you wish," she spoke audibly soft, a musical voice, and rose from his side leaving him alone in this white walled room.

Back in his clothing, all except his socks and shoes that he could not find, Zyleon moved about the small area, massaging his chin. Could it be true, he pondered, that this ancient race has the secrets of healing? It warmed his heart to think of Kuranna free of her ailments. He dropped his arm, causing his hand to rub against his hyper-band, "Ah yes," he said, hopeful, and tapped in the message, "Autumn, where are you?" Uncle Zyleon. Send. The screen remained blank. He tapped a little less ardently, Momma. Send. "Nothing," he scowled.

Minutes later a panel moved providing a doorway in which Thorb stood. He was dressed in a long flowing robe that absorbed the soft glow of light emanating from the walls themselves, Thorb motioned for Professor Zyleon to follow him.

"Where are my team members," he blurted out.

"They are here and are well. You shall see them soon enough." Thorb's diamond eyes flashed with amusement. *"Come, bu tutal ~ my friend,"* he wagged a slender, six-fingered hand toward the Professor.

An apprehensive curiosity filled Zyleon as they walked through a long, white corridor lined with many unrecognizable plants; his bare feet sunk into soft, warm, moss. It felt peculiar, as if it moved in tiny circular patterns beneath him. Crystals framed windows that stretched past a garden of such unusual, enticing color that he stopped to gaze upon its splendor.

"Please, Professor, come," Thorb said, laying a cool, gentle hand on his shoulder. *"We shall go out into the garden and sit."*

Zyleon was too fascinated to sit still. Each plant held a beauty indescribable to the folks back home, let alone the telepathic communication. The scents were exhilarating; each aroused a separate feeling completely. The thought occurred to him that an alignment of the magnetic field and vibratory rates of light, sound, and even scent frequencies could cause an organism to rearrange its cellular structure, healing diseased tissue, something medical science experimented with on Earth. He looked intently at Thorb and considered how youthful he felt. "How did you heal me?" he asked.

"With a blending of *appo's* ~ teas, and crystal energy manipulation," Thorb answered in his melodious voice.

"Is it possible for you to heal all disease?" Zyleon felt like a child before a king.

"Va ~ yes, it is possible."

"My wife," he asked expectantly.

"Va."

Professor Zyleon's face flushed at the multitude of feelings racing through him. This alien was telling him that he could make Kuranna feel well again. "Thank you," he said, a small breath of air catching in his throat.

Thorb sat patiently keeping his mind open to the musings and intense emotion of Professor Zyleon, it delighted him to experience such curiosity and eagerness, something a Targian rarely practiced. It was uncomfortable for him to block communication between him and his companions, but he needed to gain the Professor's trust last, ensuring their survival came first.

Dawn surveyed the campsite. "Nice place," she said, wrinkling her nose. "My name's Dawn." She reached out to shake hands with Foster.

Foster raised her hand to his lips and said. "My lady, you are very welcome, and it would please me if you would stay for morning meal." He watched with amusement at the flushing of her cheeks.

"Thank you but —" She paused, staring into Foster's bright twinkling eyes. "Woo wee, that thing stinks." She waved a hand in front of her face. Then feeling a little self-conscience, she turned back to Daj, swinging a hand toward Hank, "by the way Daj, this is Hank, he planned this whole encounter, so I guess he's the real hero."

Daj and Hank shook hands vigorously. "I find the lady's company pleasing." Hank inclined his head never leaving Daj's eyes, *"I am Targian."*

Daj felt his eyes widen, startled by the introduction, quickly searching for Dawn's face, saying. "Don't let the girl fool you, she's a rip of a wizard in disguise." Everyone laughed.

"Daj, you should never give away a lady's secrets." Dawn winked at him and laid her bow down on the ground getting a better look at his torn and bloodied pant leg, she took a sharp intake of air, "Daj you're hurt," she gasped and immediately cupped her nose.

"Just a scratch, nothing to get clucky about," he looked at Foster, whose eyes were watering from the stench.

"Come on then, mates; give a hand with this creature." Daj gestured to the aliens, holding his nose and tactfully switching the subject. "Our lady," he bowed in jest to Dawn, "can stoke the fire."

"Only if you're okay," she said, looking him in the eye.

"Right, my little red plum, I'm fine, really," Daj, said tipping his Barmah hat, and blew her a kiss.

"That's very brave of you." Dawn acknowledged, feeling more confident about their situation.

Foster handed Dawn a small stick. "Throw this in the fire to cleanse the smell," he instructed, plugging his nose with his free hand.

Dawn took the stick giving it a sniff. "This smells good," and left the stick under her nose, making eye contact with Foster again, *"and you are more than a saving angel."* "What?" Dawn started; she had not seen his lips move.

Foster bowed his head and said nothing more.

Dawn pulled the stick away from her nose and looked at it with raised eyebrows. Life was not what it used to be, she thought, and raised the stick again to her nose.

Daj and the two aliens had carried the wodevil some distance down wind of the camp. Although Daj was surprised at how little straining he did, it seemed the aliens were quite strong, almost as strong as the stink of the beast.

Daj had his sticky, bloodied bandana wrapped around his face, but it only muffled the stench. His stomach lurched and eyes watered each step of the way, so when Hank suggested dropping the carcass and washing in the creek, he was more than willing.

When they stepped into the maroon-tinted, warm water of the creek, Hank handed Daj a small blue stone. *"Wash with this, it shall cleanse the beast from you."* Hank's slender fingers slid across Daj's fingers. *"You are a strong specimen; TaChoo shall find ootau ~ comfort, in you."*

"Aash ta bow!" Foster admonished Hank.

Daj glanced up from where he squatted washing his arms and noted the look of disapproval on Foster's face, "Hank," he cleared his throat, "A bit of a beaut, eh?" Both aliens looked toward Daj, their eyes shimmered and danced before him, seeming to cause his head to spin. "Ugh," Daj placed his hands on the ground for balance, "tone it down mates, I didn't mean, any disrespect." Daj panted and stumbled away from the waters edge and sat down under a tree, holding his head as if he'd just taken a heavy blow.

A hand rested on his shoulder another on his brow, *"kolum trey."* Daj felt a return of equilibrium, *"TaChoo is beautiful,"* he heard Foster in his mind.

Daj lifted his head, placing his arms on his knees. "You blokes sure do pack a punch. I never saw it coming, one of your many magical tricks — if I were to venture a guess."

"Something akin to that," Hank chuckled.

Daj stood and headed back into the unusual colored water, rinsed off his face and bandana and picked up the stone he had dropped. It purified the air around him, removing the stench from his skin and his clothes. He placed it in his tee-shirt pocket, thankful for the gift; he thought of Professor Zyleon and wondered what bizarre experience he was having, and what was Nacoo doing and had anyone found Autumn? Seeing Dawn again grounded him and brought his mind back to their mission. He gently patted the pocketed stone, wanting to study it, understand it, and apply the knowledge gathered. Any good geologist would surely be interested in it. He looked around at his surroundings marveling at the beauty. What a strange and awesome place this was.

Dawn smoothed out her cloak when she spotted the men walking back up the hill. The stick worked perfectly to deodorize the air, but the stewing berries and brewing tea from Foster's pack perfumed the air with a fresh sweet aroma, even more delightful. She sighed and checked things over. Foster mysteriously placed instructions in her mind before they had left. She was to place the berries in the hard bread-cups, and scoop two spoons of the tea on top. Then place half of the sprig of loc, the stuff that looked like dill, on hers and Daj's cups, saying it would energize them for the long ride ahead — she wondered if Daj knew where they were going and combed her fingers through the tangles, of her strawberry waves.

Autumn awoke to a soft breeze kissing her face, and for a moment, she thought she was home in her own backyard, except that the sky was wine-colored with not one sun but two. She lay still, stunned by the exquisite garden she was in, flowers of shades and hues more vibrant than Earths swayed gently around her, their aromas tantalizing her senses to the point of mouth watering. Autumn sat up, running her hands over the robe she now wore, of silky white material, and the only thing she had covering her. A small surge of panic crept into her thoughts. She bolted upright searching for her equipment, causing her head to sway, and she quickly lay back down.

"I have brought you a cup of *appo* ~ tea, to aid with the space-sickness," said Farstar, appearing from the shadows of the room, sitting down next her on the bed of flowers. "All of you *komi* ~ humans, shall need this to oxygenate your blood," he smiled warmly at her.

"Where are my clothes and equipment?" Autumn pulled the silky robe up around her neck.

"They are being cleansed."

Autumn regarded Farstar, tightening her fingers, "I need them back."

"They shall be returned to you," he said, with cool self-control.

"Who changed my clothes," Autumn asked, trying not to show her discomfort. Her voice trembled.

"It was I. Now you must drink your appo while it is still warm." He pushed the cup closer to her amused at how quickly her emotions changed.

Autumn closed her eyes for a brief moment. "You," she whispered, warily taking the teacup, the aroma had an immediate calming effect, and the taste was luxurious. "Mmm," she hummed, fear dissipating, "How do you do that?"

"What?"

"Just appear." She gazed into his luminous eyes, feeling giddy.

"Our race is adept at manipulation of physical placement; you may think of it as the fourth dimension, you may see it as — visions." Farstar held Autumn's gaze, reaching out he touched her cheek. *"You find this garden to your ootau ~ comfort?"*

"Yes," she answered. He held her with his mind; his touch sent warm sprays of pleasure through her. He was exquisite. Catching herself, she cleared her throat "Ahem," and placed the empty cup back in his hand. "I would like to learn more about your planet, my curiosity is hardly containable." She faltered, feeling as if she were in a dream state.

"Va ~ yes, you shall." Standing, Farstar held a gentle hand under her elbow, he could feel her shudder, and it pleased him. He pulled her close, enjoying her human scent. *"You are strong and fertile; I shall share with you, the aresh ~ essence, of my race."* He led her to a bed of ginger-colored clovers knowing her mind was his.

The scented breeze was enticing as they lay down upon the small golden flowers, Autumn's mind shifted into a lucid state. It was as if her awareness had climbed a thousand steps of a pyramid and that everything was open to her, all she had to do was ask. Tiny electric shocks pulsed inside her brain, knowing Farstar was orchestrating what was happening, with each pulse, she glimpsed images of his home and race and the trouble they were suffering from. This entirely, taking place within moments. A deep stirring of passion unlocked its doors. Desire for what this alien offered flooded her consciousness, an explosion of information poured into her mind, and it was almost too much to bear, until she once again felt Farstar's gentle touch on her. She tucked her head in against his chest, letting tears flow freely.

Farstar smiled a thin gray-lipped smile.

IV

Thorb's gaze never left Professor Zyleon; he could feel the enthusiasm surge through the robust little man, which Thorb found refreshingly pleasant.

"Why have you brought me here, Thorb?" the Professor asked, rubbing a purple-mitten shaped leaf.

"We need you," Thorb went deeper into Professor Zyleon's mind, *"Professor, our race has need of new aresh ~ essence."*

"New essence," Zyleon eyed Thorb suspiciously.

"Life," Thorb said.

Zyleon stood for a moment trying to determine if this was a threat, "how will my life be used?" He asked, looking intentionally at the leaf.

"You are — as you would call it, a treasure." Thorb pressed his thin lips together.

"Treasure," snapped Zyleon.

"Va, we influenced the circumstances in your lives to bring you and your team to us. We find each of your companions a fine specimen th…"

"My people are here!" His voice reached a higher octave. "Where are they?" In his agitation, he ripped the leaf he held between his fingers; purple sap rapidly stained his hand.

"Be mindful of how you treat the vegetation!" Thorb shouted in the Professor's mind, which made him sway and sit down hard on the bench across from him. *"You shall listen now; and gain knowledge."*

"Many pardons," Zyleon apologized.

"Targ is very different from Earth," he said, the aggression gone from his voice. Thorb watched the Professor closely.

"I shall listen," he uttered, feeling a bit woozy.

"Thousands of years ago in your measured time, we shared common ground on your planet, the sanctuary known as Kandoria, your excavation site. Komi ~ humans would come to us for healing and pleasures of the mind." Thorb felt Zyleon's thoughts shift to Kuranna and he allowed room for

consideration and answered his reflection, *"va, as you have wondered, Kuranna shall arrive soon for healing, she, of course shall be under the affects of fresh artu, making her transition easier."* He regained Zyleon's attention and continued. *"When warring broke out between Earth beings, Targ closed our temples. Only an elect few were chosen to share our gifts in exchange for spiritually intelligent, strong specimens."*

Professor Zyleon gritted his teeth at the word specimens.

Thorb paused, *"Ah — Professor, quiet your rage. We have harmed no one, and would you, not call us, specimens? Your ancestors need fresh aresh ~ essence, and you need our forgotten knowledge to further your Earth's well being."* Thorb shifted his bare feet across the mossy floor, *"Is that not why you chose to come on this expedition? Your inquisitiveness is of great value to us."* Thorb touched a cool hand to the Professor's forehead, *"The egmur must be cleansed from your body before you fall asleep and think you are dreaming."*

Professor Zyleon's mind lay in a fog as thick as the darkest night. Like static lightening, images of a beautiful being flickered in and out of his vision. The female alien that spoke to him earlier, carefully cleansed his hand, and with each swipe of the cloth, his head cleared but brought on an incredible thirst.

A delicate-figured male emerged out of nowhere, handed him a glass of orange-colored liquid, saying, *"drink,"* and he did. The beverage's flavor reminded him of watermelon but had no succulence to it. So unusual he thought, starting to feel better.

A few moments passed before his tongue could form words into speech. "When will I see my people, Thorb?" He lowered his head, feeling meek.

"They are enjoying their own experiences. It shall depend on how engaged they are in their — adventures." He offered a gentle smile.

"My wife — will she know what is happening?" Timidly he glanced at Thorb. *"She shall be given knowledge."*

"Exactly — what do you mean by essence?" Zyleon asked once again, hands folded not wanting to touch another unfamiliar plant.

"Aresh ~ essence, is our very being, our life force." He paused and sat down beside Zyleon, *"We share an intimate existence with Targ, our planet. This awareness allows us to grow in knowledge, creating a world that works in unison."* Thorb sent this knowledge into the Professor's mind.

The Professor observed images, like a holographic recording inside his mind, of Targ and Targians living together, exchanging energy, being of one mind and order. "Amazing," he whispered.

"Much starlight passed between Targian creation and kom ~ human, creation but bestowment from the Most Ancient of Ancients, granted our Targ to create your race from ours. The making of a denser life force was just an experiment. However, you have become so much more. We enjoy watching with pleasurable interest, our extensions of us progress." Thorb melded a little deeper with Professor Zyleon's mind. *"But sadly, we discovered that our denser family lost their ability to remain as we do — spiritually open."*

"Some of us have, my Kuranna is one," Zyleon said, rubbing his chin.

"Va, to a certain extent, but your world has a long journey ahead of it to reach a full state of awareness, we see improvements and again one day soon, we shall be able to share common ground." Thorb sent visions to the Professor's mind of Kandoria's early history, operating as an experimental laboratory and later as a healing temple.

He watched the Professor's face change with the understanding. Pulling back from his mind, he showed him images of his team. *"First, we must secure our ability to procreate physically. Our abilities with healing have permitted us longevity but our lighter form has weakened us. You are our code, our pattern to a stronger physical existence."*

"So we are here to procreate," Zyleon sighed, massaging his baldhead.

"In a matter of speaking, va, Targ can accelerate and develop physical form using a simplified natural process." Thorb motioned for Professor Zyleon to stand.

Zyleon stood, thinking how crazy it all sounded. The planet Targ is a sentient being, one that he descended from — his bloodline, his history, and his origins.

"Va," Thorb smiled answering Zyleon's thought, *"our universe is vast and continuous with much to learn before we return to the Breath of Life. Now Professor, it is time to show you the rest of my home."* Thorb placed his cool hand on Professor Zyleon's shoulder.

"So it wasn't actually my friend Dawn I was with?" Nacoo fumbled over his words, slightly offended.

"Av ~ no, I created that image to entice you," her slender fingers held his tight.

They walked on through a passage of white stone that was warm to the touch. The wand hummed inside of his jacket, and he felt for his hyper-band. "Are any of my colleagues here?" Nacoo asked, anxiously.

"Va ~ yes, they are in their own ootau ~ comfort." Clamora stopped and placed her fingertip in a small depression in the wall. A door opened, exposing a room filled with lush vegetation. The furnishings appeared to be a part of the plants themselves. She led him to a leaf-covered, chaise lounge and motioned for him to sit.

Nacoo cautiously did as instructed. The lounge gave under his weight, forming to his body. Clamora raised his legs up and he stretched to his full length. Just go with it, he thought, as she removed his boots and socks.

"I will bring some *appo* ~ tea," she whispered in his ear.

The lounge shifted, enveloping him, oddly relaxing him. The wand hummed against his chest, he put his arms above his head and closed his eyes, drifting in a haze of semi-consciousness. He breathed in a captivating, unfamiliar scent, taking him deeper into relaxation, ghostly fingers travelled over his body, it surprised him at how deeply comfortable he was, given the peculiarity of this place. Nacoo lazed in this state of pleasant awareness, feeling as if time itself had stopped. All his concerns were as gentle waves rocking him on a deep blue sea.

A distant chiming voice broke through his enchantment. *"Wathu ~ awaken, Nacoo,"* and through silted eyes, he saw Clamora handing him a cup of *appo*, he thought, tea.

"This is cu," she smiled.

"Thank you," he said, groggily, the flora absorbing his sonorous voice.

By the gods, she was radiant. He smiled back, sitting up and feeling the lounge move with him. "I take it Jax is a pilot," he said, attempting to make conversation. The tea tasted sweet.

"Va," she waved a glowing hand over the lounge and it began to reshape itself. *"You may have any image you wish."*

Eyes of gem fire held his.

For the first time since she had re-entered the room, Nacoo realized a robe was all that covered him. Startled, he looked down at his legs. The foliage had repositioned him, pulling him deeper into its warm mysterious depths. He finished his tea in one swallow and closed his eyes, thinking, "this is just an illusion."

"Do not worry, I know your thoughts and shall comfort, you." Clamora lowered her head to Nacoo's and kissed his ear. *"You are my choice, strong and well bred. We shall share aresh ~ essence."*

Nacoo's head was in a cloud. Her fingers soothed him, she hummed softly, and aroma of many kinds scented the air. "I don't want this to be a dream," he shook his head to clear it.

Clamora raised an orange colored flower to his nose. *"Breathe deep,"* she smiled, *"I am glad you find ootau ~ comfort, in me."*

The fog lifted from Nacoo's mind, instantaneously, and he held this stunning alien in his arms. Her body was luminescent and soft as the softest silk. Her mind touched his and he hungered for more, he wanted to give to her... to comfort her, pleasure her. His mind tickled with energy, surges of electric heat ran through his frame. Thoughts of this strange new planet entered into his existence, it was the highest of exhilarations. New information poured into him, was Momma getting this? He smiled, and a new wave flooded his senses. Clamora spoke to him in her musical language and he understood that she needed his density, his form, his essence to bring balance back.

His body raced with tremors, explosions of delight met her every touch. She was mystery and intrigue unsurpassed by anything he had ever encountered. He felt her touches deep in his mind, *"Clamora, you are exquisite,"* and as he thought this, a great wave of pure love overcame him. The whole planet loved him.

The tea had made Dawn's head swim; she looked at Daj, he slumped forward in the saddle, holding on to the horse's neck. Foster held the reins. Hank lowered a hand to Dawn, lifted her up into the saddle, and held her from behind. Her head lay at the base of his chest. Odd she thought Hank looked gray.

Hank held Dawn close enjoying the feel of her human warmth against him. *"Oa cal tretch,"* he motioned for Foster to follow him to a vine-camouflaged entranceway, *"I must take her to the shram sy,"* Hank said, eagerness in his voice.

"Pah," Foster spoke to his tutal, *"The child shall be strong."*

Hank smiled.

Daj awoke thinking of Autumn, her dark honey hair flitting around her face and eyes that a man could find enriching and peaceful. She was a skilled colleague and a good friend that he so admired. Comfort and peace in those eyes — sparkling like the sun on the water — oh, how he desired to sink into her soul.

"Welcome," he heard, rolling his face away from the pillow.

"Morning," he sat up rubbing his head. "This has been one roo of a ride! Do you know where my hat is?" he asked, without looking up, almost afraid to see her.

A slender, six-fingered hand, pale-gray in color handed him his Barmah. *"I am TaChoo."*

Daj's mouth fell open, but no words came. He looked up at the most magnificent creature he had ever seen. "I must be dreaming, Hank certainly was right about you," he said, his words issued forth.

"We have transported you to my sleeping room. I am a child of Thorb, our planets communicator, or leader, as you would call him I am rah ~ sister, to Foster." She gazed steadily at Daj. *"Drink this appo ~ tea, you shall need it."* TaChoo slid her fingers down his forearm before handing him the cup. *"You are virile,"* she smiled, sensing Daj quiver at her touch.

"Transported? Where is Dawn? How about Professor Zyleon, Nacoo, and Autumn, I'm not sure I should drink this tea," Daj said, still rushing his words together, he shook like an old ship docking. "Coward," He thought, fitting his hat, avoiding her crystal eyes.

"You shall feel better if you drink. Travel by horse, as you know takes a lot out of one's self." TaChoo sat down beside Daj letting her mind probe his. *"I can become Autumn for you if it pleases you."* She teased the back of his neck. *"I can be any thing of ootau ~ comfort, for you."* She felt his mind shift.

Daj sipped the warm, sweet tea. Taking pleasure in her alien touch, fingers extraordinarily cool on his skin, relaxing, saying to himself, *"you are as splendid as they come, stay just the way you are,"* he dared a look into those radiant eyes and felt a deep stirring in his mind.

"Your colleagues are here, enjoying their own adventures. Let us enjoy ours." TaChoo pulled his hat strings from under his chin and knocked it off his head, letting out a small laugh. *"What a funny thing to cover such delightful hair."*

Daj reached up running his fingers through TaChoo's spider silk hair that shone like the full moon; he let his fingertips move over her thin gray lips. "Bottler," he said, mesmerized. She smiled and with her smile, everything fell away.

He stood dressed in an open white robe, standing in warm, maroon-colored water on a sandy beach. The sun penetrated his skin; it felt good on his face, as did the cool hands touching his body. Daj felt TaChoo's mind link with his, such a bizarre feeling, water washed around his bare feet, how odd he thought, that the sand felt like moss. Sharp tingles raced up his legs as if he were waking too early from sleep, a peculiar sensation of rain trickled down, on the inside of his body, causing him to shiver. As he stared into her diamond eyes, he completely yielded his will to her.

TaChoo hungrily devoured his surrender, sharing her aresh, giving him knowledge of the planet of why she had chosen him. She wrapped her mind around his, entwining her very soul with his, moving him, bringing him to the pinnacle of joy.

Hank held Dawn's hand, beckoning her with his mind. *"We must move to the shram sy ~ birthing room, jist vek ~ small one. Our seed must be transplanted into the planet to incubate."* Hank held Dawn with ease, carrying her down a dark, warm hallway.

"What are you talking about?" Her head was full of cotton and she felt as if she were floating.

"Our aresh ~ essence, is strong together." Hank embraced her lovingly.

"What seed?" Dawn's memories flashed back to the beach house. "What's going on?" she moaned, fear gripping her heart.

"Do not be afraid," Hank placed his fingertips on her forehead and whispered a strange word, *"vuel."*

Dawn gazed into Hank's diamond, alien, eyes before falling into darkness.

Farstar held Autumn's hand as they walked through the garden. He listened to her hum and felt her contentment. A *trevi* ~ desire, to share with her again surfaced but knew he would not until Targ took their seed from her womb. He pulled her close, placing an arm about her shoulders; she reached up and held his hand, it was as it should be. A surge of joy swept through him, the planet called to him, and he desired to answer.

Autumn hummed the lullaby her Aunt Kuranna sang to her as a child. She missed Aunt Kuranna and the days she had lazily sat on the porch swing, sipping tart lemonade, listening to the birds and Uncle Zyleon tell stories, in similar fashion as ol' pa had. Stories of their great grandparents and their way of life, he'd show off his collection of magazines, proudly. One in particular she remembered, was a science magazine with page after page of new inventions, the world at the time was having an oil quandary, and everyone was in on the race to find an alternative form of transportation. In another magazine, a group of environmentalist held up a sign that read, "We Are Earth Savers," and showed a protégé of the now recognized ozone filtration system.

Farstar's grip tightened around Autumn's hand and thought she felt an upwelling of eagerness come from him. "Is everything alright?" She gazed into those glowing eyes, his fingertips touching her brow.

"Vuel ~ sleep, zifla ~ angel, sleep a peaceful sleep," Farstar gathered Autumn in his arms, levitating; he took passage to Targ's birthing room. Vines wound their way around Farstar's body as he stood before a leaf-covered wall; he lay Autumn in the soft, lush branches of the vines, which gently cradled her form. *"Targ, your nourishment pulses through me, I give freely my aresh shared with this female. Take from her womb the seed, aresh mita rym."*

Farstar linked minds with Autumn, the planet absorbed their aresh, probing the link between them, and he was aware of Targ's vines shifting Autumn's body, prepping her for the seeds removal. A slender creeper entered her body, finding and surrounding the tiny seed. Farstar felt its life force, strong and vibrant, and he quavered with the energy flow. They were all one in this moment, all eternal, and part of this vast universe. He felt a quickening of Autumn's heartbeat, then pain. A soft moan escaped her lips; he reached deeper into her mind and experienced her sadness as she wept for the separation.

Farstar could sense the second creeper repairing the tear inside of her; he could taste the salt of her tears and desired to comfort her. *"Autumn, we are safe, all of us. Do not weep for this physical separation; you are mother to a stronger race. The planet has accepted your aresh, which now and forever mixes with the flow of its life. Be comforted and come back to me."*

Autumn awoke in a small white room, fully clothed and equipped, except for her socks and shoes. Her head felt like the inside of her pillow and there was a dull ache inside her groin area. She sat up, and glanced around. A cup of tea sat on the table beside a chair. "Yeah," she whispered and got up. "I'm not so sure I trust drinking anything more," she said, wiping a tear from her cheek.

A door slid open, and in walked a female alien. "Shish, Autumn," she spoke. *"There is someone who desires, to meet with you but first you must drink your appo ~ tea, you have had quite a night. Targ is well pleased."*

"Who are you? And where is Farstar?" Autumn wiped another tear and began drinking the tea. Surprisingly, it tasted just like Aunt Kuranna's tart lemonade.

"You may call me Clamora. Farstar is resting." Clamora held up her hand toward the open doorway and smiled.

Autumn's head started to clear when she reached the hallway. "That tea works good, have anything for cramping?" she inquired of her guide.

Clamora, in all female tenderness, laid a hand across Autumn's lower abdomen, speaking the words, "kolum trey," a musical compassion in her voice, meeting the astonished stare of Autumn's gold-flecked eyes. Clamora felt the human female's discomfort pass. *"Let us continue our journey,"* she said, amused.

Autumn walked behind this alien in disbelief. Not only did she have amazing healing abilities, but also her feet did not make impressions in the moss-lined corridor as her own feet did.

When Clamora depressed a nearly invisible button in the wall, opening a door, she gasped at the sight of Nacoo. Autumn raced inside and just about knocked Nacoo off his feet. They embraced as if they would never let each other go.

"Oh Nacoo," she laughed, wiping away tears.

Nacoo kissed the top of Autumn's head, "We thought you were lost for good," he said, his voice deep and thick with emotion. "I wasn't sure if I could believe what the aliens were telling me. It's all been so weird."

"Me too, Nacoo, me too," she murmured.

Dawn sipped her tea and nibbled on some peppery tasting fruits. Her mind wandered to Professor Zyleon and this shockingly, remarkable discovery. "It's not the Pacific we come from..." her voice saddened, "it's here," she said, as she caressed her belly.

A soft whoosh of the door opening started her back to reality. Daj stood peeking in, Barmah hat in hand, smiling from ear to ear. "Dawn, may I come in?"

"Always the gentleman," she waved him in, greeting him with a hug. "It's been a long night and your face is very welcome." Grief overtook her and she wept quietly into his shoulder.

Daj lowered his head and spoke in a low voice. "Never expected to have such a breakthrough, it's all so fantastic, like being aware of a dream you're having." He gently rocked Dawn. "I've experienced some bizarre stuff, but nothing compared to last night. TaChoo, ah... um..." Daj didn't quite know how to say it. Awkwardly, barely above a whisper, he said, "made love with me," Dawn trembled in his arms. "When she was sure I had impregnated her, she took me to a — a — birthing room." Tears welled in Daj's eyes. "This planet has an intelligent consciousness," he held Dawn steady. "The birthing room was a lush jungle; it wrapped me in vegetation and — this planet entered my mind as did TaChoo. We all became one; we all became the same, experiencing the joy and pain of creation." Daj lifted Dawn's face and looked caringly into her watery eyes. "Afterwards I was taken to a room, similar to a research laboratory only this one was full of plant life, and I watched the planet incubate the seed, my seed." He placed his forehead against hers. "We are part of a wondrous experiment."

Dawn heaved a sigh of frustration. "We are guinea pigs," she cried. "We are their eternal bank account and not much more."

"That's not true; we are part of a creation," Daj dropped his arms away.

"Oh Daj," Dawn said, not wanting to feel so bad. "You may be right, this place gets inside you and knows just what and when to do something for you, and after that takes what it needs. " But," she said, "Earth is my home and I miss it."

Professor Zyleon spent the night touring Targ. Now he relaxed in a small comfortable room that opened up to a veranda overlooking a purple-hued Targian lake. The scene reminded him of a not so long ago tour he had shared with his wife, of the newly opened, Undersea Living World Museum. They had enjoyed watching the multi-colored fish with their exotic shapes in their living habitat. The forms of plant life were a great conversation. However, right now, he was missing her and longed to have Kuranna with him, sharing the splendor and enchantment of this magical place.

He sighed heavily, rose from his chair, and sauntered outside. The air felt good against his baldhead and face, although the breather annoyed him. He decided not to let it spoil the moment. He leaned his elbows on the leafy vine barrier and watched a pair of pacu that Thorb had pointed out to him earlier in the evening.

The large golden-winged birds glided silently across the plum-colored water. It seemed odd to him that the ripples only went out from around the pacus about a foot or two and stopped. Targ's water was thicker than Earth's but even so, he mused, there should be a wider wave effect. He was sure Kuranna would have a simple answer for this world's dissimilarities, something along the lines of there are two suns and seven moons. He laughed aloud causing the pacu's with their long shiny necks to look up at him.

"Hello," a familiar voice sounded from behind him.

He spun around to look into the human eyes of his wife. "Kuranna," he blurted.

"Yes, Zy, it's me." Kuranna smiled sweetly, laughing softly. "What a trip!"

Zyleon couldn't move fast enough to fold his arms around the woman he loved.

V

Thorb stood in the incubation chamber of the newly created children. A warm sense of fulfillment spread through him. *"Soon Targ, you shall be filled with strong fresh life."* Thorb felt the creepers penetrate his skin, vegetation covered him with a smooth quickness, and he became one with the planet.

Targ sent waves of sadness and pain and of love and anger that the humans, felt, reeling into Thorb's mind. *"The children must be protected."* Targ spoke to Thorb with a grave voice and pushed deeper into his soft flesh. Tendrils crept into bone marrow and blood and together they pulsed with every breath Thorb took, they were a complete being. *"Bring more seeds, for only one female is developing."* Targ rumbled, releasing him with such passion, that Thorb collapsed into the lush growth.

Thorb rested there, in the ootau of his planet's vines, one slender creeper still attached to the Spirit Absorption Crystal in his brain, freeing his spirit to commune with the universe. He searched for solutions that would create balance between their finely tuned world and their denser counterparts, and then connected minds with Farstar. *"Send out the message; Targ desires more seeds."* Thorb thought he felt the tiniest shift of pleasure, in the back of Farstar's mind, as they freed from one another.

Nacoo overflowed with happiness at seeing Autumn alive and well. "It's so good to be with you; we were all so concerned about you." He looked at her hands. "These hands that unearthed the key to Kandoria are wonderful to hold." He flicked a black curl that laid center on his brow, looked deeper into Autumn's gold-flecked eyes, and laughed. "It is you, the real you!" His laughter was contagious and soon they were relaxed, sitting on the bench, telling one another of their adventures.

"Have you been able to use your hyper-band at all?" asked Autumn.

"Manual dictation but I have noticed a small vibration in my plug occasionally." Nacoo rubbed his upper neck.

"Do you think Momma is trying to get through? A homing beacon, maybe?"

"It's a possibility, the last contact I had was just before that exotic episode with Dawn," Nacoo felt his dark cheeks flush, "I mean Clamora."

"I never received any signals, except for a small bit of static. These Targians have interactive movies all beat to hell," Autumn joked, trying to make light of their unusual situation.

"The press would have a heyday with us. We'd be front-page news all around the world; you can see the headlines reading something to the matter of, "Human Scientists Breed with Alien Race." It's a completely new species, it's freaky." Nacoo felt a shiver run up his spine. "Do you remember those old clips of circus oddities? The most disgusting were the half-human, half-animal creatures; and you know that unless proven a fake back in that time, there was only one way it could have happened." He gazed at Autumn's somber expression. "We have to find a way to keep contact with each other in case they separate us again." He sat so close beside Autumn he could feel her warmth. "Let's exchange bungs," he said in a low voice, holding his hyper-band.

"Nacoo, these bungs are made for our own personal interaction with Momma. How do you expect it will help us say connected?" Autumn removed her hyper-band and switched it to sensory control.

"Momma was designed with children of her own, our hyper-bands. Each is made with its own signature and when removed remains in contact with its own signal," he paused seeing a look of understanding cross Autumns face. "Maybe it will give us, ah — a mental link through our hyper-bands."

Autumn removed her bung and handed it to Nacoo. "Take care of my personal diary." She emphasized.

"And mine," he plugged Autumn's bung in as did she his, together they watched their screens squiggle with activity and felt tingles in their sensory centers. "It looks as if it's going to work Autumn; the hyper-bands are in search mode." Nacoo stood and walked to the other side of the small room.

"Nacoo, I have an urgent need to follow you and ow, it burns like a bee sting," mused Autumn, standing up.

"Yeah, and that is how we will be able to track one another." Nacoo cocked up an eyebrow and grinned devilishly. "We have to find the others and exchange bungs it may be our only way of contact and possible link with Momma. We may have to steal a ship to get home so any information we can get...." He stopped and looked about the room, his eyes resting on the door button. "Autumn, let's take a walk."

"It's right down this hallway." Daj led Dawn by the hand.

Glancing around, she asked, "How can you tell? These passageways all look the same to me." Her other hand carefully held the handle of her sheathed dagger.

"My powers of observation have not left me," he laughed. "Even if you think I'm daft." They looked at each other and smiled. "Every now and again you can see a small indent about chest high and the curvature of the wall thickens slightly. It reminds me of a honeycomb hole." Daj slowed his pace.

"How about a catacomb," she said, following Daj's gaze to the small, barely noticeable indent in the wall. "Researching the dead is not nearly as creepy." The door slid open.

"Come on, we are just a roo jump away." Daj tugged her hand and they stepped inside.

"Great God, our ancestors are Targians. They colonized us and watched us grow of our own free will. Now they find a reason to bring us back into the circle of awareness. Kuranna, I must confess that I feel like a small boy about to set sail into the vastness of uncharted territory." Professor Zyleon rubbed his chin. "The simple truth revealed."

"This does explain many of the biblical links," she paused. "Miracles and phenomenon," Kuranna sipped her tea. "This is really good tea, you should settle down and eat with me," she said calmly.

Zyleon looked fondly at Kuranna; her white hair accentuated soft blue eyes. "Yes, yes they do serve good food," he sat across from her and gazed into a bowl full of small red berries. "My group is being harvested. Autumn…" His voice trailed off.

"Autumn is a grown woman, Zy, capable of holding her own. Certainly, the rest of your team has the cool logic needed for a situation such as this." She set her cup down and reached for his hand. "Do not waste your time with worry it is a dead-end street."

Zyleon enfolded Kuranna's hand in his. "It is so nice to have you with me. You know how to put anxiety in its place," he chuckled. "Do you remember all the maps we created, reasoning out where and what needed to be placed? All the dead-end streets of worry and inhospitable mountain terrains of lies, dead oceans of anger and selfishness, deserts of sadness and grief, and the all time favorite," Kuranna voiced with him, "the road to happiness." They laughed, "The only thing holding those maps together were the pins we poked into them." Professor Zyleon raised his cup. "Cheers to you and me, survivors of the colony."

Farstar waited for Clamora in the garden of Seven Moons. Retra, the fourth moon, was a shimmering, multi-hued orb, one of his favorite sights of the ever-changing universe he lived in. There was a transformation happening within him, a curious sense of wonderment and longing, unlike the desire Targ gave to him. He searched to connect with Autumn; sensing her shudder when his mind touched hers. She was in the western observatory staring out across the surface of Targ. He experienced her awe at the vast beauty of his home and desired to be with her. She was so full of questions, wishes, and hope.

"She is a great ootau to you Farstar, Targ is well pleased with the children." Clamora moved silently into the room, *"Do you think she desires to produce with you again?"* A look of keen awareness crossed her face, and Farstar felt her try to probe his thoughts.

"Clamora you have shared aresh with the offspring of our ancestors, do you not find it alluring?" He questioned her, staring hard into her eyes.

She turned away from his stare and looked out at Retra and the horizon's curving line of moons. *"Va, I find Nacoo,"* she paused, *"delightful."*

Farstar saw a slight shift of Clamora's shoulders and wondered if she also discerned that tiny change within. *"They are in the western observatory wex wa ep, Targ trevi ootau."*

An understanding crossed between them when their eyes met. A new sense of awe filled Farstar, and this time he opened his mind to hers. She too marveled.

Autumn stood, arms crossed, looking out the window. "It's very beautiful out there; parts of it remind me of home. Do you think the air is breathable?" She turned to face Nacoo.

"Things are growing, but from some of the vegetation I've encountered, the air mixture may be to thin for us to walk around outside." The corner of Nacoo's lip twitched as he spoke. "When I was in the birthing room with Clamora, vines actually entered and connected inside of me. It allowed me to feel every thing she went through, to be inside her thoughts..." he turned away from Autumn.

"I know," she whispered, holding herself.

"We should keep searching for the others."

"Yeah, let's do that."

They started down the corridor away from the direction they came. "Maybe we will have better luck finding someone this time." Nacoo said, hopeful, as they walked.

"Professor Zyleon's face would be nice to see."

Nacoo nudged her with his elbow, "Do you see that?"

"What?" She sucked in a breath, startled by the two ghostly figures coming toward them.

"Don't let them find out about the bung," he gripped and held her hand firmly.

"Nacoo, mel li ga ~ come with me," Clamora called to him in his mind.

He cursed under his breath, feeling his head start to spin.

"Nacoo," Autumn grasped for his slipping hand. "Nacoo," she yelled again, his fingers no longer touching hers. She felt a small tug at her sensory site and bowed her head.

Long smooth fingers ran along her jaw, *"come Autumn, we have many things to do."*

Farstar savored his touch on her skin, he was glad to be with her again.

"**D**aj, are you sure you know what we are doing?" Thick vegetation covered the walls, darkening the hallway.

He thought of the Professor, emulating, he said, "Girl, you should know better than to doubt me; I just might be a better guide than Radin." He turned and winked at her.

Dawn cuffed his shoulder, "Why are we here?" she asked as they entered a room of plush forest moss. They walked toward a dim glow in the wall across the room. "Radin explains what he's doing," she teased, flicking his hat.

"Look," Daj's face glowed blue in the eerie light.

Dawn took a sharp intake of breath, "Oh God!"

"Our babies," Daj smiled warmly at Dawn. "TaChoo showed me this room; she called it the growing room. Incubation room is more like it. She explained that Targ would be the womb for our children, they will be the beginning of a stronger Targian race." He embraced her shoulder, pulling her close. "I'm a dad."

Tears streamed down Dawn's face, she looked upon more alien than human structured fetuses, past their first trimester. Thick, burgundy, vines pulsed life into four babies and tentacles cradled, suspended, and moistened their bodies "How can this be? It's only been," she stopped, feeling a little sick, and looked at Daj, "how long have we been here?"

"I don't know." He answered, puzzled and squeezed her shoulder, "Come on Let's get out of here." He turned her away from the growing children and back out into the corridor. "What do you think the others are going through?"

Dawn dried her cheeks on her sleeve, "Do you think those other babies are theirs?" She sniffled.

"Foster told me they were on their own adventures, I wonder if Momma is still recording? That will be a story to read about, if we ever get back to Earth." Daj slid his fingers into his pockets, his brow furrowed under his hat.

"Earth," Dawn repeated. "How do they get inside our minds and create such realistic life? Are those — babies," she paused. "Are they real? Are we in some laboratory somewhere all drug induced? How can I work under such pressure?" She laughed a childish laugh. "How the hell are we going to get back to normal?"

Daj laughed with her. "Let's take a peek," he pointed at some crystal-lined windows. After a moment of searching, Daj pushed his finger into the depression on the wall. A door opened into a conservatory full of blooming plants. "It smells great in here." Daj took a deep breath, felt a familiar swirl in his head, and turned to see Hank catching Dawn as she collapsed into his slender gray arms. "Here we go," he whispered just before his knees buckled, landing him on the floor.

VI

"*Greetings Nacoo, it is good to see you again.*" Jax stood next to the Sunstream a slender hand on Clamora's shoulder. "*We…*"

Nacoo burst out, interrupting Jax. "Are you planning on flying me somewhere?" Nacoo rumbled, "because if you are, I'd like to fly first class!" Nacoo roared with laughter, slapped his knees, and then promptly sat on the floor.

"*How much artu did you give him?*" Jax asked Clamora, watching with delight at Nacoo, now curled up in a ball holding his stomach, as another round of robust jollity escaped him.

"*I used the aroma artu-moc to relax him,*" she said, squatting next to Nacoo and putting her hand on the back of his head. "*Let us board the Sunstream; we must transport you across Targ.*"

Nacoo looked into those faceted eyes, and unable to resist or stop laughing, he followed Clamora and Jax onto the Sunstream. He sprawled in the backseat of the airship, trying seriously to control himself. He attempted to sit up straighter, but when the ship lifted, both holders, more like vines, came down, locking him in his seat. A few minutes had passed before he was able to somewhat manage the hilarity, yet the smile was not so quick to fade.

The planet's surface was spectacular; displays of blue sand and purple scrub-bushes dotted the land. As the suns reflected off the surface, they re-colored the hills of dark to light orange. He could see trees with leaves of dark purple as tall as the virgin redwoods on Earth. The grasses were jet black in color.

The distant horizon held four — no five — moons. "Fascinating," he uttered under his breath.

"*There are seven moons,*" corrected Jax.

"Seven is the number of wisdom and insight, but not so lucky for gamblers." Nacoo said, chuckling, thinking of that silly superstition, and glanced at the cobra tattooed on his arm.

Jax and Clamora looked at each other curiously.

"Would you ne ootau ~ take comfort, in being lucky?" Clamora asked.

"No, I would take comfort in sailing that deep red sea." He answered, pointing out the window.

"We need to get him to the sweep," Jax spoke to Clamora. She nodded in agreement.

Nacoo felt a brief vibration of Autumn's bung, careful not to cling to the sensation, in case those silver haired aliens honed in on it, or on her. He let his mind start to analyze the knowledge he had learned about the planet and language, and how he always heard them in his head. It would be nice to write it down in his personal journal, but he kept hope that Momma was recording. Autumn popped into his mind again, just as the ship entered the vine-covered docking bay; he trusted that they would be able to gather clear information from each other's footage.

The corridor's color reminded Nacoo of crystallized air. He ran a scarred knuckle down the wall as they walked. "What kind of material is this?" he asked, eyeing Jax.

"It is called ry. It is a mineral that balances with Targ and allows us to live in harmony with our planet, something Earth dwellers have yet to completely understand."

"The environmentalists back home are always looking for more compatible ways of doing things." Nacoo rumbled, stifling a smile and almost running into Clamora.

"This is where we need to be," Jax gestured through a doorway. *"Come in and ne ootau with us."* Jax walked in behind Nacoo and Clamora.

"Part of the reason for Kandoria is to share and receive knowledge." Jax motioned for Nacoo to sit. *"Would you accept a gift from Targ, to help carry on our work at Kandoria?"*

Nacoo gazed into the Targian's shimmering, pupil-less eyes. "What kind of gift?" he asked, still feeling a bit silly, but cautious.

"An implant to go along with the key," Jax patted Nacoo's pocket that held the wand, *"and enable communication between us."* A slight smile formed on Jax's lips, *"we trevi ~ desire, you to aid us in reconnecting with our*—" he wavered. *"History,"* when he finished speaking he took a cup of appo from Clamora.

Nacoo also took a cup, unsure of what to say.

Clamora rested a hand on his shoulder. *"You shall learn much,"* she said, lightly touching his sensory site.

Nacoo turned and looked at her. "I would rather not go through that kind of pain again." Why did I say that? he thought, cringing at the idea of giving Autumn away.

Jax looked concerned. *"The procedure is similar to what happened in the shram sy ~ birthing room so do not fear, Targ creates an implant in your brain center from your own body, Targ then starts a process called, shoek. It is transference of energy, which works with the pineal and pituitary glands, this enables you with the use of abilities much like ours.* Jax grinned teasingly. *"We, of course, are born of Targ and have a very strong connection."* He chuckled taking pleasure in Nacoo's befuddlement.

"I need to think about this," Nacoo said and should have known better than to drink the tea. He felt the now familiar swirl in his head. Clamora placed the palm of her hand on his brow pulling his head back against the chair. "Please let me...." his voice trailed off. Vines began to curl their way around him, holding him securely. The room turned into a shroud of dense vegetation, his skin began to feel slippery, and he moaned like a small boy bracing for an injection from the doctor, "nooo..." Nacoo felt a small prickle at the base of his spine as a creeper entered his body.

Thorb sat at the head of the dining table. *"Kuranna, I trust you have found ootau ~ comfort, with your surroundings,"* he expressed great enjoyment speaking with her. *"Professor Zyleon mentioned your psi abilities; it is a pleasure for me to speak with you."* He plucked a flower from his plate.

"That sounds just like my Zy," she winked at her husband, "it must be the crow in him." Kuranna sipped Targian wine from a most unusual glass. Its shape was akin to a ram's horn but it actively swirled in a smoky gray cloud. "I have found Targ to be of great interest," she answered, tasting one of the pink flowers; it was bittersweet with a zippy after-taste. "Very good," Kuranna smiled at her host.

"Professor Zyleon, I wonder have you decided on the offer of Kandoria Overseer yet." Thorb relished the Professor's *new food* tasting facial contours.

"Yes, I have decided to accept," he said, chasing a purple pea around his plate. "It will be a great honor to work with you reestablishing Kandoria." The pea's taste reminded him of fennel.

"You understand the procedure you are to undertake and how that shall change you."

Thorb looked hard at Professor Zyleon.

"Yes, entirely better for communication purposes." He grinned at Kuranna, thinking of how often she had read him so well.

Kuranna blushed under her husbands loving gaze, "I also agree, but am concerned for the others."

Thorb touched deep inside Kuranna's mind. *"Gentle persuasion is sometimes necessary to use."*

Kuranna stared into Thorb's eyes of lightening. *"The start of a new era,"* she thought and watched Thorb nod in agreement.

Daj sat in a booth made to resemble one of his old college haunts, Cassia's Pub. Beside him sat TaChoo drinking dark Targian ale. "Dark ale has always been my favorite." He tipped his hat back and finished off the pint, it was good.

"I know," she smiled, seductively.

"Why are we here?" Daj waved for another round.

"Is this not one of your fondest memories? I trevi ~ desire, to share in the ootau, of this experience of — um — your best one nightstand." She giggled, acting out the memory of the woman he was thinking of.

Daj's smile spread across his face. "This could get interesting," he said as he paid the server, winking at TaChoo.

"Daj, Targ would take ootau ~ comfort, in giving you a gift." She drank heartily from her mug then placed a hand on his knee and kissed him with a foam mustache.

He licked the foam from his lips. "What kind of gift?"

"A gift of communication, of abilities similar to mine," she ran her hand up his leg resting it in the crease of his jeans. *"Targ is pleased with you,"* TaChoo slid her hand back and poured herself another full glass.

Daj was starting to feel quite relaxed. "Does it mean I will be able to *experience* your memories?" He really was enjoying himself.

"Va."

Daj leaned close to her and grasped her hand. "Dance with me, TaChoo." Her eyes flashed her approval, and she followed him to the dance floor. He held her around the waist, swaying back and forth, and for the first time he noticed how very alike they really were. "You my lady are a true gem," he murmured, taking pleasure in the ambience of the night.

"And you are quite the gentleman." She said, leaned her head against his shoulder, letting his emotion flow through her; it was extraordinary to ride the current of his way of thinking.

"Do you know what I'm feeling?" Daj whispered in TaChoo's dove-gray, angular ear. She smelled, lightly, of the forest.

"Va," she whispered back.

Surprised by her answer, "You do?"

"Va, I do find you rather enjoyable, you are easy to sense. After you receive Targ's gift you shall be able to connect with my senses and that is an incredible tangle of touches." She pushed deeper into his mind.

Daj felt soft movement in his head. "It feels like a butterfly fluttering around." He closed his eyes, yielding as she slid even further into his mind. "Mmm," he moaned, lifting his chin up.

"We shall be able to share together," she pulled back and led the way to the booth.

He held her hand, until she was sitting, and then scooted in beside her cool body, grabbing and downing the rest of the ale in his mug. The thought crossed his mind that if he were able to touch her mind then he could touch other parts of her as well. His lips curved into a smile. "That's just too damned exotic; this whole planet is exotic," he said, blithely, feeling the influence of the dark ale.

"Does that mean you are ready?" She looked at him curiously.

"I'd really like to explore you in depth." He watched her lips part to drink slow and long. "I'm game." He pushed her fine silver hair away from her face. "What do I do?"

"Just relax." She pressed her cheek against his fingers.

The room dimmed around him, vines crept up his legs and back, cradling his head. He could feel a hot touch at the base of his spine and the butterfly flutter of TaChoo in his mind. He tried to reach out to her and felt her push deeper. Small shocks ran up his spine and he could sense Targ inside him. Daj felt a creeper snaking its way into the base of his brain, connecting to him. It was hot, and he tried to resist, relaxing when he sensed TaChoo's mind caress.

God she felt good. Images of the universe raced through his mind. He could smell and taste everything at once and understood that he was spirit, that the gift Targ gave to him enabled him to use abilities beyond physical restriction. He watched the past and the future of Targians and Earth dwellers, and learned how he would help herald in a new era for all races. Pure ecstasy filled his being; he was triumphant. TaChoo nudged his mind, and he felt the tendrils slide from his body.

Dawn's notebook was filling up fast with sketches and notes of Targian tombs and remains. She was so absorbed in her findings that she never noticed Hank observing her. He slipped into her mind to find her speculating about the skeletal structures of Tuvah, the previous communicator.

Dawn methodically circled the ossuary; she was captivated with how similar the aliens were to humans. She carefully scraped a small dusting of bone and placed it in her hyper-band sample container, closing it and hoping Momma could analyze it for her. The hyper-band did not respond. "Damn," she cursed, and stomped her foot. "This is so frustrating, a great discovery, and no way to evaluate it." She looked around the sepulcher and stomped her foot once more. "How am I to interpret any of the writing without Nacoo or you, Momma?"

She walked over to the adjacent sarcophagus and noted. "By pressing the crystal on the brow of the effigy the lid of the sarcophagus opens allowing access to a well preserved skeletal frame." Dawn scraped bone, sketched, and noted, "a clear, hardened, substance covers the eyes that I cannot remove with gentle force. A large crystal, octagon shaped, orchid in color, rests in the center of the skull. It too has the same substance of the hardened covering. There is a soft glow in its middle and gives me an icy finger, creeping across the head sensation, if I lean too close. "Well, I will have to leave that for another time," she verbalized to the dead alien. "Maybe I will find more answers down the tomb shaft." She brightened her shoulder lamp to chase the shadows and eeriness farther away.

"Here we go into the darkness," she chanted, trying to quell her apprehension. "Here we go one step at a time, to find the treasure keep," her voice echoed masking her footsteps. "The chest he buried someday to find, but instead he lies in a grave dug deep. Legend is told his soul still protects the gold of Lord..." Dawn stepped lightly thinking she heard a sound behind her. Panic threatened to overtake her; she swallowed hard, hand on her dagger, spinning to shine the light into the face of a smirking Hank. "Damn it, you scared me," perspiration beaded on her forehead.

"I just thought you would find ootau with my company." Hank beamed at her amused, feeling her fear subside. He said, *"you become quite intent on learning."*

His eyes glittered like stars in the lamp's glow, and reflected off his skin, giving him a ghostly appearance. Dawn shuddered. "You have to quit scaring me!" She growled irritably, turned, and walked away. "I'm in a strange world without my colleagues, doing the best I can to maintain my sanity and —" She whipped back around and yelled at him. "YOU KEEP FRIGHTENING ME!" Breathing hard she glared at Hank. "And I want to learn more about Targians, considering I have offspring." She blew out a hard breath and resumed a stomping walk.

"You wish to learn, so let Targ assist you," Hank glided up beside her.

"Why? So far, Targ has just taken and not given. That's not very cordial." They entered a circular room; in the center was a round fire pit, flames of misty blue wisped as high as twenty feet. "Oh, how beautiful," she murmured, mesmerized.

"This is where Targ keep's memories of those past," He slipped his arm around Dawn. *"It is a place to gain wisdom,"* Hank reached up touching her thick, curly hair, excitement flashed through him. *"Targ desires you to be a part of him, of me, of all. It is a gift that you shall share with your companions and offspring."* He desired to kiss her but could feel her resistance.

"How do I receive this gift?" She faced him, "What do you mean, share?"

"It shall allow you to communicate as our race does, and enable you to increase your knowledge, what is it similar to — ah, access to the akashic records. As for receiving this gift all you need to do is ne ootau ~ take comfort, Targ shall do the rest." Hank touched her freckled face, a growing anticipation in him.

Dawn reached up and held his hand, as suspicion edged in. "Comfort is a word you use when strange occurrences happen. It could be just another "fantasy" conjured up to please you or this planet." She felt his arm loosen. "This, not knowing what's happening is maddening, you must understand." Dawn did not want him to let go; confusion was not a good friend.

Hank probed gently into her mind, apprehension filled his being, this was not as entertaining as startling her. He desired her to take Targ's gift, and he looked steadily into her eyes moving deeper, trying to find the answer for her trust. Thorb had warned them to secure Targ's wishes, but he could not allow illusion to be his shield. *"You shall be aware and we shall stay together,"* Hank permitted love to flow from him, *"do not be afraid, you are pleasing to Targ, you are pleasing to me."* He found it gratifying to perceive her answer, a slow moving snake of resolution wound its way into his thoughts.

"Yes," she spoke softly. Dawn put her arms around Hank and lifting up on her toes, tilting her head she pressed her full lips against his thin, cool gray mouth.

Hank responded with eagerness, longing to share aresh with her. He called out to Targ as he caressed her shoulders and back. *"She has accepted,"* he sent out.

Targ's vines curled around them, and Dawn held tight to Hank. Experiencing him, in her mind, coaxing her as tiny shocks ran up her spinal column. Tendrils found the place for implantation and Targ began the transference of energy. She moaned with the explosion of introspection that flooded her. The planet pulsed in her — creating a more powerful way of being. Dawn took comfort in the vines of the planet.

As the tendrils slowly left her body, she felt Hank's feathery movement still within her mind. His promise good, he had stayed with her. Wiggling her fingers, she let the room gradually come back into focus; enveloped in Hank's arms.

Hank cupped the back of her head with his hand, locked an arm around her waist, and pulled her even closer; he kissed her passionately, sharing a long exchange of new energy. Aura light and color danced within their minds, tumbling over waves of ecstasy and pure spiritual contact. Touches of fire and ice raged in his body. He sensed her exploring his mind and as she investigated, he desired her more.

Autumn surveyed the docking station. Other than the material of the spaceships, fueling tanks and vine-covered floors and walls, it looked very much the same as one of Earth's docking stations. Shuttles hovered about, and crews busily worked on parked air cars. She was aware of the small, continuous vibration inside her sensory center and she thought of Nacoo and his Sunstream stories that always kept her entertained during the lulls of work. Autumn nonchalantly walked over and stood beside a thick, woody vine. The vine grew corpulent, forming a barrel shape. Farstar was using an extension vine to fill a small craft. "What kind of fuel is that?" She peered through a slit at the top of the vine barrel noticing a warm woodsy aroma.

"It is muraht, a mixture of Targ's secretion and minerals left on the beach from the ugla fish after their breeding frenzy." Farstar held the thick, pulsating vine in his hands with a strong, tender grip. He sensed Autumn's curiosity. *"Ugla fish come out of the sea many times during the sixth moon's turning, they shimmer a rainbow of color under Yeth's light until they find and share aresh ~ essence, with all the others that have the same patterned rhythm. When the first sun's light starts to shine they return to the sea until Yeth shines again.* The vine pulled itself out of the shuttle and Farstar then placed it on the ground. *"Ish,"* He spoke to the vine and it retreated into the swollen barrel. *"During the rise of the second sun we go out and collect the dried residue left by the ugla. When the crystallized minerals, or residue, combine with Targ's secretion it creates a high-energy plasma fuel, it is very effective and efficient."* He cupped Autumn's elbow and helped her into the air ship. Following behind her, he seated himself in the pilot's seat.

"What a great use of resources. Humans are still working on repairing the damage done to Earth." Autumn paused, "I remember a well-known group of Druids, teachers that gave educational lectures and classes on the healing and perceptivity of Earth. My second year at Mabel University was when I took their class; the Druids taught how thought could be a very destructive or constructive force, proceeding to prove it by using healing energy to aid the recovery of animals and plants, of course, they are very skilled." Autumn smiled and continued, "they had the class sit in a circle around an ailing plant and meditate. We sent our thoughts to heal it and as we watched, that afternoon, complete healing occurred. It was magical. They concluded by telling us, that, that same thought transference would assist in mending Earth. The class was given event and time schedules, to join Earth healing circles for the rest of the semester. It was an exceptional class.

Farstar flew the small craft out of the docking bay and toward the setting suns. *"All of our teaching is learned through Targ. It is more of a knowing, a sharing of wisdom for all."* He pointed at the forest below them and smiled. *"Autumn I trevi ~ desire, to share aresh with you, but I cannot."*

Autumn rolled her bottom lip over her teeth and gently bit down; logic defied her. She thought it actually enjoyable to be here, sitting next to an alien that created such commotion with her senses. "Me too," she whispered.

They hovered above the treetops gazing at the sky's soft indigo glow. Farstar experienced that small twinge again; and wondered at the feeling. He could sense her awe as the Targian suns set; her light brown skin reflected their radiance, he entered her mind and understood that she would become a part of Targ soon, a part of him, of all.

"Farstar, this sunset is breathtaking." Autumn couldn't break away even as the darkness came. "Thank you," she whispered, not wanting to say anything more.

Farstar landed the craft in a small cove. *"Would you enjoy walking the beach?"*

"You've got to be kidding! Yes, I would love to," a rush of childlike excitement arose in her.

"You shall need an air mask," Farstar said. The air mask consisted of a tiny air tube connected to a small, clear box containing a quartz gelatin. The tube, which hooked around both ears, attached to a small nose cover, the set-up, resembled a pair of sunglasses. *"This shall form to your nose ensuring good air supply."* He let his finger rest on the bridge of her nose until the material shaped to her nose completely. *"Mel wa ep ~ let us go."*

Autumn trusted Farstar would not hurt her, but that first breath of air through the tube made her feel a bit lightheaded. "Okay," she grasped his hand for reassurance. As she jumped down onto the moist sand, she asked, "Will it be okay for me to remove my boots?"

"Va ~ yes," Farstar grinned enjoying her eagerness to feel the planets surface. It would allow Targ an easier connection.

The sand was warm and soft, giving under her weight; she cuffed her pants and observed the color of the sand turn an even darker maroon with each footprint she left behind. She ran up to the water's edge and back to Farstar, tagged him and ran to a large tree, laughing with delight as she leaned against its midnight purple bark.

Farstar stood in wonderment at Autumn's behavior. Probing her mind, he discovered that it was a human game of chase. He smirked devilishly and decided to show off a bit by levitating over to her. He watched her eyes sparkle with amusement the closer he came to her. Gently he pressed his body against hers in a gesture of capture; she mocked a struggle, easily relenting to his hold. Farstar could no longer resist the urges he felt, he lowered his face to her neck and kissed her. She consumed him.

Targ's vines wrapped around their legs, Farstar groaned as the planet entered him. He understood that implantation was necessary for the replenishment of his planet and had become carelessly lost in this new emotion. *"Autumn, Targ desires to give you a gift,"* he groaned again, louder as Targ slipped deeper inside him. *"If you take this gift it shall enable you to communicate and...aaaah,"* tendrils crept through his brain. *"Communicate and use similar abilities as Targians, we shall be able to touch each other's aresh ~ esse..."* panting he gave in to the planet.

Autumn felt feelers touching the base of her feet. Vines held her in place; she strained to get away, tendrils touched her face and tickled the inside of her ears. She shook her head and tried to wiggle free. Farstar's body pressed hard against hers as the vines entwined them. She thought she heard him whisper, in her mind, to be calm; his eyes silted dreamily, his mouth formed into a slight smile. "Okay," she whispered back, holding on to him. Squeezing her eyes shut, she felt Targ enter her.

The soft lilac sunlight of Targ's morning touched Kuranna's snow-white hair. Zyleon watched for a moment at the rhythmic breathing of his sleeping wife before climbing out of bed and into the shower. He thought of how nice it would be to be able to fix a surprise breakfast in bed tray for her; it seemed a long time ago that he had done such a thing. Although he wasn't sure yet what her favorite Targian food was, he decided to give it a try.

Quickly he disrobed and walked to the saucer-shaped dip in the floor at the far left corner of this unusual cleansing room. He studied the walls, searching for some kind of on off valve; he stepped closer and placed his hand on the wall. Instantly he felt a tingle in the back of his head, and the wall swirled beneath his hand. Startled he pulled his hand away and the tingling stopped. He stood gazing at the wall, rubbing the back of his neck. "Wish this thing came with instructions," he whispered and impulsively placed his hand back on the wall, thinking of a nice warm shower. It worked. A warm maroon mist sprayed him from all around. *"Thanks Targ,"* he thought and this time felt that swirling sensation on the bottoms of his feet.

The bizarre shower was a quick one so as not to disturb Kuranna's sleep. He tiptoed across the bedroom and out onto the veranda. Remarkably, a small buffet lay out in front of where he now stood. It was full of the most exotic food he had ever seen, *"thanks to the chef,"* he said in his mind, picking up a crystal plate.

"You are welcome, Professor Zyleon," came a voice from deep within his mind.

Zyleon shook his head, startled by the sound. "That will take some getting used to." He looked up at the drifting, chiffon-yellow clouds and considered if this decision to share in Targian life would really be for the betterment of Earth. The adjustment to knowing that the planet could share all his most private thoughts was unsettling.

This great being of mystifying wonder now monitored all his physical, mental, and emotional conditions, but more than that, Targ could intercede with his life at any time. Zyleon looked down at the plate in his hand and reminded himself that as a scientist his goal was to uncover truth and apply the knowledge learned. He theorized about how Targ thought of his most intimate feelings. Whistling softly as he carried breakfast to his wife.

Nacoo, semi-conscious, reclined on board the Luna-Sea. Warm ocean mist sprayed over his body with each rocking movement of the anchored boat. The gentle slap of water reminded him of Baxter strumming his guitar, practicing the music of Twilight River, designed for the play Space Deep. Nacoo could hear, in his mind, the slow rhythmic beat that could bring an audience to a moment of self-truth, and than steadily quiet until only the sounds of soft flutters filled one's ears and one's eyes with glittering tears.

Nacoo opened his eyes to find his brother looking back at him.

"Mind if I share that dream?" Baxter chuckled.

"Baxter?" Nacoo said, feeling the daydream lift from his mind.

"Yes," Baxter cocked his head to one side, giving Nacoo's swim trunks a curious glance. "Nice colors." He handed his twin brother a Twilight River drink. a drink the two of them had concocted in celebration of the play's success.

"How's mom?" Nacoo took the drink playing along with this new adventure. "The last time I visited, she was teaching a class from home, on the antiquated art of pottery making." He sat forward, elbows resting on his knees, feeling a subtle tug inside his sensory center. Nacoo sensed Autumn was thinking of him, and reflected on if they had implanted her with this alien technology.

"She is using hieroglyphics to teach with, she says it puts her in the mood," Baxter looked out across the water. "This is one beautiful planet; they will be stupefied back home, I imagine they will want to do a documentary almost immediately." He looked at Nacoo's face, which showed a sudden grip of reality.

Nacoo stared at his brother, almost dropping his glass. Could it really be him? He spoke tentatively, "Yeah, I figure we will receive our fair share of recognition." He stood, getting nose to nose with Baxter; familiar, human onyx eyes stared back at him.

"I couldn't believe it; I was space-napped from Vax-Space Station-Twelve by a beautiful woman named Clamora and her friend Jax. I felt like I was in a fog as they coerced me to come with them, saying you needed me. They also explained to me about an implant placement that would enable unrestricted breathing, and not to be concerned about how I came to be here, but I think whatever it is, it does more than they told me." He stammered, disquieted, paused, and clicked his teeth on his crystal glass. "Do you have one?" Baxter took a deep swig of his drink.

Nacoo grabbed his brother by the shoulder, "Yes, I believe I do." Not letting go, he said, "Did you see anyone else?" His grip tightened then relaxed.

"Yes, Mrs. Trowley. She said she was coming to see Professor Zyleon and…"

Nacoo interrupted, "Baxter that means we need to get back and find them." In Nacoo's excitement, he nearly fell overboard, precariously rocking the Luna-Sea.

"Hey, be more careful!" Baxter gripped the canopy rail. "At the moment I don't feel like swimming in this red water."

"Where did they take her?" Nacoo began to pull up the anchor. "Is she the only one you saw?" Sweat trickled down his face.

"Yes," Baxter said, in his resounding voice, not so unlike his brothers and started the engine, heading back to shore. "Jax said they were on an adventure, whatever that means. He also said he will be waiting for us at camp and something about testing all of us."

"Testing for what?" Nacoo thought.

"How the implants are working," Nacoo heard Jax in his mind, *"this is new for all of us, and we shall not trevi ~ desire, anything to go array for our Earth friends."* Jax stood on shore waving to the men. Nacoo could see him grinning and suddenly felt an urge to strike him. This invasion of his sanctity went against the very heart of his humanness. It was so otherworldly — alarming.

The Luna-Sea berthed at the tree-formed dock; red water gleaned over small, polycrystalline pebbles lining the shoreline, making them shimmer with the luster of polished rubies. Baxter shook Jax's hand, "Something smells good." Nacoo stood beside him, staring at the crest of the eastern hill, avoiding Jax's eyes.

Baxter's gaze followed his brothers. "It appears we have company."

Jax spoke aloud, "va ~ yes, I believe you know the female."

Nacoo's implant tingled, and his sensory site hummed with warmth. "It's Autumn." Delighted, he and started to run.

"Very good, you are adapting well, Nacoo." Jax laughed and turned to Baxter, *"I am brewing appo ~ tea, but if you are hungry we can find some verva fruit to comfort, ourselves with."*

"It's fascinating to watch your eyes reflect the landscape around you." Baxter sucked in a little air. "Maybe you should wear sunglasses when you visit Earth." He was unsure of how he was feeling about this odd turn of events in his life, even if the food was palatable here. "What does verva fruit taste like? It is edible, right. Do you think everyone will want some?" He asked in a rush of words and nodded toward the distant, enthusiastically embracing friends.

"Va, our food is agreeable with your digestive system and we shall find enough to share." Jax chuckled, amused by Baxter's uncertainty about understanding and using his newfound telepathic abilities. *"It is easier for me to speak this way; you also have the capability to link with others. With practice, mind touch becomes familiar and you shall know who it is, just as you recognize the sound of someone's voice. Try it,"* Jax coaxed.

Baxter gave Jax a quizzical look amazed at how receptive Jax was, and thought. *"Can you carry on conversations with more than one?"*

"Va, you can be open to all or none, except for Targ. Just use your imagination, see a door opened or closed." Jax noticed Baxter's eyebrows press together in deep thought. *"Come, we shall practice as we search for verva."*

Farstar probed Nacoo's mind and sensed the closeness between Nacoo and Autumn. It was a new sensation, their friendship being so different from what he experienced with her. He pulled back when he felt Jax's mind touch.

"We shall ish, ne ootau, and appo," Farstar glanced at his fellow Targian already past the large, amethyst-leafed uva tree. He wondered if Jax felt the change as he and Clamora did.

"Baxter and Mrs. Trowley are here," Nacoo was saying.

"That is good news Nacoo," Autumn responded. She glanced back at Farstar as they started to walk, staying close to Nacoo's side. "They put an implant in my brain. Did they implant you?"

Nacoo slid a large muscular arm over her shoulders. "Yes, have they questioned you about the bung?" He spoke in a hushed tone from the side of his mouth.

Autumn looked up at him. Shook her head no and asked, "how about you?"

"No," the corner of his lip curled, and he pulled her closer.

Farstar watched as the two walked. He tried a mind touch with Autumn but she was too engrossed in her conversation and blocked him out. He felt a small prickle up his spine unlike when Targ touched him and he desired to remove Nacoo's arm from her. "Are you two thirsty? Would you care for a drink?" he asked aloud, disguising his discomfort.

"Yeah, sure, that sounds fine." Autumn turned to look at Farstar and Nacoo released her.

A surge of pleasure rippled through Farstar when her eyes met his and watched, with satisfaction, as the big man's arm slid away.

"I will, so long as you don't put any drugs in it." Nacoo stopped, leaned his back against the big purple leafed tree, and wiped his forehead. "Another Twilight River drink would be nice." He surveyed the camp and water's edge. "Where did Baxter and Jax go?" he asked, uneasily.

"Try to mind touch him," Farstar flashed a challenge.

Nacoo smirked at his new Targian friend. *"What if I can not?"* he said, his eyes steady on Farstar.

"Than he is preoccupied with another ootau, you must continue to try until he feels your mind touch." Farstar was beginning to enjoy himself.

"So what you are telling me, is only one person at a time can get through."

"Va, until you learn to open your mind more and with the exception of Targ."

"So the planet knows everything?"

"That is the Targian way. Now you should try to reach your nua ~ brother." Farstar nodded. *"One Twilight River drink is on its way."* He gave a slight smile, sensing Nacoo's curiosity.

Autumn walked over and sat by the water's edge tossing pebbles in and watching the ripples. The water was of thicker consistency, making short broad waves. Targ was an interesting place with so much to learn, but she felt as though her future was a part of something she was not privy too and found that very disturbing. A new feeling, a nudge in her mind made her sit up and look around, *"what,"* she responded, startled.

"It is I, Nacoo. Care to take a dip with me?" His solid, brown frame glistened in the pink-filtered sunlight. *"Farstar tells me the water is cool and safe. Shall we believe him?"* Nacoo towered over her, holding out his hand. *"Be my guinea pig; let me feel your mind touch."*

Autumn took Nacoo's hand. *"Yes, a dip will be nice, and I will gladly be your guinea pig."* She laughed, stripping down to her bra and undies.

Nacoo dove in; the water was tepid and refreshing, it seemed to instantly sooth his mind. *"Autumn, have you located Dawn or Daj?"* He asked, breaking surface in time to see Autumn dive in. It was odd that the waves disappeared before she reappeared.

"No, nothing yet but I have a suspicion we will be seeing them soon." The water stroked and kneaded against her skin. *"This water has a calming affect, doesn't it?"* Autumn opened her eyes making out the shadow of Nacoo's treading legs, *"and to think I can communicate with you like this is — about as thrilling as space chuting."* Laughing in her mind, she yanked on Nacoo's feet, pulling him under. They surfaced face to face grinning like children. "Race you back for another dive," Autumn sputtered, already starting to swim away.

Farstar watched the two climb from the water and took great ootau in their joy. For it was well with Targ, the water allowed full contact with the humans, allowing the planet to freely explore them. Farstar's thin gray lips curved into a furtive smile.

VII

Daj tried to focus; the world had gone fuzzy as fresh peach skin, his mouth felt dry as a dead dingo's donger and to top that, he had to whiz like a half crazed brumby. "Bloody 'ell," he moaned, rubbing his forehead and face. He tried to focus again only to realize it was by far still night, standing slowly, he stumbled to the cleansing room door. A soft violet glow filled the room and he could hear water running causing the urge to go even greater. He hurried over to the bowl shaped vine that he used as lavatory. His urine immediately absorbed into the vine, he thought, what goes in must come out, his stomach turned, and he tried to erase the thought.

"When you are done come and join me, it shall relieve your — hmm, what do you call it — hangover."

Daj looked over at TaChoo, she lay in a floor depression surrounded by red foam, her skin glowed, and she reached a slender six-fingered hand out to him. His robe fell to the floor and he stepped into tepid red water. With a thought he was in the mist of her mind, a snake coiling, tongue flicking, touching every part of her that he could, soft groans escaped her, and he wound his way deeper.

Daj found treasure in this new form of lovemaking, TaChoo was completely his, he stretched his mind, caressing hers with thought-form fingers, seeking, searching every crevice, and only stopping when she shivered. Memories of her life sifted through his being, he watched her grow in Targ's womb, play, learn, and grow with other Targian children. She was the last of Thorb and Maruth's offspring, Maruth having died in a spacecraft accident.

Daj felt TaChoo move in rhythm to his investigation. He sensed her body locked with his and plunged more fully into her mind. Tingles passed through his mind, he felt her nudge further into him. He pulled her close and whispered with his mind, *"share essence, with me, TaChoo."*

"Our destinies are entwined, I take ootau with you, and with you I share my aresh." TaChoo murmured.

Daj pulled back from her mind; it felt like pulling gently back on the reins of a horse.

She rested limp in his arms, spent with pleasure. He lifted her out of the tub and carried her to the bed, where he used his physical senses to take in and burn this image of her in his mind to keep forever.

While they rested, Daj felt a prickle inside where the implant lay; he rubbed his head with no relief, then he felt the creeper, it had entered him without his knowing. Panic crept up in his throat. He wanted to run, but vines wrapped around his arms and legs holding him in place. He looked over at TaChoo cocooned in vegetation. Daj tried to move but the vines were cocooning him, too. Targ purged his mind, at first in a low vibratory rumble, gaining in frequency, and then tendrils moved about inside his body sending small jabs of electricity in all directions. It felt as though Targ was trying to reconstruct his system. Daj moaned as sparks flew behind his eyes, fire flashed in his groin and his breath crackled. His heart pounded, his mind struggled to be free and then... darkness.

The vines released them and they slept.

Thorb stood watching the children play, his smile reflecting memories of youth. Targ was ever diligent, attending to the needs of these newcomers. He sighed at the thought of the two new female offspring that now formed in TaChoo and Dawn's wombs, which pleased the planet, yet Targ demanded more. Thorb could not keep the humans away from each other for much longer, without a disturbance. The one called Nacoo was being quite a challenge, and he feared Targ would put him in Farth, a place no Targian or human should have to go.

TaChoo's first offspring returned Thorb's gaze. The child was now able to sit without assistance of holding vines; creepers held fast to her spine and neck and would remain in place until her physical body finished growing. Thorb remembered his release day, how awkward it felt to walk without Targ, but Targ was always with him and guided his movements, tendrils tickled the soles of his slender, gray feet with each step he had taken, comforting him, as the planet always did.

"I shall call you Ashruba," the child cooed and patted the mossy growth beneath her. *"You shall keep Targ comforted, for your feet give him massages,"* he looked at her swirling, smoky-green feet, *"and your thoughts are for his pleasure of learning."*

Thorb turned his attention to Farstar's child. *"You, I shall call Moonracer."* He laughed as the child whisked at the air with hands and feet. Hank's child slept cupped in the living bed, *"Po is your name."* Clamora's child rocked back and forth on hands and knees. *"You shall be Winston."* He felt love for all, *"Grow well, and grow strong."*

He would wait to name the other offspring until Farstar and Clamora conceived and all were in Targ's womb, he released a deep breath, *"Targ,"* Thorb called out, moss covered his feet. *"The four oldest are named."* Thorb straightened his arms out from his sides, palms outward and lifted his head; he yielded easily to the fine satin tendrils entering his feet.

"They are noble names."

"Copaa rit Targ," Thorb was grateful for the acceptance. *"It has been a long time since I have had such an honorable task."*

"They perfect me, I hunger for new knowledge." Targ sent tendrils snaking into Thorb's brain. *"I require more seeds,"* Thorb whimpered as the planet absorbed his fresh memories. *"The time of transition nears Kandoria waits."*

"Va," Thorb answered, throwing his head back and took ootau, as fresh waves of energy jolted through him. *"I wish to converge with you."* His body convulsed as Targ penetrated him with spider-web tendrils. *"Aaah,"* he released a breath. Thorb began to explore through the eyes of the planet, his spirit soared though rock, water and sky. He plunged into the depths of Targ, pulsated with the rhythm of the planet's life. Frequencies of light, sound, and color, tantalized him; Targ seeped throughout his being conquering him completely.

"Hank, how much farther is it?" They had been hiking through this oscillating underground passageway for a couple of hours.

"The opening is not far." He probed her mind a little harder. *"Do you feel the difference in mind touch,"* Hank looked at Dawn with intensity.

She pursed her lips and wrinkled her nose. *"I feel a faster vibration in my head."* Dawn let out a long sigh.

"Each mind touch has a different vibration; you shall learn this as you learned physical voice tone." Light shone in from an opening onto the cavern wall. Hank ceased walking and turned Dawn to face him. *"When you go back to Earth you shall find telepathy a tutal ~ friend. Jist vek ~ small one, you shall never be alone if you work at this."* He kissed her forehead and they resumed their stride.

"You make it sound as if you are not coming with me." She looked questioningly at him.

"There shall be times when we cannot be physically together, but with Targ we are conjoined spiritually. You shall have a profound bond with our offspring and very soon you will feel Po's mind touch."

"Po?"

"He is our first offspring," Hank grinned.

"First," she stammered. *"Are you saying there are more?"* They had reached the opening that looked out across a meadow, multicolored flowers and grasses reached for the suns that shown from an orchid sky. "Oh, this planet is heart-stopping," Dawn, said in a hushed tone.

They stood for a moment reveling in the beauty. *"To answer your question jist vek, va ~ yes, the second forms inside you."* Hank started to walk again.

Dawn laid a hand on her belly. She was apprehensive about another birthing experience and even more so about a fast-growing child. She'd never thought of her life with children, and it was all so overwhelming, a very un-human way, it all happened so quickly. *"I don't want to be an experiment."* She put some force behind her thought.

Hank stopped, *"Jist vek, we come from the same ancestors only now has Targ asked us to find you and rebuild our physical bodies. He nes ootau ~ takes comfort, knowing we can continue to live with him. Without you, without your density we would lose more of our structure and become spirit."* Hank tucked a curl behind Dawn's ear.

"Oh," she lowered her head against his hand. *"Does this mean that every time we make love I will have to go through this?"* She could not look at him.

"When Targ becomes fulfilled it shall not be so."

A sense of trepidation arose in her; she moved away from Hank and spied a very large violet-colored tree in the distance.

"Life should not be dreadful, take ootau that Targ finds you pleasing." He grabbed for her hand.

Dawn turned, throwing her arms in the air, and yelled, "How do you do that?" She was exasperated.

Hank chuckled aloud, "You leave yourself open to me, so it is easy to feel your emotions and see the changing color of your aura." His voice was musical and he chuckled once more, quite amused by her.

Dawn scowled, stomped her foot and headed for the tree. "You stink at facial expression," she nearly screamed.

Hank, full of merriment, followed along behind Dawn watching her and knowing how surprised she would be when they rambled into camp.

Autumn placed first on the beach, stumbling past Farstar. "Come on in, show us some talent," she laughed, and continued running toward the dock. Nacoo was now in the lead, "Hey," she panted, "looks like the water has dyed your almond skin Indian red."

Nacoo couldn't let a remark like that slip away, "Yeah, it tinted you up a bit, too." He grabbed her and both went splashing into the water.

Farstar stood on the dock waiting for them to surface. He felt Targ play under his feet. The planet's urging grew stronger, driving him to be closer to Autumn. When the two broke water, he dived, his slender body sliced into the water with the slightest ripple. Targ's warm liquid entered him much quicker than the feelers did. Little points of electric popped throughout his body; he rolled and swam closer to the bottom, vegetation brushed against his chest and legs, calling to him. He rolled over once more, allowing his back to touch the aquatic plant life; they pulled him down, exploring him, it felt so good to be in the vines of Targ.

Dawn stood there, stunned, looking at the dripping Nacoo and Autumn.

Autumn wiped the water from her eyes; she grabbed Nacoo by the arm shaking it and pointed to Dawn. "Do you see her?"

Nacoo looked up right into the eyes of his favorite colleague. "Dawn," he boomed. In one leap, he had her folded in his arms. "I have missed you, are you alright? Is it really you?" He pushed on her small shoulders and stared into her eyes.

Tears rolled down Dawn's cheeks as she gazed into his onyx eyes. "Nacoo," she wept, and returned his embrace.

"I think it's my turn," Autumn said, with a joyful tremble in her voice.

The women hugged, then all three hugged, laughing and looking at one another.

Hank drank in the emotion coming from this gathering. It was fresh and appealing, and Hank was always in for good entertainment. He put on his best grin and reached out a hand in human gesture. "Greetings," he spoke aloud.

Nacoo reached out a hand, never letting go of Dawn. "You must be Dawn's, uh, how was it put to me, ah yes, tour guide. Ha, ha, good to meet the Targian that has kept Dawn safe, Nacoo's the name." His large hand enveloped Hank's slender one.

"Va, I am Hank." He smiled, wincing slightly from the grasp but curious about the passion that surged from this large man, *"Ishag ootaut ga."* Hank slid further into Nacoo's thoughts, savoring this man's zeal.

Nacoo stared hard into the intense glow of Hank's eyes. He could feel his energy wash through his mind and understood that he had just told him he took comfort in Dawn. He pulled back fast in his mind, blocking further penetration. He noticed Hank sway and released his grip.

"This is Autumn," chirped Dawn, her eyes moist.

Hank bowed, not caring for another handshake. "You are more of a delight to my eyes, now that you are not made from memories," he said to Autumn, taunting Dawn.

"I'll explain later." Dawn ignored the comment. "It's been quite a travel thus far, and there is so much to talk about."

Autumn took Dawn by the hand. "Come on, I need to get back into my clothes. Nacoo thought he had me beat, but I proved him wrong." She gave Nacoo a quick glance and pursed her lips, razzing him.

Nacoo reluctantly let Dawn go and followed the woman into camp.

Jax sat cross-legged in front of Baxter. *"Feel Targ beneath you."* His vibration was tranquil. *"Use his knowledge,"* Jax relished Baxter's response. *"Targ shall create through you and supply you with your needs."*

Baxter relaxed, thinking of his hiking pack; he could sense Jax playing at the edges of his mind, coaching him to go forward with this meditation. Vines slithered up and around his shoulders, great warmth gathered at the center of his back, and he became aware that Targ was intimately weaving what he desired.

Jax took comfort, watching the development of Baxter's pack. He searched his mind to find a memory that would be pleasing to him. A flicker of ardor made him stop and examine a memory. He imaged Dawn smiling up at him. Jax pulled back from his pursuit, hearing Baxter moan.

Targ entered Baxter; heat rose from his feet to his head and made a connection from his implant to the now fully formed pack on his back. Gradually he came around to know his surroundings; Jax sat across from him grinning from ear to ear. "What," he asked groggily.

"You look as though you have had one to many Twilight Rivers. Targ is pleased with your first creation. Now shall we fill up our packs with plentiful harvest?" His laughter lifted up through the trees.

Baxter tried to examine the pack on his back. *"How do I take this off to fill it?"* he asked, sounding a touch flustered.

"Just lift it off your shoulders. Targ shall relinquish his hold until it is put back in place, but don't leave it off for too long or you shall find yourself tripping over vines in search of it."

"I must be dreaming." Baxter stared into Jax's glistening eyes. *"So you were saying how Targ picked me to be, um, what was it you told me I would be?"* He delicately removed the pack at the verva bush and started to fill it.

"Keeper of Resemblance, you shall learn how to probe a person and find their strongest ootau, then give them their trevi ~ desire." Jax shifted his bursting pack and started to walk.

"Have you found my ootau?" Baxter already knew the answer.

"Va," Jax smirked, and picked up the pace.

"So what you are saying is Targ only explored me so profoundly to try and understand why I felt so empowered." Daj kicked at the sand.

"Va, he needs to completely understand kom ~ human emotion for our new race of children.

"Will it always be this way?" Anger bled into his words.

"It is the Targian way, not Earth's." TaChoo tried to understand this fresh emotion. *"We must find ootau during this time of transition and we must accustom ourselves with each others mind touches."* She glanced up at the curve of the shore.

"Just one more way to control us, eh?" he shouted in his mind.

TaChoo staggered under the blow. *"Daj,"* she slowed her pace. *"You were selected because Targ knew you would protect him and our offspring, his minerals now pump through your veins as they do our children. He needs your knowledge for the betterment of not only our lives but Earth as well."* She paused looking out across the ocean. *"The suns are starting to set; do you see the chul's? They fly back to nest and care for their offspring. Soon we too shall return to the shram sy ~ birthing room."* She said quietly, and resumed walking.

"Birthing room," Daj snorted. "Are you capable of carrying a child like a human woman?" He tossed a stone into the red water. "Targ has already programmed my system to be some kind of super hero back home, so why can't he program you?" This time he threw a fist full of stones, forcefully, as they rounded the buttery colored, moss-covered cliff. "No bubbles," he shouted, "and Targ took Dawn's baby too!" His rage spewed with the intensity of an erupting volcano, he kicked vehemently at the water. God, he felt so helpless. When he finally looked up, he could see a small blue fire in the distance. He stood still for a moment, breathing heavily. Autumn came to mind.

"I am Targian and cannot be changed." TaChoo stood behind him and felt his distress, when she tried again to touch his mind she could not.

"Who is touching me?" A familiar voice asked.

Startled, he responded, *"Daj."*

"Hello Daj, it's been awhile," tinkling laughter rang in his head.

Daj tipped his hat back and subconsciously reached for his hyper-band. *"Autumn,"* hope filled his thoughts.

"That's right cowboy; it's me, Dawn and Nacoo." Daj started to run sending sand flying in every direction, "Autumn," he shouted, his anger forgotten.

Three figures ran toward him. His feet could not move fast enough; he stumbled, caught himself, and bounded onward. Sweat rolled down his face. His shirt was moist when they reached each other.

"By the great gods it's good to see you Daj." Nacoo grabbed him roughly around the head, looking deep into his eyes. "It's really you," Nacoo bear hugged him, the men clapping one another on the back.

"Right," Daj stepped back and reached for Dawn, she slid into his arms squeezing him with fervor. He kissed her forehead and then looked into the gold-flecked eyes of Autumn, and he couldn't hold the tears as the two enfolded arms around one another. "It's so good to see you." He half sobbed, half laughed into her dark honey hair.

Foster stood waiting by the docking bay doors. Today he would escort Professor Zyleon and Kuranna back to Kandoria. He smiled warmly, feeling honored that Thorb had offered him the chance to expand his knowledge of learning for Targ. He contemplated Earth and the changes that would occur for the human race. They had long since discovered Lemuria and Atlantis, but were not yet aware of how to use such ancient wisdom bestowed upon those long-ago cultures. They would start a slow transition according to the planetary alignment; Targ would need full cooperation with the Galactic Intelligence for the continuance of both species.

Foster eyed the pilot, Trombula, as he readied the ship. The magnetic attractor started to rumble and the ship levitated. Air currents blew his thin silver hair away from his face and he stepped back. The docking bay was always a busy place, crews prepared flights continuously for home planet and interplanetary flights. His thoughts drifted to Maruth, his zaf, she had taken ootau in exploring the Grehaz civilization, one of fluid motion. He smiled remembering the way she mimicked their movements, with hands over her head she would dip down and back up swaying her hips the whole time.

He chuckled and wondered of TaChoo and the task she undertook. *"TaChoo,"* he called and waited for her mind touch in return.

"The water is calm under the setting suns, nua."

Foster felt uneasy. *"The water is calm, but you are not. Are you in need of healing?"* He looked down the empty hallway.

"Interpretation of human emotion is challenging. Daj finds discomfort with Targ's interaction with him and our offspring's development. He has immense love for his tutal's, but mostly for the one called Autumn who returns his love. I feel I have not enough knowledge to continue."

Foster heard footfalls from the curve of the corridor. *"Stay with him TaChoo, rest tonight; share his love for it shall please Targ."* Thorb, Professor Zyleon, and Kuranna came into view. *"Vah, rah,"* he departed from his sister's mind. Foster greeted the trio with a bow and with a sweeping motion held an arm out pointing the way into the docking bay. They walked down one ramp and up another, into the waiting ship.

Kuranna grasped Thorb's hand, *"I shall hope to see you again soon."* Her smile was pleasant as she looked into his diamond eyes.

"In the second wake of the third turning moon, Poc, I shall visit. But for now Trombula shall assist you." Thorb inclined his head to Professor Zyleon, *"Your team shall be returned before the second wake of Unares's, our fifth moons rising."* He nodded again and retreated from the ship with just a mere glance at Foster. *"Fly well jant,"* he said to his son.

"Professor Zyleon," Foster pointed to a seat directly behind the pilots. *"This shall be your seat and Kuranna; you shall sit across from him."* He directed her to the chair behind the co-pilots seat.

"No pods this time?" Zyleon questioned.

"You shall be given rup appo ~ tea, to help you endure the trip; we shall ish ~ return, through a gravitational wave, space-time." Foster felt Professor Zyleon's curiosity, *"today we learn of each other and in many suns and moons to come we learn of technology."*

"Yes, yes, of course you are right, a human mind can only learn so quickly." Zyleon returned a knowing look to Foster. The implant would increase his level of knowledge without any study, which he found a very intriguing design.

Trombula handed Kuranna a cup of appo and she speculated just when, in Earth terms, the wake of the fifth turning moon would be.

VIII

Clamora passed through the tunnel opening, levitating across the meadow toward the cliff. She was to meet Jax at the Path of Crossing and return to camp with them. Curiosity took over at finally being able to spend a little more time with Baxter .She increased her pace, he really look did like Nacoo; Targians all had a similar body structure, females being a bit smaller, but they all had distinguishing facial features, she reached up and touched the fern leaf marking, under her right ear. Getting used to the human form was a test, all to itself; a flicker of a smile crossed her face. Thinking of Winston, he had Nacoo's strength but Targ formed the cells of his body structure, ensuring pure connection to the planet.

She loved the way she became one with Targ and was sure Winston would enjoy this pleasure. Her bare feet pressed into the black grass, as she now stood off to one side of the Path of Crossing. Clamora closed her eyes, raised her arms, and faced the suns; the grass slithered up between her toes, climbing up around her ankles to touch the hem of the spar-thread robe she wore. She allowed the suns to warm her and decided against lifting the hood over her head, heat penetrated her skin and she thought of the way Nacoo's body felt much warmer than her own. It was good that Targ had started to create a stronger Targian race, and she desired to comfort the planet.

Jax noticed Clamora standing in the sun pose. *"Taking ootau during the setting suns is prelude to pleasures."*

Clamora turned toward Jax, his eyes reflecting the amber light. *"Quite unusual and interesting pleasures,"* she waved at him.

Jax frowned.

"That's Clamora, isn't it?" Baxter shielded his eyes, squinting.

"Va," he said aloud, shifting his pack.

"Hello, Clamora," Baxter called, making out her long thin nose and lips, silhouetted against the two suns orangey glow, and a twinkling in her eyes.

"You are learning well." She returned Baxter's gaze, desiring to explore his mind, *"Jax is a good teacher,"* she bowed to Baxter, sensing Jax's eyes upon her.

Daj could not take his eyes off Autumn. She and Dawn sat side by side on one of the dark cherry red, mossy logs that encircled the campfire. They were engaged in conversation, heads tucked together with the blue flames capering off their hair. It was good to be with his colleagues again. He stood with arms folded across his chest, hat tipped back, and a silly grin he seemed incapable of wiping off his face. Autumn looked up briefly, tossing a stick at him. "Autumn!" he liked the way her name hummed in the back of his throat. "Watch where you're throwing things," sounding injured but his smile gave him away.

"You're staring." Autumn gave an appreciative wink and returned to her conversation.

Nacoo's large hand grasped his shoulder, causing him to jump, "Daj, sorry, didn't mean to startle you. Come on, Let's join the ladies." Nacoo spoke in a low tone as he sat on the log next to Dawn, "Always a beautiful Dawn."

Dawn glanced up at Nacoo, his straight row of white teeth, bluish in the firelight, flashed brightly against his dark skin. She flushed, not saying a word.

Daj grinned at Nacoo's comment, tipping his Barmah to the women. He sat down next to Autumn, the half circle was cozy; he tilted his head back, gazing at the stars that were becoming visible. The nearest moon shone pastel yellow against the fading horizon. "Does anyone know how to read these stars? Look," he pointed to a small cluster directly above them, "we can call that group Zyleon's team," Daj chuckled.

Dawn pointed to a bright star over the water, "Yeah, and that one we'll call roo." Everyone laughed.

Moonlight mirrored off the dark water and all eyes were upon a silvery figure emerging from its depths. Gooseflesh crawled over Dawn's body. "What the hell is that," she breathed.

Daj jumped to his feet, removing his dagger to face whatever this might be. Nacoo stood and stepped up beside him, a tower by his side.

"*Nacoo,*" Farstar called out and watched cautiously as the big man placed a hand on Daj's wrist, lowering the blade.

"It's okay," Nacoo, said, "he's with us.

As the bare-skinned Farstar entered the firelight, Autumn's heart skipped a beat. He was so beautiful. She turned her attention to Dawn, hoping her expression didn't give her away. "Dawn, this is Farstar. He's the one that rescued me back at Kandoria."

Farstar inclined his head, red droplets of water rolling down his face and body.

Dawn blushed.

Autumn moved closer to him. "Farstar, I would also like you to meet Daj, our team geologist." Autumn wrapped her fingers around Daj's arm as she introduced him. "*I'll go find your robe,*" she offered to Farstar, feeling a bit uncomfortable.

Farstar nodded.

Autumn smiled at Farstar and raised a finger to the men. "I'll be right back."

"*Dawn, please come with me,*" Autumn directed her thoughts to Dawn.

Dawn started at the feel of Autumn's mind touch. She stood up and the women walked away from the fire's light.

Farstar poured tea from the kettle, studying Daj as he did so. He knew this was the man in Autumn's memories and felt an uneasy stirring within him.

"You sure can hold your breath a long time." Nacoo said. He took the cup from Farstar, eyeing the alien's slightness.

"*I am Targian,*" Farstar said, forcing his hand to stay steady as he handed Daj a cup. He would have to consult with Clamora about this strange new feeling.

"Having appo without us," TaChoo's musical voice rang clear. Hank stood behind her gazing intently at Daj who had flinched at her words.

"*Please, take ootau with us,*" Farstar inclined his head to his fellow Targians and continued serving the steamy brew. "*The darkness comes swiftly. We must teach our new friends to create covers for sleeping or as Nacoo speaks of them, tents."* Farstar smirked and handed a teacup to TaChoo, motioning for her to sit.

TaChoo glided over to Daj's side and faced Nacoo. *"I am TaChoo, cula ~ daughter, of Thorb and rah ~ sister, to Foster."* Her eyes shifted past his right shoulder. *"Jax has brought food and company."* She admired Farstar, *"are you in need of moon energy?"*

"The drying of Targ's water in the moonlight is nourishing."

TaChoo gave him a perceptive look.

The small troupe turned their gaze to the three forms entering the circle. *"Ah, I must brew more appo,"* Farstar considered, occupying himself with the task.

"Baxter, I see you have once again met up with the beautiful Clamora." Nacoo held his brother's steady gaze.

"Just a few minutes ago," Baxter answered. He sat wearily on a vacant log and looked up at Jax. "How do I release this pack?"

"Speak the word, ish and the vines shall return to Targ," Jax watched with good humor as Baxter spoke the word. Verva fruit fell in all directions, causing snickers from the Targians and gawking stares from Nacoo and Daj.

"It's good to see you cobber," Daj said, tipping his hat.

"Likewise," Baxter picked up a fruit, a twisted smile on his lips, curious about the naked alien.

"That was impressive," Daj whistled softly.

"Quite," said Nacoo, staring at his brother.

"Daj, Baxter, please meet Hank," TaChoo motioned to them, *"and,"* she waved her hand toward the newcomers. *"This is Jax; he is one of our most skilled pilots, and next to him, Clamora. The one serving appo is Farstar and I am TaChoo."* She nodded to Baxter, allowing him to feel her amusement.

Everyone offered greetings.

Inside the tent, Autumn rummaged around in her backpack for something to give to Farstar to wear, as she didn't know where he'd laid his robe. *"Dawn, when Nacoo and I met the first time, we exchanged bungs. We think it's a good idea; it may help us to keep some control over our situation."* She raised a finger to her lips in a hush gesture. Autumn removed Nacoo's bung from her sensory site and handed it to Dawn.

"It feels funny to talk like this," Dawn whispered, pulling out her bung, feeling a tweak of leeriness, handing it to Autumn. Dawn pushed Nacoo's bung inside her center, smiling feebly. *"It won't scramble them, will it?"*

"It shouldn't, but you'll feel a pull, burn or tingle and know which way to go to find him. Try not to think about it in case the Targians can read us better than they let on." Autumn grasped a towel. "This will have to do, they are probably wondering what happened to us by now.

"Autumn," Dawn whispered. "This planet is frightening. It rapes your mind as well as your body." Tears threatened to come. "I don't want to be separated again." A rustle sounded by the tent door and with a jump Dawn reached for her dagger. Fumbling she squeezed the blade, cutting her left index and middle fingers quite deep. "Aaaahhh," she howled, as blood splattered her pants.

Autumn started as the door flap flew open. Farstar moved swiftly toward Dawn, eyes flaming. He reached Dawn just as she collapsed from the sight of her dangling fingers.

Autumn watched in horror. Farstar kneeled down, his body glowed a vaporous, cherry hue. He clasped Dawn's bleeding fingers in both hands. "KOLUM TREY," his voice rang in her ears and the very atmosphere shook with their power. The radiance around him took on a pinkish tint, and he placed one hand at the back of Dawn's head; Autumn mimicked him in her shock. An orb of silver light encased Dawn's hand, instantly connecting the bones, nerves, and muscle. Autumn stared in awe as he raised her nearly healed fingers to his solar plexus and said, "mienco." Heat waves lifted from Dawn's hand and as Autumn watched, the wounds laced up and disappeared. Farstar's hand holding the back of Dawn's head moved to her brow, "Wathu ~ awaken, and ne ootau ~ take comfort." Farstar dropped his hands and became very still.

Dawn opened her eyes and looked directly at the alien in front of her, mouth open in bewilderment. She flexed her fingers, astonished and murmured, "how..." Gasping she looked down at her stained pants and mended hand, and back up at the motionless Farstar.

"I don't know," Autumn, murmured, staring at Dawn's bloodied dagger.

Neither woman dared to move.

Nacoo heard a loud voice come from the tent the women had gone into. His sensory site prickled intensely. Pretending to stretch, he tried to rub it away. The vibration was a bit different from former hums, it almost numbed the area; he turned his head away from Jax, who was teaching them to create covers for sleeping and glanced behind him. TaChoo whooshed passed him, silent as deep space. He watched her enter through the flap, and then turned back to the group. All the Targians were looking where TaChoo had vanished. Nacoo bolted toward the tent, fear collecting in his chest. Daj was right beside him. The men rushed through the opening to find Farstar kneeling in front of Dawn.

"Don't touch her," Nacoo boomed, fist raised.

"*SHHH,*" TaChoo warned, "all is well, do not harm him."

Farstar's luminosity turned emerald.

"What's wrong with him," Dawn rubbed her newly healed hand, still sprawled on the ground, she carefully wiped and sheathed her dagger.

"*He is regenerating. A wound such as was yours warrants much energy. Targ shall nourish him.*" TaChoo motioned for Dawn to stand. "*Come, Jax is waiting.*"

"Who are you?" Dawn stood slowly keeping her eyes fixed on Farstar.

"*TaChoo,*" she stated.

Autumn watched intently as the grass under Farstar's ankles, moved almost imperceptibly. She felt Daj wrap a secure arm around her shoulder. "*What happened?*"

"*She almost sliced her fingers off and Farstar healed her right in front of my eyes.*" Autumn looked into Daj's moss-green eyes.

They stood together in silence for a moment, watching the glow of emerald-colored energy swirl around the Targian.

"*Foster — healed me.*" Daj flapped the stained, ripped cloth of his pants; he again felt the wodevil sink its teeth into his flesh, and he winced.

Autumn lowered her head, "*Daj…*" she choked back a sob.

"*She'll be fine, we all are,*" he pushed her hair gently away from her temple.

"Daj, I'll be out in a sec, okay," Autumn trembled, *"Farstar needs..."* she faltered, letting the words hang.

"Are you sure you'll be right?" Daj pulled her a little closer; he didn't want her to stay.

"Positive," she gripped the towel firmly as Daj released her, seeing the hurt and concern in his eyes. She held her breath as he and Nacoo left the tent. "I'm sorry," she whispered.

"Allow him to come to his surroundings on his own, Autumn." TaChoo's mind touch reached her.

Farstar's silver hair, almost dry now, hung forward, covering his features. Autumn kneeled in front of him, watching the swirls of color fade with the return of his normal dove-gray complexion. She observed the grass withdrawing and he quavered. His breathing shallow and his slender fingers twitched. Autumn longed to touch his face and look into those star crystal eyes, now closed and black in color. The tips of the seven crescent moons along his jaw line crossed one another, stretching from the slant of his sharply curved chin up to the summit of his angled ear. She stopped her reach mid-way, not touching the first crescent moon impression.

"That one is named Badu for its color of jade. You give me great ootau, Autumn." Farstar opened his eyes, absorbing her trevi. *"Moonracer, our son carries the same mark upon him."* A smile played on his lips.

"Moonracer — our son," Autumn took in a breath, continued her reach, and touched the tip of his cool chin. She leaned forward, embracing him.

Farstar was experiencing yet another new emotion; he permitted the surge of energy to flow freely as he returned her embrace. He wished to share this great welling inside of him, not quite understanding how it could be so separate from Targ.

Autumn pulled away from Farstar an inquiring look upon her face. *"Farstar, do you love me?"*

"I ne ootau ~ take comfort, in you," he answered, unsure of this human meaning.

"Comfort — all right then, come on, if you're ready, the others are waiting." She avoided his questioning look.

Outside, Baxter hugged Dawn, gently folding her in his arms, breathing in the fragrance of her hair. "It is good to see you," he said softly, then clearing his throat, "Clamora, Jax this is Dawn, she is…"

"She is the anthropologist of the group, the one who wishes to study our dead, little yet does she know how to access Targ's memories." Hank interrupted, putting on his best jokester's grin, which was contagious. Hank faced Autumn and bowed low, miming flipping a hat with his hand. *"My lady,"* he looked up at her. *"I am Hank."*

She smiled at his antics and tapped Dawn on the shoulder, "my turn to give the big guy a hug." Autumn said, reaching an arm around Baxter's solid waist.

"Farstar you should not have healed such a great wound so quickly." Jax motioned for him to sit beside him. *"Everyone, please sit. Now that all our sleeping covers… ah, tents are created,"* He glanced at Nacoo. *"We shall take ootau ~ comfort, in the food Targ has provided for us."*

"It was Targ's wish." Farstar responded to Jax.

Jax nodded to him and started the bucket brigade by handing verva fruit and alm nuts to Farstar, who handed them to Daj.

Daj felt Farstar's fingernail scratch the back of his hand, startling him as he took the bowl of nuts and fruit. He passed the bowl rather clumsily to Dawn, but her smaller hands almost missed it, causing a nut to fall to the ground. "Got it," she triumphed.

Baxter leaned over to pick up the nut at the same time and clunked heads with her. "Ow," they chorused together, laughing. He took the bowl and gently handed it to Autumn.

Autumn continued the passing of the bowl to Nacoo, noticing his hands had a few scars where Baxter's had none. *"Hope Dawn doesn't get a sore neck out of that."* Sounding casual, she smirked at Nacoo and hoped he understood her clue. Nacoo raised an eyebrow his face reflecting the blue flickering firelight.

As he handed the food to Hank, he said to Autumn, "You missed the raising of the tents. Our Targian ancestors have given us a most unusual and transfixing gift." He glanced at Dawn and then back at Autumn, acknowledging her with a wink.

TaChoo took the fruit and nuts from Hank and handed them to Clamora.

Baxter piped up, "It really is a phenomenal accomplishment to be able to connect to the ground you sit upon, form an image in your mind, and have the actual thought become physical reality." He shook his head, black curls longer than Nacoo's bounced around his face.

"Jax, the circle is complete." Clamora said, meeting the eyes of Baxter; they were so much like Nacoo's dark eyes.

Baxter found Clamora's look intriguing and he straightened his shoulders.

The verva fruit reminded Autumn of her uncle Zyleon's favorite green apple tree. "Where is Professor Zyleon?" She spoke to anyone willing to answer.

"Foster has taken them back to Kandoria; they are to prepare for each of you and the children." Jax's eyes flickered with the firelight. *"Thorb shall call you when the time comes but tonight we rest and ne ootau."* He tossed a small stick into the fire, a wispy, yellow, flame shot up from the center of the pit; an aroma of locust blossoms scented the warm night air.

"Why have you used illusions to take from us, why not just ask?" Nacoo crunched a nut. "Hey, these taste almost like walnuts." He crunched another waiting for a reply.

Snickers and sounds of agreement emerged from Daj and the women. "On Earth we try to get to know each other first, before children are brought into a relationship, but you Targian's just jump right into action." Daj chanced a look at TaChoo, her luminous eyes watching him.

"I feel so dishonored," Dawn practically yelled, throwing her short arms up into the air.

"What children," Baxter asked, feeling perplexed.

Jax tossed another stick into the fire, this time the flare was violet and smelled of mushrooms. *"Our planet is,"* he paused turning his head to look at Clamora, and then turned back to gaze into the fire, *"lonely,"* sadness filled his voice. *"Targ knows our physical structure is unable to re-populate his surface with strong Targian bodies, so we searched Earth to find..."* He steadied his gaze on Nacoo. *"Each of you,"* Jax shifted his eyes back to the flames. *"Our sacrifice is for Targ, without him we would not be able to maintain our ootau."* He tossed a nut to Baxter, who looked directly at him, continuing to explain, *"Insight was given to your tutal's ~ friends, although they seem to have lost this knowledge."* He gave each human a hard stare and resumed speaking. *"The children are seeds taken from them by using certain gentle persuasions, but they gave freely in the end."* This time he found Dawn's eyes; she lowered them.

Jax threw a third stick into the fire and emerald flames shot up higher than their heads. A mixture of lemons and grapes perfumed the air.

Daj had pulled off his boots and slid onto the ground, resting his back against the log; his feet warmed by the fire and contentedly munched nuts.

Farstar watched Daj intently, struggling with a sensation that caused a trevi in him to hurt this human. How much he had to learn. It was easy living on Targ, before the structural breakdown; a seeding took place with a wog sy tek or vesp tek, Targ had chosen for them. There was no — what was it — love the way komi felt it. Targ loved all and all loved Targ, but now Targ required another seeding from him, with the kom female that created such confusion in his mind.

Daj acknowledged Farstar's stare with one of his own. *"Is there something I can help you with mate,"* he said, drowsily.

"During the turn of Nar you shall dance with TaChoo under the second moon's violet light for all to see." He turned up one side of his mouth, still staring into those moss green, human eyes.

Nacoo stood, stretching, the fragrant air filling his lungs. His head began to swim with that familiar whirling sensation and he looked around at his brother and friends; wondering if they were under the same spell.

Daj could feel Farstar probing his mind, causing him to sway with each new thrust — he grabbed his head and moaned — he was searching for something — his mind began to feel raw. *"What is it you want,"* he whimpered. Smoke swirled around his head and he thought he saw a hazy shadow of Nacoo come toward him, and then felt a firm yank on his arm, that lifted him to his feet with ease. The steel grip drew his attention. He cursed, stumbling, almost falling to his knees, and suddenly realizing he was on the path leading away from the tents. Now how did that happen he wondered, his head beginning to clear.

"Crikey, loosen your hold," he stressed. Baxter held his arm, pacing him with long fast steps.

"No, we are not clear yet." Baxter pulled hard to the left.

"What the bloody 'ell just happened?" Daj panted, gaining a better footing.

"I think it's called the veil. It happens when a Targian tries to enter into your mind forcefully. It can be very damaging."

"How do you know that?" Daj asked, incredulously, sweat trickling down the side of his face.

"Jax is a good teacher." Baxter slowed his stride. "But if I had to speculate, I think the alien implant inside my head has something to do with it," he muttered, critically.

"I'd say you learn well. But speculation or not, how did you manage to flash us behind the tents?" Daj walked awkwardly on his bare feet.

"It's a little trick I learned in acting school, called aperture apparition. It's done by creating a gateway, an illusion of sorts, wasn't at all sure it would fool the Targians but then again they don't have the type of entertainment we have, virtual interaction. They use direct contact with the brain's intuitive glands." Baxter halted in front of a big silver-leafed bush that hid a small cave. "In here," he said, looking about and pushing Daj through its yielding branches.

Baxter stepped in behind Daj. "Jax showed this to me and told me it is a hallowed place; said it would act as a shield from the outside world, so I believe you are safe from Farstar in here." He wiped his forehead and noticed their hiding place glowed like golden honey. "Jax has given me no reason not to trust him," his large frame heaved with his breathing, "The alchemists," he continued undisturbed, "discovered an ancient library somewhere around two-thousand, seventy-two and secretly recreated working formulas. When the entertainment industry caught wind of the supposed magic this society could perform, they bargained with them for use of aperture apparition."

"So just how is it done?" Daj questioned, rubbing the tender bruise on his arm. He stared soberly into Baxter's dark, human eyes, finding reassurance that this was not an altered state of mind.

"Let's see one of your sharpay stones," Baxter held out his hand.

Daj fumbled around in his vest pocket. Finding a stone, he tossed it to Baxter. "Catch."

"Now watch this," Baxter smirked, holding the stone in his open palm.

Daj focused his attention on the sharpay stone; a soft high-pitched purring reached his ears. "It's humming."

Unexpectedly, the stone shimmered and disappeared. "Check your pocket," Baxter chuckled.

Daj dug once more in his pocket and to his amazement found the very same sharpay stone. His jaw strutted out on an exhale of breath and he closed his eyes. "How did you do that?" exasperated, he rubbed his face as if to wipe away what he had just seen.

"Do you remember your training for space flight and how you were taught to recognize different vibration frequencies?"

"Yes."

"I use a magnetic stabilizer for balancing and a vacuity post crystal for teleportation, which are my earrings." Baxter pulled back his hair and showed both ears to Daj. "I have a magnetic reversal, metamorphic chip tooth implant that I activate by pushing on it with my tongue. The current that flows between the three causes a molecular shift, which attaches to an electromagnetic pulse, an image, or thought form; you produce, as I did to get us behind the tents. It causes an actual rift and shift of objects, thus an entertainer's prized secret, aperture apparition."

"Here all this time I thought you were just an actor with exceptional skill," Daj said, raising one eyebrow and giving a half smirk to his magician friend. "I imagine you must have to be careful about chewing."

"It's taken me eight years to learn to do what we did just a few minutes ago, but I felt it was necessary to do it. Farstar had a good hold on you for some reason." Baxter's tone was wary.

"He said something about me dancing with TaChoo." Daj noticed that Baxter looked tired. "Many thanks," he added.

"That's all right," he paused, "dancing with TaChoo doesn't sound like a bad thing. She's quite a remarkable being. Strange that Farstar should want to hurt you over that," puzzled Baxter.

"Right, why don't we try to rest, you look tuckered. It must take a lot of energy to do that aperture apparition work." Daj clapped Baxter on the shoulder.

"Yeah, buddy, it does." Baxter rested his back against the den wall. He had thoughts of this strange world spinning in his head when sleep came.

IX

"*F arstar you must not let the kom emotion become a part of you,*" Clamora entered his mind. "*Targ shall heshna wa,*" she touched the back of his hand to reassure him.

"*Even with Targ protecting us, do you not feel the difference? Targ has not given such feelings to me, has he you?*" Farstar let Clamora's hand rest on his.

"*I am not without trevi,*" she bowed her head.

"*You show great displeasure around Daj. You must stay true to Targ and offer him of your knowledge,*" Jax said, gesturing for Farstar to follow him, to the tree behind the camp.

"*Av,*" TaChoo commanded. "*Daj shall return and we shall allow Farstar to finish his purpose.*"

Jax inclined his head to TaChoo, "*so it is done,*" he conceded, nodding to Farstar. "*Go to her,*" Jax felt a surge of anticipation well up in Farstar.

Jax's thoughts turned to Clamora, "*This separation my chosen one is not easy, but we shall be held together in Targ's nourishing vines for the remainder of our lives.*" Clamora matched the sadness in Jax's eyes, for she also felt the lure between them, which had grown stronger since the komi arrived on Targ.

Farstar returned to the circle. Nacoo stood quietly staring into the fire and Hank had taken Dawn to the sleeping cover, closest to the fire. Autumn slumped against the log, her dark honey hair hiding her face. He liked the aroma that scented the air from her warm body, and he gently pushed away the hair covering her features. "*Wathu bu zifla ~ awaken my angel, we shall take ootau together in the covering by the water,*" fondly, he guided the mesmerized Autumn toward the sleeping cover, but before entering, he pointed to the seventh moon's rising. "*Kinque is the moon of mystery,*" stars twinkled behind the orbs russet haze.

"It's beautiful," Autumn murmured, allowing the alien to guide her into the tent and to lay her down on the velvety black grass.

Autumn felt Farstar's hands moving like silk on glass, removing clothes, exposing their skin to Targ's surface. His cool grayness touched her warm flesh, spider silk hair tickled her face, and the grass beneath her moved in waves like a summer's breeze across a ripened wheat field.

Farstar explored every part of this human female so inviting and able to give life back to Targ. He sensed the planet's pleasure, and a great desire coursed in his veins. Targ entered through his feet, the planet was eager, yet he craved to join completely with Autumn, relishing the pleasure this moment brought, before seeding took place.

Autumn's head was clearing; her hand caressed Farstar's cool, sleek neck; he was so lean and slender, unlike her dense body. She ran a finger along his delicate spinal cord; awareness of the planet flickered and played at the edges of her consciousness. His body shuddered with each of her touches. "You are incredible." She kissed his shoulder, the grass swirled faster beneath her, and she laughed. Targ penetrated her, probing her mind, she looked into Farstar's blazing eyes, and she felt him inside, heat flooded through her being and her body arched. "Farstar," she moaned, then relaxed.

Farstar surrendered to Targ, he kissed Autumn with a consuming hunger for her kom aresh. *"My essence I give to you,"* he purred, as he explored her mind. He drank in her foreign emotions conscious that he was Targ's and could never be separate from the planet's life force. Even so, he guardedly kept a small part of this memory separate.

Nacoo slept peacefully as Clamora connected with Targ. The planet sent tendrils in through her feet and searched for the seed. *"A female shall come forth, bring the seed before Kinque's third turning."* Targ's sinuous vibration poured through her veins. A shadow of a smile crossed her lips, and she arose, going outside to sit next to Jax who heated appo in time for the rising of the suns.

"Targ is pleased with my service, but it is a difficult honor being selected to birth a new Targian race."

Jax handed a steaming teacup to Clamora, permitting his hand to linger close to hers. *"Targ shall one day allow us to dance."* A small weak smile tugged at the corner of his mouth.

Hank levitated over beside Clamora and sat, helping himself to a cup of appo. *"The suns wake up, yet the komi sleep,"* he greeted them with frivolity. *"I must take Dawn to the shram sy,"* he said, smiling mischievously. *"She is full of strength and fire. Targ's children shall be sturdy."* He took his appo, passing Farstar on his return back to watch Dawn as she lay sleeping.

"Birth well my tutal," said Jax.

Farstar returned Hank's nod, turning his thoughts to Jax and Clamora, greeting them, *"pah,"* as he glided into the circle.

"Your aura is muted Farstar, are you in need of healing?" concerned, Clamora asked.

"It is cleansing nourishment of Targ that I need, copaa rit, Clamora," Farstar answered.

"Have you not seeded well, Farstar," Jax stirred the fire.

"Targ is well pleased with the kom female," he frowned slightly. *"She has two female seeds to give,"* an uneasy weariness afflicted him as he spoke.

"Targ shall take your discomfort away," Clamora said, soothingly, offering him some appo.

He shook his head no to the tea and speaking only to Jax. *"My tutal, take Autumn to the shram sy, Targ has need of my aresh at — Keiyat Garden."* Farstar sent out a strong wave of sickened desire. *"Treat her carefully,"* then inclining his head, he silently moved from the area.

Jax was disturbed. *"How can I take Autumn to the shram sy when I have not shared aresh with her?"* he asked, Clamora.

"What?" Clamora turned her face to him.

"Targ requires Farstar at the Keiyat Garden." He stood abruptly, *"Clamora,"* he faltered, *"I trevi it was you,"* he spoke to her and reached for her hand, gesturing her to stand. *"I must go and korzuk, with Autumn and learn how to carry out this tribute."*

"Targ shall guide you"; her fingertips touched his. *"Your thoughts comfort me."*

Jax had never experienced such restlessness before. He wondered why Targ would not allow Farstar the privilege of such a great birthing.

Clamora touched his face. *"Do not question Targ's love we are all created to please him."* The urge to kiss her *wog sy tek*, over took her senses, *"take this small piece of me and keep it safe within you."* She touched him deeper than she dared to go with the kom, and he returned her mind touch all too briefly.

"Targ shall not be comforted." He let his lips linger before releasing her.

Nacco glared at them from the opening of the tent, remembering how he had caught his brother's first love in the arms of another. "You persuade me and use me as some freaky cloning science project and tell me to take comfort in this planet," he thundered in a snarling tone, "and expect me to take it like a well-mannered caged animal." He stood rigid with disapproval, hands made into softball-sized fists and moving fast toward Jax. "Comfort will be taken the way it is given to me, by persuasion!" Nacoo's fury propelled him.

"HESH GA," Jax's voice crackled with power.

Targ instantly enveloped all three of them in separate spheres of protective vines. *"You have much to learn Nacoo. Clamora and I carry the same truth given to us by Targ; we are wog sy teks ~ growing room, mates. We do not harbor resentment for what, has to happen, to keep us alive. We are struggling and learning together but cannot and shall not allow such a force of energy to consume us."* Jax clasped his hands in front of him, head bowed, Targ joined with him and he became quiet.

Nacoo tugged at the vines gripping his feet, rage flooded through him as they held him fast. "Aaaggghh," he roared the vines pulling his arms above his head.

"If you do not struggle it shall be easier." Calmly, Clamora spoke to him.

"Yeah right, like I can move if I wanted too." He snorted and glowered at her through the slits of vines. "Clamora why go through all of this? Why not just have a couple nights in the sack and leave it at that? To watch you wrap yourself up in Jax's arms after sharing, *essence*," he hissed, "is just too much."

"Nacoo," a grave voice spoke in his head. *"You shall come to Farth."*

Targ's fine thin tendrils pushed their way into Nacoo's feet. He could feel them climbing, smoldering hot and icy cold feelers slithering their way up through his body. The implant vibrated with maddening intensity, as did the bung inside his sensory center and in that same moment he sensed Dawn and knew that the planet desired to understand their human bond. Thousands of tiny needles pierced his skin; his cage was becoming gelatinous, and incredibly so was he. A sober reality set in that his life wasn't turning out the way he had planned, and he could do nothing about it except give in, *"Targ, do as you will,"* he said, and as he let go, a peculiar thought settled over him, that he was a key instrument being played by a galactic god.

"Huh," Baxter sat up from his sleeping position, looking around for Nacoo. However, not seeing him, he realized something unusual had occurred with his twin brother. It was almost as if his body had shape-shifted, leaving him with a feeling of ominous imprisonment. Baxter stood up, wiping off debris from his hair and clothes, Daj lay curled up with his head next to a mossy rock, his back to him. "Hey Daj, wake up," he cleared the sleep from his throat, walked over and pushed on Daj's backside with his foot. "Come on, we have to make plans."

Daj sat up grumbling. "What," he complained, leaning forward, rubbing his sore feet. "Couldn't you have apported my boots along with me?"

"When we sneak back to camp maybe your boots will be smoldering by the fire."

"Oh, that's flamin' funny, for one who has boots on and what's this about sneaking? Are we planning on slinking into the tucker tent to thieve a cup of coffee?" He responded, sardonically, dancing from side to side, as he stood, "Ow," he groaned through a yawn, stretched, messed his already tangled hair and replaced his Barmah. "Tell me outside what's on your mind. I have to piss."

"Yeah, me too," Baxter said. He pushed through the shrub covering the entrance and Daj followed. As he relieved himself, Baxter regarded the two suns that shone in this alien morning sky, both sundry shades of hazy gold. "Anyway, I think we should head back and try to find out what Farstar has against you."

Daj picked his way gingerly back toward Baxter, who now stood on the path they had kept to last night, thinking he should have used the sharpay stones to heal his tender feet. "It felt like he was digging at my soul trying to excavate a rare gem, it actually hurt. Makes a person wonder what these aliens are capable of and what they will permit us to learn or not learn." He delicately stepped onto the grass. "Ooooh, that's better."

"Let us hope Targ doesn't grab hold of you," Baxter warned.

"And just how the bloody 'ell can I keep him from doing that, mate? This world is so bizarre anything could happen." Daj let out a frustrated sigh.

The men walked on in silence, until the camp came into view. They ducked behind the trees, conscious of the fact that Autumn's was the only tent still standing. There was no sign of Farstar. TaChoo sat beside Daj's boots, sharing tea with Foster around the still burning fire. For a few moments, the Targian bird songs filled the air with the background accompaniment of the red water gently kissing the shore.

"Who's that?" Baxter mind touched Daj.

"His name is Foster, he is TaChoo's brother. He must be back from taking Professor Zyleon and Kuranna to Earth. They sure do know how to travel fast," he smirked. *"That's something Nacoo would enjoy learning."* Daj tipped his hat, unsnapping the one side, to block the morning's brilliance and get a better look at the camp. *"Where do you suppose everyone disappeared too."*

"Don't have the foggiest idea." Baxter sheltered his eyes with his hand. *"Should we just walk up to them?"* reserved, he conveyed.

"That would be best considering TaChoo is guarding my belongings and — we have no where else to go." Daj clicked his tongue. "She does these things to my mind —" he stared at her with a child like anticipation.

Baxter hit his sore arm. "For God's sake, you look like a love-sick puppy. Let's just go and hope for the best," he growled. An odd sensation vibrated through him. His brother was far away, somewhere deep and dark.

As they approached the camp, Foster stood and turned to face them. *"The day has begun, yet you have not had appo."* He grinned at Daj, a theatrical grin. *"Take ootau with TaChoo."* He then focused on the teacup he handed to Baxter. *"I am Foster,"* he nodded and held back the curiosity to probe the mind of this new human male.

As Baxter took the drink, he said, "Yes, Daj told me of you, thank you."

"Daj, come and sit beside me, take ootau ~ comfort, drink, and allow me to heal your feet and arm," TaChoo's mind touch was sharp and clear in his mind.

Sitting next to her, he quietly drank the tea and waited for it to work its familiar magic. She rubbed otah oil on his bruised arm, and feet, when she finished he put his unscathed, trusty boots back on. Foster and Baxter sat across from them watching in silent expectation, both he was sure, thinking completely different thoughts.

"Where is everyone?" Baxter asked.

"All have their own adventure to complete," Foster answered.

"Autumn's tent is still up," he said, pointing at it.

"She sleeps." Foster plunged deep into Baxter's mind and feeling his startled resistance smiled roguishly at him. He watched and waited for the artu to take effect.

Baxter looked over at Daj, feeling a little bewildered. Was it really Daj, or was that a sculpture? His head started to spin and he could feel Foster pushing deeper into his mind. This time he did not resist.

Jax kneeled beside Autumn, Farstar's kom, seeding mate. Her hair matched Yeth's amber color, skin just a shade lighter, and the curves of her human body were thicker than the Targian female form. Almost timidly, he laid one hand on her brow and the other on her solar plexus; she was warm and solid to his touch. *"Autumn, we need to prepare for the shram sy ~ birthing room,"* he said, delicately, pushing further into her mind. She hummed with life, and he permitted ootau to exchange.

"Who is touching me?" Autumn was groggy.

"Jax," he answered, beginning to understand Farstar's meaning to handle her carefully; it would be easy to get lost in this kom female. *"Farstar cannot be with you at shram and has asked me to guide you. We must balance our minds and energies."*

"No," Autumn wrestled with Jax's thoughts.

"Targ has taken him to the Keiyat Garden for healing and rest. It is hard for him to understand...." he felt her breath coming hard, *"emotions,"* he felt her twist and bend in his mind.

"No, Farstar must be at my side, not you," Autumn stated with determined force.

Jax withdrew his energy from her but continued the touch, unsure of pulling back too fast. Her breathing slowed, and her eyes flickered open.

Brown gold-flecked eyes stared wildly about. *"Autumn, you must understand,"* Jax found himself surfing with the biting emotions she emitted. Distrust flowed from her making him quake, he desired to pull back but was eddied even deeper. *"Autumn, please allow..."* She had moved his hand from her solar plexus to her lower belly, the life force was strong, and he trembled.

"Take me to him." Angry tears streaked her face and she dug her nails into the soft flesh of his hand, causing him to wince.

"We shall call Targ." She loosened her grip. He removed his hands and her emotional current shifted, he swayed with the rush it provided. He desired to get lost in the swelling of affection she issued forth for Farstar; it confused him that she did not want to share. Targian's imparted the knowledge to all that desired it, he looked intently at her, steadying himself, and though he did not trevi to pull back from her mysterious depths, he did. *"Know this Autumn, Farstar is Targian and so shall be his children. Targ nes ootau ~ takes comfort that Farstar not to go to the shram. Targian's follow a path of honor and Farstar privileged me to assist you — that means I must,"* he felt a wave of defiance come forth from Autumn. *"Let us call together,"* he said, placing his palms down on the soft black grass, *"cover my hands with yours, and call out to Targ."* He took ootau in a new feeling of raw determination, radiating from her like a vaporous cloud; he would revere Farstar for this privilege and smiled softly to himself.

"Targ," Autumn called out. She knew those fine tendrils were going through Jax's slender palms, prickling her own, enfolding their hands tight together, and but for a moment, she felt trapped. *"Targ you betray me my honor,"* she shrieked in her head at the planet. She felt Jax sway as his energy entwined around her, growing stronger as Targ pulsed through them.

She looked pleadingly into Jax's crystal eyes. *"You steal from me the comfort he gives me."* The vibrations increased to a dizzying speed, she fought to keep her gaze steady on Jax, *"Return him to me."* Autumn watched Jax lower his head then felt a wave of electric energy, a blanket of warmth envelope her. Jax was showing her and Targ his own affection for Autumn by surrendering his experiences with Clamora and Farstar. She felt his sadness that his sacrifices brought, by staying true to Targ, for *Targ* was what mattered. *"I am sorry Jax,"* she cried, overwhelmed by his loyalty.

They stayed suspended in this glowing orb of passionate exchange for a time. Autumn felt the planet embrace her mind, and Targ moved with the beat and rhythms of her own heartbeat. She felt the essence of life growing within her and sensed the seedlings were not ready to leave her, even though they grew so rapidly. Jax was there sharing in the sweet current of ecstasy she reveled in, his presence like an umbrella, covering her, guiding her, helping her to understand how love worked on Targ.

"Take her to the Keiyat Garden, take her to Farstar, and then return to Clamora for she waits to give seed," Targ spoke in his gravelly tone to both of them.

Jax tempered his joy; Targ gave him great comfort with reward that puzzled and charmed him, and he would fulfill Targ's wishes with a light heart.

They stood together with hands still clasped. Autumn wiped her tear-stained face with her shirtsleeve, leaving a dirty streak. Jax released her hands and touched her face to wipe the dirt away. To his surprise, she leaned into him and began to weep freely. "Thank you Jax, I'm sorry for being so untrusting but…" She sniffled in his robe taking in a deep wavering breath, "It's a human thing."

That made them both laugh.

"Autumn," Jax gently touched her mind, *"Farstar is in communication with Targ because of his deep connection to you. He must give everything he has stored in his aresh to Targ. This experience shall leave his life energy extremely vulnerable. When we arrive in the Keiyat Garden, you must allow him to regenerate completely or it shall cause damage to him. Let him awake on his own and remember it shall be well."* Jax rubbed her shoulders and felt of her hair; it was strong and thick unlike his own.

"I understand," she answered, patting the wet spot she left on his satiny robe.

Together they exited the tent.

"*Jist vek, wathu* ~ *awaken and korzuk* ~ *join me for a walk,*" Hank's grin broadened with the flicker of Dawn's thick strawberry eyelashes. "*This day you ish* ~ *return, to Earth.*" The skin beneath her freckled face flushed, he really did enjoy her colors.

"What!" Dawn squealed, flying to a standing position, stomping both feet on the floor, jumping excitedly. "I'm going home!" She looked into Hank's glittering eyes with pure bubbling excitement and dashed to gather her belongings.

"*Va,*" he chuckled, captivated by her anticipation.

"What about the others?" she asked, running a hand through her strawberry waves. "What about the children," she subconsciously touched her abdomen. "What about…"

"*Baxter shall join us,*" he interrupted, "*the others must finish preparing, and the children grow in Targ for a year of your Earth time. You may return to communicate with them at any time.*" Hank reached for her hand. "*We must meet Thorb at the docking bay so our journey can begin.*"

"Our journey," Dawn squeaked. "Are you coming with me?" She pressed her lips together.

"*Va, we are to stay together and continue the work we started. There is trevi to document each others findings.*" He touched her fingertips. "*Thorb waits, wex wa ep* ~ *let us go.*" His hand slid around her small, creamy one. "*Practice mind touches, jist vek* ~ *small one, the frequencies on Earth are denser and sometimes difficult to use.*" Hank turned, picked up her pack, and led the way.

Dawn used her free hand to rub her sensory site; it had been prickling her from just after they had left the birthing room. The tugging of it made her want to grab a shovel and start digging a hole to the center of Targ, but she tried to curve the sensation, so Hank's attention would pass over it. She patted her hyper-band with hopes that Momma had information to download and aid them in keeping some human control in this endeavor. She smiled and squeezed Hank's hand. This alien relationship was terrifying, but at the same time, mysteriously pleasing, and through it all, she still upheld a need to be diligent. Dawn rubbed her neck again and thought of how uncomfortable the knowledge of using a bung had made her. In the wrong hands, it could allow anyone, access to her most private thoughts. She nearly laughed aloud.

Daj was always teasing her about finding out what her mind held within its boney walls. She remembered him planting a fake bung download onto her computer, which played a scene of them in her tent under a sheet, heads sticking out from either end, grinning ludicrous grins. She threw anything and everything that fit in her hand at him, every time she saw him, ensuing for the full week until she obtained an apology. This time she did laugh aloud.

Hank looked at her. *"Daj is funny."*

"Why do you do that?" she asked calmly although it unnerved her.

"You leave yourself open to me," his shoulder-length silver hair plumed as they walked. *"We Targians can link together and have a knowing, a transference without words, but you komi do not use this form of refined communication so we must touch you by "hearing" you. We also must touch by "seeing" your thoughts."* He squeezed her hand sensing her unease. *"We can see and sense fluctuations in your magnetic energy field, as is happening now. Using these methods we can understand what you are thinking or feeling, instinctively.*

In this way, we are able to know you. It is more challenging for us but it enables us open interaction with you and from this we are also able to form," Hank chuckled, *"fantasies for you,"* he chuckled again and started to slow their pace. *"That is why I do this with you."*

Dawn scowled at such a long explanation. She wasn't sure if he was scolding her or trying to play at flattery. *"So it's not intentional,"* she mumbled.

Hank stopped walking and glanced toward the doorway, from which the sound of whooshing air ships came. *"Targians convey spiritual and physical knowledge in a shared process, all benefit from one another's awareness. Komi experience this individually. Komi have yet to learn not to fear spiritual wisdom,"* he stared into Dawn's wide eyes. *"It is difficult to —"* he searched her face as if looking for an answer, *"love you,"* he spoke softly in her mind.

"Love me," Dawn opened her eyes wide, shocked by his words.

"Va, love you. Targians impart our love with Targ and we become as vek ~ one but komi ~ humans keep this to themselves. It is difficult to understand your emotions, so we ask questions out of curiosity or make statements of agreement to satisfy you." He looked away from her toward the docking bay doors. *"The implant you received shall aid us in understanding. Komi shall quicken their,"* his lips curved in a thoughtful smile, *"spiritual pace by learning direct frequency*

communication. "Hank kissed Dawn's forehead with patient haste. *"Come, Thorb waits in the bay.*

As Dawn kept pace with Hank, she speculated what it would be like to be Targian. Love, she thought, there are no ghosts here because everyone is a highly attuned being, but even with his explanation, she questioned at what depth he could penetrate her soul, and maybe — her curiosity growing, at what level she could penetrate him.

Archaeoastronomy-anthropology just gained a new meaning in her mind. Without these aliens, there would be nothing to discover. She could see the headlines of the Planet Awareness, "Ancestral World Revisited." The thought of explaining how, the human's ancestral civilization began, as a migration to Earth, not a form developed from Earth, stopped her self-glorification. That would take a lot of careful thought, a lengthy explanation. She smiled and tapped her hyper-band, sincerely wishing she could stop and take notes.

X

Zyleon strummed his chin. He sat at Dawn's computer watching Momma download the breakthrough information from his bung. "It's the chivalry of innovation," he said, taking a sip from the coffee Radin delivered to him.

Radin sat across from the Professor, gazing at him steadily. "The people are still leery of entering the caverns. They want you to come to the village hall and speak of the wonders and decide if you have found the Ancients Sacred Temple." Radin flushed under the Professor's clear, blue-eyed stare.

"Yes, yes they have a right to know but absolutely no press. This needs to remain quiet." He turned his concentration back to the screen.

"Will Trombula come with you?" Radin leaned forward in his chair, arms on his knees, clasping his hands together. His mind flickered back to his meeting with the alien; the shock still clung to him. He may have believed it all an elaborate hoax, had it not been for the changes in Professor Zyleon and Kuranna.

"Trombula will come," the Professor, mumbled.

"They ask that you arrive by seven," Radin stood. "They will want to know where the others are. The holy men walk the grounds of the village, chanting for their ancestors to look kindly upon them. They are troubled, superstitions are numerous among them; please be heedful." He moved toward the tent door but before he left, he paused and took a firm look back. "It would be wise to bring your wife, Professor." Radin exited the tent, glancing at the attentive men standing guard at the entrance. He had ordered them to take extra precaution guarding the tents and cavern during the past days of the scientist's disappearances, but since the arrival of Professor Zyleon, Kuranna, and the alien Trombula, he had doubled the guard.

Radin stood for a moment mulling over the situation at hand. The Professor had taken him on a tour of Kandoria and tried to explain to him about Targian time travel or "space jumping" as he called it. He never thought much about space, preferring the ground beneath him. Nevertheless, with the recent events, a trip to the planet Targ would be a matter of safety. After all, he was the head of security, and this was a major historical event unfolding.

He would need to be able to explain to the people the precautions and safeguards and why he wouldn't use The Global Space Institution of Technology. They had not conquered "blink of the eye" space travel as Targian technology used, so it would be only right to inspect the way Professor Zyleon and his team had travelled. Radin made a soft snorting noise and smirked, deciding it would be worth talking over with the others, when they made it back home.

One of the guards asked, "Will he come?"

"Yes," he said, and walked away.

Nacoo tried to focus, but pain gripped every part of him. He thought he was standing, but in what he could not tell, fingers felt for anything familiar and failed to find it. His eyes had a covering of something moist and warm. He tried to reach up and pull it off, but his whole body seemed cocooned in the material. Fear crept through him as the sound of movement came from behind. Trying not to tremble he asked in a hoarse voice, "Who is there." He felt Targ's feeler's move about in his head. A searing flame tore through his body, and every nerve screamed with agony. It left him limp and weeping. "Why do you torment me?" he questioned with quivering breath.

The covering that blinded his eyes slid off; prisms from a mountain-sized crystal, arrowed around him in this living cage, causing him to blink madly with the brilliance of it. A great whirling of air stung his body and he crumpled to the ground; sticky vines receded into the walls. The living crystal pulsed with such intensity it pierced his being. An invisible strength pushing him into a prone position, as the pulsing grew more powerful, penetrating him to the very core of his soul. He became acutely aware that this controlling force was the very cradle of the planet's life essence. Fear expanded its hold on him, and he lay frozen in the center of this immense being. A sense of agonizing apprehension grew with his every breath.

A loud and electrifying hum started inside his implant, and his body arched reflexively. The more acute the hum grew, the more spasms occurred. A cold icy tendril slithered its way down his spine, spreading its tentacles throughout his physical form like a spider weaving a web. Nacoo moaned with the ache it caused. His thoughts came involuntarily, a gush of pictures, feelings, and words taken from the vapor of his mind, he felt repulsed and violated. *"Nooo...,"* he tried to move but the force held him still, like the might of a highly effective magnet.

He shook and convulsed, tears and sweat stung his eyes, his muscles weak and throbbing. The rawness of his mind tender with each cerebration, he thought he was dying and the planet was eating his vital energy, slowly draining him of his life. Nacoo's heart panged as he thought of his family and friends. Images filled his mind of working at the site back on Earth, of his colleagues and Targians and of the planet itself. Gradually, he became aware of a steady vibration inside his vest. His mind drifted to the birthing room and the life he aided in creating. The spirited whirring grew more insistent, the wand flashed across his mind —, *"the Key to Kandoria."* He whispered, finding strength enough to touch where he carried it.

His mind was filling with images of early life on Earth and the role that these migratory Targian ancestors played. languages of ages past pervaded his mind, emotions were mixing, sending him soaring then crashing. Knowledge downloaded into him, he regained courage, the prism's drumming light intensified, and his heart beat evenly with the rhythm of the planet.

Targ had unsympathetically ravished his mind to gain understanding of his human nature. Now the planet offered him solace and Nacoo comprehended that this world was the start to his lineal existence. Its knowledge was not beyond his ability to perceive all that it was willing to share.

The living crystal slowed its humming and the gelatinous floor on which he lay began slowly to envelope him; it was warm and glittered before his eyes. Tendrils draped from him like a life-support system, and the room commenced to spin with the same fluidity that brought him inside Targ. The planet launched him away, back through the void and into the world, and he knew that the key he held in his pocket

Carol L. Davis

would open up incredible discoveries. Not only was he a player in the making of a new race, but he was a teacher that would help to keep the Earth healthy for his children and the children of continuance.

Daj sat on the porch of TaChoo's home, relaxing. He had learned to create ice and was enjoying a large glass of Targian wine; it was the first iced drink he'd had since leaving Earth. The glass beaded with condensation and dripped on his oilskin hat, which lay under the small vine table, next to the vine chair he rested in, everything, was made of vine. Daj filtered Targ's vivid, multihued desert through the slits of his eyes. His thoughts rested on the male seedling now growing in the planet's womb, and of visiting Ashruba, his first.

Her mind bubbled with warmth and playfulness. She touched parts of him that he never knew existed; it was as if her tiny hand cradled his heart. It made him want to protect her; he was sad when he left the growing room. The same kaleidoscopic, leafy vine, encircling a maroon, oval-shaped Targ that marked Foster and TaChoo's upper left cheeks, marked hers. She carried the mark of Thorb, the planet's communicator and most all the similar genetic traits of Targians. Except for the upward curve of her lips and a streak of black hair — they were his.

Daj looked idly over the landscape, viewing the jade moon Badu in the northern sky. TaChoo had spoken to him of a preparation time during this moons turning. He would enter the Tyd Sy, a room where Targ would cleanse him for the dance of the second moon. He gazed at the sky with unhurried care, allowing a slow acknowledgement that the course of history was altering and he was an irrefutable part of this change. He knew that TaChoo needed his full acceptance but he couldn't help being human, and unfortunately, humans were not as advanced as Targians.

Even after the Global United Spiritual Transformation of Twenty-Twelve, human beings still struggled to get their damnable emotions out of the way. Instead of letting the supernova stuff they were made of flow freely through them, they filtered the universal, spirit energy, selfishly, using it for personal pleasure rather than healing the world. He had to confess he was one of them.

- 110 -

The class on quantum physics and spirituality that Professor Zyleon had everyone take during orientation for this expedition was interesting enough to get him thinking a little more in depth about the world; but he never would have thought he'd be a part of this one. Daj finished his wine, took a sideways glance, and replaced his hat, tucking it down on his forehead. The suns were low in the light maroon sky and Badu was beginning the night turn. "How long have you been waiting?" he questioned TaChoo.

"*I have just arrived,*" she said, standing in the arch of the doorway wearing a silvery-blue, full-length robe.

Daj felt a sense of adoration mixed with shame as he fixed his eyes on her. "*Is it time?*"

"*Va.*"

He rose from his chair to follow her; she moved like velvet in a breeze, leaving the scent of summer rain behind her.

"*Are you comfortable?*" Foster looked back over his shoulder at the small group.

Baxter and Dawn sat next to each other in the small ship. "Comfortable as can be," Baxter sighed. He was tired and still a little bewildered, but very happy to be sitting where he was, looking forward to going home. Baxter had relentlessly badgered Thorb until he'd shown him that his brother rested in a quiet room, giving oath that Nacoo would be joining them in a short time. He laid his head back against the seat-pillow and commenced to hum Twilight River.

Hank looked back from the pilot's seat, studying Dawn. She returned his gaze. "*Are you ready to jump into the nascent black hole?*" He grinned.

"Sure thing," she said, trying to block him from picking up on the nervousness she was feeling.

"*Would either one of you enjoy a cup of moc or rup appo to help calm you?*" Foster nodded at Dawn.

Damn it, she thought, she hadn't conquered how to block herself. "Yes," she accepted, shyly, noticing the glances of the Targian's. "Sorry, just jumpy," Dawn gave a half smile back to Hank and a nod to Foster. "I remember hearing Nacoo sing that song." She turned her attention to Baxter. "He told me you had great success with the play, Space Deep, and that the music was created by using crystals, which slowly released reverberating waves of sound, made by unusual instruments from around the world. He enlightened me on how after the show, it made him feel like a cleansed and rejuvenated person. He thought the audience responded in kind.

Baxter never opened his eyes. "It's inspiring even when you are an actual part of the performance. Nacoo visited three times just to experience it, said he'd do it again." He opened his right eye just a slit width and gently patted her hand. "He will be okay; my twin intuition has stopped tweaking my brain. Thorb has also helped to calm my fears, strange to be so trusting of him. For a while there, all I wanted to do was find Nacoo, but I felt so trapped and unable to. Ah, well, that feeling has left. We will celebrate when everyone makes it back home. We'll have a real party, food, drinks, music, and togetherness." Baxter's voice faded as he drifted into sleep.

Dawn understood Baxter's feeling for his brother, for she also had felt the urgent tug to go to him. She rubbed her neck absently and sipped the drink Foster had given her.

"Do you need healing touch?" Foster's concerned voice touched her mind.

"No, no, just weary," she smiled up at him. *"Did we lift off already?"*

"Va, we are leaving the docking bay and shall arrive at Kandoria soon. You are welcome to watch just take the co-pilot's seat, it is quite a beautiful ride."

"Thank you." She rose from her seat and moved to the front of the ship, taking the seat next to Hank. An island universe filled with billions of stars stretched out before her eyes; admiration for the great God that created such a place pervaded her.

"Directly in front of you the Partagul constellation rests and just to the left the Imrak constellation. Partagul and Imrak are named after our ancient Targian warriors."

"Warriors," Dawn interrupted.

"Va, warriors but in a different sense of what you are thinking — we are defenders of Targ. From time to time, other races have tried to conquer Targ, but he is wise and his defenders strong. Imrak stood by Partagul's side as you see here in this uranography." Hank waved a gray hand at the starry expanse in front of them. *"A race called the Ockoraerions came seeking food — us."*

"Ockoraerions eat you? How ghastly," Dawn scrunched up her small freckled nose in disgust.

"They are vile, blood-thirsty beasts. Not unlike the wodevil, we encountered at the first camp," Hank grimaced. *"A wodevil is a creature spawned of Targian and Ockoraerion blood, which uses its brut strength against us, and defiles Targ with their toxic blood."* Hank stared deeply into Dawn's hazel eyes, *"Our children are bred to fight these creatures and clear Targ's surface of them."*

Dawn gasped, "Now hold on, you're telling me my children have to battle these beasts? Why can't Targ or his defenders get rid of the menace, it only took two arrows, for me to kill one — at a good distance." She shivered remembering Daj's bloody, ripped pant leg and just the thought of getting close to one of them again made her gag involuntarily.

"We require more than arrows. They sacrifice their own, spilling blood, their tainted blood everywhere, Ockoraerion blood acts as a sedative to Targ, which slows the planet's connection to us and allows the Ockoraerions time to kill our females for food and rape our males to ensure their survival," Foster said, coldly.

"Rape your males," Dawn's words sounded strangled.

"Our females cannot birth without Targ."

"Oh," Dawn's stomach churned.

Foster's voice was grave. *"But do not fear for the children, Targ shall train them and with them, be able to protect them."* Foster laid a cool slender hand on Dawn's shoulder; *"the mix of your blood flowing in them is bitter to the Ockoraerions and their spawn, but an elixir to Targ, which he now exchanges with them in the wog sy ~ growing room."*

Dawn felt a slight quiver through her body as Foster removed his hand. She could not help but wonder at the enormity her life was having on Targ, let alone the impact their discovery would have on Earth. "So Partagul and Imrak fought the Ockoraerions…" She paused, looking out at the galaxy. "Their battle etched in the universe forever."

Hank brought up an image on the screen for her to map the figures. Partagul was in the shape of a Targian holding a sword and Imrak held a trident. *"They fought bravely, chasing the beasts from our planet, many died, and Targ was numbed with their poison, slowing his healing and nourishment for us. Spawn of the Ockoraerion grew in their impregnated females, growing an army of flesh eaters. Partagul and Imrak continued to battle the beasts crying out for those lost and to cleanse the venom from Targ. At great ages, Partagul and Imrak went home to spirit leaving only a few of the wodevils alive. Today we still fight them but we are not as strong as those before us and so we searched for you and the others."* Hank and Foster exchanged satisfied looks.

Foster went back and sat in the seat beside the softly snoring Baxter, *"Dawn, are you ready to hitch a ride on a cosmic ray through a nascent black hole?"*

Before Dawn could answer Foster, Hank placed a finger on a small indentation next to the screen; she watched the stars mix with cosmic dust, heading straight for the event horizon of the nascent black hole.

Hank grinned devilishly. *"We are the gamma ray bursts,"* he laughed aloud.

Prisms of light whirled and crackled with energy all around Farstar. Sometimes a single color would target a specific area of his body. His skin would react to the penetration as if deep massage were taking place, causing soft moans to escape him. Autumn watched with fascination at what he might be going through. She had come to discover a gentle love for this alien, and felt a need to stay as close as she could.

She sat on the edge of a large, moss-covered stone, knees bent and hanging, arms straight at her sides, palms down on top of the flat surface. Moss moved under her hands, and tiny orbs of electricity began to dance all around her. A glowing white, oval shape enveloped Farstar, making it hard for her to see his finely detailed features; she stopped herself inching closer, considering Jax's warning not to interrupt the process. Autumn felt prickles beneath her palms and could feel her heart start to beat a little faster.

"Do you trevi to dance with Farstar?"

Targ's voice sounded gravelly in her mind, *"Dance?"* Her breath came short.

"The Dance of Nar, a combining of spirit and body," Targ rasped.

Autumn's mouth opened but nothing came out, streamers of silver shot right through Farstar, and every diffusion made his body shudder as if he warded off an icy cold wind. Compassion swept through her. She longed for this ordeal to be over and for them to be together, learning, exploring, and growing together. *"Yes,"* she answered and bowed her head, feeling Targ's fiery energy swarm about her, lifting her up, closer to Farstar.

"Cleansing and balancing is desired," Targ held Autumn suspended and surrounded by a warm white light. The planet entered her body this time, by way of light rays, probing microscopic areas of this female organism, changing her brain structure to accept and use Targian minerals, which would enable greater transference of knowledge.

Autumn felt like jumping out of her skin. Small jolts of heat streaked in her brain and down her spinal cord, snakes of electricity raced around inside her body, apart from her womb. Targ protected the seedlings. She sensed a change in the electro-magnetic field; it was a feeling one had just before an earthquake, a shifting of the aura body from the physical. Deep in her bones was a strange ache, heartbeats struck painful, hard, and fast, a current of nausea washed over her and then blackness...

"Wathu jant," Targ melodiously rumbled to Farstar. *"Preparation for the Dance of Nar must begin."*

Farstar lay cradled in a bed of moss; he slowly opened his eyes to a faint star speckled room. *"To dance the Dance of Nar one must have a tek, I have none."* Farstar answered the planet.

"The one called Autumn accepts you," Targ vibrated beneath Farstar, sharing in the joy that he felt.

"Our spirits shall dance the Dance of Nar," Farstar eased up from his bed allowing Targ to leisurely withdraw from his body. Having the negative vibrations cleared from his mind, he now had a shared understanding with Targ of the kom emotion, which had permeated his mind. Unclothed he walked across the Tyd Sy for the first time; he admired the luminescent galaxy shapes that covered the ceiling, and how the flowers glowed slightly and released the sweet aroma of katri and how the softest of Targ's ferns touched his shoulders, back and sides. *"This sy is enchanting,"* he whispered to Targ. Moss played under his feet urging him onward. His hands touched the leaves growing up to meet him and he communicated great love with the planet.

Autumn lay unclothed on a velvety, moss bed in this twilight-lit room. Sweet scented air filled her lungs with an aroma similar to milkweed in bloom, "mmm...," she stretched, and felt Targ recede from her body. "That was quite an experience," she said, her voice muffled by the lush vegetation. Standing she noticed two Targian females unclothed, their forms so tall and slender, gliding easily toward her. "Hello," Autumn said, recognizing them as TaChoo and Clamora. They returned her greeting and bid her to follow them.

XI

Zyleon raised his hand. "There is no need to fear our ancestors," he said, nodding to Trombula. "Most of you already know my wife Kuranna." He swung his hand toward to her. "You know of her abilities, and have found her to be a favorable person in your community." He looked around at the people crowded into this small village hall, some standing, some sitting, wide-eyed staring faces filling the open windows and doorways. Council members sat in the front rows, Radin and his men stood beside and around the small group giving them ample space for which he was most thankful. "Trombula has many times her ability." The mood of the room shifted a concentrated alertness. "He will share with us the history of our true heritage." Professor Zyleon stepped back, giving Trombula the floor.

Trombula's calming, musical voice filled the room. "A migration of our ancestors, from planet Targ to planet Earth, occurred numerous lifetimes past. They were to colonize this world. Uniformly, they erected monoliths and built vast civilizations over the strongest power fields upon this planet. It was a working creation of highly effective, electromagnetic conductors, enabling communication between Targ and the ancient, illustrious cultures. Throughout the long ages, the great knowledge, our ancestors brought with them, became lost, and they became divided from Targ. " Trombula gazed resolutely over the mesmerized crowd. " If yet you had vision such as mine," his lips curved slightly. All eyes were upon his. "Then you could see the gridlines, the fields of energy uniting together from these most powerful sources. They merge and create a single beam that carries information through space returning to Targ, you can think of it, as a monitoring system that has enabled Targian's to observe human development. We have returned to regenerate the conductors, Kandoria the first and to begin again, communication with our descendants.

"The ancient prophecies foretold this arrival," Professor Zyleon piped up. "Human evolution has changed us in many ways from our ancestral traits." The crowd shifted uneasily in the stuffy room. "It not only changed us in the physical structure but in the spiritual as well." Murmurs and whispers filled the air.

Olander, one of the elder council members, spoke with an inquisitive tone, eyes fixed on Trombula. "Our legends tell of a day when you would return, as Professor Zyleon has said, and you have told us of our beginnings and of forgotten ancestry. But why did Targ allow this alienation?"

"A great war broke out on Targ, and many returned to aid my planet." Trombula shifted, his fine silver, hair, brushing his slender shoulders.

"Is this also why Kandoria was sealed?" Olander leaned forward studying the alien before him.

"It is the prelude to the reason. For thousands of Earth years, human history proves how a great many empires enjoyed spiritual intelligence and material productiveness. They did this by utilizing their links with one another, a link such as Kandoria, the Great Pyramids, and other power sources. War continued to rage on Targ. During this time it diminished the Targian-Earth people's abilities to properly utilize the conductors and caused a —" Trombula hesitated, "shorting out of the connection they had established. When Targ recovered, he found that most of his children on Earth had forgotten him. He was lost to one of the most glorious of civilizations ever wrought, by the ruin and destruction of knowledge." Trombula paused.

Olander sat back in his chair. "You speak as though Targ is an entity, very intriguing, please go on," he said, with a cynical tone.

A ripple of troubled whispers, spread across the room.

Trombula pressed his fingertips together. Lowering his head, he continued, "Targ being saddened, sent a new group to Earth in search of anyone who remembered him, and instructed them to leave evidence of our stay, such as petroglyph's, telling the legends of the ancient cultures that once ruled the world and finally to close the last remaining portal, Kandoria. Some of the olden Targians stayed to ensure the continuance of such things as astronomy, healing, and psi abilities but above all — spiritual wisdom, to the re-evolving Earthlings."

Lifting his head, Trombula made a sweeping motion with his hand. "Now today, once again Targ reaches out to his children." He stepped back.

"Genetically speaking, this is why Kuranna is able to use her psi gifts," Zyleon said, placing a hand on her shoulder. "Her abilities are inherited traits of our ancestors."

Kuranna stood, smiling at the people. "Kandoria will be opened once again to the elders of your tribe." She locked eyes with Olander. "You will experience deeper spiritual truths and re-learn the old ways to teach your people." She lifted her face to the crowd. "As soon as our findings are disclosed to the scientific community, Kandoria will be the center of the world's attention. So we are asking for hushed tongues —"

"When will the others return?" Marlo, another elder council member, hastily interrupted her.

Kuranna scolded Marlo with her eyes, "— until the return of Professor Zyleon's team," she finished, frostily.

Marlo lowered his eyes. "We expect a ship within the hour." She glanced over the assembly of people. "Please allow us to return to the caverns and welcome home our first arrivals." People started to move from their seats and standing positions, excitement replaced fear, and children searched the skies for the spaceship that was coming. They did not know they would not be able to see it.

"Please follow us," Trombula spoke to Olander and Marlo. "The others shall be called in turn." He could feel the disappointment spread through the other council members but there was no argument.

Surrounded by Radin and his men, the party of five was ushered out the back door of the building. *"Our first arrival is in the home stretch."* Zyleon grinned at his wife; he truly did enjoy being able to communicate so intimately with her. She responded with a nod. *"We have begun a new era."* He felt a little tug on his heart for the Earth, "What a great time to be alive." his voice was thick with emotion as he spoke to the small party.

"This is Targ's star-charting chamber; you shall come here and connect with Targ allowing him to map a path to and from Earth and other planets. For yourself, you shall be given knowledge about each being that is to enter your craft

— *which is of course* — *the passenger ship, Sunstream II."* Thorb absorbed Nacoo's excited bewilderment. *"The key you carry needs to be activated each time you enter and leave Kandoria. It holds the information gathered for and from your passengers. This information is passed to the Keepers of Resemblance to assist understanding the beings to engage in imaginations."*

"Other planets, other beings," Nacoo ran a large hand through his black curls.

"Va, there are many throughout the cosmos, some we do not desire to know, some we know well."

"So the wand is a communication device." Nacoo removed the wand tenderly from his vest pocket, gently turning it over in his hands. *"It's the key to exploring the cosmos."* His thought at being the first human journeyman to record it all was an extremely tantalizing prospect. His heart pounded, blood rushing in his ears; he looked at Thorb, flushed and speechless.

"Va and you are the Keeper of the Key." Thorb probed deeper into Nacoo's emotions, pleased to find Nacoo returning his query. *"You are learning well."* He glided effortlessly across the room coming to a stop beside a chair formed of roots and resting vines. *"Come,"* he invited Nacoo to sit.

Nacoo glanced around the room, cranberry-colored light rays filtered in through dense vegetation. A thick, buttery moss-carpeted floor caressed his bare feet; the walls flourished with silvery leaves that reflected the warmth of the two suns. He moved slowly toward the chair, apprehension mixed with curiosity. The satiny moss slid between his toes with each step, and he wondered what had happened to his boots. The chair arm held the imprint of the wand he held, which vibrated steadily now. Without question, Nacoo placed the wand into the depression.

Thorb placed a hand on Nacoo's shoulder. *"Your boots are placed at the doorway of your new home, here on Targ. They are not to be worn in this sy ~ room."*

Nacoo felt puzzled. *"New home?"* he questioned.

"Targ shall release memories of your transition slowly. It would be too overwhelming to know all of what has transpired. Targ has restructured your system to withstand and perform this privilege as you shall soon experience, please

sit and become vek ~ one." Thorb, with a hand still on Nacoo's shoulder, gently urged him toward the chair.

Nacoo turned his large frame around and sat amongst the vines. He looked up at Thorb, expecting pain, but instead he felt comforted. His scarred hand clasped the wand and he laid his head back closing his eyes. Warmth ran up his spine and into his head and he spontaneously astral projected into deep space, charting and exploring the cosmos's many wombs. Planets soared into view and then away, one galaxy after another, in a most spectacular design, information downloaded into his memories. He knew every gateway and star system in the heavens. *"Amazing,"* he thought. *"To be Kandoria's Keeper of the Key."*

Daj waited dreamily in one of the small ports that connected to a woody, vine-covered, spherical platform. He could see, in every direction, the star-splattered vastness of space; it was as if he sat inside a spyglass, which amplified a sensation of being in the very heart of the universe. Nar's violet luminosity danced off the Arch of Melding's intricately carved depictions of the birth and existence of Targ. As Daj studied each individual carving on this massive moving root, a story unfolded in his mind. It was instant knowledge, as if his memories and Targ's were the same.

He felt calm as he glimpsed around at the others, all in the same positions, unclothed, cross-legged, with palms down, touching Targ inside their small circular docks. Nar's lavender glow illuminated each one, as the beams fanned out radiantly from the top of the Arch. Daj let his gaze fall upon Jax, his hair translucent, his body slender, and colored a tint of pink in this moonlight. Daj watched him rise and walk across to the center of the circle, meeting Clamora there. Her hair swayed gently as they placed palms together and lifted them out and upward at an angle. They stood tranquil, intent, gazing at one another.

A steady reverberation started like the rolling of the ocean and then the floor opened. Daj stared in awe as they hung in mid space among the stars, Nar's dark purple light enveloping them; the light's energy raised the air temperature, touching his skin like an immersion into a warm bath; immense pleasure engulfed the very core of his being, as he shared in their union.

To his fascination, the light absorbed Jax and Clamora, leaving the center of the circle reformed and unoccupied. He watched as Farstar took his position and waited for Autumn to place her palms on his. Daj thought Autumn was more beautiful than he remembered and let loose his passion to join with Targ's swirling energy. Autumn's small five-fingered hand looked so dark compared to Farstar's pale six-fingered hand but it did not matter as they raised their arms. Daj felt sadness for never having told Autumn how much she meant to him and in response to his feeling, love from Autumn returned. Daj smiled as he shared in Farstar and Autumn's unification, watching, transfixed as the two disappear within the light.

Daj heard Targ speak in a deep rumbling voice, *"go, and stand on the center star of the circle, beneath the Arch of Melding. Daj, jant ta Targ ~ son of Targ, korzuk ~ join, with TaChoo and dance the Dance of Nar."* He rose gazing steadily at TaChoo her eyes penetrated his soul and lifted him. He placed his palms against hers and felt Targ's energy bonding them physically to one another. They lifted their arms so their fingers pointed at the stars on either side of Nar. Thickening moonlight surrounded them, weaving between their bodies with the consistency of a heavy cream. The light emitted a corporal electrical charge, connecting them, touching their souls, as the Arch of Melding slowly spun around them.

The deep purplish-blue light sparkled in TaChoo's crystal eyes, and he felt the warmth of the surrounding color come into him, humming with waves of spiritual intensity. Daj melded with TaChoo, their bodies glued together, hearts beating as one, their essence, reaching deep into one another's most sacred of places. They buried these holy parts of themselves in each other's mind like a pirate's treasure. Only they shared a map and key. The floor opened beneath them and immediately they were floating in the infinity of space, enclosed in this violet-lit bubble of pure elation.

Daj easily absorbed every moment of TaChoo's life as they turned in their ball of light, and he willingly offered his to her. Together Daj and TaChoo drifted, delving into the spirit of their interconnectedness. Communication between them would be a steady flow, learning from one another and they would always know if one needed comfort, healing, or rest no matter where they were, or what they were doing. His hands tingled against hers; he leaned into her and breathed in her beauty. *"We are one,"* he whispered, and together they danced the Dance of Nar in the radiant, indigo light of the Arch of Melding.

"**W**ake up Baxter, we've arrived home," Dawn smiled, staring down into the misty, onyx eyes of her flight companion.

Baxter cleared his throat of sleep. "The Earth is my playground, so let's play."

Hank was the first off the ship, Dawn and Baxter followed. Foster stood at the door and nodded his head to the three. *"Ne ootau bu tutal ~ take comfort my friends, I shall return when Unares turns,"* the trio waved to Foster as he closed the ship's hatch.

Dawn watched the craft silently rise. It shimmered slightly then seemed to evaporate in front of her as if time and space had no meaning. She stood for a moment in this cave mouth. Feeling a bit disoriented, she rested a hand on her hyper-band. Curious, she removed it from her belt and found to her delight, the screen was active. "Hello Momma." Send. Dawn couldn't help but grin as Momma responded, "welcome home." Excitedly she tapped. "Was all information received?" Send. The screen lit up again. "Still downloading," Dawn's enthusiasm grew. "It's good to be back," she sighed. "Now how do we get into Kandoria?" she asked Hank, noticing both her companions staring at her.

"This way," Hank waved an arm and disappeared inside a fissure. *"I trust all is in working order."*

"Yes," she answered. Dawn breathed in the familiar scent of Earth and ran her fingers over the rock walls. The cool, hard surface felt nice. Baxter's heavy footfalls echoed in the grotto and gave her a terrific sense of relief, *"This is a good world to live on, huh,"* she playfully elbowed Baxter in the side.

"Hey," Baxter laughed, nodding.

Hank stopped walking, having reached the back of the small cave, focused, and scanning for something on the wall in front of him. *"Ah, here it is,"* he said, pressing a very plain-looking spot on the wall, and like a magician's trick of illusion, a doorway appeared. Both Baxter and Dawn peered at the place Hank had touched and then at each other.

"Must be the eyes," Baxter said in a low tone. Grinned at Dawn and clapped Hank on the back.

"You are perceptive," Hank chuckled, disappearing through the doorway.

"Are you ready for this, Dawn?"

"Ready or not we are here, there is a lot of work before us," she paused. "Momma's downloading now, and I am anxious to get back to camp and work with humans again." Dawn murmured softly, "It's been a real strange journey, it kind of feels like a dream or…"

Baxter interrupted, "or coming out of an interactive movie."

She took his arm, walking through the doorway together.

"Come over here and stand beside me," Hank motioned them closer.

Hank's eyes glowed in the darkness and Baxter became aware of the now familiar shift inside his head. He sensed his arm slipping away from Dawn's as she tried to tighten her grasp, but Hank's eyes beckoned him onward. An electrical pulse passed through him and as he stepped forward, the pulse quickened. For a moment, he wanted to crouch down and get ready for the next great wave. In the next instant, all was normal, and he found himself standing in front of Hank.

Baxter looked around, dazed by what had just occurred. *"What happened to Dawn?"* He questioned Hank, searching for her.

"Being Keeper of Resemblance starts now; Dawn is your first trial." Hank motioned for Baxter to sit on the bench in the room they had entered. *"Because the Keeper of the Key has not yet arrived, the information needed to start the process, shall come from probing her mind. We shall perform a triad. First, we connect, it is what you just experienced, second, while keeping your mind open, you shall begin to probe Dawn's mind. While in her mind, we shall seek the areas of her brain, which cause temporary memory lapse. This enables us to take her to a safe place where she shall awaken at the end of her fantasy. Third, we seek the areas that create controlled hallucinations. Next, you shall feel like you are dreaming but it is her thoughts you see and feel, the deeper you probe the closer and more intimate you get.*

It is here imagination begins, allow her memories, thoughts and emotions to guide you through her journey, it shall be very real to her so you must be careful in your treatment of her. What you shall be doing is a form of psychic mind manipulation; the brain is a storehouse of thought energy that you release, like the playing of an instrument, which releases music, so the mind releases thoughts." Hank paused and studied Baxter, *"let us begin."*

Baxter remained linked to Hank while reaching out for Dawn. He felt her mind open to his call. Before he spoke, Hank moved him deeper inside her brain, plunging into a sea of warm pulsating matter. Tiny electric sparks surrounded him, and images of Dawn walking into the room where they were, became very clear. He watched her lay down and Hank took him even deeper... deeper inside her brain and again they dove into a crevice of sparkling matter. This time he gazed upon tiny balls of energy that opened before his eyes, showing him Dawn's hopes and dreams, desires, and concerns. It felt so real he reached out and touched a bubble that burst open, forming a tiny book; he absorbed its contents then touched another and another absorbing them all.

He watched Dawn's astral body rise from the bench and picked a memory of an old orchard, where she liked to play as a small girl. As he began to experience her memory, a vision of her wearing pink shorts and a purple tank top came into clear view. Baxter's awareness of her was as keen, as if it were his own. Even tasting the apple she bit into, it was crisp and juicy and the sound of a familiar voice rang in the air. "I'll race you to the stream," a child giggled.

"Susan, you know you'll lose," Dawn yelled, racing after her friend.

Baxter touched another bubble, sensing Hank smile.

XII

The flower blooms were as large as Autumn's head; she filled her lungs with their aroma. Farstar's home was lush with life, and she thought of the transplanted twin seedlings from her womb and fixed in Targ's. What a report this would be, she thought, in anticipation of returning to Earth. She brushed past a large, yellow-leafed shrub, and sneezed. "That's a first." She rubbed her nose, inspecting the dark brown powder that stained the sleeve of her robe. Pollen hung thick and heavy in the air. "Aahh-choo," she sneezed again.

Autumn hurried to get inside, sneezing, and disrobing as she went, her head clouded, eyes itching. She hurried to the cleansing room, pressing the butt of her hand against her forehead. Dizziness drove her to stop, and with a jolt, she hit the floor knees first. For a moment, she thought she sensed Dawn lying on the grass beside a slow flowing creek, under a blazing sun — "Aahh-choo," she swayed and strove to get up, without success.

Autumn crawled into the cleansing room and pressing her palm against the wall managed to think the water on. It misted over her body, head drooping; she felt incredibly nauseated... the sun hot on her fair skin. "Get up Dawn," Autumn mumbled. "You are burning your pretty..." She rubbed the back of her neck, rolling her head against her hand. "Get out of the sun..." Autumn's body slumped forward, water misting over her; in her mind, she lay beside Dawn. When she reached to touch her, there was only vacant space. She struggled to open her eyes, which were swelling shut, and breathing was becoming exceedingly difficult with every beat of her pounding heart.

Her thoughts were imprecise, vague, and unclear — what was happening? Was she dying, had death found her at last? Then through the fog, a hand reached over and touched her... Farstar had found her... no not Farstar, she felt confused. This touch she did not recognize... it hurt deep inside... the implant...

She drifted half way between waking consciousness and sleep. Something cool rested on her forehead and even through her ragged breathing, she could smell a scent similar to a pine tree running with sap; it comforted her, easing the fear. She heard children's voices singing, laughing, and splashing of water in the distance. Whose vibration… was it… she tried to mind touch Dawn, but… what… who… Baxter touched hers. Someone else was there with him… Hank… it was Hank! Startled, Autumn took a sharp intake of air and started to cough.

Hands pressed on her forehead and solar plexus. *"Autumn,"* called a voice. *"Autumn, open your eyes."*

Autumn's eyes felt grainy and the skin of her cheeks were as tight as if she had just come in from a hike in the desert. She tried to focus on the voice that seemed so far away. "Who are you?" Her throat constricted and burned.

"Rory," answered the strange voice.

"What is going on?" She felt a chill go through her.

"You brushed against the fet leaves sprinkled with satt powder, which is what discomforts you."

Autumn glanced around the room. "Where am I?" She shivered.

Rory removed his hands from their resting places and positioned them on her shoulders. *"Kom females are very warm and beautiful."* He pushed hard against her, almost touching his nose to hers. *"Farstar shall come to me so long as I have you."* A glimmer of almost human greed flashed in his mind. He moved back to his sitting position on the bed. *"Does Farstar know your secret?"* A cruel grin played on his lips.

"What secret?" Autumn said, realizing she was naked, clutching the cover as she sat up.

"That you are not using your personal bung," his grin widened.

"How do you know?" She coughed and as she leaned forward called out in her mind, *"Farstar."* Fear gripped her heart when silence answered.

"He shall not hear you nor shall Targ," Rory chuckled with great pleasure.

"Targ!" Autumn cried out, felt nothing, and closed her eyes.

"So now let me answer your question, when one is under the influence of satt, all hidden becomes — uncovered." He placed a hand on her thigh. *"Your secret shall stay secret as long as you oblige me."* Rory's grip tightened. *"Through*

you, Farstar shall feel powerless." He clenched the cover and wrenched it from her. "*He shall feel what it is like to be unable to give ootau.*" Still holding Autumn, Rory pulled a small bottle from his robe pocket and cracked it open, forcing it under her nose.

The smell of wet dirt filled her nostrils. She tried not to breathe, wrestling against this invasion, but he held fast and instantly her limbs became weak — too weak to fight. She cringed inside, shrinking away from Rory's rough touches. Although she expected pain, there was none.

Farstar trembled where he stood, aware of Autumn's fear, and confusion. "*Targ, is there naught you can do?*"

"*Rory is disconnected.*" Targ rumbled in Farstar's mind, "*he carries much disillusion in his heart for you.*"

Farstar felt the discomforting passion of his closest companion.

"*Rory, Smoot, and many others have returned.*" Targ curled a vine around Farstar's leg.

"*How is it possible for him to keep her in silence?*"

"*It is wearisome; he uses other planet's substances and magnetic pulse, barring connection.*"

Farstar twitched as if wounded. "*He allows her emotions to come through.*"

Targ entered Farstar, sending waves of calm throughout his being. "*She is kom and not fully trained. Do not let this be a weakness in you; beware of losing indifference, for it diminishes your abilities.*"

"*She fears him.*" Farstar tried to send her the tranquility Targ offered, but the distress returned, he lifted his head and thundered, "*RORY,*" clenching and unclenching his fists and felt Targ retreat from him.

"*Farstar, do what you must.*"

"*RORY,*" Farstar challenged again and as he did, he knew Rory took much pleasure in his uneasiness.

Olander stared at Trombula, still not believing he was actually seeing an alien.

"Trombula, you would look quite stunning in full ritual dress," Marlo said, speaking a bit too fast. "Do you perform rituals on Targ?"

Trombula answered, amused by their curiosity of him. "*Va* ~ yes, we have many, all for different reasons," he chuckled under his breath.

Kuranna brought in a tray of tea and placed it on the small table, which the chairs comfortably circled. "Gentleman, please enjoy some moc-tea; it has a taste all to its own," she smiled sweetly and began to pour.

"Thank you," Marlo accepted a cup.

Olander took a cup, sniffing the steam. "It smells a little fruity." He nodded his thanks to her.

Trombula bowed his head gracefully. "On Targ, *appo* ~ tea, is a ritual drink," he glanced at Marlo and sipped his tea.

"Kuranna has taken it upon herself to learn many of the brews and food dishes served on Targ, and she makes it all taste good." Zyleon approved, winking at his wife, and watched, grateful, as her newly, steadied, hands poured the golden fluid. "Cheers," he lifted his teacup in the air, "may the mystery of your own spiritual universe unfold." Zyleon relaxed as the council members enjoyed their drinks.

"What do Targians eat?" Olander studied the crackers on the tray.

"Those," Kuranna replied, "are from our kitchen; you are welcome to them." She delicately took one, flipping it front to back. "Food on Targ is similar to our own flowers, fruits, and vegetables. No flesh is consumed because Targians do not have the enzymes to digest it —" the look on the two council members" faces made her hesitate. "It makes them sick like milk does to you, Marlo."

"How did you... oh," Marlo flushed.

"Heh, heh," Olander patted Merlo's shoulder, affects of the moc tea were starting to show, as the tense lines around his mouth relaxed.

Trombula was thoroughly delighted with their change of mood. "Gentlemen, please follow me to the entrance of Kandoria; adventure awaits you." His voice jingled with merriment.

Zyleon stood with them. "Please excuse me, the landing party waits." He gave Kuranna a quick kiss on the cheek. "That tea is better than warm, butter rum brandy," he grinned and rushed out the door.

Kuranna smiled, knowing that when the doors to Kandoria closed, a fresh misting of artu and Trombula's mind probes would give Olander and Marlo the best ride of their lives. She laughed quietly, understanding how Trombula could enjoy it so much.

He could see her as she stood, quivering, staring out a window — where was she — she called to him — trapped — alone, she called out — Nacoo... he opened his eyes taking in his new, reminiscent of home surroundings; reaching up he touched his sensory site and felt its vibration against his fingers. Autumn had filled his dreams, visions of an alien towering over the top of her, and cruel laughter rang in his ears. He thought she was most probably on the other side of the planet, because of the intense directional tug of the bung. Now he just needed a way to search for her. Presently, through the haze of waking, it hit him. "The Sunstream II," he stretched and sat up, feet touching the softness of the floor.

Nacoo hastily padded his way to the cleansing room, rested his hand on the wall and thought of a misty shower. A maroon spray cascaded forth, cloaking his mass. The vapor touched his skin like a cat's whiskers and he remembered Targ touching his essence even more profoundly than Clamora. The planet had changed his chemical structure — altered him. He stepped out of the moon-shaped dip in the floor and critically studied his form in the reflecting screen. He ran a finger over the cobra tattooed on his right arm. Deciphering symbols and signs, the greatest passion in his life, was nascent, and now that passion — was literally exploding into new worlds. Nacoo pulled on his field pants, tee shirt, and vest; he had tied his boot strings together to carry just in case he encountered rough terrain.

An urgency to find Autumn sliced through his heart as he walked swiftly toward the docking bay. He whistled to keep from running. Every now and again, stopping to touch a diagram screen, not being fully acclimated with this living dome, it delayed him, yet it amazed him to know that this knowledge of even how to find a screen, on these bare walls, was by implant and not acquired by learning. His breath came hard in the last part of the trek as he hurried along. When at last he did reach the platform, he scanned the launch area for Jax. *"Jax, are you here?"* He almost pleaded.

"Va, Nacoo what would ootau rit ~ comfort you?"

Seeing Jax wave, Nacoo sprinted toward him, relieved. *"Jax is the Sunstream II ready for flight?"* he asked, wiping sweat from his eyes.

Jax cautiously eyed Nacoo, *"av ~ no, but there is another craft at hand."* He probed him, a bit surprised when Nacoo permitted him to feel his concern for Autumn; he had expected this encounter to be about Clamora.

"Autumn needs help!" Nacoo blasted out causing Jax to sway.

"Easy bu tutal ~ my friend, we shall travel together. Mel li ga ~ come with me." Jax led Nacoo to the nearest craft. *"We call this one the Planet Traveler,"* he smiled, still touching Nacoo's mind, sensing his acute focus. He glimpsed a map of stars in his mind's vision; Nacoo had already set a course. Jax once again discovered determination, a strong emotion, to be as thrilling from this big man as it was from Autumn.

Nacoo leapt into the pilot seat. *"She calls to me,"* he fumbled with the controls.

"How," Jax asked, feeling waves of impatience pass from Nacoo.

Nacoo slammed his fist into the panel; his voice boomed in the small craft. "How the hell do you work this machine?" His sensory center burned with insane intensity.

"Place a finger firmly on the nosh," Farstar sounded, from behind them, his voice rich with resolve upon entering the ship. He was dressed in a silvery-emerald green cloak, with a finely crafted, crystal sword slung across his back. A hoary finger-nailed hand pointed to the nosh, a small black triangle on the panel board. "Press it," he commanded.

"You dress as a warrior, but no alarm is signaled." Jax locked eyes with Farstar just as the Planet Traveler began to tilt into a lift.

"Rory has ishta ~ returned." Farstar grasped Nacoo's seat when the spacecraft jerked sideways.

"Are you not a pilot?" Jax yelled, falling into the co-pilot seat.

"A little instruction would be nice," Nacoo yelled back. Sweat trickled down the side of his face.

"Nacoo how is it that you are connected with Autumn?" Farstar studied Nacoo's face.

"She calls to me in dreams," Nacoo said, feeling the bung tug him toward the north. With a finger on the piloting screen, the tiny Planet Traveler sped away from the launch corridor.

"Her connection is strong with you." Farstar gripped the seat with both hands.

"We shall find her," Nacoo growled and raced toward the Jasper Mountains.

Daj wiped his brow with his sleeve and replaced his perspiration-ringed hat. The ride up this mountain path was just what he needed. A smile crept across his weathered face, and he felt that familiar spiral of excitement in his gut. This celestial planet called Targ was his for the discovering. Equipped with hyper-band and camping gear was all an adventuring geologist needed, he patted his horse's glistening neck. "We are almost at the top, horse." Daj swayed in rhythm with the horse's gait, whistling a pub tune he learned from Tanner Jones. Now there was a bloke, who could weave a tale. He would quit talking at the most exciting place and give a dry little cough, gently tap his empty glass on the counter until Daj or one of his mates would buy the storyteller a refill of dark ale. That wrinkle faced, Tanner Jones really knew how to work it, that old codger never left the pub sober and always had a tip of the hat and smile on his face for anyone. Daj pulled back on the reins, having reached the summit.

He dismounted, dropping the reins to the ground and walked to the ridge. Daj tipped his hat back and placed a hand on his hip. A soft high-pitched whistle escaped him, making the horse whinny. "Horse, this is gorgeous, just look over there," he said to his mount, pointing to the adjacent mountain. "That's what a fiery sunset looks like on Earth." Leaves in varying shades of purple and multiple hues of gold stretched for miles, with compliments of a dark red sky. Daj closed his eyes and listened to the sounds of Targ, a melody of what he thought of as bird conversation and — a strange sound mingled in the air — almost like the whirring of Momma. Opening his eyes, he surveyed the terrain, fingers laid across his quiet hyper-band. Off in the distance, a glimmer of light caught his eye; he pulled his Barmah down, blocking the rays of both suns and giving him a better view of a small airship. "Horse, it's a real UFO," he chuckled, studying the incoming craft.

The craft came close enough for Daj to recognize Nacoo sitting in the pilot's seat. "Well, I'll be kicked by a roo!" He placed a hand on the rim of his hat extending the shade for his eyes. The craft hovered for a few seconds before descending straight down into the trees, vanishing from sight. In a hop, he was back in the saddle. "Let's go find out what's up. That's Nacoo piloting that craft." He made a clicking sound with his mouth, slapped the reins down, and pulled his heels in, as the horse started into a gallop, heading down, toward the area where the ship landed. Daj tucked his hat tight on his head, enjoying the power of the animal beneath him, feeling free of restriction. Together they raced onward toward their destination.

The trees started to thin after a few minutes of hard riding. Daj loosed his rein hold and relaxed his body, slowing the horse to a trot. Rays of maroon light filtered through the leaves in wider gaps now. He surveyed the area, trying to spot anything out of the ordinary. With a wide swing of his leg and a grunt, he was out of the saddle. Daj stretched the threatening soreness out of his muscles then led his quivering mount to a small lea and dropped the reins. "You stay here for a bit," Daj said, removing the haversack, which contained the healing potions TaChoo sent with him. She'd given him the knowledge, with thought transference, on how to apply each one and taught him how to tap into the healing energy of the planet, when he needed too. He considered the mages of myth and their fascinating tales of using nature and conjuring up magical beings to aid them during their adventures. Somehow, he found reassurance with that thought and tossed the bag over his shoulder.

Daj pondered his theory about the philosopher's stone. Maybe at one time, when people actually used the powers of the mind, this stone could indeed create gold. He fancied that the energy used in healing was the same energy those alchemists of old used in the process. He considered it would be like using Baxter's performing arts tricks. He flicked his hat, laughing at himself. "Ah, but anything is possible if you only believe." By this time he stood at the opposite edge of the meadow from his grazing horse, his eyes rested on the spacecraft, which sat, upon a large circular, landing stone. Daj advanced warily and circled the craft cautiously; it was all too quiet for his comfort. He tried the door, but it would not respond to his voice or touch. "Well this is a bit on the mysterious side," he spoke in a low tone, shifted his bag, glanced around, and tried a mind touch. *"Nacoo,"* he said, hopefully.

Silence answered him; the ship was warm beneath his hand, so if it was Nacoo he saw piloting the craft, he couldn't be far, unless Targ swallowed him. He shrugged off the thought of a man-eating planet and decided there must be a better explanation. Daj surveyed the area, noticing a very old tree with some sort of carving, encircling the trunk from the ground up, to just overhead high. On closer inspection, it appeared to be writing of some kind. He touched the tree tracing the marks with a finger the tree touched him back. *"Targ?"* he asked. A strange melodic voice answered, *"av."* Then something hard cracked against his skull and blackness crept in.

XIII

D awn's eyes fluttered open. "Why did you do that?" She sat up looking from Hank to Baxter. "Give me something to throw; you two are in a plethora of crap with me!"

"Hank, I see storm clouds forming above her little red-head," Baxter took a step back.

Hank grinned, *"We should run..."*

"Yep," Baxter was the first one into the hallway. Hank fast behind him, they vanished behind an aurora borealis curtain.

"Oh, that's it, run like cowards." Dawn yelled after them, stomping her feet, following them through the curtain.

"It's delightful to hear those feet of yours," Zyleon commented.

"Eeeee..." Dawn squeaked, startled. "Professor Zyleon, what a wonderful surprise." Tears welled up in her eyes.

"It's good to have you home." He laughed as Dawn wrapped her arms around his stocky frame. "It looks as though you were doing some chasing, have the boys been misbehaving?" His voice sprinkled with humor as he turned and shook hands with Hank. "I've heard much about you, pleasure to meet you." Then he grasped Baxter's hand. "Welcome home son."

Dawn glanced around the side of the Professor where Hank and Baxter stood, pretending to be shy. "They tripped me as soon as the door was open," she pouted.

"Tripped you," Zyleon suppressed a chuckle. "Think of it as a learning experience for the betterment of mankind."

Snickers erupted from the in-the-doghouse boys.

"Ah-hem," Zyleon cleared his throat. "Let's go to the meeting room and discuss this — tripping."

Dawn shot a look of disapproval toward the boys and lifted her chin in a mocking gesture, "Professor, you look very well, and it feels fantastic to be home." She walked arm in arm with the Professor amazed at his new stride and with each step, they took, she grew more eager to start work. "As soon as possible, I would like to start filing some of the information gathered and analyzing the specimens collected." She cooed, glowing with enthusiasm.

"Here we are." Zyleon entered the room he had so recently left. A fresh pot of tea and crackers sat on the table with a note; he picked it up and read it aloud. "Welcome home kids, enjoy the refreshments. See you soon, Kuranna." He smiled, waving an arm for everyone to sit. "So starts our new adventure, life shall never be the same. We shall walk this path of enlightenment; this path of truth, clearly revealed. Never again will we tread upon the shores of the past, but forever forth, reach for the heavens."

"Brilliant my good Professor, your memory serves you well." Baxter clapped a hearty clap. "That is the last scene from Space Deep, a play of phantasmagoria depth and done splendidly for those of you not familiar.

"So starts our new adventure," Hank agreed, raising an empty teacup. *"Life shall never be the same."* He rested his eyes on Dawn. *"Dawn I ask your forgiveness for — tripping you — it was Baxter's first practice. Your energy is — ah — excitable and..."*

"Excitable! Excitable..."

"Your face is turning cherry red," Baxter teased.

"Va and this is why we..."

"Damn you, you used me without my permission! I thought we might be past that!"

"Even your freckles are a very dark red now." Baxter ducked a flying cracker.

"This is why we did it," Hank shouted, excitedly, "because of the fire inside you." He ducked a handful of flying crackers, grinning from ear to ear.

Zyleon chimed in. "If Baxter is to be a Keeper of Resemblance, then he must be able to overcome strong, ah — fiery, excitable energy." He put on his best grin, rocking on his feet.

Dawn slammed down into the chair, arms crossed. "You could have asked," she sulked.

"No my girl, you work with puzzles all the time, even a hint would have blown the whole thing right out of the water. Ka-bloom, ka-bang," Zyleon threw his arms out in front of him, "ka-plowy."

Everyone chuckled.

"Now on a more serious note, there is much to do and as quickly as we can. However, rest for the night is necessary; it will adjust everyone to the Earth cycle. Baxter you are welcome to use Nacoo's tent or the back of the mess tent and Hank — Trombula has expressed an interest in having the company of a fellow Targian and maybe it is best if you stay inside, until you familiarize yourself with our camp and the village. Your sleeping room is set up next to Trombula's beyond the transport room; I'll show you the way." Zyleon stood and shook Baxter's hand. "Therefore, if everything is under control between you kids, breakfast is at seven," he said, giving Dawn a warning look. Raising a finger to his lips, he shushed the protest that was ready to flow forth from her. With the other hand, he gestured to Hank in a hurried motion, to follow him. "Come on with me Hank; we'll get you settled in."

Dawn stomped passed Baxter. "I owe you boys one." She glared at him.

Baxter grinned stupidly and walked along behind her.

Autumn felt hollow like the inside of this cavernous tree her captor had brought her to. *"What is it exactly that you want Farstar to do for you?"* She icily mind touched Rory, per his menacing instructions, to use only telepathy.

Rory sat untroubled considering the kom female that sat bound to the chair in front of him. *"Inquisitive are we."* He leaned forward, placed an elbow on his knee, and rested his willowy, gray colored fist against his chin. *"We shared the wog sy ~ growing room, together."* Rory swooped and turned in Autumn's mind, taking pleasure in her annoyance, *"We learned everything together and took ootau in our friendship until Thorb sent us on a journey to the planet Dyeck. We were to trade spar-thread for fruit tree seedlings that Targ desired to naturalize."* He repositioned himself so that the outside of his knees touched the inside of Autumn's knees.

Autumn tightened her jaw. *"Do you really think this is beneficial for relations?"*

"And by that you mean…"

"Thorb will hear of this and inform Professor Zyleon, and I'm sure that will not make Targ happy —" She tried to shift away from his pressing knees.

"We are supposed to be reconnecting not disconnecting." Autumn glared fiercely at him still struggling to free herself.

"Come now, is it not feasible for one to have individuality. Komi are famous for it." Rory fed on her resistance. *"Mmmm... you delight me."* He leaned back in his tree formed chair and locked his fingers behind his head. *"Thorb is well-informed, for Farstar has connected with Targ and shared this knowledge of your unexpected departure, and your dear Professor Zyleon shall be told soon enough. You so easily forget how differently time works here. And as well, I no longer answer to Targ."* Rory grinned, devilishly, reveling in her growing ire. He could sense Farstar very near and knew she could not; it was a challenging game to play.

Autumn wrestled against the invisible chains that held her. *"Bastard,"* she said. She gritted her teeth tight together, growing tired.

"When you gain full ability to allow the left prefrontal parts of your brain do the thinking, there shall be no such — impishly, delicious feelings like those you are sending. He basked in the scorching looks she shot him. *"You are bound by my superb ability to manipulate kinetic energy, or in all your cunning, did you not figure that there is an opposite of levitation."*

Rory's sinful laughter filled her ears; she bowed her head and felt a small twinge of regret. Her title of Archaeoastronomer was losing its appeal fast. Being face to face with this pompous alien was like being back on Earth at a government-controlled dig. *"Get on with your story,"* she sighed.

"Very well — um, where were we —, ah, va ~ yes, after our arrival we met with the Dyeckian trade overseer a creature of great allure and intelligence. Not unlike yourself, Autumn." Rory slid a hand up the inside of her thigh and took gratification in her discomfort, knowing Farstar was sensing her great surge of panic. *"They took very good care of us, and how we took pleasure in it. Dyeck was so different from Targ it felt good to have a taste of free spirit."* He massaged her leg, pleased with the fright it caused. *"You see we benefited in more than one way during our visits with the Dyeckians. Farstar and I set up a deal to continue trade and each time we brought them something they would give us anything we asked for, and ask we did."*

"Speaking of asking, a drink would be nice." Autumn said, pressing her dry lips together.

Rory got up and stood in front of her for a long moment, enjoying the way she squirmed inside and the way she defiantly looked at him.

It gave him everything he desired. *"Va, of course,"* he walked over to a door behind Autumn's chair. *"Smoot, please bring some appo."*

"Talking too much," Smoot raised a silvery eyebrow.

"When you bring the appo, come in, and sit with us."

"That shall be my pleasure," Smoot turned on his heel, hair and robe flowing as he levitated quickly around the corner.

Rory returned to his seat. *"We shall have company for appo."*

"Are you going to release me from these damnable chains?" Autumn followed his coruscate eyes.

"Mmmm… va," he dropped his head and became very still.

Autumn could feel currents of air, akin to ropes untying, swirling around her shoulders and arms. She flexed her fingers and hugged herself. *"Thank you,"* she said, relieved.

"Farstar was a dutiful son of Targ and always reported back to him. He never could keep a secret from this planet." Rory lifted his head, voice ablaze with conviction. *"Did you know that?"*

"He loves Targ," Autumn said.

"As well," Rory looked up at Smoot carrying the tea tray.

"So why are you doing this?"

"Because our aresh is korzuki ~ joined, together I trevi him at my side. Zaqurahs should never betray the connection they share." He motioned for Smoot to place the tray on the small table beside him.

Smoot grinned at Rory and planted himself next to Autumn, carelessly spilling a small amount of steaming tea on her leg.

Autumn sucked in a short breath.

"You shall have to excuse my tutal here." Rory grinned back at Smoot. *"He finds you to be a fascinating creature."* He leaned forward, rubbing the wet spot just above her knee.

Autumn swung, barely missing Rory's face. *"Who betrays whom?"* she sizzled with anger.

Rory was contented with her outburst. *"Farstar shall do as I ask, as long as I have you."* He looked at her haughtily. *"And,"* he spoke slower, *"there is still some trading to do. Trading that would secure a better and more prosperous relationship with the Dyeckians."* Rory handed her a teacup. *"Maybe I'll keep you."*

Rory's eyes sparkled with amusement and his laughter rang in her head. *"Death would be a better friend,"* she sneered.

"*Tutals are found aplenty but none as true as death.*" Rory leaned back and lifted his cup in the air. "*By the time Farstar finds this safe place we shall be gone. You are such a beautiful specimen and accordingly shall fetch a nice round of cret on Dyeck and so zifla, to avoid flight discomforts please enjoy your appo.*" He spoke with a touch of sarcastic humor.

Autumn lowered her eyes, taking the teacup, "*I'm not amused.*" She sipped the spicy drink, knowing she would be asleep and unaware of his touches before long. Sensing the unseen bonds fall away, her kidnapper held out a beckoning hand for her to take, she rose up unsteadily, feeling cold hands grasp her arms.

"*She is so warm,*" Smoot spoke close in her mind.

"*Autumn,*" Rory cooed, "*mel li wa ~ come with us.*"

Autumn propelled forward grasping his icy hand.

A sleepy eyed Dawn pushed back her tent flap, startling one of Radin's men. "You okay," he asked, choppily.

"Yep, just headed to get breakfast," she smiled, lifting her face toward the morning sky. "It's so nice to feel Earth's sunshine again."

There was an awkwardness between them before the guard spoke again, "Aliens go," he pointed toward the food tent looking a bit nervous.

"Have you seen Professor Zyleon?"

Straightening up, he conferred slowly, "Professor Zyleon very hungry," a crooked smile crossed his face.

Dawn stifled a giggle, knowing well the respect they held for the Professor. "Thanks," she said, bobbing off toward the tent.

People were filing in and out of the tent, each of them shyly glancing at the two mysterious visitors. Dawn couldn't help smirking as she had the food server spoon some bread pudding onto her plate, mouth salivating with anticipation of good old, bad for you, Earth food. She picked up an orange juice and headed toward the left back corner of the tent, where Professor Zyleon, Kuranna, Trombula, and Hank all sat. She was glad she wasn't the last one to join the meal, noticing as Baxter entered the breakfast line. Waving, she teased him, mouthing, "nyah, nyah," and then suddenly felt a small pang for Nacoo, wondering how he was getting on.

Baxter waved back at everyone and grabbed a tray, his attention drawn to the food choices before him.

Tied-back door flaps and rolled-up window covers allowed the bright early sunshine to spill in across the metal tables. Hank admired the golden highlights reflecting off Dawn's hair a smile played on his lips and with a whimsical mind touch, he caught her attention. *"You shine fiery as your sun."*

Blushing, Dawn averted Hank's starry eyes. "Good Morning," she said, cheerfully, resting her gaze on Kuranna. "You are looking quite well, Kuranna."

"Nice to see you again, Dawn," Kuranna's voice was warm and welcoming.

"Morning girl," Professor Zyleon said, his baldhead glistening. "I'm not sure if you've met Trombula here." He pointed at the Targain sitting next to him. "He will be assisting Baxter as Keeper of Resemblance among other things."

"Pleasure to meet you, Trombula," Dawn wiped at the sweat that tickled her top lip.

Trombula nodded.

"Gosh, it's hot out already and it's only seven-thirty," noticing that Hank and Trombula were not perspiring. Lucky dogs she thought.

"What is a lucky dog?" Trombula mind touched her.

Dawn's mom had taught her not to talk with her mouth full, now she laughed at this, putting to memory Trombula's voice. *"It is just an expression."* She tried to send him the feeling of it.

Trombula laughed aloud, causing everyone to look at him curiously.

"Va, we have much to accrue about your culture," he said aloud. He took a bite of melon, allowing the sweet flavor to cover his tongue. "This is delicious," again he verbalized, expressing in a singsong voice.

"Melon is one of my favorites," Baxter toned, settling in next to Dawn. "Morning everyone," he said. He held a glass of juice up and drank deeply, smacking his lips when he finished.

Kuranna pushed her plate forward. "You look well rested, Baxter, and hungry too."

Baxter's tray contained a plate of mixed fruit, two muffins, a bowl of oatmeal, bread pudding, a cup of nuts, and three kinds of juice. "Yeah," he answered with a ravenous smile.

Everyone got a chuckle out of that.

Kuranna and Trombula were looking at one another, giving Dawn the impression that they were communicating. She felt a mind nudge hers and looked up to see Professor Zyleon studying her. Lifting a finger to the side of her lips, checking for escaped food just in case there was something there, she questioned. *"What?"*

"Crazy idea you had exchanging bungs like that, but a good one."

"It was Autumn and Nacoo's idea." She could not hide her surprise from the Professor.

"So how is the connection?" He looked very serious.

"It's bothersome at times. Last evening it started its — burning, pulling sensation, and hummed most of the night, dreams of Nacoo filled my head." Dawn glanced at Baxter. *"Is he coming back to Earth soon?"* She chewed on some toast.

"Uh, girl, we'll talk later at the workstation." He patted his big mustache with one hand and gave the other to his wife.

Kuranna accepted his hand and they rose from their seats together, each grabbing their trays. "I will see you all again very soon. But for now —" she said, nodding at Trombula, "we have business to attend."

Trombula stood, bowed his head, and stepped away from the table with the grace of a sauntering deer. He seemed to shimmer with every movement like sunlight warming the dewy leaves of summer. Dawn must have let her mind linger too long on his splendor, for he turned, grinned wistfully, bowed his head, and said. *"You give me ootau."*

Dawn felt fire in her cheeks as she looked into Trombula's sparkling eyes. She was grateful for the loud slurp that sounded beside her, tearing her attention away, as Baxter finished his last juice. It completely amused her at how fast Baxter had eaten.

"I must get to work too," he said. Grabbed up his empty tray and started behind the trio. "See you for dinner." His voice carried a note of anticipation to begin his day.

Hank eyed Dawn. *"Dinner on Earth has a nice sound to it, does it not jist vek?"*

Dawn felt Hank's playfulness. He was teasing her again, and that made her feel all right. "Well, Let's see if Earthly work sings to you," smirking, she teased back.

"*He used a hor trap,*" Farstar held the crystal sword in quaking hands, ready to battle, energy hissed around the blade his eyes danced with valor but the room was empty and he feared for Autumn. "*It was meant for me, to keep me disoriented.*"

Nacoo squatted beside Jax, concerned by what had happened. Feeling an intense tug, he could almost hear Autumn scream. "*They are leaving Targ.*" His mind twitched with irritation. "*Can you help Jax?*" A dark spot, spreading outward had appeared just above his temple, a laser hit — poison — Nacoo wrestled with his thoughts, "*What the hell is a hor trap?*"

"*It is what you would call a magnetic scrambler of brain waves. It is a strong weapon used among defenders of Targ.*" Farstar knelt beside Jax, placed a hand on his brow and solar plexus, "kolum trey," he toned, inclining his head, and repeated in a clear, concise voice, "kolum trey," there was a minute of silence, softer, "kolum — trey —," Farstar moaned and his body shivered as the energy left his body. "Assist *me, Nacoo, Rory's magic is powerful, place your hands on mine, and send healing.*"

Nacoo's large bronze hands covered Farstars. He closed his eyes, not knowing how to send healing, but he tried by imagining Jax standing, smiling at him. A tingle started in his fingers growing warmer with each inhalation of breath. The air crackled around them, a connection taking place between it, and their bodies, his hands began to feel hotter as they hummed with this intense energy. Nacoo opened his eyes and could see waves of color, like heat rising off hot pavement. It was beautiful; he willed the waves to enter through their hands and into Jax. Nacoo could feel a slight strain on his arms and noticed Farstar starting to slump. He thought more clearly, seeing Jax healthy and full of vitality, energy pulled through him in torrents of burning arrows, he heard himself moan.

He wasn't sure he could keep this up when miraculously another pair of hands settled on top of his. He didn't look up but could feel a fresh wave of energy surge through him.

Farstar raised his head speaking in a thunderous voice, "WATHU, JANT TA TARG," then became very still.

Nacoo suddenly felt cold and shivered, dazed, he repeated the words wathu, jant ta Targ. He thought it meant, awaken, son of Targ. "You alright," a familiar voice echoed through a tunnel. "Hey," a warm hand grasped his shoulder bringing him back to the room; he looked up into the face of his friend, Daj.

"Good timing," Nacoo rubbed his hands shaking from the experience. "How did you know we were here?" He asked, fatigued.

"You the pilot of that ship out there," he chuckled, clapping Nacoo's shoulder.

Nacoo grunted.

Jax stirred and lifted up on his elbows, "I am *ootauto* ~ comforted," his voice a dry whisper.

Daj handed Jax his water canteen and stepped around to Farstar, resting a hand on his brow, "kolum trey, Farstar."

The four of them rehydrated and rested, not speaking until Nacoo heaved his body off the floor. The burning from Autumn's bung was relentless. "We have to go now," he said, holding his hand out to Jax.

"Where are we going?" Daj asked.

"To find Autumn," there was a note of graveness to Nacoo's voice.

A few minutes earlier, Daj awakened on the ground, just outside the door; he now touched his head and felt the wound, left by the unseen attacker. "Who has her?"

"His name is Rory," Farstar answered, heading for the door.

Once outside Daj sent a mind touch to his horse to go home to TaChoo. The idea of being able to understand an animal, alien or not, and have that animal understand him was still very mind boggling. Let me introduce to you — the animal whisperer, he jested, entering the ship, but before he could sit, the ship was moving.

Nacoo's face was set in stone, a determination Daj had never seen in his colleague. He let his mind drift to Autumn and felt a tingle pass through him. She was a good friend to all of them, but now he wondered if there was more in Nacoo's heart for her than friendship.

Farstar felt Daj's fleeting passion for Autumn and shifted the sword on his back, refusing to look into his eyes. He was grateful for the healing Daj had given and even a bit comforted by his presence, knowing his chances were better with him than without. *"I am ootauto, Earth tutal,"* he spoke softly to Daj, his tone unassuming.

Daj grinned and tipped his hat to Farstar's back. He heard Jax say something about the planet Dyeck and thought, another world to discover, wasn't his life just a grand adventure; he eyed the crystal sword and hoped that it would not have to be used during their search for Autumn.

Rory motioned to Smoot. *"Bind her to you until a deal is made."*

"As you say," Smoot answered. He beckoned for the still-drugged Autumn to stand, taking her by the hand, leading her to the back of the ship. He placed his hands on either side of her head, *"heshna lef wa,"* he chanted, sliding his hands to her shoulders staring into her eyes, *"protection bind us."* He pulled her head close, their cheeks almost touching his lips very near to her ear. Smelling her kom scent, he probed her neural system, needing to know how long until the effect of the appo wore off.

Autumn tried to focus on her surroundings. The words he'd spoken had sounded distant and meaningless. Smoot's face swirled in front of her, and she could feel his cool breath on her face. She sensed energy roping them close together and swaggered with its force. She found a focus point, on his thin gray lips, but then he pulled away. Autumn jerked when Smoot turned and started to walk; she had no choice but to follow him. The strange energy drew her with him as they passed through the ship's external door. Autumn grasped him, losing her balance, struggling for breath.

"Relax and let the implant work." Smoot's voice was calming.

Autumn, gasping, centered her attention on a group clustered at the base of the ship's lift. The beings were darker skinned and slightly heavier than the Targian body structure. The one talking to Rory held a staff with an emblem that resembled one she had seen at the ancient temples of... her mind drifted.

The pain of breathing had eased by the time Smoot came to a rest, just behind Rory. Wide, black eyes, irises rimmed in fire red, stared at her. She made a conscious effort to hide behind Smoot.

Smoot felt Autumn's discomfort. He took pleasure in being her protector, having her so close to him, a shield for her fear. *"Welcome to the planet Dyeck,"* he said, probing her neural system once again, sensing the moc appo losing its affect.

Rory spoke fluent Dyeckian with gestures toward Autumn, making her even more uncomfortable; Autumn thought of Nacoo and his ability to speak many languages. She covered the sensory site, squeezing her cupped hand between neck and shoulder; a hopeful source that the homing signal worked at such a distance, unwelcome tears stung the corners of her eyes. *"What is happening?"* She asked Smoot.

Smoot, saying nothing, turned and followed Rory toward a knolled structure; Autumn felt the tug of energy, a horse pulled by the reins. *"Where are you taking me?"* Angry, she glanced back at the group of hungry-looking Dyeckians then took a step closer to Smoot.

"We are to take ootau at Eth's mound."

"This is not comfortable," she said, suddenly very homesick for planet Earth.

Dawn plugged in her hyper-band, watching as the recorded information downloaded. Momma whirred with its familiar and reassuring sound. She studied the scenes as they unfolded, grateful for having used the tiny box every chance that she'd had. Now she opened a new file, starting from the day Autumn had disappeared behind the cavern wall.

"Jist vek, may I probe your mind for the learned information about using this machine." Hank stared at the screen with a look of interest on his face.

Dawn pushed her chair away from the desk. *"Thank you."*

"A pleasure?" he sent a feeling of inquisitiveness along with his answer.

"Certainly Hank, I appreciate you asking me this time, instead of just doing it." Dawn closed her eyes, rested her elbows on the chair arms, relaxed, and waited for the mind rush.

Hank relished the pounce approach; he calculated his time, waiting until Dawn started to become impatient then dove into her mind. She gasped as he quickly hurdled into her warm, multi-faceted energy field. Currents whirl pooled around him and he plunged deeper, searching for the information, passing memory bubble after memory bubble. He heard Dawn moan as he propelled forward, knowing that the awareness of what he was doing was intoxicating. Hank touched a bubble and became a part of Dawn's world, her education of the work she was doing. He immersed himself in the knowledge, absorbing, refining, and attuning this archaic kom way. Targ would be pleased with him; he twirled through Dawn's neural mesh and took pleasure in her quivering reaction.

Hank slowly started to pull away, when a high-intensity thought impulse struck him like an exploding shaft of light, confusing him. Nacoo's voice pervaded the energy field with a fierce determination, channeling its way around his mind. Hank struggled to move forward getting caught up in a spider web of unfamiliar emotion — a mixture of anger, defiance and fear — Autumn was sending a message to Nacoo that reminded him of a homing signal — Hank reached out to her. *"Do not fear he comes."* A great discomfort encompassed his heart, and he stumbled over an electrochemical path in Dawn's mind. She jerked involuntarily.

Hank again tried to move forward, but an intense magnetic pull dragged him away — away from Earth, away from Targ. A driving anticipation to reach Autumn overwhelmed him, a sense of her fright surged through him. *"Autumn, he comes,"* he cried out and in a feverish effort fell from Dawn's mind.

"What the hell was that?" Dawn panted. Sweat rolled off her forehead.

Hank sat frozen in his seat, eyes distant and unseeing.

"Hank, are you all right?" Her sensory site raged with vibration. The realization sunk in that he had found her secret and experienced what she was feeling. *"Hank, listen to me,"* she paused, *"Nacoo's hung is in my sensory center. You must have tripped over it."* She nervously waited not knowing how it had affected him. She grasped his hand, disquieted. *"Come back to me Hank, please come back, I'm sorry Hank — Hank — Hank."* She shook his shoulders.

Hank was in restructure mode. The uncontrolled flood of thoughts and emotions that he just experienced shocked his system. A slow sense of him returned, diligent and careful. He cleansed his mind of as much of the kom emotion and confusion that he could without Targ.

Understanding seeped in when he heard Dawn explain. He sorted out the gathered information and started to come back to his body, giving her the comfort she needed.

Dawn felt Hank lightly squeeze her hand. She smiled, consoled by his touch.

"Hello," Zyleon stepped into the tent, snapping them both out of their quandary. "Coffee smells good," he sauntered over to the table to pour a cup. "Have you started the download?"

"Yes, Professor, it's been very interesting so far."

Hank winked at her reassuringly.

"Momma's hyper-band recordings are static filled but readable." She said trying to sound composed.

Zyleon eyed her over the top of his mug. "Let me understand, you four have traded bungs…"

"Three," Dawn interrupted.

"So my niece, Nacoo, and you have switched."

"Yes, Professor, but please explain to me how you knew? Nacoo's bung is still in my sensory center." Dawn felt perplexed thinking that maybe, all this time, Daj really had spied on her most intimate thoughts.

Hank chuckled, *"That's easy to answer,"* he looked at Professor Zyleon before he continued.

Zyleon nodded and said, "Let's hear it." he sat down at the desk that rested back to back with Dawn's workstation and spun the chair to face Dawn. Her face glowed oddly pale, and the look in her eyes was a mixture of worry and humiliation.

"Uh," she groaned and tried to look away from the Professor's stare.

Hank started, *"you should all ready know the answer to this, just think about it. When an unauthorized, personal connection interruption occurs, Momma automatically switches the homing device on. Therefore, when you placed the non-owner bung in your sensory center, Momma could only make a static record, thus sending the signal home to begin the search for the rightful owner. Professor Zyleon received that message."* Hank smiled, satisfied with the Professor's approval.

Dawn dropped her head, relieved that her personal stuff was still personal. "Oh," she sighed, visualizing the tiny intricate connections that made up the bung and sensory site. She remembered that if bung removal took place and the bung not directly imputed into the hyper-band or Momma's docking port, within a few minutes of that removal, the activation of both bung and sensory center started. "So what you're saying is the bung's homing system has become me."

"Exactly," Zyleon patted Dawn's knee and noted the perspiration that beaded across her top lip.

"Professor, we have to go back," Hank spoke aloud, with a dead calm.

"Why?"

"Autumn is in danger."

"How do you know this?" Zyleon's voice filled with concern.

"The molecular network of the mind works with universal frequencies and during times of change or disruption the neuronal pathways become a frenzy of activity. During my quest for knowledge in Dawn's mind, the bung started transmitting and caught me in its energy burst, thus creating a bridge — an instant connection between Autumn, Nacoo, and me, a pyramid of thought transference occurred. Nacoo is trying to find her." Hank paused, *"He is being drawn toward the planet Dyeck."*

Dawn's heart fluttered.

Zyleon studied Hank, fascinated by how Targians had a way of explaining experience. He pictured Autumn in his mind. The last time he had seen her smile was at breakfast on the morning all this had started. Now he tried to remember their last conversation — *today we discover what no one else ever has* — he shifted uneasily, still staring at Hank. He swallowed the lump forming in his throat. "Notify Thorb upon arrival, give him all the information you have gathered, he'll need it."

Hank bowed his head.

"Dawn, by the sounds of it, Nacoo's bung will guide you, so, you'll have to go. But damn it all, if you can find them, stick close with Daj and Nacoo." Zyleon sighed, "Report back as soon as there is any news," he said. "I wish I could go with you, but there is to much happening here that needs my attention."

"Yes, Professor," Dawn bit her bottom lip, her mind filling with anxiety.

"Trombula shall give us use of his ship; we shall go immediately."

Zyleon caught a flash of grimness in Hank's diamond eyes as he bowed his head.

"Good luck." Zyleon faltered, "Autumn is very dear to me." He shook Hank's hand. "You are all, very important." He patted Dawn's shoulder, "It'll be all right." He quietly left the tent.

Farstar turned his gaze toward the golden, spar-thread potion bag Daj held. A delicately crafted pattern of TaChoo's symbol, an oval-shaped maroon-colored Targ, encircled by kaleidoscopic leafy vines, adorned the pouch. He watched Daj pick out one of the small gourd-shaped bottles, apply some of its oil to the back of his head, and replace his hat. Farstar mind touched Daj. *"Do you need healing?"* he asked.

An awkward moment passed between them.

"I'm fine," Daj, sighed, pulling the bag strings tight, retying it to his belt.

Jax placed his hands palm down on a glossy maroon panel and began to chant just above a whisper. Nacoo watched, transfixed, as Jax's hands appeared to melt into and become part of the ship. "By the gods," he stammered under his breath, still not quite accustomed to the alien way of doing things. Nacoo instinctively relinquished the controls, as the ship transformed into a silent, camouflaged flying machine, by way of Jax's unseen manipulations.

The ship dropped slowly, unnoticed, into the Dyeckian forest. *"Not even air disturbance."* Daj mind touched Nacoo, *"And how about that trick."* He pointed to Jax's reforming hands. *"That beats Baxter's in a roo race any day."*

"Glad you're here, Daj." Nacoo looked into his human friends eyes. *"Let's go get Autumn."*

Farstar's voice, stern and commanding, entered their minds. *"If you trevi ~ desire to stay free keep close and quiet. The Dyeckians do not take kindly to unannounced visitors."*

"Shall we instruct you with a yentch?" Jax asked the men, while he belted on two, three-pronged tridents. Four inches in length with starred tips and a crescent moon knuckle guard trailing back to the wrist.

Nacoo steadied his gaze on Daj, apprehension growing, Daj nodded. *"Yeah,"* Nacoo answered.

"You use an upward thrust motion." Jax held the yentch underhanded and made a violent upward thrusting motion. *"Now to make your own for you to practice with, reach into the panel; Targ's ship shall connect with your energy and create a yentch to fit your fist, in the same manner sleeping covers are made. Wait until you feel no movement before retracting your hands."* Coolly, Jax directed, pointing to the glossy maroon panel.

Daj was first. Taking a deep breath and closing his eyes, he laid his hands palms down on the panel. A familiar sensation touched his fingers. Tendrils threaded their way inside him, pulling his hands into a gelatinous soup. The feelers triggered his fingers to curl around the forming handles. They grew warmer, his body drawing strength from this extension of Targ. Daj thought back to the creation of the tents and Baxter telling his version of the vine-induced backpack. They had all laughed. For a brief moment, he was lost in the sharing of that happiness, his mind picturing and drinking in the affection between his friends. Daj pulled both his hands out when the swirling stopped. The weapons were complete, and he stepped aside for Nacoo. "That was a buzz," he murmured, honestly.

Daj felt Farstar's gaze upon him, sensing that painful stab he had encountered from Farstar before. Daj tried to ignore the sting by concentrating on Nacoo; he couldn't help the way he felt. Nacoo stood hunched before the panel, hands immersed up to his wrists, shiny, thick, black waves of hair laid over his calm expression, and Daj looked down at the weapons in his own hands. This wasn't something he'd signed up to do. A ripple of homesickness swept over him, and he wondered if he would ever see Earth again.

An arm reached across his shoulders. *"Dyeckians are a culture of traders. They would rather have us trade you, than fight. So be of good heart my tutal, maybe a Dyeckian female shall find you alluring."* Farstar stroked his hair mockingly.

"Let's just get this done," Daj growled, annoyed, avoiding Farstar's burning gaze.

Nacoo stood to his full height, a good five to seven inches over the group. He took in his surroundings, gasping, as the poisonous atmosphere stung his lungs. He could feel Targ's implant readjusting for the non-breathable air, but still he wanted to panic. He gasped again, noticing this time that the air was cool, and smelled similar to wood smoke. He heard Daj catch his breath and looked to see him bent forward, holding his knees. A small cough escaped his friend, and he quickly started to lose that sick pasty color. *"Thank Targ for the implant,"* he soberly commented to Daj.

"Right," Daj answered, straightening, sucking in air cautiously.

"Mel li ga ~ come with me," Farstar commanded, quickly gliding into the cover of the woods.

Jax pointed for Nacoo and Daj to step in behind Farstar, levitating in after them as they headed toward the mounds.

Nacoo knew Autumn wasn't far from him now; he shuddered at the thought of his colleague held by this altogether new and strange race of aliens. His sensory center drummed in rhythm with his heart, and he did not know which was louder. Coarse vegetation scraped his bare arms; blood trickled from the cuts, splattering small drops on the brown colored-leaves — something in the forest followed — licking up the warm liquid, grunting with hunger.

Jax's awareness heightened; his body, protected in aura armor, shimmered as he levitated across this rough terrain. He could hear the heavy-footed creature that followed them; he could sense its desire to feed and knew it would continue to follow them to the edge of the forest, but no farther. A Dyeckian stalker rat stayed in the shadows and fed on the severely wounded and dying. Its teeth could snap bone in half, and if its prey were unlucky, enough to still be alive when it started to feast, it would watch helplessly while its tormenter rolled in the warm spilled blood.

Jax noted the now dried blood on Nacoo's powerful arm; he thought of the children and the blood that flowed through them. Targ had chosen well.

Farstar stopped at the edge of the tree line and looked out across the morass. Nacoo came up behind him breathing heavily. *"We must move above the ground."* Farstar pointed, indicating the way to go.

Daj came to a halt beside Nacoo, a bit winded, and leaned forward. *"Whew."* He took off his snapped up hat, wiping the perspiration from his forehead. *"Bizarre isn't it, he wants us to fly."* Daj looked out across the expanse of soggy clay that lay in front of them. He could clearly see an ominous, rain curtain, hanging low over the iron-tinted wetness, *"Appears as if we are in for a good soak."*

Nacoo watched an updraft of cloudy air. *"Bad weather doesn't make for good flight."*

Jax looked behind him into the murky eyes of the stalker rat, whose razor-sharp teeth dripped with gelatinous, yellow saliva. It snapped its jaws emitting a low snarl. Nacoo and Daj turned to look, startled by the sound. All they observed were rustling leaves.

Farstar stood silent; unmoving, he could sense a growing discomfort in Autumn.

XIV

Autumn awoke with an urge to pee. Hank's echoing words, *"do not fear, he comes, Autumn, he comes."* A disquieting blackness surrounded her and at first, she thought she was still in the ship. After a time, she recalled walking toward Eth's mound. Smoot had whispered something, and she had collapsed into his arms. Autumn could still feel the bindings that held her to him. She knew he rested to the left of her.

The room was cold and damp, smelling of stale smoke. She fanned her arm, cautiously, out away from her body, inching her fingers across an oily dirt floor. The unseen matter collected under her fingernails causing her to cringe. Autumn sighed, and brought her arm back to her side. She lay on some sort of coarse fur, and she flinched at the thought of bugs. Rolling onto her right side, she stretched her top leg out into the charcoal gloom, her bladder protesting.

The sound of movement came from the direction she faced. She froze, listening — hot prickles of fear raced over every inch of skin, heart thundering — she held her breath. Even Smoot's breathing was barely audible, and then there it was again, a shifting. She strained to see into the tarry darkness, not daring to move, or breathe. She could roll up against Smoot to wake him or she could scream — something grabbed her ankle, making her recoil in fright.

"Forget about me all ready?" Rory chided.

Autumn's breath returned with a flare of ire behind it.

Rory kept hold of her ankle. *"Sit up,"* he demanded.

She felt the energy pull against Smoot and scooted closer to him.

Rory grabbed Autumn by the face, his cheek almost touching hers, *"Eck mita tra, heshna lef wa."*

Energy swirled around her, and she unwillingly tucked her face into Rory's shoulder, inhaling his woodsy scent.

He had control now and bid her to stand while Smoot slept. His eyes penetrated the inkiness. He held Autumn firm around the waist directing her out into a passageway and up a flight of stairs. Light from a dust-smeared window filtered its way down to them, dimly reflecting off walls that were a smooth, polished coal. The roughly cut stairs they walked on were made of the same material. Heat from Autumn's breath warmed Rory's shoulder. He loosened his grip on her, now that she could see her feet, but he did not let go. He knew the Dyeckians would jump at the chance to have her, and he could not let that happen. He needed her to do his biding.

They entered a room just at the top left of the stairs. There was a large fur rolled up and placed against a wall of rough-hewn, stone. In the center of the room, a small fire pit smoldered from use by an earlier occupant. A round stone table stood knee high to the right of them. Straight ahead stood a three quarter partition that Rory walked toward; behind it was a hole in the floor. He pushed Autumn away from him and turned around. *"Relieve yourself."*

Autumn didn't have to think twice about squatting over the hole. Her muscles ached from holding it for so long, and it took a moment to relax enough to go. She ignored the fact that Rory stood a couple of feet away. The easing of pressure made, if only for a moment, this alien world seem better.

Beside the door hung a long, coarse fur coat, which Rory walked toward, towing Autumn behind him. He took it off its hook. The coat had hung on a human-size, rat-clawed foot. Autumn shuddered with revulsion.

"Disrobe and put this on," Rory shoved the coat at her.

She let it drop to the floor. *"No,"* Autumn wore nothing under the robe. Her stomach tightened at the thought of the dirty thing against her body.

Rory grinned, grabbed her throat, and untied her belt. *"Va,"* the robe fell to the floor and he kicked it away. He could feel her hot blood pulsing against his hand. A desire grew in him as he feasted his eyes and felt her defenses rise. It felt euphoric knowing that he could take her; he reveled in her distress and knew Farstar was sensing it — it felt so satisfying — she choked for air, shaking him from his indulgence, he backed up, letting his hand drop. *"Cover your body,"* he hissed.

Autumn stood defiantly before Rory, not able to bring herself to put on the coat.

"*Come now, you wouldn't want the Dyeckians to see you before payment, now would you,*" Rory said, greasily.

"You bastard," Autumn slammed her fists into Rory's chest. Fire flashed in his eyes.

He shoved her to the floor, grabbed the coat, and threw it on top of her. "*Cover yourself, and no audible speech or you'll stay here for the animals to feast on you.*"

Autumn reluctantly slipped on the coat; it smelled of smoky leather and was rough against her skin. She glanced at the discarded silken robe. Despondent, she rose to her feet. The energy ropes lessened their intense pull as she stepped closer to Rory. "*Satisfied,*" she ceded.

"*More than you know,*" he taunted.

Autumn followed behind Rory as they made their way outside, through semi-empty streets lit by the bloody sky. All the buildings were a duplicate of the mound they had come from, except for the markings on the doors. She watched a creature resembling a spiky-shelled turtle dive into murky water, as they crossed a bridge. Rory grasped her around the waist, keeping her very close to him. The streets on this side buzzed with activity, vendors selling wares akin to a farmer's market on Earth, smells of cooking food made her mouth salivate and she wondered if Rory would know she was hungry, the way he knew she'd had to pee.

Rory stopped in front of a slouchy, dim-eyed vendor, never loosening his grip on Autumn, as a markedly inquisitive crowd loomed around them. He spoke to the vendor with quick confidence; the vendor answered, never glancing away from Autumn. Rory sounded frustrated as he continued to talk, finally taking Autumn's hand in his, and permitting the vendor to examine and even touch her fingers. Excited whispers filled the air. He felt Autumn cringe then picked up an apple-shaped fruit. He moved speedily through the bustle of the very animated, very curious horde.

Autumn hid her face in Rory's shoulder, now thankful for the long, heavy coat. Rory moved fast and to her surprise, levitated her inches above the road. He intensified the orb that shimmered protectively around them, but even with all his shielding measures, she clutched him tightly, feeling as though her life depended on it. The contempt she felt for him settled somewhere in the back of her mind.

Rory slowed, having pulled away from the hubbub; they landed softly just to the side of a much worn door. *"Va ~ yes, I feel your hunger,"* he said, taking a couple of bites from the fruit and handing her the rest. *"Eat,"* he said, calmly. *"When we enter King Tri's, mound, there shall be a selected few sitting in a circle. We shall stand together and wait for a Trader to secure a bid. From there we shall enter into King Tri's personal chambers; the Trader shall follow. At that point, King Tri shall collect the offer from the Trader then you must allow them to look upon your beauty and to —,"* Rory paused, *"to touch you."*

The fruit tasted sour as Rory's words tumbled into her mind. *"Touch — where? Why?"* She asked, horrified, letting go of him and tucking the coat closer around her.

"They have never seen or touched a kom ~ human, before so the deal was made. Necessary provisions for me, just to let the good King Tri and highest bid Trader to look upon you and touch your body." Rory stopped and took Autumn by the shoulders, staring hard into her eyes, *"they shall honor their word, and you shall let them if you honor Farstar."* A gleam of gratification flickered in his mind, and he bent close to her, licking off a droplet of juice that rested on her chin. She jerked away and he laughed. *"Be good, and soon we shall be off this planet."*

With the thought of Farstar, a fleeting bubble of hope rose inside her, she wiped the spot Rory had licked. *"I'll do it for Farstar,"* she said.

The smell of stale smoke and dirty bodies lay heavily in King Tri's dim and creepy mound. Chills ran up and down her spine, and she shuddered against all the eyes that were upon her.

"**W**hat do you mean Daj and Nacoo are gone; gone where?" Dawn stomped her foot in fiery temperament. "Professor Zyleon isn't going to like this," she huffed.

"They travel to Dyeck. Foster and TaChoo as well prepare to journey and trade with King Tri of Dyeck," Thorb spoke, unemotionally.

Targ tickled Dawn's feet and she sighed, "Professor Zyleon asked that we go." She looked in Hank's direction.

Hank waited for Thorb to continue, also enjoying Targ's touches.

"*Rory, Smoot, and others have become disconnected from Targ and have continued trade with Dyeck. This time Rory has involved Farstar in his trading by keeping control of Autumn.*"

"Keeping control," Dawn snorted.

"*Rory has severed all links between Farstar and Autumn, except her emotions... but there is a connection between Nacoo and Autumn that guides them.*"

"What do you mean severed?" Dawn asked, subconsciously rubbing her sensory site.

"*When a Targian leaves Targ and does not come back for aresh bonding, discomfort settles into their hearts. They, not unlike a human living apart from their planet, gradually lose their connection, their ootau. If Targ could enter them, linking takes place, nourishing them, soothing them.*"

"Why can't Targ enter them?" Dawn sunk her feet into Targ's mossy ground.

"*Rory and Smoot use an Ockoraerion dust as a barrier,*" solemnly, Thorb said.

"*Ockoraerions,*" said Hank. He thought of his wog sy zaqurah, Smoot, and wondered how he could use something so vile against Targ. "*We shall go with Foster and TaChoo,*" he spoke with conviction.

Jax released Daj from the energy binding, which had enabled Daj to levitate beside him. Now Jax needed a moment to rest, as did Farstar. They had taken cover in a large clump of feathery, dirty yellow grass that grew taller than Nacoo. Squatting on his ankles, Jax glanced at Farstar, then at the men. "*Use mind touch with each other,*" Jax instructed, and then both Targians became eerily motionless.

Nacoo sat next to Daj as they waited for Farstar and Jax to regain strength. "*Baxter will want to learn how to levitate,*" he chuckled, handing his water jug to Daj.

"*Did your implant vibrate?*" Daj asked, swallowing a mouthful of water. "*Thanks.*"

"*Yeah, similar to an old motor,*" Nacoo shook his head, "*a little less intense than the bung.*"

"*What?*" Daj checked for his bung.

"Autumn exchanged bungs with me when we first arrived on Targ. We thought it would help us find one another. Later, Autumn exchanged with Dawn, and you were to get Autumn's bung. We never got a chance to be alone for the exchange to happen. The homing signal works very well." Nacoo capped the jug.

"So you're guiding us on this trip." He now understood why Nacoo acted so drawn to Autumn, *"damn."*

"Farstar and Jax don't know." Nacoo's steadied his gaze on Daj's moss green eyes. *"For now Let's keep it that way."*

"I'm surprised they haven't found out," Daj tipped his hat to Nacco, *"but I'm with you, mate."*

"Thorb has made me Keeper of the Key," Nacoo pushed a bluish colored stone around with his finger. *"Each time Targ gets inside — each time —"* he sighed*"; it changes me…"* Nacoo inclined his head and stopped the stone in front of Daj. *"Does it make me less human?"* he implored.

Daj picked up the stone and tucked it in his vest pocket. *"Freska Sharp once told me that human didn't come close to describing me."* He smirked at the memory, *"Now there was a woman with a stone soul,"* Daj patted his pocket. *"One night Freska the untouchable asked a favor of me. Said I could have pick from the top shelf, any one night, all night, if I obliged her. Never could turn down a good offer. She wanted to go to Jar Top's yacht party that weekend; to pump up business for her restaurant — but the stipulation was she needed to bring a date. That's when the fun started. We ate, drank, danced and we talked to everyone, life of the party, that one."* Daj chuckled.

"The first evening we slept apart but the second, she was putty in my hands. Woo, wee, what a night. Freska Sharp was quiet the next day even thanked me for the escort real nice like but the next weekend when payment came due, with every glass she poured, a foul and very disturbing stream of words corrupted my ears. The best insult she gave was," Daj put his hands on his hips and jutted out his jaw imitating her, *"human doesn't come close to what you are, you're a fiendish, muck sucking, rubbish heap of a slimy beast. Oh yes, that was a good, top shelf night."*

Nacoo was grinning. *"You're a sick dog."* It felt good for a few moments to forget about where he was and what he was becoming.

The heavy rains sheeted the distant sky but only misted in and around the small group's resting place.

Farstar was the first to come out of his stupor, gracefully rising. He looked toward the Dyeckian village; a painful expression shadowed his face.

Jax roused from his altered state, meeting the eyes of his fellow Targian. *"Your discomfort is great."*

"Jax, you are the only one that can be seen without disguise. You shall find us a path to her." Farstar could not contain the trembling; *"her emotions are strong."*

"Va, Farstar," Jax bowed his head and vanished into the thick grass.

For a moment, Farstar watched the two dozing men, slumped against each other in a circle of flattened, moist grass. Then the aching began again. He was unable to stop the building unrest coming from Autumn. He knew Rory bound her to him and that whatever he was trading had much to do with her; he could sense Rory's contentment, pulling Farstar deeper into his maze of the unknown.

Getting only curious stares, Jax levitated passed the vendors selling from their doorsteps and those that lined the coal-slated road. He stopped at a table where a buzz of excited conversation caught his attention. Listening to the Dyeckian tongue, he discovered that this particular vendor traded fruit for a touch of the strange female, and the Targian who owned her, took her to King Tri's mound. It was just what Jax needed to hear. He went past the group to within sight of King Tri's door; there he dropped into a meditative state and remote viewed the scene, taking place inside King Tri's mound.

Rory and Autumn were in King Tri's personal chamber, Rory was bowing his head, a gratified look on his face. King Tri and a single Trader bowed back, the deal done. Rory held Autumn close to him, her head buried in his chest, and swiftly headed for the chamber door. Inside the main room sat a circle of Dyeckians and Traders lying about on furs, drunk on their highly intoxicating drink, gog. They watched critically, hungrily as the two crossed through the room, danger shadowing their faces. Rory exited the mound, already levitating at a rapid speed. Smoot waited just beyond the trees with a ship — they were leaving the planet.

Jax snapped back into his body and raced to Farstar. *"We must hurry,"* he spoke to all of them, crashing through the grass. *"They are leaving the planet."*

Daj and Nacoo barely reached the standing position when they were collected in an energy orb and whipped through the sedge. In a blur, they were through the woods and stumbling back into the ship.

The Targians sparkled and snapped with energy. Nacoo dropped into the pilot's seat, trying to ignore his hair standing on end and remembering the dream of Autumn wrapped in a fur coat.

"Devils black forest," Daj cursed, his head still spinning. *"That has space-chuting all torn to shreds."*

Nacoo pressed the nosh, Jax slid into the co-pilot's seat, *"Nacoo can you sense her?"* he asked. *"We must find her."*

"Hang on," Nacoo toned, mapping a new course.

Jax's smile showed his fatigue as he fell into a stupor.

"Rest well," Nacoo empathized, now consumed with the burning throb of the bung.

Autumn stood shivering under the heavy coat she wore as the tradesmen did their bidding. They shouted deafeningly, Rory forced her face up and walked her around inside the circle for all to see. He grabbed her hands, turning them over and opened the lower part of the coat, exposing her legs. He slid his fingers down along her shins and tapped the tops of her bare feet. It drove the tradesmen into a spitting, slobbering frenzy of madness, trying to out do one another. *"You are worth even more than hoped for,"* Rory said, pulling her hair back away from her face, exposing her neck and ears. The Dyeckians and Traders thundered their approval, grabbing one another, and yelling until King Tri stood up.

There was an exchange of words between King Tri, Rory, and Trader Umbra, who sat nearest the door.

"The highest offer has been taken; we shall go into King Tri's chamber now. Walk slowly and wait for them to part a way for you. You are not to be touched by anyone else," Rory uttered, returning his arm snugly about her waist and to his wonder she wrapped both her arms around him, tucking her head in against his chest. *"If you are touched by another Dyeckian or Trader,*

you become tainted and you shall never see Farstar again." Rory held his head high, relishing Autumn's trepidation.

The queasy feeling that had started in her stomach moved to her head, making her dizzy with fright. *"Rory, promise me that you will take me away from here."* She dug her fingers into his side, terrified that he would leave her here alone.

"You are full of surprises," Rory parleyed, velvet tongued. Autumn's human emotions were strong and made him sway. He allowed her some comfort. *"Va, Autumn. You shall ish ~ return, home with me, just do everything asked of you,"* his voice maliciously sweet.

It was quiet inside King Tri's chambers; furs covered the arching walls and steps that led up to a raised bed. A fire pit crackled with flames, small tables with pillows encircled it. King Tri poured some gog into four cups and spoke to Rory and Trader Umbra.

"He wants us to drink; you must release your hold on me."

Autumn held Rory with such tension that her muscles ached. Reluctantly, painfully, she loosened her grip. He moved away from her to retrieve the cups; she became aware of a growing anticipation between King Tri and Trader Umbra as they talked together. Her eyes met the King's and watched the red ring around his iris widen. She gasped and jumped when Rory handed her a cup made of gemstone.

Trader Umbra stood Autumn's height; coarse dark hair fell unkempt past his shoulders, covering part of his tawny face. Large fluid amber eyes, unblinking and full of a savage eagerness, stared at her, his tongue-moistened lips parted showing two rows of shiny, black pointed teeth. Autumn shuddered.

"Drink," Rory moved away from her until he felt the energy cord pull. *"Drink,"* he said again, with more force.

Autumn held the heavy cup with both hands and shakily raised it to her lips. They intently watched her every move. The drink was bitter with an after burn; she coughed and heard them laugh.

King Tri was first to touch her, taking the cup, and just tapping her fingertips. She stepped forward and Rory stepped back, keeping the distance between them. King Tri spoke to Rory never taking his eyes off Autumn, eyes that were now glowing solid red.

"Remove the coat," Rory commanded, rocking with the force of emotion streaming from Autumn's pleading eyes. He smirked. *"Remove the coat."*

Autumn lowered her head, and swirling from the Dyeckian gog, fumbled to untie the cord. The King's breathing increased; Trader Umbra took a step closer. She held her breath, closed her eyes, and diffidently opened the coat; it slid off her shoulders, crumpling around her feet. She heard approving sighs and felt King Tri's breath, fast and hot as he circled her. He ran a finger down her back, talking and grunting joyously.

"He says your skin is as soft as spar-thread, and he likes the way you shiver."

Autumn focused on Rory. *"Bastard,"* she cursed, vehemently, continuing to stare at him.

Rory absorbed it all.

The King began rubbing with both hands, exploring every part of her, rumbling with the pleasure of it. Autumn's stomach tightened and she swallowed hard. After a couple of very long, torturous minutes, King Tri started speaking, weaving his fingers through her hair.

"The King desires to buy you and keep you for himself."

This provoked Trader Umbra into action by grabbing Autumn's arm, causing her to wince.

"Trader Umbra says he shall get what he paid for." Rory looked upon Autumn's defenselessness and felt the deepness of her shame. He took a step forward.

The Trader was rough with his touches; Autumn recoiled sending him into a seething fit of words.

"He is telling you to stand still." Rory took another step closer.

"He is hurting me." Tears stung Autumn's eyes.

"He enjoys it."

Trader Umbra grabbed Autumn's face, forcing her to look at him. His breath smelled of stale gog; hungrily he sniffed her neck, her breasts, her groin, digging his bony fingers into her tender flesh. Then he bit, hard and deep into her thigh, blood spilling over his face and down her leg.

Autumn screamed, tearing at the Trader's coarse hair in an effort to yank his head away from her leg.

King Tri's powerful hands seized Trader Umbra's, all too eager for more, shoulders, causing him to release his jaws ungenerously.

Rory quickly picked up the coat and wrapped it around Autumn. He bowed to King Tri and Trader Umbra.

Autumn felt sick, collapsing in Rory's arms.

King Tri nodded, satisfied.

Trader Umbra licked her blood from his reedy, grimacing lips.

Rory rushed through the circle of drunken under-bidders, directly outside and raced for the trees, where Smoot would be waiting.

Autumn moaned, clinging limply to Rory, as they ascended into the ship. "Rory," she gasped, "it hurts. It hurts so... bad." Pain shot up her leg into her back with a paralyzing influence.

Smoot was up above the trees, and headed for Pik, the small planet they claimed as home; in the same moment, Rory began to heal Autumn. Rory knew if he didn't work fast that the Trader's venom would reach into her brain, putting her into a controlled state only Trader Umbra's blood could reverse. He could not lose her. *"Autumn,"* desperate, he called to her, *"Autumn you must enter my mind,"* he waited for a response. *"Autumn, do it now."* He shook with the exertion.

Autumn heard Rory calling from far away, but something inside her said his was not the voice to follow. A great force commanded she come to her master but abruptly a mesh of energy threads tangled around her mind, pulling her into Rory's thoughts and quickly immersing her in the reality of his being. He wanted her to find something — but what — a cloudy vapor turned into a vision of Trader Umbra's dreadful, bloodied face. Fear and confusion blindfolded her, and she began to drown in this sea of hot, pulsing terror.

She wondered if maybe she were dying, when a distinct, shielding power encircled her, and suddenly, Farstar was standing majestically in front of her, in full warrior's attire. Autumn reached for him trying to form words out of the chaos churning in her mind — another powerful flash and she found herself back in Rory's mind embrace, and facing what he wanted her to find. It was a tiny bit of his life essence. As she took a piece of his shimmering liquid crystal, a tremendous shudder slammed her back into her body. She sat up violently, fully conscious, in a pool of sweat, gasping for breath.

Rory buckled, exhausted.

Autumn gulped for air, eyes wide with panic — where was she? What just happened? Rory lay crumpled beside her, there was pain in her heart, and she grasped at her chest, weakly swinging her head from side to side. Clenching her stomach she crawled to the back of the ship, gut rolling and bile stinging the back of her throat, the remainder of the fruit and gog splashed to the floor, and with that, her memories returned.

She wiped her lips with the back of her hand; head hung low and started to weep. How had it come to this? Why had she been the one to find that stupid wand and fall into the hands of crazy aliens? A deep rolling moan escaped her throat, her face wet with tears, *"Why?"* she asked.

Smoot's calm, musical voice broke through her pity, *"because Targ chose you."*

Autumn looked up at the back of Smoot's silver head and back down at Rory. Rory had given her a piece of his essence to keep her from a danger she did not understand. He had saved her life. She could not stop the sobs.

XV

Daj sat beside Farstar, who kneeled on the floor head slumped forward. The orb of energy faded, leaving the familiar gray tone of his skin in its place. His hair splayed across his silvery-emerald green robe. Daj touched the material, and sensed Farstar quaver. Dawn popped into his thoughts and of how she had snuck around his workstation, unnoticed, and zapped him with a laser pen. He had jumped, crashing his knees into the underside of the desk, and in a flurry had set chase.

Daj chuckled under his breath, which gave way to a memory of a teacher, a healer, a person of exceptional sensitivity, one that could tell when the energy around him was touched — even without the physical touch. He studied Farstar and wondered if that man was part Targian?

"Hope She's all right," Nacoo said, breaking the silence.

Daj looked passed Nacoo out into the galaxy that lay before them. "How's Jax?"

"He looks close to coming out of it. It's a funny feeling to look at the stars and find them all familiar, never having seen them before. They put a map of the entire universe inside here." Nacoo tapped his skull.

"Do you remember the night we all celebrated around that huge bonfire by the lake watching Dawn and Autumn dance, so drunk they could hardly stand?" Daj snickered.

"Yeah, that was the day we discovered the cavern." Nacoo fingered the instrument panel, turning their direction southward.

"He was there that night and danced with them." Daj pointed to Farstar.

Nacoo was silent for a moment. "We all danced."

"They left their calling card in us," Daj said, tapped his forehead, noticing Farstar's finger twitch. "Farstar is coming around." Daj resisted the urge to touch the aliens robe again, waiting to see Farstar's pupil less, diamond eyes, open.

Farstar struggled to regain strength from the drain of carrying Daj safely back to the ship and against the onslaught of Autumn's agonizing emotions. He had felt Rory's aresh touch his own and then wrap itself around Autumn's, fully aware that Rory had kept her alive this way, but in doing so joined with her, without zaqurah sharing.

"You need healing?" concerned, Daj asked.

Farstar shook his head no. *"Listen to me,"* he urged, raising his head, *"during our development in the wog sy ~ growing room, we share Targ's nourishment with one another, a continual link of imparted knowledge. As we age we choose a seeding tek ~ mate, but there was only one female in our group, so three went without a wog sy teks."*

"We also choose a zaqurah ~ companion to korzuk aresh ~ join essence with, and to journey the path of life with, Rory —" Farstar sighed, *"and I, are zaqurah's, and in being so, we can give to one another parts of our aresh in time of great need, this includes giving to each others linked mates, seeding mates and offspring."*

"As you have experienced…" Farstar gripped Daj's forearm, *"the exchange of aresh with TaChoo, you understand how you are vesp ~ linked, together."*

"I think so," Daj answered, attentively.

"You now have the ability to keep her zaqurah alive by giving her a part of your essence." Farstar searched Daj's face for signs of understanding and continued, *"Rory has given Autumn a part of his aresh, and he is now always vesp ~ linked, to her and her to him."*

Daj let the words sink in. *"what you're saying is his link with her is permanent, as is yours with his, and therefore you share her together — with him — in more than just companionship."* He felt a cold shiver run his spine.

Daj suddenly felt weak. Autumn had been close to death, but for the sacred healing Rory had shared. *"Rory…"* he stared at Farstar unable to finish.

"Va, for he has kept her from death," Farstar bowed his head.

"So you will know everything that happens between them," Daj said, barely audible in his mind.

"Va," a sense of helplessness exchanged between them.

Daj rested his hand on Farstar's arm and tried to give him reassurance. *"We will find her,"* he tightened his hand and felt Farstar tremble.

"The signal's gone," Nacoo, boomed, "there's nothing!"

Jax steered the hovering ship slowly in a circle, intently watching Nacoo.

Nacoo just kept shaking his head. "Nothing, it's lost." *"Daj,"* Nacoo mind touched him, *"do you think you could pick up her signal?"*

"How," Daj questioned.

"Let's exchange bungs."

The men eyed each other, a moment of anxiety passed through them.

"It can't hurt can it," Daj agreed.

Nacoo smirked, *"that depends on the distance."*

The Targians watched curiously as Nacoo and Daj exchanged the small objects from the sides of their necks. Nacoo's reaction was small compared to Daj's, Daj hollered and grasped at his neck. It felt like a hundred bees stung him all at once, "AHHH… BLOODY 'ELL," he went down on his knees, bringing both Jax and Farstar to their feet.

Nacoo held up a hand to stop them.

Daj rocked back and forth for a moment, cupping his neck, one hand on top of the other, whimpering and staring directly into Nacoo's eyes. *"I believe we need to turn this ship around,"* Daj said, through clenched teeth.

"Good man," Nacoo boomed, turning back to the panel and hastily piloting the ship in the direction Daj pointed.

Farstar and Jax looked at one another with new understanding of how these komi were connected. Farstar smiled.

Foster stood in the closed circle of tradesmen, before King Tri, speaking in his tongue. "We search for knowledge —" Foster inclined his head. "What may we entice you with, King Tri?"

King Tri gazed at Dawn, his lips curling. The Dyeckians and Traders talked amongst themselves, while greedily eyeing the newcomers, all apart from the one closest to the door who dwelled on his earlier loss. He still salivated over the first sweet taste, left in his mouth, of the previous female, human's blood. The female that now stood in King Tri's trading circle was fully dressed. His eyes focused on the soft, creamy white flesh of her neck. Beckoning to him like a beacon of light to a galactic sailor on the dark star sea. Trader Umbra's venom flowed and he swallowed thickly; standing, he took a forward step, and so did King Tri.

"Covers for sleeping made from the finest spar-thread," he walked around the group never taking his gaze from Trader Umbra. "Alm nuts, verva fruit, and scent of katri flower," King Tri forcefully pushed down on the shoulder of Trader Umbra as he passed.

Umbra responded with a deep-throated gurgled growl, shifting his shoulder violently away. He wiped at a small bit of drool forming at the corner of his threadlike lips, and returned to his seat, glowering at King Tri.

The room went quiet and Dawn's hair stood on end.

The King continued his circle. "Some cu and the females," he conveyed in a rumbling, authoritative voice.

"King Tri, the females are not for trade," Foster countered, respectfully.

"Everything is for trade. The one that came before you exchanged observance of his female, for Ockoraerion powders. What is this knowledge you seek?" Tri stopped beside TaChoo and grinned at Trader Umbra now sitting tense and ready to leap.

"What is his name?" TaChoo faced King Tri. She had to be sure they were on the right path.

"For a touch of your silken hair," he taunted.

TaChoo grasped the King's hand defiantly and rubbed it down the side of her head. "His name, good King," she hissed.

A rumble went around the room as the tradesmen watched King Tri run his fingers through TaChoo's silver hair. "Rory," he imparted.

Giving him a look of warning, Foster clasped King Tri's hand, making him grunt, from the untraded for touch. He deferentially dropped his hand away from TaChoo's face.

The King resumed his loop then stopped and stood between Dawn and Trader Umbra, by the door. Dawn stepped closer to Hank. "She is like the female Trader Umbra and I observed."

A shiver of fear shot through Dawn. She gasped as she looked into the King's intense fiery eyes.

"Where has the female been taken?" Foster insisted.

"For a touch," Tri said, knowing the laws of trade by heart.

"Dawn you must allow King Tri to touch you." Foster sternly cautioned. *"He shall not harm you."*

Dawn met Foster's gaze and nervously nodded, understanding it was vitally important.

"Va, for a touch," Foster bowed his head.

Dawn pressed her lips together.

Tri gently touched Dawn's cheek, enthralled. "Soft," he rasped, nostrils flaring, his fingertips exploring her ears and twisting her strawberry waves. Pulling slightly he leaned forward, smelling her scent, tormenting the tradesmen.

A low growl sounded from behind the King, he smirked mockingly and let go of Dawn's hair.

Hank locked calculating eyes on King Tri.

The King sneered. "Go toward the dim star," he answered.

"We honor you with the wares requested." Foster turned, "wex wa ep ~ let us go," he spoke to the group.

King Tri spoke threateningly to the tradesmen, and they opened a passage just wide enough for one person at a time to pass. Trader Umbra stood by the door, slavering, as he watched the last of them leave. He would have another taste.

While Foster and Hank unloaded the goods, TaChoo and Dawn surveyed the street lined with merchant goods. The Dyeckian vendors and passers by all stared with those creepy red-ringed irises, giving Dawn the chills. She stayed close to TaChoo, glancing over the strange items laid out on the tables and ground. *"Why did King Tri want to touch us?"* Dawn questioned.

"The Dyeckians consider touching a high honor..." TaChoo picked up a string of oval stones, the vendor rubbed his hands together with anticipation. *"It empowers them and causes a stirring..."* TaChoo spoke to the vendor still holding the string of stones. The vendor answered and TaChoo sighed, allowing the vendor to explore her fingers and forearm in payment and greedily ogling Dawn.

"A stirring," Dawn urged.

"When their fingertips touch a Targian a chemical transference takes place, it does not harm us but does create feelings of strength and vitality in them, once felt they try any form of trading to touch us. They live by the law of trade. When the King touched you, a deeper transference took place; he received greater empowerment as he did from Autumn. TaChoo turned her head peering through the crowd. *"Ew buja ep ~ we must go."*

"Who are the Traders?" Dawn asked stumbling over a statue, causing her to fall and scrape her knee on the stone road. "Damn it," she cried out. When Dawn started to stand, a hand grabbed her by the arm. She thought at first it was TaChoo, but this hand clenched her painfully, dragging her with enormous speed away from the crowd — away from TaChoo. Her unseen assailant pulled her recklessly behind one of the mounds and forced her down into a dimly lit, dank, tunnel. In the blur of movement, she realized her attacker was the Trader that had stood beside the door of King Tri's mound. He covered her mouth smothering her startled shriek and locked the door they had just come through. Dawn bit down hard on his hand, drawing foul tasting blood, she coughed, and the Trader struck her sending her crashing to the ground. He kicked with both feet, rolling her curled up body farther into the passage. With every strike, he let loose a sequence of angry sounds.

Abruptly, Umbra stopped his attack and yanked her into a standing position, grabbed her jaw and forced her head against the damp wall. He held her there for a few moments, nose quivering, smelling her sweat and blood. It enticed him.

Dawn's head swam from one of the blows; blood trickled into her eyes, stinging them. Pain grew in complaint all over her body, and a feeling of foreboding crept its way into her mind.

Umbra ripped open her vest exposing more of her creamy skin; he licked the blood that covered her cheek, growing ravenous, saliva dripped from his black mouth. He searched out a fleshy spot just below her collarbone, savagely, sinking his teeth into her tender flesh. Umbra shuddered with the deep release of his venom, a blinding rapture, euphoria, gripped him.

Dawn arched. An intense scorching pain shot its way to her head. She slumped against the Trader losing consciousness.

Soon the venom would take hold, and reverence was his, for marking another human servant. Umbra released his jaws tasting her sweet blood and growled triumphantly.

TaChoo turned to see the Trader disappear with Dawn and she called out with urgency to Foster and Hank.

Umbra carried Dawn over his shoulder, down through the northern tunnel, the wild driving frenzy in his mind calmed by the release of toxin, now flowing in her veins. He smiled a bloody satisfied smile and whispered all the things he would have her do for him. He walked for an hour, passing an occasional doorway lit by a glow stone, before he had to shift her weight to his other shoulder. Umbra had the stamina and determination that few came close to. He thought about the first human female; she was close to being his servant. It made his mouth salivate; knowing that she would always carry his venom inside her and just a small second bite would complete the process. He made the decision to seek her out and set his bane free in her veins. Having marked two female human servants would set him above the current High Mark Trader. He rumbled with a gurgling laughter.

Above ground, three Targians levitated, tracking the Trader. Hank had entered Dawn's mind and was using her as a homing signal. He could sense the Trader's poison sledging through her mind and knew soon, she would be unable to resist the Trader's commands. They would have to fight to get her back, and then to get her back to Targ.

Umbra stopped walking, as the female was gaining consciousness. He laid her up against the cold stonewall, opening her vest wider, and admired the bite mark, still oozing with his venom. It gratified him to know that only his blood carried the antidote.

Dawn's stomach turned over and before she was fully aware, she was spewing its contents on the floor beside her. The pounding behind her eyes made her not want to open them, pain racked her body, and her heart felt like it was on fire. "Oh God," she moaned.

The Trader leaned his head, mouth close to her ear, his breath putrid, saying something she did not understand. He ran his black tongue over the blood caked on her cheek, and down to her heaving chest then she felt his warm, sticky drool, seep into the open wound. His coarse hair scratched her skin and she felt his teeth once again, sink into her flesh. Oh, God, she thought, he's eating me alive.

Umbra took his time, savoring the moment. As the poison from his bite filtered its way into her muscle, blood dribbled down his chin and the frenzy took over. He bit deeper, and venom gushed from his mouth. He held a hand over her mouth, stifling her screams; she pounded on his head and back driving him deeper into the fury of his rage. Then suddenly she became calm and let her arms fall to her sides, he moved his jaw around in circles, biting and sucking at the warm moist flesh, she whimpered pitifully and he relaxed, pulling his mouth away from her, pleased. He took her by the arm and she followed him, she would follow him anywhere.

Hank felt the sudden shock of Dawn's pain and knew the Trader injected more of his corruption into her body. *"He has begun the second stage,"* Hank said to his companions, knowing that time was waning, and soon she would not remember them; they had to get to her fast. *"We are coming, jist vek ~ small one, we are coming."* He pushed his way into the darkening crevices of her mind.

Thorb stood at the well of Kandoria with Professor Zyleon and Trombula. *"The second turning of Poc is at its zenith, but I come without ootau."*

"I presume the search is not going well," Professor Zyleon massaged his head and blew a forceful breath out.

"The children are released from Targ and soon shall be allowed to join the quest."

"Children," Zyleon said, startled at the rate in which Targians developed. He knew that their bodies were at the physical ages they would stay at until death. He looked at Thorb, who appeared to be thirty years of age, but underneath he was centuries old in Earth terms.

"The children have a deep intergraded vesp ~ link, with their dutom's ~ seeders," Trombula stated.

"Va, and in times of great discomfort their seeders aresh begins to flow through their veins with a magnetic pull. This is true for anyone sharing essence but is strongest in the children," Thorb added, gliding beside Professor Zyleon.

Trombula pressed an indentation in the wall, which opened a door to a small docking area.

A scattered crew worked around them as the continued on.

"Po and Frox have exchanged with Targ the knowledge of danger that their dutom's are in."

"Whose kids are they?" Zyleon questioned.

"They share aresh with Hank and Dawn."

Professor Zyleon stopped in his tracks. "What the hell kind of danger are you talking about?"

Thorb pressed into his mind. *"They sense the venom of a Trader flows in Dawn's blood. The children of Farstar and Autumn also sense the Traders venom flowing in Autumn."*

"Bless it man! What do you mean by that?" Zyleon was highly agitated now.

"A Trader's venom is stimulated when he is allured. It becomes a consuming drive to mark — bite — his chosen victim, thus releasing a toxin into their bloodstream. Both Autumn and Dawn allured him. The children sense Autumn has escaped his clutch for now, but Dawn is under the Traders" control."

A prickly heat crept its way over Zyleon's head. "What can I do to help," he asked.

"You are Overseer of Kandoria and your assistance is needed here. Please express comfort to Kuranna and Baxter. Trombula informs me, they progress well," Thorb steadied his eyes on Zyleon. *"I shall send message when they have been found."*

Zyleon watched as Thorb boarded a small ship. He gritted his teeth and wondered if he could keep the council reassured. "This discovery just keeps getting more complex by the minute," he hissed under his breath, mustache flaring outward.

Trombula gazed at the Professor. *"We live in an infinite universe with many others."*

Zyleon watched the ship vanish before his eyes. "Yeah," he sighed.

XVI

Rory watched the rhythmic movement of Autumn's breathing as she lay beneath the cover. Shadows chased each other around the sleeping room, crossing over him as he sat on the floor beside her; he played with a piece of her coppery hair and sensed his own aresh in her. He'd never meant to allow Trader Umbra to mark her; she was only to be touched, not bitten.

She would have to learn to use protection from Traders Umbra's further attempts; Rory knew he would search her out, always, just as his zaqurah Farstar would search for her, always. He closed his eyes and sat in stillness during the next few hours that Autumn slept, aware that he also would seek for her, always. Rory stayed until her breathing changed, leaving her to awaken alone. A new human emotion washed over him as he closed the door — sadness.

Autumn gradually came to her senses, remembering the ship landing on some small, red desert planet. While being carried to this room, she blurrily remembered seeing a city that bustled with activity and had wondered for a few moments, if they had time traveled back to Earth, during the era of the great Incan Empire. Smoot placed her on the sleeping cover that she now stretched her legs across; she could feel an ache where the Trader had bitten her, and ran her fingertips gingerly over the spot, stomach tightening when she felt the raised flesh.

A round, stone table rested under the only window, which filtered in light through a slatted shutter. Dust particles floated on the beams splaying to the floor; she flipped the sleeping cover off, creating an air current that spun the dust in circles. Next to her lay a beautiful, deep purple spar-thread robe. She stroked the softness of the material as she covered herself with it and tied the cord, wondering if Smoot had removed the fur coat. She couldn't remember anything but Smoot's crystal eyes and gentle smile as he laid her down.

She padded lightly across the smooth, stone floor, stopping to look around the sienna-colored room before she opened the door. Autumn felt a growing sense of apprehension. She wondered just how safe this place was, and what might be waiting for her out there. She touched the wound on her leg and shivered.

Outside a hot refreshing air welcomed her and from where she stood, which was a tremendous height, she could clearly see the great stone temples scattered in the near and far distance of the flat land beyond the city.

Autumn gasped awe struck, as she overlooked this magnificent city. It was carved, horseshoe shaped, from a mountain of sandstone. Two small waterfalls issued forth from a cliff, cave mouth, and flowed into a star-shaped bathing pool resting at its base. Streaming water sparkled atop yellow bricks, and large red ferns lined the walkways forming the fan of a shooting star. The pool had an encirclement of luscious green trees, akin to palms, shading the pool and making it look very inviting. One of the most exquisite sights before her was the carved curving staircases, under sheltered cliffs, that led to decorated balconies and arched doorways such as the one Autumn just exited.

From her small curved balcony, she regarded the beings milling about below, most of them, she thought, were Targian or Dyeck. Autumn leaned over the railing and squinted to get a better view of the smaller ones, laughing, thinking they looked almost like Rock Dwarfs. She pondered if she was the first human to see this glorious place. A slow realization sunk in… she was standing on the highest of the balconies and that the beings below, noticing her, had stopped to stare. Suddenly, she felt very exposed and pulled her perspiration-dampened robe, tighter.

"Let them look," Rory's voice came into her mind.

Autumn flinched but remained gazing at the city below. "Where am I?"

"Pik," he answered audibly.

"It is beautiful."

"You are correct in naming the Rock Dwarfs. Many of Earth's mythical beings are real in other parts of the universe."

"Fascinating," she breathed.

"Would you take ootau in bathing?" He asked, *"The water is healing."* Rory thought of the toxin still flowing in her blood.

Autumn sensed Rory probing the edges of her mind; she continued to stand with her back to him, but did not try to block his mind touches. There was a new connection between them, and her curiosity of discovery out weighed her uneasiness. *"You saved my life —"* she hesitated, *"thank you."* Turning, meeting Rory's brilliant eyes and yet another realization sunk in, the shooing star that crossed the bridge of his nose and landed on his right cheekbone matched the garden below. This place was Rory's world, *"Yes, I would take comfort in bathing."* Autumn shyly smiled.

Rory gazed upon Autumn, her robe moist, hanging heavy on her shoulders, and the honey highlights in her hair darkened with wetness. *"Mel li ga,"* he rose from the engraved wooden chair he was sitting upon and glided past her down stairs.

Autumn felt Rory's coolness as he passed beside her, but the usual pull of the energy bindings did not jerk or wrench her about. Nice, she thought, freely following behind him, to the bathing pool. Targians, Dyeckians, and Rock Dwarfs, all stopped what they were doing to watch them. Autumn stayed an arm's length from Rory as they walked, sensing his pleasure in her discomfort. "Why does it please you," she blurted out.

Rory was silent until they reached the edge of the pool, where he turned to her and quickly, fervidly disrobed her, once again rendering her vulnerable to strange eyes. *"Do not ask me that again,"* he growled, pushing hard into her mind.

Autumn winced and scanned for a way to escape, her gaze finding Smoot standing in the gathering crowd.

"Remove my robe," he demanded heatedly, absorbing her humiliation. *"By this act they shall all know that you are mine and shall not harm you."*

Resigning to his will, as the safest thing to do, Autumn untied Rory's belt and pulled back the matching dark purple, spar-thread robe from his shoulders, Autumn blushed, exposing his slender, pale-grayness.

Rory grinned cruelly and grabbed her by the arm, pulling her close, so that their bodies touched. Her skin was hot against his and he felt her shy away, he led her into the soft green water, wading waist high to the center, where they climbed a couple steps up onto a stone block.

There he pushed her down, water covering her body and face. She coughed as he pulled her head back up and placed a large, smooth, moon-shaped crystal behind her head and neck. He held one hand over her brow and the other over her solar plexus.

"Kolum trey," his voice rang through her head; she arched her body from the shock of it. Immediately the bite on her leg turned to fire, as did the bung in her sensory center. She heard Rory thunder out words she did not know — or was it — was it — she screamed in her mind, the Trader was there — there in her mind — teeth tearing into flesh, venom, a surging flow of lava through her veins. Autumn tried to open her eyes only to find Dawn standing over her; she was speaking the language of the Trader and smiling sweetly at her. Oh God, oh God, Autumn thought, we have to get away, we have to get away.

"Autumn," she heard her name called through the cloud of fear. *"Autumn, come back to me."*

Rory lifted Autumn into a sitting position, her eyelids fluttering, her breathing coming hard. The crystal had absorbed more of the poison with surprising rapidity. Smoot had entered the water to assist Rory by placing both palms just below her shoulder blades, sending healing, and comfort throughout her mind. Rory cupped water in his hands, spilling it over her head, soothing her spirit. *"Autumn, you are safe,"* he said, serenely.

Autumn fled through a dark tunnel, she could see a glimmer of light growing stronger — gasping, — she was going to make it. Then suddenly, she was sprawling through the air, closer to the light, the light of Rory's eyes. Autumn leapt off the stone, wrapping herself around him, shaking and crying, "Oh God, Rory, he has Dawn."

Rory looked up at Smoot. *"We must teach her soon."*

Smoot bowed his head to his tutal and waded through the water, waving for the quiet crowd to dissipate.

Rory levitated Autumn out of the pool to where their robes lay and covered them. This time his feet touched the ground as they walked; she held him as if she were terrified of falling into the vast darkness of space. A desire grew in him and he sent her comfort. Rory was formulating a plan, Trader Umbra would pay dearly for his dishonesty, and Farstar would help bring it to fruition.

Once inside the high room, Autumn could not bring herself to release Rory. At least with him she felt a little bit safe. *"Please stay with me,"* she spoke, beseechingly.

Her kom emotions were powerful and he swayed under their energy.

Autumn pushed her way deeper into his mind like a little girl hiding beneath the bed covers. *"Rory, I am so terribly afraid."*

Rory bowed his head, faint with her overwhelming passion.

"He has Dawn," she shook at the thought of her friend captured and under control of that beast. *"Don't let him take me,"* she pleaded.

He desired more and entered her mind. Swirling with the craze, diving deeper, deeper... she was weeping, he could not stop. *"I shall stay,"* he hungered for her human reaction; it drew him into the sacred, hidden crevices of her mind. A place only Targians dare go, and in her weakened state, she did not resist him. Sobs wracked her body now, as he absorbed her most intimate memories. Here, deep within the sacred parts of her, Farstar's aresh burned brightly. Autumn slumped in Rory's arms.

"Rory, please stop," she whimpered.

He was riotous with the desire for full immersion, but her human mind was too frail. Rory felt Farstar's life force push him away. He laughed sardonically. *"It seems we share the aresh of a seeding mate, Farstar."* Rory pulled back, wild with longing.

Autumn moaned, woozy from Rory's invasion, but there was a moment when she felt Farstar's mind caress, and now she called out to him, *"Farstar..."*

"Av, not Farstar," Rory shushed her, touching her bareness, smelling her muskiness, and tasting the salt of her tears. He explored with his mind her human cellular frequencies and could feel her feeble attempts at escape. *"The Targian women on Pik cannot conceive without Targ's assistance, but you Autumn, shall incubate my seed."* Rory opened his mind, releasing his passion and felt Autumn yield under his force. At last, he thought, sharing takes place.

Farstar sat in an unmoving state; a turmoil of emotions hailed from Autumn. The Trader had set into motion a change within her, a clutching fear of the mind, but another fear settled upon him as his own essence, given to her during the Dance of Nar was touched and absorbed. Rory was going too deep; he was going to damage her with his craving.

"Autumn, I am here." Farstar pushed at Rory, blocking further penetration of her mind. He heard his laughter and thoughts of his intentions, Farstar trembled, feeling Autumn's frailty, and yearned to give her comfort. Unnoticed by the others, Farstar cradled his head in his hands; he would do as Rory asked for the protection of Autumn.

Daj tumbled the little blue rock between his fingers. "I don't think it's too far now, just a roo jump away," he said, thankful that the burning sensation in his neck had changed to a strange low-key vibration.

"That could mean years to us," Nacoo grunted.

"Time is of the mind," Jax conveyed.

"That's hard to fathom, considering we are from Earth, where everything runs on time. Daj grinned, "Except for the sky-buses."

"Trying to be funny," Nacoo grinned, giving his friend a knowing look.

Jax wrestled with the idea of late sky-buses. *"Do they elude your time?"* his face contorted in a bewildered expression.

Nacoo busted out in laughter, "Ha, that's a good one."

"It's just a joke, Jax," Daj joined Nacoo in the amusement.

Having cleared his mind, Farstar smirked at his fellow Targian, *"good thing you are not an Earthling,"* he chided.

"You are right, Farstar," Jax agreed, still looking baffled.

Nacoo pointed to a star beginning to appear on the horizon. "I believe there is a planet just north of that dim star, and if I am correct, that is our destination."

"Your knowledge is correct," Jax replied.

"Feels that way to me," Daj sat back, put his feet up, pulled his well-worn hat down over his eyes, and crossed his arms. "Since my services are not needed, wake me up when we get there." Daj fell immediately into a dream of Autumn resting in a darkened room. There was another presence in the room, a cunning presence seeming to engulf her in his energy.

"Autumn," Daj tried to mind touch her, *"Autumn, it's Daj."* He noticed, out of the corner of his eye, a flash of silver. *"Farstar,"* he

whispered, and in his dream state, looked around the room. It was small and sparsely furnished; the walls appeared to be sandstone, as did the floor. Hot and dusty, he thought. A strange painted symbol topped the arched doorway; Daj stared at it, trying to decipher it. Cupped in a backward letter cee a figure of a man lay on the bottom, mist rising from his abdomen and forming the shape of a woman surrounded by wavy lines. The woman reached out with an open, upward palm, in which a luminous gem rested.

"Beautiful, isn't she."

Daj jerked his eyes away from the painting, *"What?"* he asked, directing his gaze fully upon Autumn. She was breathing deeply, and he watched a trickle of sweat roll down the side of her tanned face. *"Autumn,"* he tried to shake her, remembering he was still dreaming.

"She is the beautiful woman in the painting and she incubates the Queen of Pik in her womb."

Threatening laughter filled Daj's head, and the presence in the room came into clear view.

"Rory," Daj questioned.

"Your instincts serve you well."

The next thing Daj knew, he slammed back into his body, awake and quickly back on his feet, ready to fight.

"Have a bad dream," Nacoo eyed Daj.

Daj rubbed his neck, "happened to you too, eh?"

"Yeah," Nacoo patted Daj on the back, "it's just a little insight."

"Farstar, Rory claims Autumn incubates the Queen of Pik," Daj said, somewhat shaken.

"It shall be the first time a Targian is birthed by a kom." Farstar turned his gaze to the fast approaching planet.

Jax and Nacoo glanced fretfully at the two behind them.

The whole situation made Daj feel uncomfortable.

The ship tilted downward, cutting smoothly through the atmosphere of Pik. Jax scanned the sandy reddish-brown landscape. *"We shall land between the village and the city."* He pointed to the swiftly appearing flat-topped, pyramid-shaped houses that dotted the landscape.

Daj whistled softly.

"It's right out of the ancient past, come to life before my eyes," Nacoo said, stunned.

The small group gazed upon a burnt-orange terrain, distanced by hills of rusty-coral, with quiet admiration as they waited for the dust to settle after their landing. One by one, they climbed out of the ship, each gasping, adjusting to Pik's air. With each step Nacoo and Daj took, a chalky cloud rose up around their feet, leaving their impressions behind them.

Farstar and Jax levitated just an inch above the ground.

"Before we go any farther I shall teach you how to levitate." Jax landed in the sand with a poof.

Farstar hovered silently, observing the mesa carved city. Two massive palm trees stood on either side of a thickly built, arched entranceway. Yellow-bricks formed the fanned-out walkways that teemed with activity. Farstar focused his attention on two figures moving toward them.

"First you must remove your boots and feel the ground beneath you." Jax waited as the men readied themselves.

Nacoo had not laced up his boots, so pulling them off wasn't a problem. Daj on the other hand hopped around in circles, trying to keep his balance and kicked up a powdery swirl around them. Nacoo coughed.

"Stuff it up." Daj threw him a look of annoyance.

Even in the shade of the ship the sand burned, "very hot, very hot, hot," Nacoo chanted, skipping from one foot to the other.

"Ouch," Daj cringed.

"When you are ready, still yourselves and become aware of the air around you."

Both men closed their eyes, trying to ignore their discomfort.

"Sense the space of air between the ground and your feet. Feel it as if Targ were touching you." Jax gently probed both of their minds and allowed them to experience his slight elevation off the surface.

Daj sensed vibration in his implant and imagined Targ moving under his feet raising him up. The feeling reminded him of hovering in his air-car and having the air-car beside him move, faking the feeling of his air-car, shifting.

Nacoo allowed Jax's energy to flow through him, sensing the lift; he swayed and opened his eyes. Again, he felt a repelling force push him up, farther away from the dusty surface, and automatically he put his arms out for stability. "Whoa."

Nacoo's deep voice caused Daj to open his eyes and look at him, amazed to see his friend floating. "Now this is an ace of a trick," he said, realizing his feet were not burning anymore and that he too hovered in the air.

"How do we move?" Nacoo asked, regaining his poise.

"Imagine yourself walking." Jax directed, hovering in a straight postured manner, moving backward, and forward, coaxing them to try.

Daj started to move his right leg forward but quickly changed his mind when he lost balance.

Nacoo moved in a circle, rocking back and forth until finally after a half dozen attempts he moved forward, proud as a boy catching his first fish.

Daj went backward at a high rate of speed, crashing into the ship, and sending Nacoo and Jax into a fit of laughter. He mumbled but was happy to see he still hung in air. His second try went more smoothly.

"They come to greet us," Farstar interrupted their practice.

The three lined up beside Farstar and directed their attention toward the two Targians that approached.

"Rory, Keeper of Pik, nes ootau ~ takes comfort in welcoming you," the greeters bowed their heads.

Farstar and Jax recognized the two from their time together living on Targ. "We welcome his comfort," Jax spoke aloud, inclining his head.

"We bid you, mil li wa ~ come with us."

The four of them glided behind their escorts. Daj stayed behind Nacoo, concentrating on stability as they moved along and occasionally eyed the progress Nacoo was making. About as good as himself, he thought, wavering slightly. He rubbed his neck with a desire to float higher, and before he could stop, he was above Nacoo's head. "Crikey," Daj, he spoke to himself, "tie that roo down," slowly returning to an inch above ground.

"You learn fast Daj, but one must be careful to understand what impulse can do," Jax smirked.

Sweat stained Nacoo's clothes and stung the unhealed cuts on his arms. Pik's sun, burned relentlessly in the hazy yellow-orange atmosphere of the planet. His skin prickled with the heat, and he was tiring fast. *"I need to walk, Jax."*

Jax glanced at Nacoo. "Just imagine the soil touching your feet," he said.

"Yow!" Nacoo hollered, his knees slightly buckling when his feet contacted the scorching surface. For a moment, he hopped around, before quickly sliding on his boots.

"Not so easy is it, cobber." Daj mocked a cough and waved away the dust that Nacoo stirred up with his hotfooted dance.

Remembering his desert survival training to keep covered, preventing rapid evaporation of precious body moisture, Nacoo removed a bandana from his vest pocket. As he tied it around his thick chock of black hair, he caught Daj's knowing look, noticing the dark ring of wetness around his hat. "Levitation takes a lot of energy," Nacoo said, uncapping his drinking bottle and taking two long swigs of water. "I think I have blisters," he gave Daj a sideways glance. "Do you have enough water?"

Daj nodded. "Yes, and I have mineral caps if you need them." He too felt the drain from such intense exertion but decided he could make it to the shade of the trees before he touched down. *"Ever notice that Targians don't seem to perspire?"* Daj half grinned, snorting air through his nose.

"Maybe they have an implant for that too," Nacoo huffed sarcastically.

When they entered the city, to the stunned amazement of Daj and Nacoo, a group of Rock Dwarfs, just as astounded by the humans, ushered them under the shade of the trees and set to wetting their feet and surrounding bricks, cooling them from their walk.

The Targian, whom Farstar recognized as Cres, took his leave of them. Urna, Cres's companion, spoke aloud. "When you are comforted, I shall take you to your sleeping rooms. When the sun dims, Rory invites you to the Eating Hall." He pointed across the bricked courtyard, passed a very inviting pool, and came to a dark red, stoned, arched doorway. "You can refresh yourselves in the healing pool; disrobe before you enter the water."

Daj and Nacoo looked at one another. "Sounds good to me," Daj murmured, gawking at the Rock Dwarfs and the other dark-skinned, red-eyed aliens.

Nacoo towered over the Rock Dwarfs as they busied themselves carrying water, sometimes bumping into him, offering him water to drink. Nacoo felt his implant hum as he searched his mind for the language of these beings. "Euba sac?" he questioned.

"What?" asked Daj a bit startled.

"I asked if the water is safe." The smallest female Rock Dwarf grabbed Nacoo's hand and shoved a cup in it.

"Uh," a gruff voice sounded from the female dwarf.

"You're bloody cunning," Daj said to Nacoo, accepting a cup from the same female. She smiled with a row of tiny, yellowed, square teeth, and pushed the cup up toward him as high as she could, giggling.

"I think she likes you Daj," Jax piped up, accepting water himself.

"She has a beard." Daj looked quite appalled at the idea.

Farstar grinned. "Komi," he said openly, watching a Rock Dwarf wet his feet. He heightened his senses and scanned for Autumn, searching for a connection. A tiny flicker of her energy breezed through his mind, and he knew she was near. It comforted him. Finishing the water, the smallest female took his cup. Catching his eye, she quickly glanced up at the highest balcony, and just as quickly, she offered him another cup of water. Farstar bowed his head with the slightest movement and gently pushed the second cup away. He looked toward the highest balcony and understood that was where Rory kept Autumn. A fire danced within his spirit. Soon, he thought, he would see her. A shiver of anticipation scuttled down his spine, *"We are ready,"* he said to Urna.

Led by the smallest female Rock Dwarf, Daj and Nacoo followed her through an expertly dug tunnel, which descended into the cool depths beneath the mesa. Nacoo, now refreshed, levitated, cross-legged, grateful for his new ability to float and for the relief he felt from the heat. He marveled at the workmanship of the Rock Dwarfs and memorized the number of phosphorescent stones that lined the low ceiling walls. He wanted to be able to get out of here if he had to.

The tunnel opened into a large, dimly lit vaulted room, miniature waterfalls flowed mistily down the Indian red tinted walls, and into a small, naturally formed, pool centering the area. In here, Nacoo could stand to his full height. "This is some kind of pretty," he said.

Daj noted the tiredness in Nacoo's voice. "Appears as though she wants us to go into our room," he pointed to where the female Rock Dwarf stood beckoning them to come.

Inside the sleeping room, two rolled-up furs lay on the floor, on either side of a small table, which held a bowl full of strange fruit and two drinking containers. On the left side, a doorway led into a cleansing room, complete with spring-green, silken spar-thread robes.

Nacoo was pleased to be able to stand to full height in the rooms, although he did have to duck coming in and out of them. "I'll give it three stars," Nacoo sighed.

"Etta," the female Rock Dwarf thumped her chest, "Et-ta."

"Nacoo," he tapped his chest. "Daj," he pointed to Daj who tipped his hat in greeting.

"Naacoo, Daazz," Etta tried to pronounce their names then pointed out at the pool, "euba sac," she smiled shyly at Daj, showing her small row of yellowish teeth. Stepping back through the doorway, she unfastened the fur that covered the entranceway, separating them from one another.

Above ground, Farstar and Jax settled into their room located midway up the cliff. Farstar delicately laid the crystal sword on top of his folded defenders robe; he ran his fingers over its vibrating blade, forged in the belly of Targ. *"Pah,"* he spoke softly.

Jax handed him a common robe. *"Peace,"* he repeated, *"wex wa ne ootau in the healing pool."*

They made their way to the pool, disrobed, and entered the crystal-infused water. Farstar found a spot where he could gaze upon the balcony the female Rock Dwarf had shown him, then immersed himself up to his shoulders.

Jax waded across the pool and engaged in conversation with a small group of Piks residents, occasionally glancing at Farstar and sensing his longing for Autumn.

Umbra landed his ship on the yellow sands of Pik. Dawn watched, waiting in a semiconscious state for the Trader to call upon her. She'd tried to remember what had happened, and why she felt such bitter revulsion toward him, when she knew that at any moment, and for any reason she would give her life for him. Things were so fuzzy and nonsensical except for the distant voice in her mind, which chanted the words — *jist vek* ~ small *one* ~ *jist vek* — seemed to reassure her, ground her to something — if only she could remember.

Just out of view, tucked behind a concave dune, a Targian spacecraft landed. Hank concentrated to keep the link open to Dawn. *"She tries to remember,"* he spoke to Foster and TaChoo as they readied for the task that lay before them. Hank clasped securely in his hand the blowpipe and dart laced with oil of egmur for sleeping, and athic to dehydrate the poison in her blood.

Hank gathered in his will, focusing on his task to release Dawn from Trader Umbra's prison. *"Jist vek* ~ *small one* ~ *jist vek,"* he called to her in soft, whispering, cries, *"we come."*

TaChoo tucked her yentch and blowpipe into her belt then skillfully dipped three darts in a mixture of egmur and artu, to weaken Trader Umbra's body and mind, and athic, to desiccate his venom. *"I am ready."* She covered her head and belt with a long spar-thread wrap, glancing somberly at her two companions.

Foster gazed at his sister. *"Rah, after you make well of your darts,"* lines creased his forehead, *"I shall extract three vials of the Trader's black blood."*

TaChoo nodded.

"A vial for Hank to administer to Dawn," Foster turned a firm gaze on Hank.

Hank acknowledged Foster with a slight sideways nod.

"And TaChoo shall carry the second vial for Autumn. The third vial I shall carry as a precaution, for a Trader's venom only needs a scratch to enter the bloodstream." Foster received feelings of understanding from both his companions. *"Wex wa ep, let us go,"* he said, leading the way.

Umbra planned to enter the city via the tunnels where his Dyeckian accomplice, waiting inside, would give shelter to him and his second servant. This would give him time to find a way and furtively impart the next round of his bane to his first servant. "Arr, arr," he laughed and roughly grabbed Dawn by the arm.

Dawn winced from the pain of his grip but stood willingly and stared into his large, amber eyes. "What will you have of me," she asked. Her voice was monotone. Although she did not understand his

Carol L. Davis

words, she understood that he wanted her to follow him. She did so freely.

The Trader tied a water belt around Dawn's waist and placed a heavy supply pack on her back. He dug around in another pack, searching for something — something — she thought, searching her mind, what was it — something? The Trader covered her head and shoulders with a sheer, black veil then handed her cloth wrappings for her hands. She complied with his wishes. He wanted her completely shielded from curious eyes, and she would remain so until he commanded her to remove them. Dawn looked down at her pants and boots, hoping in an uncaring way that he approved.

Trader Umbra reveled in his cleverness, knowing the Dyeckians of Pik would nearly trade him their lives, for a touch of the human female. "Arr, arr," he growled a raspy laugh while he activated the ships weather shield. He pushed Dawn toward the door and closed it behind them, triggering the locking system. Satisfied, he started their trek across the arid land, to the Dyeckians room.

Foster glanced behind them as they levitated across the hot sand; they left no impressions, unlike the two they were following. Foster, TaChoo, and Hank rested a moment in the shade of Trader Umbra's ship. *"They are not far from the city,"* Foster divulged, his sensitive eyes noticing the colorful signatures that their footprints left in the sand. *"Dawn is burdened and walks quickly to keep the Trader's pace."*

"The heat is a great discomfort to her." Hank allowed Foster and TaChoo feel his mounting concern. *"Wex wa ep,"* he urged, continuing to speak to Dawn through a constricting haze.

TaChoo glided behind Hank, thinking about how Daj had returned to her the horse he had ridden to Jasper Mountain, delivering the visual message about his search for Autumn. Now as they drew closer to the city, a stronger sense of him filled her. *"Daj,"* she tried mind touch. *"I am outside the city; we track Dawn and Trader Umbra."* TaChoo felt a small stirring then nothing more.

Umbra stood a few feet from the mesa's cliff edge, a steep drop if one were to lose footing. He scanned for telltale signs of the trapdoor that would lead him into the Rock Dwarf tunnels. Dawn was the first to notice the circular indentation in the sand and strangely knowing that was what he searched for, pointed to the spot. He gave a good yank, which sent sand scattering off the top of the door; it surprised him at how easy it opened. Sand fell into the opening; Umbra felt a rush of cool air escape the tunnel, and he stared hard into the darkness. The face of his collaborator came into view, his hand held in mid air, shielding his eyes from Pik's ever-brilliant sun, his lips twisted in a shocked expression. They exchanged startled looks and a few words that excited the Dyeckian greatly.

Dawn sighed with welcome relief as the revitalizing moistness of the passage eased the tightness in her parched throat and cooled the wetness of her body. Yet she did not stop or ask for a drink of water, perceiving that it would anger the Trader. She stayed, obediently, a couple steps behind him, down an almost perfect cut of stone stairs. Dawn let her cloth-covered fingertips slide over the chill damp of the walls. When the tips were saturated, she brought them to her lips, rolling in her dried-out bottom lip and over the top of her teeth, sucking at the moisture the cloth had collected.

The oddly familiar metallic taste jogged something in her memory, a name — someone named Daj. Dawn struggled to recall more, but they had arrived at their destiny. The Trader grabbed her arm and brusquely pushed her into the room the Dyeckian had brought them to; the Dyeckians greed-filled eyes followed her until the Trader snapped at him and stood in the doorway, blocking his view. She was tired and sore and wanted to rest, but all she seemed able to do was stand staring at the chamber wall, waiting for the Trader's next command.

The Trader closed the door flap, walked into the burrowed-out room, and in his silent commanding way, conveyed to her to unburden herself of the packs and coverings. Dawn neatly folded the cloth wrappings, placing them on the room's only stone table. Next to that, she laid the water belt across the top of the pack; she touched the water container and looked at the Trader, who watched her intently. "May I," she surprised herself by asking. The Trader's amber eyes flashing with superiority, he nodded, yes. Dawn raised the bottle to her mouth gulping the warm water. It soothed her parched throat and she released a satisfied moan, and even though she could see the Trader's narcissist, self-satisfied expression, she didn't care. She closed her eyes, continuing to drink until she drained the bottle.

Dawn put the empty container back in its holder and returned the Trader's gaze, completely hypnotized by him. She sat on a pillow as instructed and proceeded to remove her boots along with the rest of her clothing, carefully folding each piece and placing them on top of the wrappings. A crazy thought danced around in her mind that she really didn't like being neat, yet she was compelled to be so.

The Trader had a solemn look on his face now, as he clenched her lower arm with his spidery-fingered hand. His fluid eyes stared steadily into hers, his small square nose almost touching her rounded one. She did not flinch as he lowered his head, sniffing her injury. She braced herself for the pain of his bite, but it did not come. Instead, he yanked her toward the cleansing room and directed her to sit down in a stone-carved tub, filled with freshly flowing water. Dawn allowed herself to relax. The water felt good to her bruised, aching, and bloodied body. She leaned back, sinking up to the top of her breasts, being mindful to keep the laceration exposed for the Trader to examine more closely.

Umbra skillfully cleansed the wound in an unusual manner of gentleness. Opening his mouth, he disgorged a sticky black substance, swathing the lesion generously. He was proud of his accomplishment and keeping his servant clean and free of infection would ensure lucrative dealings. She slept while he worked but that didn't bother him. He imagined his two human female servants sleeping side by side in his own chambers back home on Feljoa. Swallowing noisily, he reveled in the idea that his distinction at such a feat would encompass the whole of his planet. Pleased with his work, he laughed cruelly and left his second servant alone in the room.

Trader Umbra put on a long, hooded cloak, untied the door flap, instructed the Dyeckian who awaited him in the passageway to guard the door, letting no one in or out until his return, offering him the reward of touching the human female, how and where he wanted. He stuck a disc on either side of the doorway, activating them with the disc he held in his hand. A foul-smelling, poisonous vapor curtained the opening, and he sneered at his henchman, showing his sharp rows of pearly black teeth. He pulled up his hood so that it shrouded his face and quickly disappeared into the corridor.

The Dyeckian narrowed his red-ringed eyes and gazed at the Trader's venomous fumes that blocked the doorway. He grumbled, moving away from the offensive odor, feeling cheated at his chance for a few extra touches.

Outside on the surface, the dimming red-orange haze of Pik's nightfall was swiftly approaching. Foster grabbed the handle to the trapdoor, flinging it open. A gust of chill air rushed up to meet them. Hank was the first to enter the tunnel; TaChoo, and Foster quietly followed.

XVII

Thorb communicated with Targ. The planet's tendrils connected deep within his brain. *"The children are restless."* Thorb spoke gently. He could feel Targ's discomfort as a physical part of himself and he longed to give Targ ootau. *"They are strong."* Thorb's body pulsed in rhythm with the planets; Targ gathered knowledge from him, so he waited, giving himself freely, exchanging energy, and taking pleasure in the process.

"I have grown nine and they are perfect. They shall journey in the company of Clamora," Targ's voice rumbled.

"Va, Targ," Thorb felt Targ's silky tendrils move slowly through his body caressing and nourishing him as they withdrew, Thorb desired to stay cradled in the vines of the planet but knew the children awaited Targ's decision.

Starshine, Daj and TaChoo's second stood grasping the docking bay landing handrails. *"They ready a ship for us."* Hopeful, he pointed at the closest one to them.

"I can sense the poison that flows in my zaf's veins growing stronger," Po spoke to Starshine. The longer they waited, the more restless and uneasy about his seeder's fading connection became.

"We shall go," Starshine opened his mind to his eight tutals sending out encouragement.

"It shall discomfort Targ," said Moonracer, empathetically.

"Zaf needs much healing," Frox responded, shifting closer to her brother, Po.

Ashruba and Ryla who stood beside the twins, Treya and Coxy, took a step closer to watch a pilot fueling the ship.

Winston, who stood to the right of Starshine, leaned his forearms on the railing. *"I shall pilot my bua's craft."* His tone authoritative, he was gesturing to the newly completed Sunstream II. It sat closest to the docking doors, shining in its entire splendor, smooth, glistening silvery-maroon that would awe any Targian; Winston thought of his father and took courage in being the offspring of the Keeper of the Key. The group unified with Winston; he stood upright and crossed his slender, muscular arms. *"We shall go,"* Winston gave Starshine a nod.

"Va, you shall, Winston," Clamora's voice rang strong, *"but not without me."*

The nine turned to face Clamora. Seeing Thorb behind her, all bowed their heads to both their elders.

"It shall be dangerous, zaf," Winston raised his head.

"Targ has felt your concern and offers his ootau." Thorb spoke kindly, still vibrating from the planet's energy.

The children all looked intently at Thorb. He could sense their eagerness, yet they waited in veneration of him and for his sanction. He smiled, knowing they would have left without comfort from him or Targ, for the pull to restore balance flowed powerfully in their blood. *"Fly well, children of Targ."* Thorb bowed his head, closing his mind to all except Treya. *"Upon your return, you shall dance the Dance of Nar with Foster; Targ takes comfort in you, Treya."* Thorb caught Treya's expression of reverence and accepted the pleasure she sent.

Treya being the first seeded twin of Farstar and Autumn took the mark of distinction to be the chosen mate to Communicator Thorb's jant. Foster had come with TaChoo on many occasions to the growing room, patient and silent, observing her grow and learn, until the day before her release from Targ. Foster had entered the room alone. She had watched Targ entangle him in vines, and Foster had opened his luminous mind to her. She shared his rapture at being one with the planet. That day Targ created a link between them.

As soon as Winston entered the Sunstream II, he took his place as pilot. Po sat next to him in the co-pilot's chair. Starshine stood behind them waiting for Quinni Clamora, the last to enter, and closed the door behind her.

"Let us begin our journey." Clamora sensed the stirrings of anticipation in the children.

"Zaf," Ryla spoke to Clamora, *"remember who it is, piloting this craft."* She grinned as Winston sped out of the docking bay and into the vastness of space.

Autumn sat on the sleeping roll, watching Etta, the small female Rock Dwarf, mix up a tonic for her sickness. This Rock Dwarf would tend to her needs during the high sun rotation, but at low sun rotation, Rory would be her keeper. Autumn hugged her knees wrapping the silken purple robe tighter around her; she rocked gently back and forth, humming a few notes of nothing in particular.

Etta scooped a half finger measure of leaves from the third and final container; her small stubby hands worked the pestle with care, crushing and grinding until a fine powder remained in the mortar. Etta glanced up with a motherly softness when Autumn had started to hum; she knew it was a beginning to Autumn's acceptance of what she had endured. Etta stood up on her chair and lit a vessel of oil on fire; the flames danced across the surface and emitted an odor of musty tomes into the air. She grunted and placed a stand, cradling a stone bowl, over the top of the fire and proceeded to mix the powder and water together in the rapidly heating container.

Autumn rested her head on her knee, still watching Etta. The aroma of decaying wood reached her nose, stimulating a long-forgotten childhood memory. One of her favorite places to play was inside a small thicket of very old woods behind Uncle Zyleon's house. A game of dig and discover kept her occupied for hours. She would dig down into the soft duff soil, building walls and searching for clues of whatever mystery lay beneath.

Smoot opened the heavy wooden door, bringing Autumn out of her reverie. *"It is time for learning,"* he affirmed, amiably.

Autumn cradled her face between her knees. Etta gave a little spat of alarm at Smoot's sudden appearance, but then relaxed and continued to stir the potion.

Smoot gracefully sat down cross-legged in front of Autumn, his back straight as he leaned forward, resting his elbows on his knees. He offered his open palmed hands to her. *"Place your hands on mine,"* he instructed. When she did not respond, he tenderly pushed further into her mind. *"Autumn, we must try again."*

Autumn slowly repositioned herself, mirroring Smoot; she laid her hands, palm down on his. *"Okay,"* with faint sadness, she answered.

Smoot curled his sixth finger of either hand, around Autumn's pinky fingers, and speaking Targian words, intoned *"hesna ga, lef ga, cutra ga, uckri ga."*

"Protect me, bind me, strengthen me, encase me," Autumn repeated as singsong as she could muster. She felt Smoot's energy pass from his hands, into hers; it created a tingling sensation all along and up her arms. The energy moved across her shoulders, flowed down through her body, and returned to her shoulders, entering her mind. Autumn allowed Smoot to reach further into her mind, showing her how to draw energy from her surroundings and into her aura field, to create an Orb of Protection. She breathed deep and slow, her concentration centered in the middle of her brain. A hot prickle crept down her spine, she wanted to let go of Smoot's hands, but his magnetic force held her strong.

"Uckri ga," Smoot closed his eyes and lifted his head, a whisper of a moan on his lips.

Autumn had not until this point, felt such a powerful stream of energy rushing throughout her body. It felt frighteningly good. *"Encase me,"* she repeated, the words surged forth, rocking her with intense force, she reflexively lifted up her chin exposing the soft creaminess of her throat and released a long, low moan. An explosion of red lit up the back of her eyelids, and a current of hot sparks jetted from her base chakra. She opened her eyes and clearly watched the creation of a translucent, ice blue orb encircle them, an iron shield of energy, invisible to the outside world. *"It's wonderful,"* she said, softly.

Smoot lowered his head, taking comfort that Autumn could now protect herself from Trader Umbra and others. He looked upon her, shimmering in this field of armor, and thought of the Queen that grew inside her womb. A sleepy wave of affection drifted over him, and he found himself staring deeply into the golden eyes of Autumn. For a moment, he was entranced with her kom beauty. He could sense her lightly nudging the edges of his mind, sending sprays of warmth into his thoughts. He knew he should not let her go beyond this point, but it was his trevi of knowledge won. Smoot opened his mind to her.

Autumn smiled. *"Copaa rit,"* she thanked him. Smoot's mind was the playground of a caring, savant being. A friend she felt safe with,

"You have protected me amiably," Autumn reached further, into his mind noticing an upward curl of his lips; he was enjoying her investigation.

Suddenly an overwhelming sense of mounting gratitude arose from within her belly, a tiny voice desiring to give in return for his kind attention.

"This child I carry shall be named Mooti in honor of your sheltering love," said Autumn, entranced, and she glimpsed a look of surprise cross Smoot's face. *"Your care is gentle and I desire that you care for Mooti, as you have cared for me."* Autumn continued to shower Smoot with affection until she understood what the child inside her desired, a perfect solution to show her gratefulness — *"Mooti is to be your mate."* She felt warmth happily stir in her womb.

"This is a great ootau you have imparted upon me; I shall accept Mooti when she is grown. Smoot sent an energy stream of his astonished pleasure to Autumn, sensing the minute vibration of the Queen of Pik.

Autumn understood that when the time came for a favor, she had only to ask.

Etta was speaking to them with the sound of frustration in her voice. Smoot had reveled too long, but Autumn had given him the unexpected tribute of being her confidante. *"Copaa rit,"* Smoot slowly withdrew his energy from Autumn, *"ish,"* he gently squeezed Autumn's hands.

"Return," she repeated. The protection orb dematerialized.

Etta handed Autumn her daily cup of potion, growling something under her breath that made Smoot chuckle and bow his head to her. Etta pointed at the door, ordering Smoot to leave. Just as gracefully as he had sat, Smoot stood, inclining his head to Autumn and glided silently out of the room.

Etta urged Autumn to finish the licorice-tasting tonic that she'd had to drink from the day of conception. Rory insisted it was to protect the child's blood from the foulness of Trader Umbra's bane. She licked her lips and handed the cup back for Etta's examination, only this time she seemed agitated and without checking it, hurriedly placed it on the table next to the cooling pots. She grabbed Autumn's hand, grunting and urging her up, wanting her to follow.

Autumn stood, feeling a bit woozy from her experience with Smoot. Despite that, she followed Etta into the cleansing room, noticing her glance around the room as if checking to make sure no one was spying. Etta climbed into the tub of water, waving her hand for Autumn to join her. It made her feel a little funny climbing into the water to stand next to a very small Rock Dwarf, but that soon diminished when Etta slammed a fist into the side of the sandstone wall. Abruptly, the bottom of the tub opened and both of them plunged into a pool of water just below. Autumn, coughing, surfaced in time to see the bottom of the tub slide shut, leaving little light in which to see.

Etta tugged immediately on her sleeve, paddling over to the side of the pool, climbing out of the water and onto the cool floor, grumbling. Autumn couldn't help but laugh, seeing Etta sitting there like that, her thick, copper braid flipped over her head and short, fuzzy beard, dripping wet, and a scowl on her blocky face. Autumn's laughter only caused more grunts and urgent yanking on her hand. "Okay, okay, I'm coming," she said, pulling herself up and out of the pool.

Etta's hairy little hand grasped Autumn's once again, leading her down into the damp coolness of the passageway; water rivulets trickled down the sides of the walls, making soft dripping sounds, rhythmically timed with her water-laden robe, which swished heavily against the floor. As they made their way through the cool duskiness, she thought of how nice it was to be out of her stuffy little room and breathing deeply of the moist air. It felt good, but she was rather curious as to where they were going. It seemed out of character for Etta to take a risk that might lead to Rory's disapproval, unless this was something he planned or even better, maybe it was a rescue. She laughed aloud at this, causing Etta to scowl at her in the dimness, and raise a finger to her bearded lips. "Okay," Autumn whispered, rubbing her neck, feeling for the first time since the healing pool incident, a vibration inside her sensory center. Oh sweet Dawn, she thought sickly, sensing a tiny spread of compassionate warmth in her womb.

After a few minutes of walking and the occasional slip on the gently sloping, stone corridor, Etta stopped before a hole in the wall that emitted a small ray of bright light. She pointed to the hole and peeked through it, then pointed at Autumn, then back at the hole. Autumn sighed and carefully knelt down to eye level with the hole and peeked out. At first, all she could see was the dark orange sunlight sparkling off the city's healing pool and streams. When her vision adjusted, a form came into view that sent shivers convulsing through her. Farstar's luminous diamond eyes stared back at her.

Farstar was in astral form hovering near the ceiling in the room with the highest balcony. He sensed Autumn's energy in the room and took comfort that she was close, Glancing at the table and its clay containers; he perceived the same female Rock Dwarf's signature he had encountered at the gates of the city. Drifting closer to the sleeping fur, Farstar recognized Rory and Smoot's energy impressions, Smoot being the more recent. An innate signal stirred within Farstar's spirit, and he quickly followed the familiar sensation, moving away from the sleeping fur and toward the cleansing room.

As he entered the cleansing room, a stone-grinding rumble, came from the tub and all the water it held emptied through its bottom with a solid splash. Farstar stared, mystified as Etta and Autumn clambered up and out of the hole. Autumn's dark auburn hair fell damp about her shoulders, complementing the water-darkened, royal purple robe she wore. His heart skipped a beat as he looked into her golden eyes. Realizing she could not see him, he desired himself to materialize.

Farstar shimmered into view, stopping Autumn in her tracks. *"Zifla,"* he warmly greeted her, absorbing her beauty and astonishment. *"Angel,"* he said again, and for the first time since her capture, he was able to give her ootau. There was a slight movement from behind Autumn, a quick glance revealed the female Rock Dwarf considering him with an intense contented look on her face. Then abruptly, a tremendous yank pulled him away, slamming him back into his body. Alarmed he braced for danger.

"Come on Farstar, it's time to go to the Eating Hall."

Daj's brilliant green eyes stared into his. Farstar immediately looked away and up at the highest balcony in time to see the door open and Smoot enter. He grabbed Daj's arm, shocking him with the residue of his passion. *"I shall have her back."* Farstar snarled, viciously, returning his stare to the stunned Daj, his eyes huge, round, and black. Comprehending what he had done to Daj, Farstar hastily whispered, *"kolum trey,"* sending a ray of healing into Daj's arm, and shaken mind.

"Ootau oa rit bu kom tutal ~ comfort to you my human friend." He apologized, genuinely.

Daj shook his head. *"That was roo kicking,"* he said, standing up and causing the water to ripple around Farstar's lean, gray chest.

Nacoo covered his thick muscular body, observing the gazes of the slighter Targians that Jax had just left. Jax himself admired Nacoo and once again thought of Clamora being his seeder tek; they had given Targ strong children. *"The Targian females of Pik find you appealing, Nacoo."* Jax gave him a sly smirk.

Nacoo grinned back. *"Think I can ask one of them for a date?"*

"Date," Jax looked puzzled.

"Earth talk for taking comfort with a female," Nacoo draped his large arm over Jax's slender shoulder and headed for the Eating Hall, water glistening on his hair, in the dim orange light of night. *"Is Farstar going to be all right?"* Nacoo asked, with a backward glance at Daj and Farstar.

"I do not know," answering, Jax absorbed the compassionate energy that flowed from this big man.

Farstar followed Daj out of the healing pool, glancing up at the balcony. Autumn's robe clung to her as she stepped down the stairs behind Smoot, her head gracefully turning, searching the grounds. *"Daj, look up at the highest balcony, Smoot escorts Autumn to the Eating Hall."* Farstar sent Daj his unrestrained excitement.

Daj swayed with the force of Farstar's thoughts. Looking up in the direction Farstar indicated. He could just make out two figures moving down the stairs and that both wore the same color purple. *"Farstar, you forget that I have, human eyes."* he reminded him, and picked up their robes of spring-green, spar-thread from beside a tree. *"Here, put this on and Let's go get some tucker and grog,"* Daj said, eyeing Farstar warily.

"Some what," Farstar suddenly wore a curious expression.

"Food and drink," Daj answered, with a jittery chuckle.

Farstar and Daj caught up with Nacoo and Jax at the dark red archway of the Eating Hall. Daj, still a bit tense from the power Farstar had shown, sidled in next to Nacoo. "Aliens," he mumbled, sticking his thumbs through his front belt loops.

Nacoo gave Daj a long scrutinizing look and decided not to ask what had happened.

Urna and Cres led them into a large vaulted room, seating them in ornate, crystal inlaid, kingly chairs, placed around the end of a long, narrow stone-hewn table. The top polished to a mirror finish, reflecting the multi-colored glow lights that lined the center of the table.

Farstar scanned the length of the table, noting the lights were just low enough, enabling a direct line of vision to the head throne. Urna settled in next to Jax and Daj on his right side, directly across from Cres. There were others filtering into the Eating Hall now. The sound of their voices filled the room with a chattering din. Their robes shimmered, splashing a rainbow of color around the reflective, clay-red table.

Farstar quietly observed the small female Rock Dwarf as she climbed up into the second stately chair, to the left of the head of the table. She glanced at Farstar, and he nodded his recognition of her. She shyly looked away and kept her face turned toward the tunnel opening, behind and to the right of the head throne, which bore Rory's shooting-star symbol.

A mixed crew of servers scurried about the table, placing clay bowls filled with wir buds and putja roots before the guests. A gloved, female Dyeckian filled tall, slender, crystal flutes with Dyeckian trepaa wine, being carefully attentive to Nacoo. Nacoo, having found a taste for the wine, drank two glasses quickly. He flashed a brilliant, white smile at Daj, who seemed to be enjoying the wine equally well. On Nacoo's third refill, the empty seat between himself and Cres was no longer empty; a golden robed, Targian female sat elegantly poised.

"Nacoo, it looks as though your date has arrived," Jax chided.

Nacoo emptied his third flute.

An abrupt hush fell over the table as Rory glided in and speaking so all could understand him in their own languages, announced, "I take pleasure that all of you have joined me here, in this fine Eating Hall." He gazed over the crowd, resting his eyes on Farstar. "Tonight we are honored with the presence of my companion — Farstar." Rory lifted his flute filled with the thick, peach-colored trepaa wine, in gesture of a cheer. "Stand with me and take ootau, Farstar," Rory grinned impishly.

Farstar stood, pressing the tips of his fingers firmly on the tabletop, raising his filled flute up and outward toward Rory. "I take comfort my companion." Farstar kept his voice steady, with the same speech translation for all at the table, and sensed Rory's pleasure with him; he brought the flute to his thin gray lips, tilting it back, draining the fluid, as did Rory.

Farstar gazed upon Autumn as she entered through the tunnel opening behind Rory's throne. The hand that held the flute trembled and the server asked him to lower it to the table. He did so, never taking his eyes from his vesp tek.

The gathering of Dyeckians, Targians, and Rock Dwarfs all raised their flutes and loudly expressed their cheerful approval.

Autumn stood in front of her queenly chair with her head inclined, and Smoot at her side.

Rory raised his six-fingered hand, quieting the crowd, and then placing his hand on her shoulder, pronounced, "Now, take ootau with Autumn." He stared fiercely at Farstar. "Incubator of the Queen of Pik," Rory felt desire burn in Farstar and lifted his chin taking in a deep breath of satisfaction. *"Zaqurah, I offer you a few moments with your mate, in return for a korzuku."*

Farstar lost constraint and answered, *"Uc rit trevi, zaqurah."* He shifted his gaze away from Rory's look of triumph and locked eyes with Autumn and in that, fleeting moment felt her essence link with his.

Distracted by Smoot's gentle tug on her arm, directing her to her seat beside Etta, Autumn looked away from Farstar. She quivered inside, wanting to run to him and feel his arms around her. It was almost too much she thought, sitting down. *"G'Day Autumn,"* Daj's slightly drunken but familiar voice sounded in her mind. She looked up noticing for the first time Daj, Jax and Nacoo.

"Hello," she returned, enthusiastically, almost leaping from her chair.

Smoot placed a cool hand on her leg. *"Not yet,"* he said, responding to her connection with the three, bowing his head. Then he made his way to the empty, regal-looking chair directly across from Autumn, to the right hand side of Rory.

Etta patted Autumn's hand, giving her a sympathetic smile.

Jax, Daj, and Nacoo felt an unusually powerful energy emanating from Farstar as he unflinchingly held up another full flute of wine. "I take great comfort with Autumn, Incubator of the Queen of Pik." Farstar declared and being able, sent Autumn his passion.

"As do we," Jax chimed in and everyone at the majestically adorned, banquet table, cheered.

Autumn blushed, lowering her head, only to feel Rory's cool fingers lift her chin. She closed her eyes, wishing this were all just a dream and wanting to be back on Earth with the team, working, playing, and just being. *"Rory,"* she said, feeling his cool fingers slide up along the curve of her jaw to her ear. *"I would like to visit with Daj and Nacoo."* Autumn took a short breath and opened her eyes. Rory's face softened with her acknowledgement of his touch; Autumn hoped that was a positive answer and offered him a curt smile.

Farstar clenched his hand, down by his side, observing Rory's tender caress of Autumn's face.

Rory turned his gaze to Farstar, absorbing his companion's unfettered, almost human, emotion. "Let us eat," he said, glancing around at his lavishly set table and at the many cheerful guests. He raised his crystal glass, inclined his head, and sat down.

Another round of supporting cheers and celebratory laughter for the unborn Queen went up around the table.

Autumn felt the familiar vibration of her child within her womb, and she laid a hand across her belly. *"Oh, little Mooti,"* she cooed. *"This is all for you."* She looked up into Rory's strangely curious face.

"She speaks to you," warmly, Rory asked.

"From the day of conception," Autumn answered.

"Mooti is a very good name," he glanced at Smoot with a wily smirk on his face.

"Rory — about my friends..." she tilted her head toward the end of the long, glittering table.

"They are very fond of you; I can see their colors of affection brighten when they look upon you." Rory responded to Autumn and glanced at Smoot, sensing his amusement with the men. *"There shall be a visit."* Rory followed Autumn's expression as she turned her head and smiled ecstatically at her colleagues. He sensed their joy at seeing one another but felt displeased by the fiercely ardent energy exchange between Autumn and Farstar. It triggered a raw, vicious emotion in him to drag her away. Instead, with condescending control, he reached over and

with mild force turned her head toward him. *"Do not linger,"* he said, dangerously low.

"Yes," Autumn answered, frustrated. She glanced at Smoot, who kept an open connection with her, per Rory's instructions, and caught a flicker of concern within his steady, crystal gaze. Autumn felt the solid pat of Etta's hand on hers. The small Rock Dwarf offered her a flute of trepaa wine she had mixed with some potion. Etta's presence was calming, and she took the drink.

The table swarmed with activity as the servers set dishes with a variety of food before the guests. The clinking of glasses and eating utensils, laughter, and an occasional belch filled the atmosphere.

Nacoo was on his fifth flute and appeared to have grown a permanent smile; he looked at Daj with his short, messy, straight black hair and shining green eyes. Nacoo held his flute, tipping it slightly toward him. "No oilskin tonight," Nacoo boomed.

Daj clinked Nacoo's glass. "Have to look my best," he winked and finished his fifth flute. "This is some really good wine," he hiccupped. "We'll have to take some back to Earth."

The female Dyeckian, not letting this opportunity slip by, said, "For a touch." She smiled sweetly at Daj, stroking the wine container with gloved fingers.

"Right," Daj looked into her red-ringed eyes and could have sworn he seen them getting redder.

Jax laughed enjoying Daj's bewilderment. *"She is eager to trade you wine, for a touch. It is how you buy from a Dyeckian."*

"That's just bloody wicked," Daj slurred, still mesmerized by her reddening eyes.

"Komi ~ humans," Farstar added to the conversation.

"Cheers," Nacoo rumbled and downed his sixth flute, eyeing Daj to see if he was keeping up.

"Zaqurah," Rory mind touched Farstar.

Farstar looked up to see Smoot offering his hand to Autumn in gesture to follow. *"Va,"* he responded, watching as Smoot led Autumn away from the table. He tightened his jaw.

"Mel li ga," Rory stood and quietly glided into the tunnel that opened behind his throne.

"Jax, I am bid to korzuk with my zaqurah." He looked into his tutal's eyes and then at Nacoo and Daj. Giving Jax a fleeting smile, he said, *"vah,"* and without hesitation left the table.

Nacoo and Daj, blurry eyed, watched Farstar silently leave them. "How about we get a bottle of wine and take it back to our room, Nacoo." Daj's head wobbled as he spoke.

"How about two," Nacoo's smile increased.

"Right," Daj hiccupped, "Hey red eyes, what does it cost for two bottles of wine?" He straightened his posture and reached to tip up the hat that wasn't there. The Dyeckian female's eyes burned solid red and spoke a single word Daj did not understand. "What did she say," her eyes captivated him.

"Two," Jax chuckled.

"Cheap trade," Nacoo's robust laughter filled the air.

"Jax, go ahead and tell her it's a trade." He sat back in his decorous chair giving Nacoo, a drunken arrogant, smirk.

Nacoo leaned forward, placing his large arms on the table, teasing to get a better look.

Jax enjoyed their festiveness and set the deal with the Dyeckian female.

She groaned in anticipation and hurriedly removed her gloves, gaining the attention of all the other female Dyeckians, left serving in the Eating Hall. Her fingertips made contact with either side of Daj's warm facial skin just below his eyes, which seemed glued to hers. The female Dyeckian moaned, slowly sliding her fingers across his cheekbones and down his stubble-haired jaw line. His breath was hot on her hands and surprisingly, Daj reached up and touched her face, sending her into near ecstasy. A loud gasp from the other Dyeckian females echoed around the table. Their eyes were large and glowing red. The female Dyeckian allowed Daj to explore her face, trembling uncontrollably under his touches and she wondered what he would want in return for such pleasure.

Daj couldn't resist the urge to continue touching and chuckled at the way she reacted, with a violent shiver, and a soft, low purring sound. Her eyes became a deep sunset red and her skin a cool slate; he was entranced. Daj slid his fingertips over her dark, alien lips, down and under her oval chin, and up under her shadowy hairline, then in his intoxicated state he pulled her down to his lips and kissed her.

There was a thunderous cry around the table, and Jax pulled Daj away from the female. *"In Dyeckian custom touches are like gold to you on Earth. You have just paid for more than she can offer. I suggest you request her personal service so that she shall not be shunned by the others,"* Jax said sternly.

"Way to go buddy," Nacoo shook his head, leaned back, and crossed his arms. "Sheesh, you are truly remarkable," he half laughed.

Daj looked apologetically at the female Dyeckian now holding the chair arm, catching her breath. "Talk to her Jax," Daj stammered over his words, and watched as the female shakily put her gloves back on, avoiding his eyes but nodding to Jax then hurriedly disappeared into the cluster of waiting female Dyeckians.

Urna and Cres had made a discreet departure during Daj's trade, along with many others, leaving the Eating Hall nearly empty. The Targian female sitting next to Nacoo remained. *"Shish,"* Jax mind touched her, pleased to find her mind open.

"Shish," she bowed her head to him.

"I am Tamara; Rory asks that you take ootau with my services," she lightly breezed across his mind.

The Dyeckian female returned with two containers of wine, handing them to Daj with a bit more self-control. Daj took the bottles, smiled drunkenly, and stood wavering for a moment. "Thanks," he nodded to the female, still waiting to be of service. Daj looked her up and down then back at Nacoo. "If I was still on Earth, I'd..."

"Take her back to my place," Nacoo interrupted, raising his eyebrows at the Dyeckian female, sending both men into a fit of inebriated laughter.

"Yesss," Daj said, gasping for air. The whole idea seemed incredible to him. "Just call us space tramps," he said in a singsong voice.

"Argh, that was terrible," Nacoo stumbled away from the table meeting Daj by the exit and resting an arm over his shoulders. "Shall we," he bowed throwing his arm out in a, "you first," motion, nearly toppling them. Another fit of laughter broke out between them, as they continued on their way, oblivious to the three who followed them.

XVIII

Alone, TaChoo glided toward the Dyeckian standing guard outside the trapped doorway. As TaChoo drew closer, she could see the eerie red shine of the Dyeckians eyes in the dim glow of the tunnel. Enticingly, she loosened her wrap, hearing him grunt as she let it fall to the floor. Teasing him with a flirtatious smile, she guided the spar-thread wrap over the top of his buckled sandal. The cloth snagged on the buckle just as she had desired it to. TaChoo looked down in feigned surprise and in his tongue, said, "It seems that I am caught." She made a tinkling sound. "Could you release me," she whispered seductively to the Dyeckian, leading him into a trade. She lowered herself from her levitated position, to the ground with a soft whooshing of her robe.

He rumbled, "For a touch."

TaChoo stared into his reddening eyes and smiled shyly. "Where," she questioned.

The Dyeckian pulled off his gloves. "Your throat," he said, hungrily.

TaChoo unwound the wrap from her head and neck, exposing the pale gray flesh under her long, silver spider-silk hair.

The Dyeckian pushed her hair aside, eyes blazing, and touched her tender flesh. In the moment of his delight, Foster hit him with a boreal, an orb of energy that knocked the Dyeckian unconscious. TaChoo rapidly untangled herself from him and hurriedly walked over to stand by Foster and Hank at the doorway; all three of them produced an Orb of Protection and walked into Trader Umbra's room.

Hank found Dawn sleeping inside the tub of continually flowing water, in the cleansing room. He pulled out his blowpipe and dart, took aim, and made a perfect, deep, hit into the black, salve-covered bite wound.

Dawn gasped looking about wild-eyed, grasping at the air then the sides of the tub. She tried to sit up, and water splashed to the floor. Bewildered, she searched for the Trader but her eyes focused instead,

on a slender gray face. She loosened her hold and stared at the face
— she was so tired — so very tired. She gazed with heavy eyelids into
Hank's compassionate, diamond eyes. "Who are you," she whispered,
before the effects of the egmur kicked in and she fell into a dreamless
sleep.

Hank quickly bundled her up in his arms, surrounding her in his
Orb of Protection. "*Jist vek*," he kissed her bruised forehead and
swiftly moved out of the cleansing room.

"*Take the pack.*" Foster draped the backpack over Dawn's
unconscious body.

"*Ne ootau tutal, we shall obtain the Trader's black blood.*" TaChoo
bowed her head to Hank, and followed him immediately through the
doorway.

"*Travel well,*" Foster sensed Hank's deep unease as he guarded his
speedy retreat.

"*We must leave this tunnel before Trader Umbra returns.*" TaChoo levitated
passed the Dyeckians still body. "*He shall not be of good reason or humor.*"
TaChoo was grateful that the retrieval of Hank's seeder mate was so
swift and simple. Trader Umbra would not be so easy to deal with.

The two traveled downward for a few minutes, silently passing
closed doorways and a single Rock Dwarf snoring loudly under the
luminescence of an orange glow light. They heard the sound of water
and muffled voices as they rounded a corner. Cautiously they entered
into a large underground cave; a misty waterfall flowed into a small,
naturally formed pool, and in it sat Daj and Nacoo, each with a container
in their hand. TaChoo smiled. "*Shish, Daj,*" she mind touched him.

"Shhh..." he lifted the bottle to his mouth taking a long swig of
Dyeckian wine. " I think I'm hearing things," Daj whispered, with
exaggeration.

TaChoo's chiming laughter filled Daj's head.

Nacoo swirled the little bit of wine he had left in his bottle. "I
didn't hear a thing," Nacoo laughed, resting his head against the edge
of the stone. "This feels great."

Daj lowered his now empty bottle and blurrily looked about their
surroundings. "I think I'm hallucinating." Making an unflattering
sound, he stood clumsily, splashing Nacoo.

Nacoo caught the surprise in Daj's voice and heaved himself out of the water. His eyes followed Daj as his friend staggered toward the far tunnel, where he eyed Foster's silver hair fluttered in the breeze, caught up by the roiling mist. "Hello," he boomed, waving a hand, noticing that TaChoo stood beside him.

Daj reached TaChoo, swaying drunkenly in a sopping-wet robe in front of her, not quite trusting his eyes; he touched her face, just to make double sure he was not seeing things. "You are real," he slurred, awkwardly folding her up in his cool sogginess, saturating her robe. "Did you know they have real Rock Dwarfs here?" He asked, his dripping black hair falling in his eyes.

Nacoo shook Foster's hand erratically and grinned at TaChoo rocking in Daj's arms. "We have a room," Nacoo waved an unsteady arm, causing Foster to duck. "Come on, it's over here," he rattled, cheerfully, trying unsuccessfully not to stagger toward a doorway on the other side of the vaulted grotto.

Foster stepped in behind the highly inebriated Daj, who clung to his sister for support, as they followed the somewhat unsteady Nacoo; he rather enjoyed the momentary comical experience of the two komi, and he sensed TaChoo did also. *"Be careful rah that you do not get stepped on,"* Foster said, chuckling at TaChoo's whimsical smirk.

Jax met them with a welcoming smile at the covered entranceway to the room, beckoning them inside. Tamara and the female Dyeckian sat beside one another on a sleeping fur, cups of tea in their hands. *"Ne ootau,"* Jax waved a long slender arm toward an empty sleeping fur. *"I shall get you some appo."*

The room was very warm, and the heat went straight to Nacoo's head; he fell to his knees, arms at his sides, in front of Tamara and the female Dyeckian. Then doing a funny little wobble, he tipped forward, landing with his face on the pillow between them, unconscious and snoring. The two females beamed at one another.

Daj let go of TaChoo and crumpled into a pile on the opposite sleeping fur. "Come here," he made a pathetic attempt to grab TaChoo's fingers before he also found his way into the world of insensibility.

Jax handed Foster a cup of warm sprig of loc tea. It felt good to his cold hands. *"Farstar is not with you."*

"Rory asked for ootau in a korzuk," Jax handed TaChoo a cup and sat down beside her on the sleeping fur, his mind open.

"Farstar shall comply with Rory's trevi," TaChoo stated, sipping her steamy appo.

"He shall comply to be near Autumn," Jax said, empathetically.

"Autumn is conceived with the Queen of Pik, before korzuk?" Tamara asked, aloud, incredulously.

The female Dyeckian tore her eyes away from the sleeping Daj and looked at the group, a twisted smile on her lips.

Foster and TaChoo exchanged curious glances.

Jax sighed. "Va, Tamara, it seems Rory shared aresh with Autumn to keep her from succumbing to a Trader's venom." Jax spoke audibly, giving a warning look to the female Dyeckian.

The Dyeckian female shifted uncomfortably and warily eyed the door; she did not intend to trade with a Trader.

Tamara inhaled sharply.

Jax glanced at her, then at the wet-robed, thunderously snoring Nacoo. *"Rory seeded Farstar's kom tek to carry this child for him. Farstar honors his zaqurah with a korzuk and the giving of his mate as the Incubator of the Queen of Pik. It is a new Targian age. I shall remain concerned for them all,"* Jax said, wondering how the child could live without Targ's nourishment and how Farstar and Rory could have korzuk without the planet joining them together.

Foster nodded perceptively to Jax, sensing his uncertainty. *"It is so between companions, whatever the conditions."* He finished his tea and continued to speak, *"we track the same Trader, who infected Dawn and stays a search for Autumn. His first marked. We shall..."* he paused, *"extract his black blood."* Foster spoke, venomously, walked over to the small table, refilled his cup, and sat on a pillow propped up against the wall.

"The same Trader," Jax questioned.

"When we arrived on Dyeck seeking knowledge, King Tri roughly distracted Trader Umbra from Dawn, telling us they had observed Autumn for trade of Ockoraerion powder." Foster scowled. *"After Dawn was taken Hank kept his mind open, linking with her, allowing us to trace Trader Umbra's energy signature to his ship."* He stared at the drunken men and with a flare of his slender, six fingered hand, he chuckled, *"komi."*

"Targ knows of this?"

"Va, Thorb has informed him."

"Is Rory to be taken to Farth?"

"Av," Foster said, with a sympathetic glance at Nacoo.

Jax clicked the rim of his teacup with a dark fingernail. *"Dawn is well?"*

"Ishag nes ootau li Hank ~ she takes comfort with Hank," TaChoo answered.

Tamara stood, her golden robe shining. "We must inform Rory of Trader Umbra."

Jax inclined his head and spoke to the female Dyeckian, "Daj shall sleep until the sun brightens. Wait for him to call upon you." She looked relieved and hurried to catch up to Tamara, not wanting to be alone in the tunnels.

"We shall rest with our inebriated tutals," Foster chuckled, scooping up a handful of alm nuts.

Winston landed the Sunstream II beside the smaller Targian ship on Pik's sandy yellow surface, with the accomplished style of a well-travelled pilot. Clamora climbed out of the ship and hovered an inch above the torrid sand. She waited while the nine readied themselves before their travel into the city. Ashruba, Daj's first-born, scaled down the ladder, followed by Autumn's twins Treya and Coxy. *"Mita trath ta bir rit efen ri resh ~ be mindful of how you spend your energy,"* Clamora warned the children.

Po's face appeared in the ships doorway, *"ze aw lyx, Quinni ~ do not fear, Elder ~ Targ fli yoxa wa vos ~ Targ has taught us well."* His voice rang clear and rich with an ancient courage.

Starshine, Ryla, and Frox trailed Po out of the ship and out into the arid atmosphere of Pik.

"Zaqurah," Winston tossed an octagon-sided, orchid-colored crystal to Moonracer. *"Kav ti reh rit ~ this is for you,"* he said to him, before they descended to the surface.

Moonracer felt the energy of the Absorption Spirit Crystal grow hot in his palm. *"Kav ti Dox Minoni Tuvah's Ackon Parge Gamo ~ this is Olden Communicator Tuvah's Absorption Spirit Crystal."* He felt his own, still moist and developing, Absorption Spirit Crystal, buried deep in his brain vibrate in rhythm with Tuvah's hardened Absorption Spirit Crystal. *"Why do you give this to me?"* Moonracer inquired. Tuvah's Absorption Spirit Crystal melted into his hand, spreading its fiery arrows of power up his arm.

"You shall know when the time comes, companion," Winston picked up his pack, *"wex wa ep,"* he said, anticipation in his voice.

When everyone was gathered, Clamora spoke. *"You must use caution in seeking the Trader. Be careful you do not allure him for he shall find a way to release his venom in you."* Clamora's sharp-sighted eyes picked up a movement coming over the top of the heat-waved dune. *"His black blood is the tonic we seek; do not spill it,"* she commanded, observing the shimmering figure, start down the sandbank. *"Ne ootau in the city, learn, and be wary, jant's and cula's ta Targ..."* Clamora trailed off, inclining her head, to the nine then rapidly propelled forward, toward the advancing shape.

Hank's arms ached from carrying Dawn, but he refused to release his hold on her even when Clamora and the nine reached him.

"You are a great comfort to see," Hank opened his mind and released his protection energy orb.

"Uc rit puta oa ga ~ as you are to me," Clamora touched his tense arm, sending healing energy through him.

"Copaa rit," he thanked her, *"Foster and TaChoo are within the tunnels. They seek Trader Umbra."* Hank transferred a visual image to her of the trapdoor at the top of the mesa.

"Let me carry my dutom for you, Bua," Po shared comfort with his father and for his seeder.

"I must be the one she sees upon awakening," Hank said. He rested a moment while Winston opened the access door, belonging to the smaller ship.

"It shall give her ootau." Hank painfully shifted Dawn's, sleeping, perspiration-drenched body, over his shoulder, so that they could ascend into the ship. He gently laid her down on the sleeping pillows in the pilot's cabin and kissed her forehead with quivering lips. *"Vuel, jist vek ~ sleep, small one."* Hank's muscles trembled from their over-exertion, but he made his way to the door, poking his face out of the opening.

The group looked at him with anxious stares.

"She rests and so must I," Hank breathed heavily.

"We are here to bring the komi back and search for Trader Umbra," Clamora answered.

The nine looked around at one another and reached a silent decision.

"Frox and I shall take ootau with you," Po said, feeling the strong pull to comfort his seeders. Frox agreed and followed her nua up into the ship.

Clamora watched the door close. *"Pah oa rit,"* she said, as she and the seven began their trek to the city of Pik.

"Peace to you," Ashruba repeated, sending ootau to her wog sy tek, Po and Frox, her wog sy zaqurah. It was their first separation; she glanced at Starshine, Po's younger vesp zaqurah, and Moonracer, Frox's older vesp tek, with empathy.

They acknowledged her glance and continued along with a new sense of mounting anticipation. *"The Olden Ones spoke with great reverence of the separation time, when Targians migrated to Earth. We shall honor this separation and be Targ's strength as he intended with our creation."* Moonracer said, touching his palm where Olden Communicator Tuvah's Absorption Spirit Crystal had embedded itself so comfortably.

Inside the ship, Hank sat in a stupor beside Dawn. Po and Frox readied cu appo to aid in strengthening their dutoms, when they awoke. A sense of expectation developed between Po and Frox; it was the first time that they would administer healing, a test of true ability and ascendancy bred into them.

Farstar leaned against a stone-carved balustrade that rested beneath one of the Mesa's many ledges. An updraft from the city below wafted at his silken robe. Both he and Rory sipped a Targian brew of appo, the tea of korzuk. Farstar let his bare six-toed feet touch the polished sandstone floor, as he walked back into Rory's extensive library of writings and artifacts from around the known galaxies. He scanned the room, noting that Rory had carefully placed objects from Targ and Earth side by side on a shelf by themselves. One of the objects, Autumn's hairbrush, still glowed with her energy signature.

Rory studied his companion. The seven crescent moons that lined his jaw, each sparkling in their corresponding colors to the Targian moons, stood out against his pale gray skin. *"For thousands of Earth years we Targians have gathered knowledge for Targ. Our venturesome visit of late has become a prophecy fulfilled."* Rory refilled both teacups and motioned for Farstar to sit on one of the large fur pillows neatly placed about the room. Farstar chose one in the center of the round library, and Rory took comfort on the pillow in front of him. *"Komi are frail creatures as I have experienced."* Rory stared steadily into Farstar's eyes, sensing his unease. *"They are so easily manipulated with thought frequency, yet Targ requires their density to continue a sharing of aresh with us."* Rory placed his cup on the floor beside him.

"Uc rit roz ~ as you have," Farstar responded, starting to feel the tea's warmth spread through him.

"Uc ew roz ~ as we have, zaqurah," Rory corrected, and bowed his head. *"You were to freely, have given me, the sharing of Autumn, before korzuk, but Trader Umbra's dishonesty fell upon me.* Rory sighed, regretfully, *"Our aresh now grows inside her womb; the cells of the Queen Child communicate with her and link all our aresh, even in part Trader Umbra's essence."*

Farstar clamped his teeth tightly together.

"The Queen Child is gaining in Targian and kom wisdom. Already she has vast knowledge of many worlds. She shall rule Pik with insight and strength." Rory hesitated, *"I ask that you stand by my side zaqurah, let us create a new world,"* he added exuberantly, holding out his hands, palms facing Farstar.

Farstar placed his palms against Rory's, and their joining began. *"As we are companions, I shall stand beside you."* Farstar agreed, knowing that Rory spoke the truth, for Targ had not linked Rory with a mate. Hence, in being Rory's zaqurah, it fell upon him to allow the sharing of Autumn's essence and their seeding.

A current of crackling air began to whirl about them, and Farstar plunged into the vaults of Rory's mind. Rory conceded, and in return, Farstar allowed his companion to take comfort in the deep recesses of his mind.

Sparks of kinetic energy formed around their bodies, until a small stable vortex was established, leaving the two inside a hollow of space, unseen and unheard by the outside world, a shared sacred space. Light strings of particle interaction penetrated one another's neural systems, their thoughts connecting, bubbles of memory being played out, moving them through the vast interplay of their lives.

Farstar began to experience Rory's sense of loss, when he had failed to return with him, on their last trade trip to Dyeck. Rory had become accustomed to King Tri's crafty ways of trading and soon found he was in a position that triggered his search for Targians eager to assist him in moving goods, and touch trading. When his extended lapse from linking with Targ began to make him feel more confident that he could live away from the planet, Targ had sensed his change and started to make it hard for him and the others to gather wares and nourishment, desiring them back in his vines.

King Tri had laughed at Rory and told him of the Traders dealings with the Ockoraerions. King Tri had said he could supply him with a powder that would create a barrier between Targ and Rory, and those wishing to be independent of Targ. By Rory's acceptance of this, the Traders gained a more secure holding in the dissenting Targian trade. Rory then needed to find a home for his rapidly expanding faction. He offered his Targian cohorts the essential nourishment of Targ, the Dyeckians his touches, freely, and his personal favorite, he offered the Rock Dwarfs, healing and crystals for satisfying their lust for gems, in trade for tunneling and carving out homes, for those who wished to live on Pik. Rory was true to his word and gained the respect of all Pik's inhabitants.

Rory had kept a continual eye on Farstar, knowing of Targ's plans to reconnect Kandoria and the group of komi he had chosen. The night when Targ's selected group went to Earth, for implantation of the frequency crystals in the komi, he watched Farstar dance with Autumn around the bonfire. After Farstar's departure, he had probed Autumn's mind and implanted a part of his own frequency into the crystal. Soon after, he began to experience human emotion, balanced only by his Targian heritage. It was a feeling he desired to impart with his zaqurah, to share in the wonders he was learning. The longer his separation from Farstar, the more agitated it made him, soon he devised a way, once more, to have Farstar by his side, and the sharing of the kom female.

Rory and Farstar embraced this sacred companion's voyage, exchanging with one another the missing time between them. Sensing

Farstar's devotion to their powerful camaraderie profoundly pleased Rory and for a moment caused a ripple in their magnetic thought field. Targ held no sway over this korzuk but without the planet's sustenance, grounding their energy, it was a new phenomenon. Both aliens became acutely aware, entering together into a lucid state, a field of transparency where their minds blended with their bodies of light, peaceful, and loving sensations undulated through this new fantastical, spiritual realm.

Farstar felt another emotional ripple come from Rory. He wrestled with the impression, trying to curb its energy, pulling back and away from Rory as he did so. An orb of multi-colored light began to shine between them, separating their minds and astral bodies. He felt Rory's mind grasp at him, but Farstar had begun his descent back into the physical world. The orb of light continued to grow, surrounding them and completing the transference back into the warmth of the library. Farstar stared into Rory's shining eyes, their palms still pressed against each other's, a twitch of a smile played across Rory's lips and he knew they had accomplished a never before, complete, joining without Targ. Farstar trembled with the strangeness and felt the same tremble exchange through Rory's hands.

"Zaqurah," Rory spoke after the vibrations eased. *"I shall brew fresh moc appo."* He slowly lowered his hands, but did not immediately stand.

A moment of triumphant harmony lingered between them.

"I did not know we could reach such a great exchanging of spirit." Farstar stood without hurry, as did Rory.

"I have long hoped for this day." Rory pulled a sapphire container from a shelf, *"I did not trevi to return."* He scooped a handful of moc tealeaves out of the jar and tossed them into a pot of simmering water. *"You are strong, zaqurah. I felt you pull me out of the depths and ground us back to this world."*

Farstar sighed, *"It has only been a short while since the planet entered me."* He felt Rory waver. *"I shall miss Targ,"* he said, somberly, and from the balcony, Farstar looked down upon the city of Pik.

"Drink this and then, return to your room. I shall have someone call upon you for your visit with Autumn." Rory handed Farstar a cup; *"Our journey begins*

anew." They stood in silence, Pik's sun now spreading bright-orange rays of light throughout the quieted city.

Umbra growled, recognizing the scents of the three Targians who had brought the second human female to King Tri's mound. He brutally kicked the unconscious Dyeckian as he passed by, his foul mood increasing with each step he took. Umbra snapped his teeth upon entering the sleeping room, knowing the female was gone, along with his gear. Enraged, fists clenched, he catapulted back into the tunnel, viciously attacking the Dyeckians still body with such force it slammed the Dyeckian up against the stone tunnel wall.

He sniffed the air, seething with rage at whomever he should track, the two that went in the direction of the grotto, or the one that took his servant. He pulled up the hood of his cloak, deciding to retrieve his servant first. That would be the simplest and wisest choice. With a flare of his cape, Trader Umbra started back up the tunnel to the stairs leading to the outside world. The sound of dripping water blunted his footfalls as he stalked through the passageway; keeping an eye open for hidden crevices and sealed doorways that the Rock Dwarfs made sure there were plenty of, he could use their knowledge of such craftiness and made a note to make a couple of them his servants.

The stairs were damp and slippery, causing him to slow his pace. He thought back too observing the first human female during the gathering at the Eating Hall. He licked a small bit of drool collecting at the corner of his mouth, remembering her taste. He'd had a perfect view of the table from the cranny in which he'd hidden. The human males were amusing in their drunken state but he was agitated by the amount of protection the female human was given. He had known Rory would be on the lookout for him, so quietly in his hidden crevice, he began to formulate a plan for securing the first human female aboard his ship.

Now his plan would take more time. He made a guttural noise in his throat. Abruptly, the hair on his body stood on end and he ceased movement to listen — he heard a slight scuffing sound, a sound of rustling cloth. Quickly he studied the area, just a few steps away he discovered a fissure big enough for him to disappear into, and like a shadow in the dark, he was gone.

"Bua is not far away," Coxy mind touched her twin, Treya.

"Va," Treya agreed.

As the group passed the cleft, into which Trader Umbra had vanished, a wave of disquiet passed through them. Clamora stopped moving and reached out with her mind, penetrating the walls around them, tuning into the dense resonant vibration of Trader Umbra. *"It is Trader Umbra's signature,"* she confirmed, *"Remember this Trader's energy imprint."* Clamora felt a quaking like leaves on a tree course through the children as they absorbed Trader Umbra's frequency signature.

"He is too far away to mind touch." Winston placed a slender six-fingered hand against the wall next to the opening. *"Shall we follow?"* he asked, peering into the crevice.

"Traders are cunning and brutal. We shall first go into the city and seek knowledge from the Rock Dwarfs, originators of the warrens," Clamora answered, descending the stairs.

"Quinni," Moonracer glided up to Clamora's side. *"The impressions I have received from my dutoms shall aid us."* The passageway curved gently to the right at the end of the stairs. *"My blood surges in cadence with the Ancient Warrior's song,"* Moonracer whispered in her mind.

Clamora gave him a knowing look. They slowed their pace as they passed Trader Umbra's venom-laced curtain and the bloodied Dyeckian. She stopped and probed his mind, feeling for the damage done. The wound on his head, she decided, needed healing. Dropping to her knees, she placed a hand on the Dyeckians injured brow but before she placed her second hand, Ryla gently pushed her away.

"Save your strength, Zaf," Ryla inclined her head to her dutom and began healing the Dyeckian.

Starshine moved closer to Ryla. *"Do not awaken him,"* he spoke directly to her. *"Sleep shall keep him company,"* he said, looking upon the Dyeckian, impassioned with disdain.

Ashruba felt her nua's wave of emotion and gently touched his shoulder. *"Bua's blood is strong in you."*

Treya levitated up beside Clamora. *"Come, let us continue,"* she said, regarding her with reverence.

Clamora resumed the lead down the cool, slight slope of the tunnel and thought of the children; they were keen and strong with a taste for truth. She also had felt Starshines" acute kom expression and wondered about the power and capability of this new Targian race. The sound of moving water resonated throughout the tunnel as they swiftly moved deeper into the widening passage.

Winston glided silently up beside his mother; his slender, muscular arms glistened with the dampness of the air, *"Zaf, you have naught to wonder. Targ commands our hearts just as he charges yours."* The tunnel opened into a vaulted room, glow lights lit the area with an array of colors; a cascading waterfall spilled down over smooth, water-worn stone, creating a fine mist above the naturally formed pool. *"Let us continue,"* Winston said, eyeing the room across the grotto. Clamora nodded and moved away from him. He shivered when his bare feet touched the cold stone but he desired to feel its vibrations and stepped down upon the first of the three, jasper-red steps, which circled the bowl-shaped depression.

Coxy, Winston's linked mate watched him as he passed close to the spray, lifting his face to its wetness, the dark streaks in his hair shining. *"You amuse me,"* she mind touched him.

"It is unlike Targ," Winston responded, thoughtfully, and maneuvered the steps up to the wide ledge to the doorway that everyone now stood close too. He opened his mind, penetrating beyond the walls and smiled, *"Bua is inside."*

Clamora trembled as she gently pulled back the door flap; it was the first time since his trip to Farth that she would be so near to him. She looked around the small room. TaChoo rested next to a drooling Daj, Foster was in a stupor, looking quite fragile compared to Nacoo's large frame, and Jax was suddenly touching her face. *"Jax,"* she said, startled.

Ryla responded to the alarm and with a lightning-fast reflex, grasped Jax's wrist. For a moment, the two stood staring at one another, Ryla then bowed her head releasing her grasp. *"Forgive me, Quinni Jax,"* she apologized.

Jax nodded and with a slight bow made a sweeping motion with his hand for everyone to enter. Foster and TaChoo awoke immediately;

Daj and Nacoo did not. *"Komi seem to enjoy Dyeckian wine,"* Jax explained, grinning at the children.

Ashruba sat beside Daj to apply healing, but TaChoo stopped her. *"Let them sleep,"* she said to everyone.

Foster raised himself to a standing position, his long silver hair slid across his silken robe. Treya felt her heart speed up as she watched him move gracefully to the table and pour appo from the warming pot. *"Quinni Foster,"* she spoke shyly to him, *"may I assist you?"*

Foster eyed her with clandestine humor. *"Va,"* he answered gently, handing her a cup to give to Clamora.

"Copaa rit," Clamora thanked Treya.

"Thorb has sent us encouragement," said Foster inquisitively, *"but only seven of the nine are with you."*

"We encountered Hank just after landing; he was in great need of rest. Po and Frox stayed with him at the ship to aid in Dawn's recovery. " Clamora sipped her tea. *" On the way through the tunnel, we passed Trader Umbra's recent impression; he shadowed into the bowels of the stone and I dared not follow."* She opened her mind to everyone but locked eyes with TaChoo. *"We shall ask the aid of the Rock Dwarfs."*

Ryla sat beside Nacoo studying his black curls then looked up at Winston who seemed just as enthralled with his seeder. *"Nua, you have much of him in you,"* she admired.

Winston curled his lips and took the cup of appo Treya offered him. *"He is much larger and darker than I,"* he said, contemplating his arm. He laughed, Ryla laughed with him.

"There is a female Rock Dwarf given to care for Autumn and protect the incubating Queen of Pik." Jax responded to Clamora.

Coxy, Treya, and Moonracer stared at Jax, confirming their sense of the danger that surrounded the unborn child, growing in their kom dutom's womb.

"This child shall be an initiate to Pik," Jax sighed.

"What of Farstar," Clamora asked.

"Rory has asked for a korzuku," Jax paused, *"a joining without Targ."*

"Farstar shall comply," TaChoo sipped her appo and looked at Daj.

Po glanced at Starshine, *"I would honor my zaqurah with a korzuku, if it was his desire."*

"I would comply," Starshine inclined his head.

A gentle and quiet understanding fleeted through the Targians as they absorbed one another's thoughts.

"I believe," Daj cleared his pasty throat, wiping at the dried spittle around his lips, "that Farstar will remain loyal to Targ." He rasped thickly, sitting up, leaning so far forward that his head almost touched the sleeping fur between his knees, "urgh — bloody 'ell, what kicked me?"

Ashruba touched his forehead. *"Kolum trey, Bua,"* she spoke softly.

Daj looked up into the scintillating eyes of his daughter, dumbstruck by her presence.

"Seems you have captivated our Bua's attention rah," Starshine said to his sister and sipped his appo to cover his smirk.

Daj leapt to his feet, bear hugging Starshine, which sent the tea splashing over Nacoo's bare arm. *"My son,"* Daj croaked, hardly believing what he was saying, he pushed the astonished Starshine back away from him to get a better look then pulled Ashruba to her feet and hugged them both. "I thought I was dreaming," Daj swayed, still feeling the affects of the Dyeckian wine, even with Ashruba's healing touch.

Nacoo grumbled, awakened so rudely. "Can't a man get any rest around here?" His voice resonated through the room.

"Wake up, Nacoo, say G'Day to your family," said Daj. His mouth felt as if tomb dust resided there.

"What," Nacoo groggily sat up, staring into the alien eyes of his daughter. Bleary eyed he continued to gaze at her, sensing a strange but familiar tingle touch his mind. "You are as beautiful as your mother," Nacoo complimented, without noticing Clamora's smile.

"I take comfort, Bua," Ryla chimed.

Winston reached down a strong hand to his father. *"Shish Bua,"* he said, in a tone similar to Nacoo's voice.

"Hello," Nacoo said hoarsely, clasped Winston's hand, standing as he did. His son's hands were smaller and six-fingered but strong. "Hello," he repeated, making Winston raise his head a bit higher in a respectful gesture.

"Va, he is larger and darker than you," Ryla giggled.

"Bua, the Sunstream II is a ship of delight," Winston mentioned, cheerily, still shaking Nacoo's hand and winked at Ryla.

"He piloted well," Clamora mind touched Nacoo.

Nacoo's cheeks darkened at the sound of Clamora's voice. A small pang of regret filled his throbbing head. "Ugh," he groaned, dropping Winston's hand. His bladder was at full capacity, and it was a great excuse to get his thoughts under control. "I'll be right back."

"Bua shall need appo when he returns," Ryla laughed sweetly.

The small female Rock Dwarf, Etta, pulled back the door flap, her eyes widening at the sight of the new Targians. She cleared her throat, getting Jax's attention, waving him out into the outer chamber.

Jax gracefully exited the room and stood before Etta. He listened to her explain that the incubator of the Queen of Pik wished to visit with Daj and Nacoo, and that they were to come alone, with her, to Rory's study. Etta also pointed, with a low grunt, to the open door flaps, saying the new visitors were welcome to have their own rooms, in the cavern.

Jax agreed and told her of Trader Umbra using the shadow tunnels and asked for her aid in locating where he was. Etta looked apprehensive but agreed to send out trackers and get word back to him. Jax bowed and disappeared back into the room, Etta feeling more comfortable to wait outside the door.

XIX

Farstar's robe fluttered across the tops of his feet as he drifted back toward his room. The words Tamara had spoken returned to him just before his parting from Rory: *Trader Umbra searches the city.* Rory assured him that Urna and Cres would keep watch outside the room, where he was to meet Autumn, and that he and Smoot would keep guard inside the room. Even knowing this, a great restlessness stirred within him.

The crystal sword lay atop Farstar's silvery-emerald-green warrior's cloak, anticipating his return. The time was right, and the closer its wielder came, the faster it hummed with an ever-increasing force. Soon and unforeseen to Farstar, the energy of the Great and Ancient Warrior, Partagul's Absorption Spirit Crystal, that Targ had placed inside the handle, would meld with Farstar's own Absorption Spirit Crystal.

Farstar sent out a mind touch to Jax, deciding not to wait for Rory's summons. *"Jax, the korzuku is completed."* Silence returned. *"Tamara relayed that Trader Umbra is within the city. I shall dress in the warrior's cloak, and return to Rory's sitting chamber."* He reached out again to Jax, pulling open the door flap to their room. Only silence.

Immediately upon entering the chamber, an alluring, soft, high-pitched hum met his ears, the crystal sword shone brightly, reflecting back to him his own diamond eyes. Kneeling down, he lightly touched its tip and felt the breath of Targ. An intense shiver ran along his spine, and a sense of longing crept over him to immerse his body into the waters of Targ. The crystal sword responded with mounting vibration.

For a moment, Farstar thought Targ had touched him back. He slid his fingertips down the length of the slender, two-edged blade, eyes absorbing its beauty, heart pounding. *"Va,"* it sang to him. He feverishly gripped the Targian engraved silver hilt with both hands and raised it, aligning its engraving of the seven crescent moons to his family mark, upon his jaw. *"I give you Partagul's Absorption Spirit Crystal;*

sing the song of the defender, Farstar." Targ was with him and had bestowed upon him a great and terrible honor. Farstar shuddered as the stored power of the planet moved inside him. A low and haunting voice trembled through his own and together they chanted, *"oo shura uc vek li rit, oo ca heshni, oo ca jant ta Targ ~ I live as one with you, I am protector, I am son of Targ.*

Partagul's Absorption Spirit Crystal emerged from the handle with an electric crackle and pressed into Farstar's jawbone. The crystal melted against his skin, filtering its way beneath the bone and up into Farstar's brain. Farstar gasped as its coolness entered his still moist and growing Absorption Spirit Crystal. A sense of euphoria touched his soul, and he lost the world around him. Farstar projected into the realm in which Partagul now existed: he was lucid, and accepting of what this prodigious warrior offered him. *"Quinni Partagul,"* Farstar bowed his head, ethereal colors moved and shifted around and through him within this vaporous kingdom. *"I shall honor you."*

An ambient mystical energy permeated his solar plexus. *"You shall honor Targ,"* the voice of the long-dead Targian echoed in Farstar's mind.

"How shall I?" He cried, tasting for the first time, the bittersweet sorrow of betrayal. *"My zaqurah nay touches Targ. My tek carries his seed of shared aresh and Trader Umbra's venom flows in their veins."* Farstar was impassioned, his astral body pulsing inside this current of spiritual power.

"Take her to Kandoria," Partagul's voice resounded.

Before Farstar could speak again, the energy realm he visited began to change in vibration, and as his high rate of descent, back into his physical body occurred, he could hear the fading words of the Great Warrior: *"Oo ca heshni ta Prest ta Wadoni , jant ta Targ."*

Etta trotted through the dimly lit tunnel followed by Daj and Nacoo. Even now, both had plenty of wine left in them. Etta slowed down and looked back at the human males. She had waited for them to change back into there peculiar looking, human clothes but Etta thought, as she studied them, it made them look adorable. She put on her best yellow-toothed grin for Daj. She was fond of the way his hair fell out from under his half-sided hat and the upward curl of his lips that made him appear as if he were always smiling. Etta giggled, glancing to either side of her, searching for one of the shadow doorways that the Rock Dwarfs prided themselves with — but she would take extra caution traveling through the shadow passageways to avoid running into the Trader.

Soon she found it; she kicked at a small protruding stone at the bottom of the wall and stepped back. The wall slid open to reveal another dimly lit tunnel. She grunted her approval and slipped through the doorway, waving for the two men to follow her. Etta waited for the cross-legged levitating Nacoo to pass through. Then she pulled a lever down to close the door, and once again, it became a solid rock wall.

Daj whistled under his breath. *"I think I'll hire these Rock Dwarfs to build my next house,"* he mind touched Nacoo.

"Yeah, they sure are an inventive bunch," Nacoo said, distantly, still thinking about Winston and Ryla. It felt funny to be a bua, as Winston had called him, and it was a very awkward experience to look at Ryla and not notice how much she resembled Clamora. He preferred not to look into Clamora's eyes when she spoke to him, feeling that if he did, he would want to hold her. Nacoo was never happier than when Etta came knocking. *"She's a cute little thing,"* he flashed a bright smile up at Daj's back, stretching to his full height. *"That feels good,"* he yawned.

"You have strange taste, cobber," Daj remarked in his best drawl, rocking his head against his hand, rubbing his sensory site, quite aware of its burning tug, now that the Dyeckian wine was starting to wear off.

The tunnel was cool, long, and curving, occasionally widening out so the men could travel side by side. Etta listened carefully for sounds other than the men's footfalls, their heavy breathing, and her long, swooshing, spar-thread skirt. Once she heard a whistle and made the men stop, until a male Rock Dwarf came strolling around a bend, which for the whole conversation suspiciously eyed the humans and grunted in Rock Dwarf fashion. Etta sent word with him concerning the Trader and report to the Targian Jax any information discovered. The rest of the walk was uneventful.

When Etta opened the wall to Rory's study in the cleansing room, the Targian Smoot greeted her with a yentch at her throat. She stood defiantly still, until Smoot lowered the weapon. Immediately and angrily, she growled at him, pushing her way past and into the study.

Humored by the little Rock Dwarf, Smoot grinned when Daj popped through the wall followed by Nacoo, who was glad to stand to his full height. *"Remain here,"* he spoke to both men, sealing the door behind them then moved toward the opening of the study. Rory nodded his approval for Smoot to have them enter. *"You may go,"* Smoot stepped aside and let them pass, flashing a smile at Etta.

Autumn barely gave Daj a chance to get into the study before she was hugging him. "I'm so glad you're here," she kissed his cheek and felt Nacoo's strong arms embrace both her and Daj. All three laughed, looking each other over, touching and hugging.

Nacoo wiped away her tears and a couple of his own, "can you believe it," he said, "another planet."

"Oh, Nacoo it's been way too long. There is so much to catch up on."

Nacoo grinned, seeing Autumn's eyes twinkle with happiness.

Rory observed the greeting with discomfort; Etta plopped down on a pillow, grumbling about Smoot's unpleasant welcome. "Please, ne ootau ~ take comfort," Rory tried to keep his voice steady.

Autumn took both men by the arms and led them over to the sitting pillows, "Nacoo the last time I saw you was — the day we went swimming." Autumn refused to let go of them as they sat, causing a very clumsy descent. "That seems like such a long time ago." She paused. "Time is strange here." Autumn glanced down at her belly, which now had a good roundness to it. "Daj, the last time I saw you, we were at the Arch of Melding," she smiled sadly at him, squeezing his arm a bit tighter. "I've missed you both so much."

Rory shifted uneasily as he watched the three of them and motioned for Etta to come to him. She reluctantly gave up her seat, getting curious glances from the pillow group, but they were too engrossed in conversation to care.

Rory needed his Targian elixir that kept his disposition on an even keel; it was one of the drawbacks to living away from Targ, something he would share with his companion when he notice Farstar's impassive side begin to falter. Rory watched as Etta mixed the precious smuggled ingredients of Targ's vine blood, and the planet's crystal mineral water together into a clay pot. He licked his thin gray lips in anticipation of the drink that nourished his mind and body so well.

Autumn glanced briefly at Rory; he appeared quite interested in what Etta was making but kept his place at the door. She spoke only to Nacoo and Daj. *"Do you think you can get me out of here,"* she flicked her eyes toward Rory and the cleansing room doorway. *"I want to go home,"* she said, with too much emotion. The men swayed, and she noticed Rory's attention shift to her, his face stony. "I would like a drink," Autumn cleared her throat and stood Rory's eyes boring into her. "What about you two, gentleman, Would you like a drink?"

Nacoo and Daj grinned at one another. "A bit of grog would do nicely," Daj accentuated.

"Tea," Autumn said, lightheartedly, rolling her eyes toward the ceiling.

"Do you have any of that tasty Dyeckian wine?" Nacoo winked. *"We will try,"* he mind touched her.

"Tea for two, coming up," Autumn genuinely laughed, winking back. As she walked over to the table to pour their drinks, she felt Rory probe her mind. He had made it clear that if she closed her mind to him, it would terminate the visit, not to mention future visits. *"What is it you desire,"* Autumn asked.

Rory desired to take Autumn away from the kom males but he sensed her happiness at being close to them. She held one hand over her belly in a protective gesture as she poured the tea. Rory sensed the child within her and took comfort that she was safe. *"Your ootau,"* Rory answered, taking the cup of elixir from Etta's small, stumpy hands.

Etta held a second cup of elixir, grumbling. She headed for the cleansing room to give it to Smoot.

"Copaa rit Etta," Rory said, pleased.

Autumn picked up two teacups and looked across the room at Rory, "Nacoo do you still play *tug*-of-war?" Autumn asked, emphasizing tug, and handed Daj his cup of tea spilling some on his hand. "Sorry," she whispered, looking deeply into his moss green, human eyes.

"Daj plays a good tug-of-war game," Nacoo boomed.

"Daj," Autumn said, surprised, and gave Nacoo his cup, sauntering back to the table to get herself one. A small thrill ran through her because Daj, her favorite colleague, had her bung, but she quickly shook off the feeling before it went too far.

"What is tug-of-war?" Rory questioned, eyeing Daj, sensing he was Autumn's bung carrier, the one he spoke with in the astral dream state.

"It's a human game played with a rope." Nacoo robustly toned.

"How do you play," Rory was curious.

"Well," Nacoo stood facing Rory, "you get a long rope," he spread his arms out in description, "and two teams of people on either end of that rope and tug back and forth until one team falls or crosses a line." He acted out pulling back and forth on a rope.

It was Daj's turn to stand. "It's made even more amusing when you tug over a mud-puddle."

Rory wasn't sure a mud-puddle sounded like much fun, but the komi seemed to express delight in the idea. "Hhmm," he said aloud, relaxed and starting to enjoy the affects of the elixir.

"So how is Dawn?" Autumn asked, rubbing her constantly vibrating sensory site.

Daj put an arm around her shoulders, putting his mouth, close to her ear and speaking low said, "Dawn is with Hank, Po, and Frox back at their ship, She's in rough shape." Daj touched her temple with his forehead. "TaChoo said they were searching for Trader Umbra, something about his blood is the antidote for her and you."

"Po and Frox," she looked incredulously at Daj.

"Hank and Dawn's kids," Nacoo spoke softly.

"Where's the ship?" Autumn began to feel hopeful.

Daj's lips fluttered against her cheek, "not far."

Having exceptional hearing, Rory began to feel the edges of anger toward Daj. "I think..." he started to say aloud, interrupted by Urna opening the door. Rory placed a hand on his yentch and spun around.

"Farstar is here," he opened the door wider and Farstar levitated through, in full warrior dress.

Autumn gasped; Daj dropped his arm away from her, a bit self-conscious.

Farstar did not stop at the door but glided right up to Autumn, landing gently on the floor in front of her and lightly touched her face.

"Zifla ~ angel," he whispered in her mind, *"I take great comfort in your presence."*

Autumn did not withhold her passion; she wrapped her arms around him and buried her face in his chest. She breathed in the faint woodsy smell of his body and felt his trembling — but there was another stronger vibration — it came from the crystal sword, slung across his back. Autumn looked up at Farstar; he had a new boldness about his spirit, *"Farstar,"* the sword felt hot to her touch.

Suddenly, Rory stood beside Autumn staring hard at his zaqurah. *"You were not summoned."*

Farstar pushed Autumn toward Daj and Nacoo and in the same moment, he pulled the crystal sword from the holding strap, grazing Autumn's arm. Sensing Partagul's energy surge through him, he slapped the crystal sword cruelly across Rory's chest. *"I come for Autumn, zaqurah."*

Rory's eyes squinted and he tightened his grip around the yentch; an uncommon brilliance blazed in Farstar's eyes, making him question his own senses. *"Targ has touched you,"* Rory growled, and for the first time felt, confused. He did not like it.

Nacoo placed his body in front of Autumn, Daj stood beside him, Smoot quickly moved so that he stood behind Rory and while keeping an eye on Farstar, never noticed Etta sneak Autumn into the cleansing room, through the door and into the tunnel. For Etta, Autumn's safety was first. She would take her to the shelter of her own home, farther beneath the city.

Dawn rested against the cabin wall, waiting for the Trader to call upon her, puzzling over the faintly familiar alien who stared at her warmly. She took a swallow from her third cup of tea, hoping to ease her incredible thirst. Two younger aliens worked to heal her wounds. While she listened to them softly talk, a tiny shift in her mind stirred tender emotions for them, — they affectionately called her, zaf. "Is that my name?" She asked her throat rough and scratchy.

Po and Frox glanced at one another, then respectfully at Hank.

Taking the hint, Hank answered, "Your name is Dawn." He watched her face for a sign of recognition. "Are you still thirsty?"

"Yes," She held out her cup for him to fill again.

Hank poured the appo mixed with athic that would aid in drying some of the poison in her system; he could sense it working not only by the changes in her aura but also by her thirst. He desired to probe her mind, but Po and Frox were administering healing and he dared not interrupt their energy work, just yet.

An image of Hank sitting on a horse popped into Dawn's mind as she studied him. There was something changing in her mind, like a shadow on the horizon slowly moving closer.

Hank sat quietly in front of Dawn. *"Jist vek ~ small one,"* he reached out; *"take my hands."*

Dawn blinked at him, unsure if she had really heard him and looked down at his gray, opened palmed, six-fingered hands. A feeling of trust crept through her, as if parting a thick blanket of fog; she put her cup on the floor and placed her hands on top of his. He was cool to her touch and a growing sense of intimacy developed between them, awareness of him inside her mind, clearing a path, showing her that the shadow was part of her, a part of her soul. *"I know you,"* she whispered in her mind.

"Va, jist vek ~ yes, small one," Hank sighed.

It was his voice in her mind; his voice had stayed with her all along, his voice…

Po and Frox stood back watching the energy exchange between their seeders. *"Zaf is starting to remember,"* Po said to his sister.

"It is a comfort," Frox responded and together in silence, watched the auras light swirl and grow clearer around Hank and Dawn.

Dawn gazed into the diamond eyes before her. "Hank," she spoke, somehow knowing that was his name. *"What is happening?"* she asked, incredulously. Slipping rapidly toward a frightening awareness, tears clouded her vision, and she squeezed Hank's hands. *"Help me,"* she pleaded, for now she could hear the Trader's irresistible command. "He summons me," Dawn's voice cracked as she began to rise.

Hank tightened his grip and stood with her. *"You must fight the urge, jist vek. I am here as are your children. Repeat what I say."* Locking his arms around her, *"hesna ga, lef ga, cutra ga, uckri ga,"* Hank chanted in Dawn's mind and he heard her repeating them. *"Protect me, bind me, strengthen me; encase me."* An icy ball of energy snapped and sparkled all around them, bolts of electricity passed through and between them, connecting them in an Orb of Protection.

Po was the first to react to Dawn's words and moved to the ship's windowed panel. He placed his hand over a red-dusted section, clearing it kinetically, to reveal the outside world. *"He is here."* Po's warrior's blood surged.

Frox began dipping blow-darts in egmur. *"We shall stay an attack until he opens the door."*

Although Po desired to fight and not wait, he knew Frox was right. His grip tightened around his yentch. He stood watching the unaware Trader walk back and forth under the ship.

Treya stood calmly next to Foster as he spoke, *"TaChoo and I shall go and seek audience with Rory. Starshine, Winston, Moonracer, shall seek audience with Autumn. Ashruba and Ryla shall seek information around the city while Coxy and Treya seek out Daj and Nacoo. Jax and Clamora you shall seek out Farstar."* Foster looked around at everyone.

"I shall go with you," Treya spoke with a warrior's inflection.

"Very well, Starshine shall go with Coxy," Foster did not look at Treya but could feel her pleasure with him. *"We shall all rendezvous back at the ships during the dimming of the sun."*

"Our journey is to find Trader Umbra," TaChoo spoke commandingly to Treya.

"Va, Quinni, I shall fight for zaf, her blood flows strong in me," Treya bowed her head to TaChoo.

Foster offered his rah a slight smile and watched as Winston and Starshine collected their bua's belongings. Within moments, everyone was out of the room and into the cavern, moving in rapid silence along the passageway leading to the city.

Winston and Moonracer were the first to break from the tunnel mouth; they gazed around at the sparkling city, adjusting their eyes to the sun's radiance and taking in the sights. *"Pik is pleasing to the eye,"* Moonracer approved, blinking.

The group stood for only a few moments, before Rock Dwarfs approached them, offering water to drink and wet their feet, although the Targians did not stand on the stone. *"We seek Rory,"* Foster spoke in Rock Dwarf tongue.

A male Rock Dwarf pointed to a well-ornamented archway just beyond the healing pool. Foster nodded his thanks, and with a whoosh of his robe was moving toward the bedecked archway, with most of the group behind him.

Ashruba and Ryla headed in the opposite direction, waving to Moonracer and Winston as they re-entered the tunnel. *"Zaf is within the tunnels,"* Moonracer said with anticipation, and swiftly levitated along the passageway that forked off the main tunnel. They traveled a curving, downward slope, growing dimmer and cooler, until they reached another division of the path. Moonracer hovered there for a moment, then suddenly turned and faced the left wall; he placed a hand against the chill moistness and began searching for a lever.

"Her blood calls you," Winston half questioned, half stated and he also took search of the wall, delighted when his fingers slid into a stone notch, opening the shadow door.

Moonracer stood face to face with Autumn and for a moment, no one moved. Then with lightening quickness, Etta held a short sword against Moonracer's solar plexus, growling a warning. Winston gripped his yentch, his heart quickened and he lowered himself to the floor, as did Moonracer.

Autumn placed a gentle hand on Etta's small, solid shoulder and waved the two young Targians inside the shadow passage. Etta grunted and stepped back, replacing her short sword in its scabbard, pushed the door lever and crossed her arms in annoyance at the intrusion.

Autumn moved closer to Moonracer. *"You have your father's eyes,"* she said admiringly, with tears in her own, and embraced him.

Moonracer responded to his zaf, sending her comfort. *"We must return to the ship,"* he spoke tenderly.

Winston explained to Etta what was happening, patiently waiting while she went through a series of grumbles; she agreed to assist them, only if she stayed with Autumn. They accepted and started their trek to the surface of Pik.

"You are Nacoo's first," Autumn mind touched Winston.

Winston smirked, *"Va, Quinni Autumn, I am Winston."*

Moonracer chuckled, getting a dirty look from Etta.

"We have just come from seeing him, there was some misfortune, and Etta here stole me away." Autumn's pace was slowing as they climbed the rough-cut stairs.

"Bua is a large, strong kom." Winston lifted his jaw, shaking his long, black streaked, silver hair.

"Yes, and a very good friend," Autumn sighed.

"Zaf, you are discomforted," Moonracer probed his seeder's mind.

Autumn leaned up against the cold stonewall of the stairway, panting from the exertion of the steep climb. *"When Farstar pushed me away, his sword burned my skin,"* she pulled up her sleeve revealing a small, purplish cut. *"I have to sit."* She sat heavily and looked up at Etta, who was now wiping her sweaty face. *"Farstar and Rory,"* Autumn slumped against the stairs, *"they…"*

Winston knelt beside Autumn, laying a hand over the mark. *"Quinni Farstar has transferred quintessence from the crystal sword into Quinni Autumn."* A look of graveness shadowed his face; Etta patted Autumn's shoulder, softly humming and looking worried.

"Targ ti li wa ~ Targ is with us," Moonracer imparted in a soothing tone. He carried the knowledge of Olden Communicator Tuvah in his consciousness and understood that Farstar needed Autumn to be in a stupor to keep her and the child protected. "Vessa," he spoke aloud sliding his hands under his mother's body. She rose into the air and so did he. *"Carry the Rock Dwarf, quickly,"* he directed to Winston, who had already felt Moonracer's urgency.

Etta's big eyes got bigger as she lifted into the air. "Ahh," she wobbled and grabbed for Winston's leg, squeezing her eyes tight.

Winston smirked at the Rock Dwarf as he held her aloft and speedily followed Moonracer. Within a small space of time, the four were on the surface and moving rapidly toward the ships.

The sun was burning brightly on a low horizon; a harsh, steady wind had swept Trader Umbra's recent tracks clean.

Moonracer stopped as he crested the hill, sand stung his skin, and he pulled Autumn closer, sheltering her face. *"Frox,"* he tried to mind touch her, *"we are near."*

Frox thrust her yentch catching Trader Umbra's leather-cloaked shoulder. Po made contact with the side of his head, and he fell back and away from the door. Frox was bleeding where his dagger had sliced her upper arm, but she did not notice as her keen instincts focused on the furious Trader.

Trader Umbra raged at the Targians blocking his path. He beckoned again to his servant to come, although he knew she tried to break free, she could not, and it angered him with a scorching fury. Blood streaked down his face, his shoulder burned and the building wind swirled sand around his body, setting him further into his wrath. He gave a last look up at his foes, memorizing their faces and then disappeared into the growing storm.

Moonracer and Winston reached the Sunstream II taking refuge from the storm. Both the young Targian's had sensed Trader Umbra's presence and took extra precaution, Winston guarding the main door and Moonracer guarding the small room Autumn and Etta now rested in. Moonracer rubbed his arm and lowered his head, *"Frox, you are wounded?"* He called out, feeling his linked mate's pain, and waited with heaviness in his heart.

Po was healing Frox's arm when she felt Moonracer's mind touch. *"I am healed,"* she sent back to him. *"Who is with you?"*

Moonracer raised his head, relieved, *"Winston accompanies me, Quinni Autumn, and Etta, a Rock Dwarf that nay leaves her side. We rest in the Sunstream II and await the rest of our group."* He hesitated then asked, *"are you poisoned?"*

Frox touched her arm, allayed, *"av ~ no."*

"Bua," Frox mind touched Hank, *"Quinni Autumn rests in the Sunstream II."*

Hank looked at Frox nodding his head; he continued to hold a weakly struggling Dawn in his arms. *"Dawn,"* his voice musical, *"Autumn is near."*

Dawn calmed and gazed into Hank's shimmering eyes, a clear picture of Autumn's face developed in her mind, "I know Autumn," she said, surprising all of them.

XX

Farstar pressed the crystal sword harder against Rory's chest. *"Zaqurah, where would the Rock Dwarf take her?"* His words rippled with fury. He had not noticed the exit of his mate. *"Would you leave her to the cruelty of Trader Umbra,"* he hissed in Rory's face.

Rory felt the presence of Targ within the blade that held him frozen where he stood. *"I do not know,"* Rory, answered crossly. Anger stirred in his heart at this betrayal and he plunged hard and fast into Farstar's mind, astonished to find his companion carried the Great Warrior Partagul's essence within him.

Farstar swayed, taking a step back from the energy Rory hit him with, and it was a hard hit. Farstar absorbed it so that Rory could share the knowledge he'd received. *"We are honored to share Quinni Partagul's aresh."* Farstar felt a part of Partagul's energy flow outward from him and mix with Rory's energy.

Rory pulled back from Farstar and bowed his head reverently in acknowledgement of the ancient defender. *"We shall search,"* he vowed.

Smoot, Daj, and Nacoo relaxed when they saw Farstar re-shoulder the crystal sword in its holding strap. Daj rubbed his neck, wanting to follow the pull of the bung; he glanced over his shoulder at the cleansing room doorway and started to move in that direction when Smoot blocked his path.

"You shall leave through the front," his tone was steady, eyes brightly shining.

"Daj is able to track her," Rory spoke audibly.

Nacoo shot Daj a so-much-for-riddles look, and stepped toward the door. "Come on, Daj," Nacoo boomed, his face tight with anticipation.

Farstar inclined his head to Rory and followed the men out into the passage, passing Urna and Cres. They continued down the hall to the outside steps that led them into the city. Farstar knew Rory would stay close to him, and he took comfort in that. "I sense Coxy is near," Farstar spoke openly to the men.

"All the children are here." Daj tipped his hat, looking around at the hubbub of Pik's inhabitants. "Foster, TaChoo, and Clamora are here and Hank took Dawn back to the ship." A Dyeckian offered a yellow root to them, as they walked past his colorfully decorated stand.

Nacoo spotted Ryla and Ashruba talking to a group of Targians and lengthening his stride left Daj and Farstar a few steps behind. *"Ryla,"* he mind touched his daughter.

Ryla lifted her head and gazed in Nacoo's direction. *"Bua,"* she smiled, eyes searching about as if for someone else. *"Starshine and Coxy have not found you."* She felt small compared to Nacoo's size.

"I didn't know they were looking for us," he said, in a soft deep voice.

"Quinni Farstar," Ryla and Ashruba bowed their heads. "Quinni Jax and Quinni Clamora are seeking you," Ryla imparted, feeling honored to be in Farstar's presence.

"Where are they?" Farstar inquired.

"In the direction of the Eating Hall," Ryla's gray cheeks darkened for not having a better answer.

"Then we shall go to the Eating Hall," he said aloud, and instantly was floating above the ground and moving swiftly away.

Daj lifted his hat, and pushed his perspiration-soaked hair away from his eyes. "I need a haircut," he complained, eyeing the quickly disappearing Farstar. "Let's move." Daj shuffled with an edge of irritability with each step.

"Do you need healing Bua," Ashruba asked Daj, levitating beside him.

"Nah, just some sleep," Daj looked at Ashruba, noticing her family mark on her upper left cheek, a kaleidoscopic leafy vine encircling an oval maroon-shaped Targ. He thought of how he never had the chance to hold her as a baby or experience any childhood growth and felt saddened yet at the same time astonished at how she came into being. Daj put his thumbs through the front belt loops of his pants and looked through the crowded streets. Farstar stood beside Jax and Clamora at the healing pool and just behind them stood Smoot, Rory,

Foster, TaChoo, and Treya. Suddenly he had the feeling he was going home.

"The Rock Dwarfs informed us that Trader Umbra is not in the city. They also took note of four leaving. Two Targians, one carried a Rock Dwarf and the other carried the Incubator of the Queen of Pik," Jax was saying, *"We must go quickly to the ships,"* he paused briefly to look up at Starshine and Coxy as they settled beside Treya, *"We must not leave without Trader Umbra's black blood."* Jax studied the group, *"wex wa ep ~ let us go,"* resolutely, he said.

The sand pelted the side of the ship making an abrasive scraping sound that caused Dawn to feel very edgy. A vague memory teased her into thinking she somehow knew this alien female that blocked her way to the Trader. The female had bound them together in some kind of energy chain that bounced her back like a ball against the wall every time she tried to walk away. Dawn wrung her hands together, looking expectantly at the door, the Trader would be furious with her if she couldn't find a way to escape back to him. She studied the young alien male guarding the door, and felt a twinge of affection for him, which made her twist her lips anxiously. "Let me leave," she pleaded.

Hank sat in the pilot's seat; he maneuvered his ship into docking position with the Sunstream II, considering that if Dawn met with Autumn, it might trigger the memories that remained clouded by Trader Umbra's noxious venom, and help regain control of her mind. Hank depressed the docking corridor button, concentrating, as the two ships locked together; the intense wind rocked them, threatening to disrupt the process. His keen eyes searched for signs of Trader Umbra, but the churning sand made visibility poor, even to him. *"Winston,"* he called, listening for the corridor door to open. *"Winston,"* he called out, once again to the Sunstream II's pilot.

"Va," Winston answered back, sensing Hank's relief. *"I am clearing away sand, Quinni Hank."*

"I shall aid you," Hank walked over to the corridor hatch and placed his hand on a side panel. The door swooshed open and a pile of sand slid in around his feet. So did the hand of Trader Umbra. Hank stumbled back pulling his yentch from his belt and as he did Trader

Umbra sliced his foot, grinning with delight for his cleverness to spread poison on the blade of the dagger. "KAPRAY," Hank howled and thrust his yentch upward, catching the Trader deep in his right shoulder spilling his black blood.

Umbra swung again, paying no mind to his wound and viciously slicing Hank's face, laughing cruelly as Hank recoiled, taking a step back. He licked at the blood splattered across the back of his hand enjoying the taste of it.

At the exact time Hank roared his warning of attack, Dawn leapt at the female. Having the Trader so close was driving her to madness. In an attempt to carry out his command to aid him, she tackled Frox to the floor. Dawn not only fought with the alien female, she struggled not to.

Po leaped over the wrestling females and lunged at Trader Umbra. The impact sent the Trader hurling into the sand-covered corridor. Po raged with the warrior strength bred into him. "You are not welcome here," he growled and charged Trader Umbra again.

Hank watched as his jant transformed in front of him and in his weakening state saw Winston and Moonracer burst through the sand-blocked door. They had an ancient brilliance in their eyes and auras. Hank fell heavily to the floor, his head hurt and he felt very sick. Trader Umbra's venom was working fast; he rolled his head to see Frox using a dart of egmur on Dawn. He gazed upon the scene with rapidly blurring vision; his thoughts reached out to his wog sy zaqurah.

Winston grabbed Trader Umbra by the throat, pushing him deeper into the sand. Moonracer kicked the dagger from his dark hand and slammed a knee into his chest. "This is for zaf," he howled. Clasping his hands together, he swung full force, connecting against the Trader's jaw.

Umbra's razor-sharp teeth just missed his foe's fists, and venom flew from his mouth landing harmlessly in the sand beside Po's feet. He kicked brutally at Po, as he felt the Targian's hands grip his legs, and fiercely snapped at Winston's arms, that now held his; he took another bone-cracking blow across the face from Moonracer, just as Frox struck him in the side, causing a cruel sting, sucking the breath out of him. Blood mixed with poisonous saliva gushed from his mouth and over the dart, that she had pierced him with, Umbra recognized the female Targian, spewed obscenities at her, and then took yet another crushing hit across the head, losing consciousness.

"Quickly, we must bind him," Po urged.

"Vessa," Winston spoke, and the Trader's limp body rose into the air.

The group entered the Sunstream II sending Etta into a fit of angry, fearful grunts; she pulled her short sword and stood guard at the door of Autumn's room. Etta would die rather than let the Trader who floated in the air take her charge. She watched with wide eyes as the Targians placed the Trader's bloodied body against the wall and started to chant. A swirl of white light flowed around them and the faster they chanted the tighter the bindings of light grew, until it formed an almost solid mass around Trader Umbra. The ship itself grew slender green tentacles that wrapped around the Trader's extremities. Etta backed slowly into the room, not wanting to see any more.

A great fatigue suddenly overcame Smoot and he fell to his knees. *"Zaqurah!"* he wailed, bundled in his leather-hooded cloak. He lowered his head and rested his gloved hands in his lap. Sand blew threateningly around him, and he grasped at his chest, sensing the pain that Hank was feeling. A thick pasty film covered his tongue, and he spat, trying to rid himself of the poison that was blackening Hank's aresh. *"Do not leave me, I am near,"* he cried out.

Rory had Smoot under one arm, and Farstar had him under the other, lifting him to his feet. *"Do you need healing,"* Rory asked, sensing Smoot's energy loss.

"My zaqurah is poisoned, we must continue," Smoot whimpered and lifted off the hot, agitated surface of Pik, using the strength of the pelting wind to propel forward.

Ryla was keeping pace with Nacoo as he labored to stay above the sand. *"Bua, I sense confusion in you."*

"I have strange feelings," Nacoo spoke as loud as he dared, to his daughter. *"Winston is using an energy that I can physically feel inside me; it's like Targ being inside me."*

"I feel it too, Bua. It is our essence connecting." Ryla tightened her cloak about her, explaining, *"You, and Quinni Baxter think intensely about one*

another when there is discomfort or great excitement. It is a disruption of your brain waves which act upon your cellular structure and trigger what you now experience."

"Yeah, but this is stronger than it is with Baxter." Nacoo raised a hand sheltering his face and squinted into the blowing sand.

"Va, Bua, the cells of his body are communicating with the cells of your body. They call upon the knowledge and strength that you have. This also gives you understanding of what he is going through."

Daj broke through. *"Cobber, the weirdest thing is occurring. I'm wide-awake seeing things happen. It's as if I'm dreaming but they are not my dreams. I think it's coming from Autumn. Anything like it happen to you?"*

"Only once when I was sleeping, and I believe that was of the first place Rory kept her," Nacoo said, restraining from shouting into Daj's mind.

"This is really vivid. I see Professor Zyleon eating ice cream." Daj said, gripping tight with a gloved hand to lower his hat, blocking the stinging sand from chafing his face.

"Is it cherry swirled," Nacoo asked, wetting his dry lips.

"Eh," Daj grunted, perplexed, *"isn't that the Professor's favorite kind. Maybe Autumn's bung is reacting to her dream like an interactive movie."* Daj tossed the idea at Nacoo.

"That just might be, buddy," Nacoo answered, pulling his hood lower, protecting his face from whipping wind.

Foster's voice rang clear. *"When we arrive, we shall enter the Sunstream II."*

Fighting against the angry storm, the small group crested the hill and started to push through the thickening air, down toward the tempest-battered ships. Soon they huddled under the hatch. Clamora, Treya, Ashruba, Jax, and Foster created a protective orb around the group to block more sand from piling up, while TaChoo, Rory, and Coxy calmed Smoot. Farstar, Starshine, Nacoo, and Daj dug until they cleared the sand away from the access door of Sunstream II.

Inside, Etta sat quietly with a hairy little hand on Autumn's rounded belly; the Incubator of the Queen of Pik would need a treatment soon, to keep the Trader's foulness from growing out of control. She turned her attention away from Autumn. A banging was coming from the hatch where one of the young Targians stood guard.

The door opened, and one by one, the small group from the turbulent outside world climbed in. Smoot instantly headed for the corridor leading to his zaqurah. Clamora, Ryla, and Ashruba followed. Rory headed for a relieved Etta with Treya and Coxy at his heals. Foster and TaChoo examined the cloud white casing the children had put around Trader Umbra. *"We must take his black blood, rah,"* Foster's lips curled in a gratified sneer. He placed his hands upon the orb and softly spoke, "Truba."

The orb ceased its swirling and cleared an opening for Foster's hands. Trader Umbra roused with the first draw of blood and viciously snapped his teeth. The vines held him tight, but Foster worked quickly, drawing three more tubes of his dark, foul blood.

Umbra seethed with a vengeance-filled soul at the ruin of his plans, but already his malevolent mind started to formulate a new one. Venom dripped from the corners of his cruel grin, and he glanced sideways at the door to where his first servant slept. The child she carried shared his black blood, both through the mother and with the antidote they would give, his first marked. A nasty, gurgling laugh escaped his throat, drool spilling down his chin and onto his shirt.

Farstar pulled the crystal sword from its holding strap, pressing it to the Trader's throat. He could feel its power pulsing through his hands, and as he stared into the fluid, amber eyes of Trader Umbra, he desired to kill him, slowly and painfully.

"Partagul is strong in you, zaqurah," Rory mind touched Farstar.

Farstar pushed the tip of the sword a little harder against the Trader's tawny throat. A small droplet of black blood rolled down its blade and Farstar sneered.

Umbra snapped his shiny black teeth, daring Farstar to thrust the blade through him.

Farstar trembled with a craving to satisfy this lust for blood, an emotion he had never experienced before.

"It feels good, doesn't it, zaqurah," Rory now stood at the doorway, closely examining Farstar, the same as everyone else in the room. *"To wield control,"* Rory bit the corner of his lip in anticipation of Farstar's decision, his own thoughts wild with excitement.

"Bua, we must keep Trader Umbra alive, there shall be no war started by us. We shall throw him out into the storm before we leave this planet." Moonracer

placed a hand on the blade and looked into the fiery eyes of his dutom.

Farstar shook with the exertion of desire to plunge the sword deep into this vile creature. He could feel a mix of Rory's exhilaration and comfort coming from his jant. He stared flintily, into the eyes of Trader Umbra. *"There shall be another day for this,"* he spoke in the Trader's tongue. As Farstar withdrew the crystal sword, deliberately running it under Trader Umbra's jaw line, ensuring his own mark upon him. It gave him pleasure to see the loathing in those tainted eyes. There was a stony silence in the ship, as the opening in the orb closed and turned back into its milky, swirling cocoon, with the retreat of the blade.

Daj had his back against the pilot's seat, watching in silent horror as the alien that had tortured his mind now wielded a strange new power that could kill him *without* a thought. Daj glanced at Nacoo, who appeared just as disturbed as he felt; glancing back, he locked eyes with Farstar and put both hands in the air. "I'm just standing here," his words rushed together.

Farstar glared, unseeing, at Daj.

"Bua, you are safe," Starshine spoke calmly to Daj.

Daj slowly lowered his arms but dared not move any other muscles. Shifting his gaze away from Farstar's burning stare, he sighted in on Foster and TaChoo working vigilantly together, formulating an antidote.

"We shall administer to Hank, first," TaChoo said, then turned and looked at Farstar. *"His need is the greatest."*

Farstar glowered at TaChoo. "As you desire," he spoke aloud, through gritted teeth. It was becoming harder for him to keep control; he craved to be in the vines of his planet.

"Zaqurah, come, I have a drink to share with you." Rory wore a devilish smirk on his lips. *"It shall ease your discomfort."*

Farstar re-shouldered the crystal sword in its holding strap, and then gave Moonracer a nod of his head. He moved quickly toward Rory, sensing TaChoo's steady gaze upon him. "Everyone must leave," Farstar snarled, whipping his robe around and pointing at the door. His daughters bowed to him and left quietly. Etta on the other hand stomped noisily out of the room. Farstar pressed the indent by the door and it closed. Leaving his hand on the wall, he lowered his head and growled, *"Give me your drink."*

Rory handed him the flask of potion he carried. *"Just a couple of swallows, tutal,"* Rory felt a craving to share more of this moment and gently probed Farstar's mind.

Farstar swallowed the familiar taste of home; it was sweet and thick on his tongue. His second swallow sent a flood of warming calm throughout him; he sighed deeply and allowed Rory to enter his mind.

Rory touched Farstar's Absorption Spirit Crystal and found that shared sense of the Great Warrior Partagul within his own mind. He felt the fierce strength of the ancients, and he shivered within Farstar's mind.

Farstar closed his mind to Rory. *"This is not the time,"* he spoke softly, and handed Rory's flask back to him. *"Autumn needs the antidote,"* Farstar said, regaining control and met Rory's diamond eyes. They held each other's gaze for a long moment. Then Farstar opened the door and Etta shuffled her way past, grumbling and taking her place next to Autumn.

When Farstar stepped out of the room and into the main ship's area, he found it empty except for Trader Umbra, who stared maliciously at him from his prison. Rage lay just under the surface of Farstar's thoughts, but Rory's drink aided him in this struggle with emotion. He heard Rory chuckle, which propelled him across the ship's interior and through the sandy corridor in time to see Smoot helping Hank to his feet.

Dawn had just received a dart of antidote that the new, familiar-faced alien female had given her, and now a very large man was sitting by her side. Dawn felt compelled to be close to him. It caused the humming in her neck to lessen, and foggy memories of him crept along like a snail in the back of her mind. She studied the smaller man with his playful grin and black hair poking out from under his oilskin hat and felt a familiar pang for him too. The big man's hands rested in his lap; Dawn's eyes traced a tattoo of a cobra up his left arm. His vest just covered his chest, and a delicate gold chain hung from his thick neck. She liked his curly, black whiskers and felt a rush of prickly heat at the sight of those beautiful onyx eyes… a song blossomed in her mind and in a hushed tone, she started to sing, "it's twilight on the river…" She noticed a slow smile tug at the corners of the big man's lips.

Unexpectedly, his baritone voice filled the small ship. "Stars are shining bright…"

Together they sang, "Our spirits soar on this beautiful, moon shadowed night…" Dawn watched a single tear roll down his cheek and nest upon that curly mass of hair. "You need a shave, Nacoo," she said, without thinking, and in the next moment, she had both men wrapping their arms around her and shouting something about, "She's remembered us."

Relief flowed from one Targian to another; the antidote was working well. TaChoo gestured to Farstar and bid him to follow her, *"mel ~ come,"* she said, and took the lead back through the corridor. She smiled to herself at the feelings Daj was having. *"Komi are amusing,"* she spoke to Farstar.

Farstar found TaChoo's mind touch refreshing and calm, assisting him to relax. He thought of Jax and hoped he was well without Targ's nourishment.

Etta tramped away, grumbling when the two Targians came in; TaChoo closed the door chanting, *"shurah."*

"You seal the door," Farstar looked curiously at TaChoo.

"The komi must be taken to Kandoria," she held Farstar's gaze. *"You are Targian, Farstar, and no matter what occurs, we shall keep the truth of Targ. We shall continue what we have started."* TaChoo touched his jaw tracing his family symbol, *"wathu Autumn, jant ta Targ."*

Farstar gently pulled the crystal sword from its holder and laid it, bloodstain up, across Autumn's brow, releasing her from its influence. A misty green blanket of energy covered her body as the waters of a great sea cover the land. Farstar threw his head back, silver hair fluttering, a soft moan escaped him, and he plunged into Autumn's mind. *"Zifla ~ angel, wathu ~ awaken,"* he touched her essence and sensed her touching back… She was coming back to him.

Autumn opened her eyes to a luminous green mist. "I am awake," she reached out touching Farstar's robe.

He lifted the crystal sword from her brow, feeling its energy travel back into his Absorption Spirit Crystal. Farstar re-shouldered the crystal sword gazing upon Autumn's human beauty, and yet in her mind, caressed her thoughts with comfort.

"Please sit up, Autumn," TaChoo held out a cup with one hand. "You must drink this." and in her other hand a dart of Trader Umbra's antidote. TaChoo's aim was true; with a flick of her wrist, the dart penetrated the side of Autumn's neck, immediately spilling its contents into her bloodstream.

"Ouch," Autumn reached up and pulled the dart from her throat and let it tumble to the floor "Why did you do that," she said, feeling dazed.

"To cleanly administer Trader Umbra's serum," TaChoo mind touched her.

Autumn flinched at the Trader's name, "Will it hurt my baby?"

"Av, the child is safe," TaChoo reassured.

Sitting up was a gradual process, one hand pushing her body up, and the other hand protectively holding her curved belly, cautiously sniffing the brew held out to her; "What is it?"

Farstar sat beside her. *"It is elixir, also an aid in removing the Trader's venom from your cells."* He brushed a small piece of coppery hair away from her mouth, *"ne ootau, take comfort, it shall not harm the child."* His cool, thin, lips kissed her cheek, unable to control the intense emotional turmoil inside him; he pulled her into his arms and wept. Autumn wept with him.

TaChoo, holding the cup, felt the power of Farstar's love for Autumn; she bowed her head and swayed with its energy. *"Farstar you are unbalanced,"* TaChoo said, concerned and waited for her fellow Targian to answer.

"We shall go to Kandoria and from there I shall return to Targ," Farstar lifted his tear streaked face and took the cup from TaChoo. *"Drink this Autumn, for you must be ready to travel back to Earth,"* he uttered, softly, with a shadow of a smile.

"Earth," Autumn put her feet on the floor, "I'm going home?"

"Va," TaChoo answered aloud.

Farstar stood, *"first, drink."*

Autumn took the cup from TaChoo and gulped it down, "Ugh, that's awful," she scrunched her nose and shook her head.

A loud knocking boomed through the tiny spaceship's room. *"That is Etta,"* TaChoo nodded to Autumn and moved gracefully toward the door.

Etta stomped heavily, passing a grinning TaChoo and right up to Autumn, tapping a foot and crossing her arms, she snorted her disapproval. Farstar laughed audibly, provoking Etta to kick him in the shin.

It surprised him at how powerful the little Rock Dwarf was. "Oowww," Farstar howled in pain and grabbed his already swelling ankle. If he had not heard, Autumn's chiming laughter, he would have been angry. Instead, he whispered a healing, and chuckled under his breath.

"Hello Autumn," the words sounded from behind the doorway.

Autumn knew immediately the melody of that voice. "Dawn," she looked up expectantly. "Dawn," she said, again with a quaver, walked over to her friend and grabbed both of her hands. Tears welled in her eyes. "I felt the Trader's venom in you." Autumn squeezed Dawn's hands. "I was so afraid that I would never see you again. It was dreadful." A tear fell from her chin, exploding on the floor.

"I know, it was a challenge to walk past him — out there," Dawn's lip trembled as she nodded back toward the door. "It really was awful, but I had the best kind of help." She shivered, "Anyway, now we are together, and we are going home," she chimed, in her girlish tone, smiling.

"Yeah, and I'm flying us there," Nacoo rumbled from the ship's main area.

Etta stayed close to Autumn as they filtered out of the room. Farstar told her she did not need to mix a tonic for Autumn. Nevertheless, she thought it a safer plan to continue the potions, and now as she stared once again at the caged Trader; she knew it was a good idea.

Umbra stared with a sadistic, glossy-eyed intent at Dawn and Autumn as they entered the main part of the ship.

"Don't look or listen to him," Dawn said, shakily.

Autumn turned her back on the caged Trader, pulling Dawn with her.

Foster stood in the corridor looking over the small gathering. *"Rah, you shall keep the komi and their mates together in the Sunstream II. Winston,*

Moonracer, and Etta shall also attend them, seeing them safely to Kandoria. Clamora shall return with Jax on the Planet Traveler and the rest of us shall return to Targ in the attached ship." Foster's face hardened, *"have all the komi go into the pilots cabin and secure the door. We must release Trader Umbra."* Foster glided over and stood beside the glaring Trader.

TaChoo spoke aloud, "Daj, Nacoo, Dawn, Autumn, and Etta, join me." She waved a hand for them to follow her into the pilot's cabin at the front of the ship. *"You shall have to stay in here until we are safely on our way to Earth."* Repeating what she'd said to Etta in her language.

"Wait a minute," Daj grabbed TaChoo's hand. "Why," he questioned.

All eyes were on her. *"It is for your heshna ~ protection."* She retrieved her hand and hurriedly shut the door sealing it. *"Shurah,"* she whispered.

TaChoo scrutinized the formation line, one Targian across from another; they angled from Trader Umbra to the outside hatch. She took her place across from Foster and watched as Foster took yet another vial of black blood.

Trader Umbra warily eyed the Targian who pointed the large crystal sword at his throat and decided not to protest to the withdrawal of blood. His black heart seethed with revenge as he studied the face of the one who stole away his antidote. He salivated at the thought of the human females and snapped his teeth. "Baugh copate," he spewed.

"Expect conflict," Foster repeated in the Trader's tongue, "from whom?"

Trader Umbra grinned maliciously, "Sa Tri," he snarled.

"King Tri," Rory answered, sneering sarcastically, "there is nothing for you to trade."

"No more talk," Farstar pushed the blade tip harder against the Trader's vulnerable throat, fighting the desire to cut his life down.

Trader Umbra's amber eyes blazed with loathing. The blade reflected his broken and bloodied, battle-scarred, tawny face, and he thought with some pleasure of how he would end the life of its wielder. Venom filled his mouth and he spat at Farstar, but the orb prevented it from making contact. For a moment, he was glad for its protection; for he was sure, he heard the blade singing a song about his own death.

"Let us put up a korax," Foster intoned to everyone and began the chant, *"maza ta heshna erra, maza ta heshna lef wa."*

In fine Targian form, all hands, palms forward, raised to heart level. A lightning bolt of energy crackled down the center of the path and began to spread forming walls on either side of the line. Everyone chanted, *"pathway of protection unfold ~ maza ta heshna erra ~ pathway of protection bind us ~ maza ta heshna lef wa."* A frenzy of energy snapped with loud cracks, whipping back and forth from Trader Umbra to the hatch.

Umbra heard the crystal sword wielder, speaking under his breath, and felt the bindings that held him prisoner break free. He slouched as the vines retreated, rubbed his throat and then his wrists. The milky orb was next to dissolve, allowing him to push the pressing blade against his throat, aside. The crystal sword wielder stepped behind him and touched the blade tip to the back of his neck, they wanted him to leave, and he was more than willing to go, but resisted the urge to run. Instead, he straightened and slowly walked to the hatchway, taking in each face and noting it to memory.

Black blood trickled down Trader Umbra's neck and painfully Farstar resisted pushing the blade all the way through. His desire to inflict a mortal wound to the Trader turned into a severe slice of his foul arm and savage shove, dropping him out of the ship.

Trader Umbra crumpled; black blood spilling onto the shifting dune, sand tore at his filthy flesh, giving Farstar a strange feeling of satisfaction. He sneered cruelly as the Trader disappeared into the storm. With a powerful thrust, Farstar locked down the hatch.

Nacoo sat in the pilot seat of the Sunstream II. A lazy smile formed on his lips as he thought about the stars in front of him. He was making history, the first human to make deep galactic space exploration achievable. His mind was filled with star charts, alien races, trade routes, and most important, the way home, Earth. "I think I will share a bottle of Dyeckian wine with Baxter when I get home," Nacoo announced.

"Here, here, I'm putting my order in; I could use a good Earthly night out," Dawn said, feeling a bit more like her self.

Autumn, who sat next to Dawn, noticed the dark rings under her eyes. "I think we should have a party on the beach and dance until that beautiful golden sun rises."

Everyone laughed.

"Why is that funny?" Moonracer asked.

"That is how it started," Farstar answered.

Moonracer turned his attention to Autumn. *"It would comfort me to dance with you, Zaf."* He bowed his head to his dutom, sending her an impression of his admiration.

"You may have the first dance," Autumn felt a stirring within her womb that traveled up into her mind, a soft touch, like the brush of a cat's tail.

"The Queen of Pik responds to her nua's voice," Rory mind touched Autumn.

Autumn shifted to look at Rory, he still held her captive, an invisible band wrapped around her mind. *"Yes,"* she answered and turned away.

"I wonder how that old boy Professor Zyleon is doing." Daj sat sprawled out in a chair. "I hope the news hasn't escaped beyond camp. That would make things difficult." He peeked at TaChoo from under the brim of his Barmah hat.

"Professor Zyleon is level headed, I'm sure he's kept the press hounds away." Dawn said, stretching out her tired legs, yawning.

"We'll have a history text written about us that kids all over the world will thrill about," Nacoo boomed, shifting up straighter in his seat.

"What are kids and what is a history text," Winston queried; a bemused expression on his gray face.

"A kom child's brain has a long development, so during their years of growing and learning, using written information, they are affectionately called kids by their quinni," TaChoo answered, steadying her eyes on Winston.

"You speak of the time factor knowledge Targ engrained in our minds, Quinni TaChoo. It is a curious thing their long development. I shall have to learn more about..."

Nacoo interrupted, "I'll take you fishing."

Daj, Dawn, and Autumn all snickered getting inquiring looks from the Targians, which made them snort and guffaw all the harder.

Kandoria

"*What is fishing,*" Moonracer accepted the good humor and smiled.

"A human method of catching food," Autumn responded her eyes sparkling with merriment.

Farstar gazed upon Autumn, touching the edges of her mind, experiencing her cheerfulness. He stayed there on the rim of her thoughts, allowing the wonder of this emotion to settle upon him. A place he would not reach again. After he went back to be nourished by Targ, he slipped a little deeper into her ebbing tide of warm human sensation.

When he had agreed to be a part of Targ's plan to re-introduce their ancestral path, he never expected to become what he now was. Sadness crept into his own thoughts and mingled with Autumn's. Farstar felt a shift of energy that kept him from immersing further, suddenly realizing that the energy was purely not her own but that of the child.

The child touched his aresh and she knew him; she let Farstar explore the wonders of her incubator's womb and the occurring growth of her tiny physical body. She understood his sadness and imparted a vision of a warrior's heart, protecting her and her mother, she sent him love, a tremendous love, and he quivered. "*It is my honor to serve Autumn and greater still the Queen of Pik,*" he spoke with clarity, visualizing this knowledge to her. She only need touch his aresh and he would know her desires.

Autumn laid her fingers on Farstar's hand, her voice full of happiness. "*Farstar, we will have time later to explore…*" She paused and sipped the drink Etta had made for her, "*rit ootau ga.*" She placed his hand on her belly, "*Mooti is also comforted.*" Autumn felt Farstar's familiar retreat from her mind and gave him a sweet smile. "*I'll have to keep a low profile back home, the science of it all will drive people mad with curiosity, and I must protect us from that risk. Stay close to me… very close…*" she pressed her lips together, glanced at Rory, and turned her attention to Nacoo, who was still boasting about fame.

"*Mooti is a pleasant name and I shall stay near,*" Farstar answered.

"Yeah, our pictures will be plastered on sky boards everywhere," Nacoo chuckled and continued, "interviewers will want to know

- 249 -

every detail about our adventures and of course want to meet the Targians."

"Sure and as soon as that happens, we humans will all but be forgotten," Daj jested.

"I'm more interested in continuing my research," Dawn commented sleepily.

Nacoo had turned in his chair so he was facing everyone, "We'll be home in about fifteen minutes our ETA." He pulled out Daj's bung. "Hey buddy, I think it's time you have this back."

Daj peeked out from under his hat. "Right," he said and met Nacoo halfway, taking his bung from his big hand. He looked shyly over at Autumn and pulled out her bung from his sensory site, replacing it with his own. It made him feel a bit more balanced, and he felt the familiar vibration of his hyper-band reconnecting with it. "It's been a pleasure," Daj handed Autumn's bung back to her and took a deep bow, glancing at a very still Farstar. He looked at Rory, TaChoo, and Hank who all seemed to be in stupors. Winston and Moonracer were both watching him with curious expressions. "They seem to be catching up on some zees," he said, more daringly playful to Autumn.

Autumn daintily took her bung from his open hand. "You are so observant," she teased. Autumn pulled out Dawn's bung looking deeply into Daj's moss-green human eyes and started to feel her homesickness dwindle. "Dawn I believe this belongs to you." She started to stand, but Etta's firm hand pressed on her shoulder. The Rock Dwarf carefully picked up the bung and carried it over to an enthralled Dawn.

"Thank you, Etta," Dawn said softly, observing a shy, crooked, yellow grin of satisfaction on Etta's dark, hairy face. Dawn rose to her feet, stretching her arms upward and let loose a huge yawn before pulling Nacoo's bung out of her sensory site and replacing her own. "Daj, maybe we should get together and compare research notes." She winked at him. "Nothing is too personal anymore."

A slow rumble of laughter sounded from Nacoo. "Give me my piece of personal, sugar."

Daj joined in the humor, "It's just so bloody intimate."

The four of them fell into uncontrollable laughter. Etta, Winston, and Moonracer stood mystified, looking upon them in wonder.

XXI

Zyleon paced back and forth across the landing dock, rubbing his smooth baldhead, then switching to his unshaven chin, which agitated him further. "Where are they," he grumbled stopping to look out through the bay door.

"Winston says they are here," Trombula answered, concealing his amusement with Professor Zyleon's impatience.

In a blink of an eye, a spaceship bearing the name Sunstream II appeared in front of them. "Whoa," Zyleon moved back a step. "That's impressive," he said, air rushing past them.

Trombula's spidery hair fluttered about his shoulders. *"Va,"* he simply replied.

Zyleon's heart gave a lurch upon seeing the first one off the ship was his greatest discovery, his niece. He was a bit surprised to see a strange little being he thought he had once seen in a book on fantasy creatures tagging along behind her. Dawn, Daj, and Nacoo came after them, each one waving, and shouting their hellos. He absently rubbed his stubble, resting his hand there for a moment, somewhat overwhelmed by emotion. All his anxieties left him like the last fall leaf, tumbling gently to a snow-covered ground; he stood transfixed in that frozen silence. Here he was a seventy-three-year-old Archaeoastronomy-Physicist Professor, watching his team walk off an alien ship.

"Uncle, it's been to long a time. It's so good to be with you again."

Autumn's voice broke into his thoughts; she stood before him, eyes twinkling with wetness. "Ah, come here, give me a hug," he said thickly. Noticing the slight bulge of her belly, he pushed her back to gather a better look at her. *"You have fattened up since the last time we saw each other."* He gave her a quizzical look knowing how carefully she maintained a steady weight.

"I carry a child." Autumn's eyes were dark with passion. *"We will talk privately."* She smiled and gave him another hug. It felt good to be back

on Earth and seeing her uncle made it all the better. For the moment, Autumn allowed her joy to flow.

"Professor Zyleon, it's bloody good to see you," Daj tipped his hat and extended a hand to him.

Moonracer stood beside Daj and bowed his head to the Professor, *"Farstar and Autumn are my seeders, I am Moonracer, their first."*

For a moment, Zyleon felt as if he were a part of a programmed show, *"I guess that makes me your great uncle,"* he responded to Moonracer. He grasped Daj's hand, never breaking his hug from Autumn. "Yes, my boy, it's good to see you too."

Nacoo's grasp was solid and his eyes moist. "I have my own ship, isn't she a beauty? And this is my son," Nacoo put a large arm over Winston's shoulders.

Hank and TaChoo stood just behind Winston and both bowed their heads in acknowledgement of Professor Zyleon.

"Good to see you," the Professor greeted them.

Dawn stood tapping her foot, arms crossed. "Do you suppose I…" she emphasized, "could get a welcome home hug."

Autumn chuckled and did a little curtsy, "Of course."

"Girl, don't ever change," Zyleon, laughed and hugged the little red head.

"Uncle, this is Farstar," Autumn reached for Farstar's hand, showing his importance to her, "and this is Rory, Farstar's companion." Autumn had slid in between the two Targians and placed a hand on Rory's shoulder. "And this is Etta, my assistant." Etta stood like a stone in front of them. The Targians nodded. However, Etta, feeling this human man was important, tried to copy Autumn's curtsy, which caused a ripple of grins.

"By God, you look like a Queen standing there Autumn, with a maiden at your side."

Autumn gazed into her uncle's clear blue eyes that twinkled with affection for her, "Uncle!" Autumn whispered and felt the blood rush to her cheeks.

Zyleon suddenly felt like a trespasser who'd set off a very loud alarm.

"Not a chance," Daj jested, breaking the sudden awkwardness.

Zyleon wanted to ask more questions but he forced himself to swallow them — for now. "Come on everyone, I'm sure you are anxious to get settled."

"The guys filled me in about the baby," Dawn mind touched Autumn. *"How are you doing?"*

"I'm really not sure," answered Autumn, honestly. *"Sometimes it's exciting, sometimes frightening and sometimes it makes me just plain angry."*

Dawn reached up and put her arm in Autumn's, hoping to convey her concern. *"If you need to talk…"* she left it at that.

Trombula fell in behind Rory as the little troupe made their way back inside Kandoria's walls. Conversation about history in the making and wonders yet to be experienced filled the corridor. *"Thorb desires a connection with you,"* Trombula spoke to Rory, *"your experiment has caused great concern."*

Rory restrained the agitation he felt at the request, answering without emotion, *"we shall speak here or on my planet, Pik. Let him choose."* Rory glanced narrowly at Daj who walked beside Autumn. They were happy and it incensed him to think Trader Umbra had cost him so much precious time with her and the child that grew within her womb. He clenched his teeth and reached for his potion. He would make things right again, he had too.

"Zaqurah, you should take ootau that she is safe. The loss of time is not the Targian way," Farstar focused on Rory as he raised the potion bottle to his mouth and desired that taste of home. *"Rory use caution while on Earth, we shall return to our own soon enough."*

"What is your own," Rory sneered.

"My existence is shared; being many parts of one…" Farstar hesitated, *"that is my own."*

At Farstar's words, Rory's thoughts transported him back to the wog sy. He remembered Targ's deep penetrating touch in his mind, a touch that even now he could not shake. Targ held his soul, still guiding him and nourishing him. Rory's Absorption Spirit Crystal tingled with the memory of his part, in Targ's re-uniting with planet Earth. His life, a tale already written, meant there would never be escape from Targ or the things that were to occur. *"You are ever the wisest, zaqurah,"* Rory closed his mind.

The days of the past two weeks had proven successful in telling a historical account of the team's experiences through the hyper-band bung technology of Momma. Now Zyleon felt it was time to introduce their findings to the International Alliance of Archaeoastronomy Sciences. "Just wait until we introduce the Targians when they ask for supporting evidence," Zyleon chuckled.

"That brings me to my point, Uncle Zyleon." Autumn took a deep breath of the humid jungle air. They strolled through, one of the many well-used paths surrounding the camp. The sun, partially hidden by slow-moving clouds, cast large patches of shade between the trees. "Uncle Zyleon, I know it's hard to accept everything that I have told you, but after we are finished with the release of this discovery, I must return to Pik. Neither Etta, nor this child, will be the subject of the world's criticisms." Autumn gently grabbed Zyleon's hand and held it on her belly. "I want you to feel her."

Zyleon closed his eyes and waited. His hand warm against her blouse. A small electric ripple moved through his palm and in his surprise, he yanked his hand away.

"Feels neat, huh," Autumn rocked from side to side. "Honestly, I thought I'd end up having a baby with someone like Daj." She crinkled her nose, "Not becoming the mother of an alien Queen." Autumn kicked a pebble from the path feeling the tiny shocks that the baby sent out. She knew Mooti was enjoying this adventure, but she wasn't too sure about her uncle.

"We just got you back," Zyleon, sighed. "What about your work?"

"What is happening to me is my work, so you'll just have to come for a visit. Pik is very beautiful and I'm sure Etta would love to show you around."

"What about that Trader, wouldn't you be safer here or on Targ?"

"Farstar and Rory have that covered, Uncle, and if you haven't noticed, Etta is an excellent body guard." Autumn gave a right sideways glance and a slight nod of her head toward the trees. "She's been with us since we started our walk."

Zyleon casually looked in the direction of his niece's nod, just making out the Rock Dwarf's movements. "She blends well with the trees. I think I would like to visit Pik and learn more of its inhabitants."

"That's the spirit," Autumn made a fist and playfully bumped her uncle's chin.

Etta quietly shared their walk back; the small Rock Dwarf was full of cautious curiosity, not daring to stray far from her charge. This new world was full of wonderful sounds and smells. She liked it so far and would do her best to remember every detail of her stay and take the stories home to her kin.

Baxter kept shaking his head. "It's not played like that, here let me show you." He took the guitar from Winston and slowly played the chords. "Practice your finger movements, and you'll be making music in no time flat." Baxter handed the guitar back to his nephew and wagged his fingers in the air.

"With six fingers you would think the kid a prodigy," Nacoo said, guzzling the last bit of his beer. "Would anyone like another?" He belched rather noisily and placed his empty bottle in the glass-recycling container.

"I would," Daj answered and continued to strum his own guitar, coaxing Winston along.

Moonracer was on his third Earth beer and beginning to enjoy the intoxication of it. "This is good drink but I grow hungry," he said as Nacoo passed by.

"Food sounds good," Radin, spoke up. "Let's go to the food tent and taste some of today's cuisine." He chuckled, feeling a little more comfortable around the aliens.

"Yes, I think I would enjoy that," Moonracer absorbed the growing self-confidence that Radin sent out. He knew that only the seven komi having implants would be able to communicate with him on a Targian level, but even so, he could amuse himself with this man. "Shall we go," he said, then touched his mind. *"My existence here is not to harm you,"* and with a half-smirk on his lips, Moonracer watched Radin change expressions from relaxed to startled.

"That's just too freaking weird," Radin gulped down his beer, wiped his dark chin with a napkin, and started for the door. "Come on," he said, looking behind him and swung his arm in a gesture for

Moonracer to follow. Abruptly, Radin's arm stopped in mid swing; he'd made contact with Dawn's shoulder.

"Radin," Dawn squeaked. "Ouch, what was that for," she rubbed her shoulder; sounding injured and glanced at Moonracer, who appeared ready to burst into laughter.

Radin felt his face burn. "I am sorry, I did not see you," he said, his rich voice thick with apology. "Are you alright?"

"I'll be fine. Where are you off to anyhow," she asked, moving her arm around in circles.

"To the food tent," Moonracer piped up, grinning foolishly.

"Good, I was just on my way in here to see if anyone wanted to eat. Would you mind some company?"

"We are always up for a lady's company," Radin answered.

"Pardon me," Nacoo boomed coming back from his beer run. "Can I get through the doorway? I have a very important delivery to make." He put on his best grin for Dawn.

Dawn bounced past Nacoo, with red faced Radin and a smirking Moonracer following. "Hey," he yelled after them, "was it something I said?" He heard Dawn's mousy laugh and watched for another second before entering the room where his son, brother, and good friend were. *"How long do you think Hank will stay in his stupor,"* he sent to Daj.

Daj stopped strumming and looked up at Nacoo, *"you're such a dingo."*

Nacoo's boisterous laughter filled the room.

Trombula sat in this small circular room with his fellow Targians, each placing oneself in a deep, open-mind meditation. This level of consciousness was a well-practiced rite on Targ. However, here in Kandoria and without the nourishment of their home planet, he wondered how long they would be able to maintain the circle. A slow, steady stream of energy flowed through their physical forms, healing and deepening their connection. This allowed him to sense everyone on a multifaceted plane and take in each Targians new experiences. What Targ had ingrained in them was now coming to fruition: a new species to aid in the survival of their planet and the return back to Earth.

Trombula touched Partagul's aresh in Farstar and remembered his ancestor with the reverence of a young Targian. Even so, this sharing of knowledge exchanged between them, there was a part of Farstar that Trombula could not penetrate. It felt as if the Ancient Warrior stood before him, nay allowing him to absorb further memories. Trombula sensed Farstar's hunger for the planet's sustenance. It prickled throughout his own body for he also desired the taste of Targ's nectar. *"Pah,"* Trombula said and next entered TaChoo.

TaChoo recounted trying to understand Daj's kom emotions and the analysis she applied to the brain structure. The same was true for Hank learning about Dawn. Trombula allowed the energy of their joy to circle through the group. The effect took its toll on Rory and he dropped his defenses. Trombula entered and touched his Absorption Spirit Crystal to extract his memory records, but once again, he felt the Ancient Warrior standing guard and he could not penetrate further. Trombula sensed thought forms of confusion in Rory, causing a ripple of its energy to swirl around him. He pulled back and rested at the edge of Rory's mind. *"Pah,"* he said. He thought he brushed against Farstar's aresh, as he pulled slowly out of his meditative state and found that when he opened his eyes, Farstar was gazing upon him.

"I shall return to Targ with all of our collected knowledge and return with instructions at Badu's first turning." Trombula stood, bowing his head and levitated from the room.

TaChoo stretched her arms, her twelve fingers splayed out in front of her, *"would anyone care to glide about Kandoria with me?"*

"I shall," said Hank, lightheartedly, as he levitated turning in slow circles.

"I shall not," Farstar, answered. He was already standing by the door. *"Zaqurah, accompany me?"* He spoke slow and easy to Rory.

Rory, the last to rise and still a bit confused, answered, *"Va, I trevi explanation."*

"You shall have it." Farstar raised the corner of his lip briefly, in a gesture of secretive pleasure, and disappeared into the corridor.

Rory followed close behind Farstar, considering what had just happened to him. *"That was most unusual of you, zaqurah."*

"As I desired it to be, you were not ready for Trombula's extraction. You are in need of healing."

"Targ's nourishment still flows in my blood, but I grow weaker without my full measure." They exited Kandoria and entered the cavern, where a few of Radin's men stopped working to stare at them as they glided past. They left them to their thoughts of fear and wonder.

"We shall go into the forest; I have found a place of high energy vibration. We shall be safe there." Farstar handed Rory a full bottle of potion. *"Drink this,"* he said, extracting a second one from beneath his robe, taking a long, comforting drink from the container.

Rory drank hungrily, emptying the bottle of its potion. *"Where did you get this?"* he asked, his face lifted to the sky with an expression of near ecstasy.

"Etta," Farstar smirked.

Rory dropped his jaw at the mention of the Rock Dwarf. *"Where did she get it?"*

"Smoot," Farstar was enjoying his zaqurah's confused curiosity.

"I shall honor them," Rory stood a bit straighter, *"the potion was strong."*

"Va, it was ordered by the incubator of the Queen of Pik. She also requested that I hesna you and the plans you have made for your seedling." Farstar felt a rush of pure exultation come from Rory, causing a small burst of pleasant laughter to escape him.

"Autumn requested," Rory triumphantly chimed, with a sensation of humility creeping through him, *"how did you block Trombula's extraction?"*

"I used getch ta fruick."

Rory smirked pensively, *"shield of parapet,"* he sighed, relaxing more as the potion pulsed through his system. *"A powerful gift from Quinni Partagul, one must be of great mental strength to use such ability,"* Rory said, realizing they hovered over the center of a raised platform, choked with overgrown vegetation. The resemblance of an ancient temple lay in ruins around them, in this very dense, undisturbed part of the jungle. Rory tilted his head, listening to the rhythmic beat of the magnetic pulses that resonated through his body. A cascading torrent of vibrant energy danced before his eyes, his mind open and sensitive to its song. *"Such beauty, it caresses the very core of my aresh."*

"As mine," Farstar replied. *"Oorah, the temple of regeneration and kinetic light travel was built by our ancestors. It is a connection to Targ, and it is how Smoot journeyed here with the ingredients for Etta to blend our elixir."*

"Journeyed here," Rory repeated, enthralled. His silken white robe fluttered as if fondled by a breeze. *"Yet another gift… zaqurah, you have unlocked the Sacred Krish. A significant universe crossing, closed by Targ, lifetimes ago,"* Rory mused, slightly daunted. The magnetic pull began to increase. He looked up, seeing the gridlines brighten. *"Are we to travel?"*

"Va," Farstar reached out, grabbing Rory by the shoulder; prisms filled the space between them, blending with the color of their eyes. A flicker of pain crossed their brows and then they were standing on the highest balcony, in front of the door that led into the room Rory had given to Autumn.

Rory looked down upon his city. *"Pik,"* he whispered in amazement.

"When Targ was healing me in the Keiyat Garden he allowed Autumn to enter into my energy presence, and at that moment, Targ had Nacoo in Farth, Nacoo carried Autumn's bung which I had no knowledge of at the time, and so because of that unobstructed connection, an interaction took place between Autumn, Nacoo and me. This interaction allowed me to explore Targ's deep, recesses of sacred memories. A place of fantastic magnitude, when I left the Keiyat Garden, I left with powerful knowledge," Farstar paused. *"More even than Thorb,"* he said, arrestingly, and leaned on the stone railing. The sun was warm on his cool skin, and he took in its comfort for a moment. *"We cannot stay zaqurah, your Queen desires your company."*

Rory felt Farstar's grip on his shoulder and once again, the magnetic pull began.

Zyleon shook Marlo and Olander's hands in greeting. "I hope this goes well, I'm as nervous as a mouse being stalked by a cat."

"You will do fine." Olander's words sounded brave, but he looked like the mouse.

"Zy," Kuranna spoke calmly. "Fredrick Meer, the authority on anthropology has arrived. I believe that is everyone." Kuranna gave her husband a reassuring smile and took her place next to him at the meeting table.

During the first few minutes, Zyleon introduced his discovery team and the tribal council members. He noted the serious expressions of his peers, as he shook each person's hand, and they settled into their seats. "Gentleman," he stated, "to get started, I wish to present to you, the bung recordings of my team members." He motioned to Nacoo to dim the lights. "Momma, activate hologram player," Zyleon spoke into his hyper-band.

From the center of the table, a hologram screen spread in front of them, displaying a carefully edited account of their physical experiences on Targ and Pik. When Momma had finished playing an hour later, Martin Elwood, the physicist expert, who had his fingertips pressed together swiveling his chair left to right, was the first to speak. "We have no time for hoaxes," he said, with haughtiness in his voice. "You better have some hard evidence backing up this flight-of-fancy program." He raised his hand in a gesture for Nacoo to flick on the lights.

Daj sat back, resting an elbow on the chair arm, thumb cradling his chin, fingers lazily spread over his lips. He wanted to tear apart Martin Elwood's skeptical sarcasm, but kept silent, as asked to do. Instead, he tipped up his hat with his free hand, and in defense, stared brazenly at the disbelieving Martin Elwood.

Martin Elwood shifted in his seat.

"With the exception of you four gentlemen, everyone at this table is a witness, and part of this phenomenal discovery." Professor Zyleon set his jaw. "You of all people," he looked directly at Martin Elwood, "should know Momma's security system would not allow for such a hoax. If my people had not been as prepared as possible for the unknown, you would not be sitting here today."

Dawn smiled at Fredrick Meer, seeing the questioning look in his eyes.

"Please continue," said Leonard Ketchum, President of the International Alliance of Archaeoastronomy Sciences. He gazed steadily at Professor Zyleon, an inquisitive nuance in his voice.

"We are prepared to take you into Kandoria, when you are ready," Zyleon said, replacing his hyper-band in his vest pocket.

Warden Gresham, the specialist in field study, pushed his chair back and stood up. "Let's go," he said, his voice quavering with anticipation.

"Please," Professor Zyleon raised a hand, "one moment." He stepped away from the table and went over to the doorway. "We would like you to meet the Targians that will be accompanying us."

There was a brief moment of stillness when TaChoo, with gracefulness, levitated into the room. "Shish," she greeted them. Farstar, Rory, and Hank came in behind her.

Warden Gresham gasped and abruptly sat back down.

Dawn stifled a giggle at the fearful, disbelieving looks on Fredrick Meer and Martin Elwood's faces.

Leonard Ketchum rose to his feet and extended his hand to TaChoo. "Hello," he said, his tone giving away his bravado.

TaChoo reached out with her slender six-fingered hand, enjoying the sense of his awe. "I am TaChoo, daughter of Thorb, the Communicator of Targ. Farstar of Targ stands to my right and next to him is Rory of Pik, to my left is Hank of Targ."

Leonard Ketchum, dry mouthed, introduced his four associates, never taking his eyes off the extraordinary being that hovered in front of him.

"Now for more — hard evidence," Professor Zyleon grinned devilishly at Martin Elwood. "Let us go into Kandoria."

Winston, Moonracer, and Etta stood just outside the doorway, having chosen not to enter the meeting room; they now met the stares of dazed disbelief, as each of the strangers passed them by.

Autumn came to stand beside the flustered cross-armed Etta, who made strange little growling noises, trying her best to intimidate these human males and making Autumn laugh softly.

The people of the village had lined the donkey cart path leading to Kandoria with offerings of foods, herbs, flowers and, beaded jewelry. *"It seems we are being worshipped,"* Hank said blithely to Moonracer and Winston, who had stepped in beside him.

"We shall honor them for their kindness," Moonracer teased back.

Rory picked up a wooden necklace, each bead carved to resemble a Targian's face. *"The Dyeckians shall find these gifts pleasing. Pik shall be the first to trade Earth goods."* He spoke impassively to Autumn, and then handed the necklace to Etta, bringing a broad, yellow smile to her small, bearded face.

"The Queen of Pik will be pleased that you are making such arrangements." Autumn anticipated Mooti's tickling shocks of recognition at Rory's mind touch. Only this time there was a sharp, burning sting. She winced and slowed her steps when a second wave of pain came over her.

Farstar and Rory, both, felt Autumn's discomfort, but Moonracer was first at Autumn's side, *"Shish Zaf, ze rit sca kolum trey."*

"Shish jant," Autumn put her arm in his; the pain was stabbing, like a blade slicing up along her spine. *"Yes, I am in need of healing. Please take me somewhere quiet."* Autumn communicated privately to Moonracer.

Moonracer stood upon the Sacred Krish of Targ, holding his dutom securely. *"We must take you to the Keiyat Garden to receive mienco."*

"How did we get here," Autumn gasped with another pain. Her mind was spinning from the fact she was standing on the violet planet of Targ.

"It is a gift from Ancient Communicator Tuvah. It is a form of apporting using cosmic rays." Moonracer levitated Autumn. *"Zaf, Targ shall assist the growth of rah, but we must hurry before your body rejects her."*

"You sound as if you knew this would happen." Beads of sweat rolled down her face, and she leaned on Moonracer for support. *"Vessa,"* he said, urgently, and they lifted higher into the air.

"Targ is connected to all his children. He knew how Rory would attempt to start a new race, for encoding took place in the wog sy ~ growing room. This knowledge is rooted very deeply into his Absorption Spirit Crystal. Targ has just recently opened that part of his mind and he is beginning to understand his role in the planet's survival."

"So how did Rory block Targ's communication with him?" Autumn bent forward breathing hard, a small trickle of warmth traveled down the inside of her leg. *"I am bleeding,"* she moaned.

"We are almost there, Zaf. Rory used Ockoraerion blocking potion. It is toxic to Targ, so in times of this silence, Targ connected with those closest to him. Rory can live apart from Targ but not without him." Moonracer entered the Keiyat Garden and levitated Autumn into a supine position. *"Healing shall take place now."*

"Please," Autumn grabbed Moonracer's hand. *"Let Professor Zyleon know what has happened. He has waited a long time for a discovery like this."* Autumn could feel Targ's tendrils entering at many different points of her body and a warm, calming sensation crept throughout her. She could feel Mooti move ever so slightly, reassured, she gave in completely to the planet, knowing her baby would be safe.

When Farstar came through the Sacred Krish, Starshine was there to meet him. *"Welcome home Quinni Farstar."*

Farstar felt recognition of Partagul's zaqurah, Imrak in Starshine. *"We are united."* He responded.

"Targ has requested a linking with you while Quinni Autumn goes through mienco."

Farstar bowed his head to Starshine, grateful that she was safe in the vines of Targ. *"I shall pay honor to Moonracer."*

"Quinni Farstar, Moonracer would die for his dutom. Honor is not necessary."

"Pah oa rit Starshine," Farstar thought of his own seeder and smiled, knowing that he would have done the same.

"There is feasting in Thorb's garden for Foster and Treya. They have danced the Dance of Nar this past turning and shall ne ootau in your return home."

"I shall feast." Farstar remembered the food that Targ provided for his feast of the Dance of Nar with Autumn. *"I shall look for you, you that are bestowed with the great honor of Warrior Imrak."* A knowing look exchanged between them.

They parted at the linking room entrance; Farstar's silvery hair fell about his fine-featured face as he nodded to Starshine, anticipation rushing through him. He was glad to be home and ready to spend time allowing Targ inside, feeding and healing him, removing the kom emotion from his tired spirit. His robe slid off his shoulders and down onto the yellow moss beneath his feet, pressing sensuously into Targ's warm touches. He began to sink. Tendrils slid over him, cleaning him with a soft gelatinous coating, as he sank lower into the soft cushion of his loving planet.

Targ entered into a ravenous Farstar. *"This journey takes me to far from you, Targ."* A ripple of electric shocks raced up his spine and into his brain, feelers spread across the inside of his skull. Impulses of magnetic energy seeped into every cell, invigorating his spirit. *"I have longed to be ~ one with you."* A single feeler pushed its way into his shared Absorption Spirit Crystal. Partagul's aresh intertwined with his, memories set free, side by side with Farstars. *"I am grateful to share such wisdom."* His spirit filled with reverence.

His body vibrated with the energy of the planet, and his mind hummed with the wisdom of the Great Warrior Partagul's life. Knowledge imprinted rapidly into his cells, methods of new communication, protection, and the entrusted role of Prest ta Wadoni ~ Keeper of Mysteries. *"I am humbled to receive this highest of honors,"* Farstar was completely open, fluid and flowing through the core of Targ, it was a sensation remembered in his beginning stages of growth, the feeling of purity.

"It is time to return," the planet rumbled. *"Continue your journey Prest ta Wadoni."*

"Pah," Farstar whispered.

Targ unhurriedly brought him back to the yellow-moss surface of the linking room. The planet's retreat, taken in measured movements, reconnected Farstar's energy body to his solidifying physical one. Vines slithered around his illuminated form. *"The growing female child shall not survive without nourishment. When she calls to you, bring her here for ootau."* Targ touched his mind like a great rolling cloud.

"I shall." Farstar answered. His fine silver hair lay moistly about his slender, gray shoulders.

"Do this under cloak, Prest ta Wadoni," Targ resonated.

Farstar stood with his head inclined, allowing the last flickers of soft crackling light to subside. His thoughts clear on his journey, a journey that would forever change many worlds.

XXII

When Moonracer had so swiftly taken Autumn from her side, she did not wait for an answer why. Etta ran after him with a speed only her powerful little legs could reach. Rory had glided easily beside her, and even after Moonracer vanished, he knew just where to go. They sat in silence, waiting on the crumbling stones of an old temple until dusk, when Moonracer made his sudden appearance, without Autumn.

Enraptured by the story of saving the Incubator and the Queen child, Etta had not noticed they traveled a clear path carved of stone. On one side a solid wall and on the other the jungle, nay touching the walkway, Moonracer slowed their pace, scanning the mountainous side as they continued onward. Etta picked up a tiny stone and crunched it between her teeth; it was rich in mineral, a good place for mining. Moonracer stopped moving and placed a hand on the mountain wall. She heard him speak the Dwarf word "gort," and wondered at his magic when the wall changed into an entrance leading underground; its stonework sculpted the same as on Pik. "Sac," she pointed at the doorway.

"Va, Etta," Moonracer spoke in her tongue. "This Earth world has been inhabited by many beings. Some left, some stayed." He looked steadily into Etta's big dark eyes. "The Ancients decided it was safer for those who stayed to remain in hiding, away from komi."

"Oti ha," Etta puzzled over what Moonracer was saying.

"Va, the Ancients are here." Moonracer stepped inside the opening.

Etta and Rory stepped in behind him.

"How is it you know these things." Rory sensed a powerful energy as they descended into the depths of the cave.

"Olden Communicator Tuvah," Moonracer answered, allowing Tuvah's aresh to touch Rory's mind.

"*A great gift, Quinni Tuvah has honored you with.*" Rory inclined his head to Moonracer and placed his cold gray hand on Etta's broad shoulder. "Etta, why do you shudder?"

Etta pointed into the silent darkness and grunted, "Oti."

The three stood face to face with a hundred of Etta's kin, in full, finely crafted armor, at the ready.

"ZANK," the most rugged-looking of the bunch yelled out, slamming his ax on his shield.

"Krumbel, urend sumesh yana wo," Moonracer spoke the words, Krumbel; legend descends upon us.

Rory gazed steadily before him. "*The ancient pact...*" his thought trailed off.

A clamorous ringing filled the cavern; until the one called, Krumbel raised his hand. All eyes were on the strangers, "Ex bach!" His voice was strong and powerful, reverberating in this dark, underground chamber.

Etta looked up at Rory. His keen eyes sparkled as lanterns were lit; she could hardly believe what was happening, her curious excitement building so that she proudly thumped her chest in greeting.

"Tuvah Moonracer of Targ is who speaks," he answered, bowing his silvery head to Krumbel.

Whispers that echoed in animated tones circulated throughout the underground dwellers, Krumbel raised a gauntlet, and like a sudden wind, silence fell. He studied the three before him and asked one more question to complete the legendary appearance of the three, "ex ru boosta."

"ETTA VO PIK," Etta yelled before Moonracer could answer. She grabbed Rory's hand, lifting it above her head, "RORY VO PIK," her enthusiasm contagious.

Krumbel grunted a laugh, "daple ru nok, luzyd."

Rory smiled, "*in Krumbel's words, truth is told, welcome,*" he cocked his head sideways looking at Moonracer. "*I wonder how the komi shall react to this.*"

"*The komi have already met Etta.*" Moonracer reminded Rory as the Mountain Dwarfs escorted them through the tunnels.

Etta held Rory's hand, jibber jabbering so fast that he could not understand her. Feeling her warmth comforted him from the cold, strange dampness. He could sense her desire to walk among her kin and reluctantly released her hand. "Go," he said, shivering.

Etta blended into the midst of the clanging throng but was back in moments with furs for her companions.

"Copaa rit, Etta," Moonracer shuddered.

Etta, with hands on her hips, gave a satisfied sigh at having aided the Targians. Now she would stay near, for she felt closer to her own home with them. She thought of Autumn and even though Moonracer told them of her safety, Etta wanted to keep watch over her, and Rory seemed so lost. She remembered finding a shivering, scared, child hiding in a wall crevice in one of the old passageways back on Pik. The child cried in her arms all the way through the shadow tunnels, to the well-traveled passages. There his tears had turned into sniffles at the recognition of the door arches, leading out into the city. Etta stayed close to Rory as they walked.

Rory heard a low rumble come from his small friend and placed his cold slender hand on her thick shoulder. Etta's compassion comforted him.

Krumbel spoke to the guards standing in front of the biggest drawbridge Etta had ever seen. She was standing before the first of many intricate workings of a great Dwarf Kingdom. Massive chains pulled taut and a long, low rumbling filled the cavern. The bridge lowered, opening the way across a chasm so deep Etta could not see the bottom. The bridge was as wide as twenty Dwarfs, which she was thankful to be close to the center and holding a levitating Targian's hand. The bridge rebounded with the weighted footfalls of this mighty warrior race; armor clinked against shield and battle-axe. She touched the short sword Rory had given her but wondered if a battle-axe would fit her hand better.

Once on the other side, Krumbel dismissed the troupe, leaving only two of his best beside him. He led the small party of six through a great hall, lined with towering stone pillars carved from the mountain itself; torches adorned each column illuminating the golden inlayed runes around their bases. The floor shone, polished to a point where their faces reflected back at them and each sound echoed a song about strength and valor. Statues with faces of a long ago past greeted them, as they entered into a smaller passageway. Krumbel pulled a perfectly crafted metal key in the form of a Targian from his pocket and placed it in the keyhole of a heavy wooden door. It creaked on its cast-iron hinges, moaning with displeasure at being disturbed after so many years.

When the door swung fully open, the two guards moved into the chamber, lighting the cobwebbed torches. Engraved on the center of the floor were four symbols. Krumbel instructed the guards to stand outside, close the door, and keep watch.

"What happened to a welcome of feasting," Rory asked Etta, gazing at his family symbol, a shooting star carved into the floor. He noticed that along with his, Etta's crest, a short-horned helmet, and Krumbel's, a seven-jeweled crown of gold, formed a pyramid lining the outside of a circle. The inside of the circle portrayed Moonracer's family symbol, the seven crescent moons of Targ.

Moonracer stood on his symbol. "It is time to unlock the pathway between our worlds; stand in your place. Be still and take comfort," Moonracer's voice reverberated with an unmistakable sense of anticipation.

"Sac," Etta questioned, cautiously stepping onto her mark.

"Sac," Krumbel grunted in reply and stepped onto his own.

"Safe," Rory repeated, in admiration of Farstar's seedling.

"Vessa," Moonracer called out. The pyramid shape they stood upon, pulled away from the stone surrounding it, and started to raise, stone ground against stone, shaking the floor beneath them. A violet light filled the room, the ground dropped out from under them, opening up into a canopy of stars, and then just as fast, they found themselves standing on the balcony of Rory's study back on Pik.

"Pik," Etta said, breathlessly.

Rory smiled, "home." His city hummed with activity below them; he stepped up to the railing, taking in the full rays of the delightfully warm sun. *"I am comforted,"* he mind touched Moonracer.

Krumbel felt his flesh tingle with the touch of the sun's rays and grunted his annoyance, shielding his bushy-browed eyes; he stepped soundly into the dimness of Rory's study.

"In ancient days our races knew each other well. Many moons have turned, and now once more we are reunited." Moonracer said, following behind the thickset Krumbel.

Etta studied Krumbel's axes that crisscrossed his sturdy back; it gave her a peculiar feeling and she once again found herself touching her short sword. She gave him a critical once over, noticing he was a stout, coarse-looking Dwarf, with long scruffy hair and a beard, unceremoniously braided, that hung down to his girded belt. Her fingers twitched with a compelling urge to comb and re-braid that muddle. She blushed when she noticed Krumbel staring at her with a mischievous twinkle in his eye.

Krumbel made a sound like a rumbling purr then turned his attention back to Moonracer.

The foretelling of this legend descends upon us." Moonracer looked steadily at Krumbel. "I ask you Krumbel shall we stand together in this new age."

Krumbel thumped his breastplate with a resounding clang. "Uh," he approved.

"There are others yet to call upon to join with us. Their doorways shall reopen soon.

"Join us for what," Rory asked curiously, still standing on the balcony in the sun's warm embrace.

"We join for war," Krumbel said in his harsh dwarf tongue.

Etta crossed the room and plopped down on a pillow; she made a small gasping sound and covered her face with her thick little hands.

"The Ockoraerions hunger once again; already they have threatened King Tri."

"I must go to Autumn," alarmed, Rory's heart beat faster.

"I shall return to Targ with Krumbel before returning to Earth. Take ootau, Quinni Farstar shall bring Autumn here to Pik, when the Queen is safe to travel." Moonracer inclined his head and placed a hand on Krumbel's shoulder, *"Pah, Quinni Rory."* In a shimmer like a wave of heat, the two were gone.

Rory looked out over his city and pulled an almost empty potion bottle from inside his robe. He had much to prepare, new escape tunnels, walls needed building, and old tunnels closed, protection for his Queen and the inhabitants of Pik. If the Ockoraerions hungered, he was sure the Traders would stand in their wake. His heart pounded in his temples as he tipped the near empty bottle upward, receiving the last of its nourishment.

Etta tugged on Rory's free hand, getting his attention; she produced a full bottle of potion from her pocket. "Faa…staa," she tried to pronounce Farstar's name. "Ro…ree," she giggled seeing the look of pleasure cross Rory's face.

"Copaa rit," Rory put an arm around his small friend and drank deeply from the nourishing elixir.

Trombula sat next to Professor Zyleon in one of the comfortable, meeting room chairs, recounting the past events of the week, while they waited for the others to arrive. "They are putting our names in the Scientist Hall of Fame, the most legendary scientific-minded men and women to ever to walk the planet Earth," Zyleon said, rubbing his chin. "Imagine us, Trombula, celebrated for a calculated discovery." He laughed sarcastically. "I find that the honor received is not the piece of pie I expected it to be. The real honor belongs to Targ."

Zyleon stared into Trombula's sparkling eyes. "We have long awaited this discovery, a treasure map to the human origins." He waved his arm through the air in front of him. "Our world has only just begun to understand a tiny portion, of what Targ has the ability to awaken in us." Zyleon felt a sensation like drops of water rolling down his skin, inside his head. He squeezed his eyebrows together. *"Did you feel that?"*

"Va, Professor, Targ nes ootau," Trombula mind touched him sending a calm reassurance.

"He takes comfort in unusual ways," Zyleon sighed, his thoughts skipping to Autumn, "First stop, Pik to await the arrival of my new great niece."

Trombula glanced up at the doorway.

"Did I hear you say the arrival of your new great niece," Dawn asked, bouncing into the room her voice jingling with merriment.

"Yes, but no arrival yet, just talking."

"Oh," she said, disappointed and flopped into a chair.

"Talking about what?" Nacoo asked, winking at Dawn as he entered the room. He had quietly followed her through the corridors just to watch her walk.

"Autumn," Zyleon answered, giving him a sly look. "So now all we need is Daj, that boy is always late," he sighed, glancing at his watch.

"That's our Daj," Nacoo chuckled.

"Professor, I thought I heard you say something about Pik too," Dawn played with a strawberry colored curl that lay next to her chin, "is that where Autumn is?"

"Not yet but she will be returning."

"Why?" asked the reliably late Daj.

"It was her decision," he leaned forward in his chair, resting his elbows on the arms. He clasped his hands together. "It's what she wanted, which is why I asked you here." Zyleon eyed Dawn, "What's your decision, girl?"

"It will take some time to set up a new drawer in Momma," Dawn twirled her hair thoughtfully, "so I've decided to stay here and continue documentation of our findings." Dawn smiled playfully at the Professor.

"All right," Nacoo slapped his big hands together. "So when I bring in the customers, I expect you to be waiting to greet me." Nacoo rumbled and raised an eyebrow at Dawn.

"Only if you bring me presents."

"I take it Nacoo, that you will continue to pilot," Trombula spoke aloud, approvingly.

"Yeah, it's kind of implanted," Nacoo tapped his head.

Daj laughed, "We've had some fantastic things happen, haven't we cobber."

"What about you, kangaroo cowboy," Dawn teased.

"I'm returning to Targ to carry out some geological studies. So spitfire don't you worry your sweet little red head. I'll be back to have some fun with you."

Zyleon laughed. "Galactic travel is on my agenda. The I. A. A. S. has asked for further investigation of these new worlds that we all shall be exploring." He made a sweeping gesture to everyone in the room. "Baxter has agreed to handle the media and Trombula will stay as overseer of Kandoria." Zyleon sat back in his chair with a confident smile, "so it sounds like Dawn is elected to keep the camp, up and running." He paused, then asked, "What do you say, girl? Can we count on you?"

Dawn's hazel eyes grew wide. "Oh, Professor," tears threatened to come at the thought of everyone leaving, but she rapidly blinked them away. "I'll be glad to do it," she said, a lump in her throat.

Trombula nodded his approval.

"Don't fret about a thing Dawn. Trombula will be at your side," Professor Zyleon gave Nacoo a jesting glance, "and Nacoo will always be available. All you have to do is ask, and I'm sure he'll gladly fly me back home to help you out, or give you a lift to anywhere. That is if you run into any problems," Zyleon conveyed, soothingly.

Nacoo's cheeks darkened. "I'll take you anywhere you want to go," he sighed deeply, "anywhere." At times it was hard to look into her eyes, so much had happened, so many deep and personal feelings threatened to sneak out. Life would never be the same for any of them. He grinned foolishly at the thought, knowing that each of them already knew so much more about one another than any of them could ever have imagined. His grin widened, "anytime," Nacoo said, realizing he had left his mind open and all eyes were upon him. "Oops," he eyed Daj feeling a bit, like a little boy caught with his hand in the cookie jar.

"Right, we understand," Daj, laughed unreservedly as did everyone else.

Farstar embraced Autumn; her rich human aroma filled his senses. *"We must return to Pik."* Her body warmth penetrated his coolness, and he pulled her closer.

"Let us share aresh before we return," Autumn played at the edges of Farstar's mind.

Farstar trembled at her touches. *"We shall,"* he agreed and plunged into her mind. He heard her softly moan her acceptance of him, and he pushed forward into her swirling depths of kom vitality. Her essence, moved within him like the sweet, warm nectar of Targ.

Autumn delighted in Farstar's thoughts. He quivered each time she caressed a part of his energy body, a pleasure to her own senses. She craved him, tumbling rapidly into his being; it was nirvana, an intense rapture of spirit intertwining with spirit. Light energy sparkled and whirled around them, tiny electric shocks raced throughout her body, a shower of icy rain, an intense desert heat, a weakness, and strength. She was acutely sensitive to Farstar's powerful presence within her. It was as if he tested her strength, every cell in her body yearned for him to saturate her with his electrifying might, *"Farstar,"* she gasped as he, with a leisure tenderness, immersed into the mystery of her soul.

Farstar's energy body shimmered, taking in more of Autumn's aresh, his Targian nature being stimulated with each movement, driving him onward. He breathed deeply of her spiritual vapor; it was invigorating, rousing a dormant memory of an ancient practice. Increasing his descent into her realm of being, caused muffled cries to arise in her throat, but he could not stop. Hunger driving him to satiate himself with her life was strong. Her sweetness was artu to his mind. He stood powerful in the midst of her aresh, ready for complete engagement; he was at the edge of her core. *"Zifla, ancient trevi beckons, shall we fulfill the call."* Farstar felt Autumn's fragile mind shudder at his words.

Autumn gathered the strength she had. *"Continue,"* she breathed, his life force was deliriously intoxicating.

Farstar's spirit burned with an untamed frenzy — the height of an ancient fiery obsession to plunge into her life core, but he knew, to continue, would snuff out the light growing dimmer in Autumn. Every moment that passed was vital. It took all of his resolve to slowly, gently pull back from the edge of her core being. He sighed, turning away his trevi and took ootau. Knowing she shared with him what her human structure would allow.

That moment of such intense awareness had left Autumn euphorically weak. She slumped against Farstar's body; allowing her thoughts to flutter uninhibited about his mind, his cool, steady breathing was soothing to her shaking, sweaty, body, but she was conscious enough to know of his struggle to keep from plummeting back into the depths of her soul. *"I am tired Farstar,"* Autumn spoke, sounding as if she stood deep inside a long, hollow tunnel.

Farstar levitated her into the sleeping room of their home. He lay Autumn down on the cushions, letting his hand slide gently over her swollen belly. He felt the tingle of the child within and whispered, *"pah oa rit, Queen Mooti."* Then disrobing, he lay down, close to Autumn, taking comfort in her warmth.

"Copaa rit, Farstar," Autumn gazed into his scintillating eyes. *"I hope that someday we will be able to completely immerse, to answer the… ancient call."* She closed her eyes and faded quickly into sleep.

Farstar had stopped Rory from exploring her core energy, a Targian act that would leave komi dead. Now he contemplated whether she was able to survive the depth he had gone, if a possibility existed to achieve such a pure state of being with her. His hunger stirred.

"Farstar," he heard Targ's voice rumble in his mind.

"Va, Targ," Farstar answered, and caressed the vines that curled around his body.

"You rage with fervent trevi, a desire I shall ease, Prest ta Wadoni." Targ penetrated the back of Farstar's neck. *"I shall link you with Amar."* Targ wound his way into the center of Farstar's Absorption Spirit Crystal and began his link with Amar.

Farstar ached for completion of the ancient practice, his mind converged almost savagely with Amar; she was a strong Targian female. She whispered in the old tongue, and he thrust into her thoughts with crazed abandon, linking, through Targ, with her aresh. There he stopped, hanging for a moment in the misty vapor of this unfamiliar embrace. A strange light filled his mind, and words of an ancient past asked if he was prepared. Amar chanted, luring him deeper into the secrets of her spirit, of the universe from which she was born. He shook with longing to gather this knowledge, as she pushed into him, searching for his core.

His body arched upward, *"AV,"* he screamed for Targ, *"AV, ISHAG TI AW AUTUMN,"* he screamed again, unable to stop the force growing inside him. *"NO, SHE IS NOT AUTUMN, AV TARG, AV,"* Farstar tried to pull back from Amar, and darkness answered his plea.

For the first time Targ tasted Farstar's tears of distress. *"Vuel,"* sleep, Targ rumbled. The planet started to heal and absorb Farstar's experience, this bond he held with such strength. The planet felt a great compassion and entered Autumn, adding to her implant, his minerals, and each time she returned for the child's nourishing, he would add more until her blood flowed more Targian than human. He would give his Prest ta Wadoni ootau, that Farstar might safely complete the ancient practice with this female.

XXIII

aj brushed the Targian soil from the clear yellow sapphire. "This must be the jemba stone," he whistled under his breath making his horse whinny.

"It is a stone of magic," Starshine said, amused by his seeder's reaction at finding the stone.

"Everything on Targ is magic," Daj chuckled, and carefully placed the glowing stone into a small leather pouch.

"The Olden Ones used these stones in potions during the war with the Ockoraerions.

Starshine glanced at the horse standing alertly on the rocky path; Daj had chosen to dig at. *"Bua, why is it that you enjoy riding these creatures of Earth?*

Daj pushed his oilskin hat up with the back of his fist. "I've been around horses all my life. My father breeds and trains them, so during my childhood years, I learned a lot about the animals." Daj dropped another stone into his pouch. "When I reached my late teens I thought I knew pretty much everything, until my father's horse trainer got hold of me. Abby taught the finer points on how riding double had its advantages; the first time with her, we never got off the saddle. She said it was one of many lessons in learning to trust a horse." Daj paused. "That horse has always been one of my favorites."

"How did that help you to trust a horse," Starshine asked, a bit confused.

"A good horse will stand right where you stop, whether you are on it or not."

Starshine probed Daj's mind for the memory of Abby. *"Bua, I should like to meet this Abby."* His face held a look of fascination.

Daj chuckled. "She's married now with a family to look after, and besides that, Earth is just beginning to learn of Targians. However it all works out, I do want you to meet your human grandparents." He grinned, continuing to brush around a dark blue jagged circle. "This is interesting," the spot seemed to be some sort of dye with a foul odor to it.

Starshine pulled back from Daj's mind and looked down at the spot. He stood quickly, glancing around the area, *"Bua that is wodevil urine."* Starshine placed a hand on his yentch, probing the area with his mind.

Daj's investigative nature took over, and he thought Dawn would be able to study something about this creature with a good sample; he quickly pulled out a small container and spoon from his pack and scooped up some of the stained soil. An icy fear trickled into his thoughts, as he remembered his first encounter with the vile, offensive creature, which Dawn had so bravely killed.

"Hurry Bua it is not safe here." Starshine's acute senses detected a trace of the wodevil's energy signature.

"Right, I'm with you, let's go," Daj strapped the pack on the saddle and mounted.

"I shall not ride," Starshine handed his steed's reins to Daj. *"Head higher up to the grove of alm nut trees, not far from here, you shall be safe if you stay in its center. Now go."* He pushed the feeling of urgency into Daj's mind.

Daj heeled his horse into action. It was not necessary for Starshine to emphasize the need to escape; he knew the threat the monster meant to him. Daj raced up the trail, with heart pounding and sweat trickling down the sides of his face. The horses' nostrils flared, dirt flying beneath their hooves as they sped away from the hostile danger they now, so closely, sensed. As he entered the grove, he caught sight of one of the hideous beasts; it was just steps behind him.

His mind filled with the painful terror of it sinking its teeth into his flesh again. This sent him scrambling out of the saddle, and as he did so, pulled the yentch from its sheath. Daj spun around, back against his horse. What had Foster said, it didn't like the taste of his blood, but that did not give him any comfort. A shadow moved through the tops of the trees, than another at their base.

One wodevil stepped from between the trees then a second. They headed straight for Daj. "Shit!" he cursed, trying to keep the horses calm. "Starshine, I could use a little help," his throat was tight. A burning arrow streaked through the air, Daj heard the solid thud as it sunk deep into the retched beast's flesh, a direct hit to the back of the closest wodevil's head. It screeched, causing the horses to rear up and bolt. Daj covered his ears, a second blaze from the base of the trees struck the beast still standing, bringing it to its knees. Daj watched with relief as Starshine stepped out from behind the trunk of the tree. He loaded up a sling, with a fiery stone he spat from his mouth, and his aim was true, connecting with the wodevil's skull. The screaming stopped.

The shadow climbed down from the tops of the trees to greet Starshine. The being was not Targian. As the two came closer, Daj thought that the newcomer looked amazingly like a fabled woodland elf, only taller. This bewitchingly beautiful being made eye contact with him, causing Daj's cheeks to darken slightly under his mesmerizing stare. "Thank you, I thought I was a goner," he said, trying to sound calm and held a trembling hand out in greeting. At the same time, he wondered if, Starshine had created this fantasy for his entertainment.

"I am Greenwood," the woodland elf clasped Daj's hand.

"I'm Daj," the hand that gripped his was light as the sun, powerful, slender, and warm.

"Bua this is real," Starshine, answered his thought. "Greenwood is from the neighboring planet Alf-heim. A place your Earth knows about in myths and legends. They along with others are our allies in this galaxy."

Daj forced himself to look away from Greenwood's smoldering, forest-green-brown eyes and at the two wodevils' crumpled bodies. "You knew they'd chase me." The beast's overpowering, rancid odor wafted under his nose, and he suppressed the urge to gag.

"Va, Bua, you were the temptation."

Daj choked and covered his nose with his bandana. "What if they had caught me?"

Greenwood looked amused. "Let me take care of that," he smiled, without showing his teeth and soundlessly walked over to the retched beasts. Speaking under his breath, a few words of an unfamiliar language, he created a swirl of golden sparkles in which the wodevils disappeared. He turned around asking Daj, "Is that better my new friend," and he laughed with mischief in his voice.

Daj was stunned.

"They would not have caught you," Greenwood answered his question, walking back to stand beside Starshine, who was enjoying this. "I am an expert archer with eyes and ears even sharper than a Targian's." He lifted the corner of his mouth with pride.

With his mind, Starshine called out for the horses to return. "Let us resume gathering stones for your studies." The horses emerged from nowhere, and with them stood a fabled elfin horse.

"Well, I'll be kicked in the balls by a roo," Daj tipped back his hat and stared at the lean beauty of the shimmering animal.

Nacoo rubbed the car-shaped, antique keychain, created into a necklace that Dawn had given him as a blast off gift. He chuckled as he flew the Sunstream II through the galaxy on his first official run.

"You shall enjoy the Grehaz," Jax said. *"They are a friendly species and always engaging in some sort of trade."*

"Foster tells me they are a fluid civilization, born of the gelatinous swamps, taking on shapes of things around them except for when they move. He said their jellylike body motion is in the ever-moving shape of an ess wave," Nacoo smirked.

"There is a flare star," Jax pointed to his right. *"It is my third time seeing one."*

"My first," Nacoo stared at the brightening star. *"It's beautiful."*

Jax darkened the screen. "We shall watch," he said, absorbing Nacoo's awe.

"I use to dream about such realities and now — here I am watching it. I just wish my Dad was here to see this," Nacoo said, somberly.

"I can change if you desire me too," Jax responded to Nacoo's mix of wonder and sadness.

"Nah, buddy, once was enough." He let loose a deep sigh as the star began to return to its normal brightness. *"Time is so different here."*

"There are many wonders in the universe. Here let me show you one," Jax swiveled his chair toward Nacoo and put his hands, palms facing each other out in front of him. *"Do this."* He started to move his hands in a circular motion increasing in speed then touched his fingertips together. In a moment, a ball of crackling light developed, and he tossed it back and forth between his palms.

Nacoo's first try created a very small ball of light. "Hey, that tickles," he rumbled aloud.

"This can happen by itself if there is any swirling of air," Jax lightly tossed his ball away from him and it dispersed in a show of shimmering pigtails.

Nacoo tossed his light ball toward Jax, but before it touched him, it burst like a balloon. The game was on! Nacoo's second ball of light was bigger, and when it hit Jax, it showered him with curlicues of glistening light.

Jax had the advantage in the beginning by creating two and three light balls at a time, blasting Nacoo with the shimmering tails of light, until the whole inside of the ship looked like a turn-of-the-century party.

By the end of the game, Nacoo had learned that by stirring the air with the fingers of each hand, he could make two balls of light at the same time. Finding the challenge of creating them as much fun as it was bombing Jax. "They would call this magical, back home," Nacoo, said, laughter in his voice. He rubbed his palms on his pants and pushed back in his chair. *"What do you call them?"* he questioned his Targian co-pilot.

"Wisp dust," Jax touched the screen. *"We have arrived."*

Nacoo straightened in his chair, heart beating a little faster. The implant training had prepared him for finding and understanding this and other alien races, but it did not prepare him for the actual physical contact.

Jax looked over at Nacoo. *"When we exit the ship, do not step anywhere except for on the mats they have put down. You shall be short of breath at first, just like on Dyeck and Pik, but do not take discomfort; the implant shall balance your air mixture rapidly. Once one of them speaks to you, your implant shall also harmonize the languages and you shall be able to speak to them. Do not touch them until they take form, unless you trevi ~ desire a burn."* Jax opened the hatch.

Remembering his prior experiences, Nacoo braced himself for the sudden loss of breath. He stepped carefully out of the ship and onto the welcoming mat. Gasping, he placed his hands on his knees and noticed the ship shared the same mat, which was moving under its weight. He took in a deep breath of the foul-smelling, gaseous air, and felt the burn in his lungs lessening and the panic leaving. *"Is this entire planet swamp,"* he asked, feeling like he was on the Luna-Sea.

"Va," Jax stood calmly before the waiting Grehaz.

A strange buzzing reached Nacoo's ears, as he stood to his full height. It sounded like a crowd of people talking all at once. He spread his legs for balance and stared at the beings before him. They pulled themselves out of the ooze and onto the mat, their bodies green, murky blobs of thick swirling gelatin. The one closest formed into the shape of Nacoo, Nacoo's mouth fell open.

"Welcome to Grehaz," the Nacoo form spoke, "I am Ott." He said, for the benefit of Nacoo, "I see Targ is nourishing you well, Jax." Ott's lips formed into a smile complete with teeth, his skin taking on the coloring of Nacoo's dark pigment.

"Va, I am ootauto ~ comforted," Jax, answered. "This is Nacoo." He nodded his head toward Nacoo, "he is our first human trade pilot and the Keeper of the Key.

"We have long waited to visit Kandoria; all is as it should be."

Nacoo looked around at the swampy landscape; large bubbles would grow out of its depths and into shapes copying the top half of him. He thought he could see them laughing. Others took on shapes of plants, trees, and beings he was not familiar with; others he recognized.

"Allow me to show the Keeper of the Key, Grehaz," Ott looked at Nacoo with swirling murky green eyes.

"I am honored," Nacoo's voice boomed, and now he was sure he heard laughter.

Professor Zyleon kissed Dawn's cheek, then bent down and picked up his packs. "You make sure you give President Cunningham the best tour Kandoria has to offer." He turned and headed to the ship not wanting to suffer a long good-bye.

"We will Professor, we will," Dawn turned to Kuranna putting on a brave front. "Let Autumn, know we are thinking of her and will come for a visit as soon as things are calm."

"Okay dear," Kuranna gave Dawn a motherly hug, "you take care now." She turned and followed Trombula, who carried her bags.

Foster received Kuranna and her luggage, bowing his head to Trombula, saying, *"Ne ootau that we take this journey together and let truth tell our story."*

Trombula inclined his head and glided back to where Dawn, Baxter, Radin and, Hank all stood waiting for the Trowley's departure.

"I will miss them," Radin said, his hands in his pockets, looking like a small boy.

"Me too," Dawn sniffled.

"I'll miss Kuranna's butterscotch cookies," Baxter said, matter-of-factly.

"Va, they were quite good," Hank, said aloud, for the sake of Radin, and thought of the first time Kuranna had baked them. The smell reminded him of Targian mashed pata, wrapped in floot leaves. She had given him one warm from the oven with a cup of appo, smiled, and waited for his opinion of his first Earth cookie. He had asked for more.

Trombula waved a six-fingered hand. "Pah," he spoke as the ship disappeared.

"That is a marvel to watch," said Radin, removing a crumpled envelope from his pants pocket. "Dawn," he handed it to her, "Professor Zyleon said that I should give this to you as soon as they were gone."

Baxter looked curiously at the Professor's scrawl across the front of it. "Girl," he leaned closer as she opened it.

"Thank you, Radin," Dawn gave Baxter an annoyed look; pulling out a piece of pink floral stationery she flipped it open. "It's Kuranna's butterscotch cookie recipe." The group made approving sounds and she giggled at how well Kuranna knew the crew. There was another sealed envelope inside the first, but on this one, it said, "Dawn, this is for your "thoughts" only." She quickly replaced the recipe and smiled sweetly. "It must be my instructions for the President." Dawn glanced at Trombula. "When is Nacoo to arrive with the Grehaz?" she asked, feeling anxious not only about meeting new alien beings, but also about having to find time to shelter her mind and read the Professor's directives.

"When the sun rises," Trombula bowed his head, *"ne ootau that we shall join with you. Now, please excuse us. Baxter and I must attend to Kandoria's*

newest group of visitors." Again, he bowed his silvery head and glided silkily from the dock.

"Yeah, all the President's men," Baxter chuckled. "I'll see you for breakfast." He winked at Dawn and sauntered after Trombula.

Radin looked puzzled; a question on his lips than shook his head.

"Hank, Radin will you two let Olander and Marlo know they can start preparations for the President's arrival to Kandoria," Dawn asked, biting her bottom lip, to stifle a giggle.

"Yes," Radin answered content to have something to do. He ambled away, whistling a soft tune.

"Jist vek," Hank led Dawn by the elbow, *"I shall return to Targ for nourishment after this task is through."* He felt her concern, *"rit ootau ga."*

"You comfort me also," she brushed a curl away from her eyes and looked into Hank's luminous ones. *"When will you come back?"* she asked, already missing him.

"I'll ish by the waxing crescent of the moon." They stopped walking and he held her warmth against him. *"Aresh mita rym, jist vek."* Hank tickled the edges of her mind, opening his to her. *"Aresh mita rym ~ essence be yours."*

Dawn returned his mind touches and hugged him even closer. *'Go before I cry,"* she whispered.

He glided from her view, leaving her in the empty corridor. Like a child opening a hidden Christmas present, she hastily opened Professor Zyleon's letter. Written inside was a date: 2152, January- full moon, place: Space Station 17 – Star room. That was it. Dawn smiled to herself and headed back to camp, thinking that maybe she would bake some cookies.

XXIV

Farstar stood next to Rory, overlooking Pik; Smoot leaned against a tree, guarding Autumn as she rested in the healing pool. Etta busied herself, cleaning alm nuts at a nearby table, occasionally glancing around the market. There was a bustling excitement throughout Pik. It was the long season, and harvested food filled every table. Trading would be good this turn of the planet, providing for the galactic event...a colossal celebration, the naissance of Pik's first Queen, an unfolding prophecy heralding in a new age.

Glossary

Targian language

Aash – beware
Ackon – absorption
Alm nuts – similar to walnuts
Appo – tea
Appo's – teas
Aresh – essence
Artu – mind altering herb/tea
Athic – dehydrating herb/tea
Av – no
Aw – not
Bir – how
Boreal – orb of energy
Bow – words
Bu – my
Bua - father
Buja – must
Ca – am
Cal – the
Chul's – sea birds, similar to gulls
Copaa – thank
Cu – strengthening herb/tea
Cula – daughter
Cutra – strengthen
Dox – olden
Dutom – seeder
Dutoms – seeders
Eck – control
Efen – spend
Egmur –sleep aid herb/tea

Ep – go
Erra – unfold
Ew – we
Farth – center of Targ
Fet leaves – large, yellow leafed bush
Fli – has
Floot leaves – similar to lettuce
Fruick – parapet
Ga – me
Gamo – crystal
Getch – shield
Hesh – protect
Heshna – protection
Heshni – protector
Hor trap – magnetic scrambler of brain waves
Ish – return
Ishag – she
Jant – son
Jemba stone – clear yellow sapphire used in protection potions
Jist – small
Kandoria – Targ's, Earth sanctuary
Kapray – attack
Katri flower – honeysuckle aroma
Kav – this

Keiyat Garden – Targ's garden of regeneration
Kolum Trey – healing
Kom – human
Komi – humans
Korax – energy wall
Korzuk – join
Korzuki – joined
Korzuku - joining
Krish – doorway, universal crossing
Lef – bind
Li – with
Lyx – fear
Maza – pathway
Mel – come
Mienco – complete healing
Mil – come
Minoni – communicator
Mita – be
Moc – relaxant herb/tea
Muraht – fuel
Ne – take
Nes – takes
Nosh – a black shaped triangle used to engage a Targian craft
Nua – brother
Oa – to
Oo – I
Oorah – temple of regeneration and kinetic light travel
Ootau – comfort
Ootaut – comforts
Ootauto – comforted
Otah – herb/tea/oil used for wound healing

Pacu's – long-necked, golden winged birds, resembling swans
Pah – Peace
Parge – spirit
Pata – a mash, butterscotch flavored
Pik – planet
Prest – keeper
Quinni – elder
Quinni's – elder's
Rah – sister
Reh – for
Resh – energy
Ri – your
Rit – you
Roz – have
Rup – calming herb/tea for space travel
Ry – mineral
Rym – yours
Satt powder – mineral/brown powder used in dispelling truth, has bad effects
Sca – need
Shish – hello
Shoek – implant process, energy transference
Shram – birthing
Shura – live
Shurah – seal
Spar-thread – silky-cotton material
Sprig of Loc – herb, increases energy, resembles dill
Sy – room
Ta – of
Targ – sentient being/planet

Tek – mate
Ti – is
Tra – mine
Trath – mindful
Tretch – entrance
Trevi – desire
Truba – cease
Tutal – friend
Tyd – cleansing
Uc – as
Uckri – encase
Ugla – fish
Uva tree – large amethyst leafed tree
Va – yes
Vah – goodbye
Vek – one
Verva Fruit – sweet berry
Vesp – link/linked

Vessa – rise
Vessa – rise
Vos – well
Vuel – sleep
Vuel – sleep
Wa – us
Wadoni – mysteries
Wathu – awaken
Wex – let
Wisp dust – space static
Wog – growing
Yentch – Targian weapon
Yoxa – taught
Zaf – mother
Zaqurah – companion
Ze – do
Zifla – angel

Seven Targian Moons Respectively

Badu – jade green
Nar – violet
Poc – white
Retra – multi-hued

Unares – sapphire blue
Yeth – amber
Kinque – russet
(moon of mystery)

Dwarven Language

Bach – speaks
Boosta – female
Daple – truth
Euba – water
Ex – who
Gort – open
Ha – here
Luzyd - welcome

Nok – told
Oti – Ancients
Ru – is
Sac – safe
Sumesh – descends
Uh – yes
Urend – legend
Vo – of

Wo – us   Zank – halt
Yana – upon

Dyeckian Language

Cret – mildly intoxicating ale   Trepaa wine – a thick, peachy
Dyeck – planet   drink
Gog – highly intoxicating ale   Wir buds – tangy flower buds
Putja root – similar to potato

Trader Language

Baugh – expect
Copate – conflict
Feljoa – planet
Sa - King
Wa – us